Penguin Education

Social Inequality
Edited by André Béteille

Penguin Modern Sociology Readings

Social Inequality

Selected Readings

Edited by André Béteille

Penguin Books

Penguin Books Ltd, Harmondsworth, Middlesex, England
Penguin Books, 625 Madison Avenue, New York,
New York 10022, U.S.A.
Penguin Books Australia Ltd, Ringwood,
Victoria, Australia
Penguin Books Canada Ltd,
2801 John Street,
Markham, Ontario, Canada L3R 1B4
Penguin Books (N.Z.) Ltd,
182–190 Wairau Road,
Auckland 10, New Zealand

First published 1969
Reprinted 1970, 1972, 1974, 1976, 1978

Made and printed in Great Britain by
Richard Clay (The Chaucer Press) Ltd,
Bungay, Suffolk
Set in Monotype Times

For Biku,
a birthday gift

Contents

Introduction

This book offers a selection of Readings on various aspects of social inequality. It is essentially a selection of contemporary writings. All the pieces in it were published after 1950, and many of them during the last ten years.

Social inequality is a broad and general problem, one which is present in all contemporary societies. In the past, societies have differed greatly in their attitudes to inequality, but in the modern world it would be hard indeed to find any society whose members are indifferent to the problem. The industrial societies of the U.S.A. and the U.S.S.R. alike justify their respective systems by the argument that they provide the best opportunities for real social equality. For the more 'backward' societies, the chief appeal of industrialization is the promise it holds of bringing inequality under control.

As one might expect, there is a vast literature on social inequality. Under various names, the problem has occupied a central position in the discipline of sociology since its very inception. It has been treated in very different ways by different scholars. Among those who have written most perceptively on the subject, few have been altogether without some kind of moral commitment. This is certainly true of the two great nineteenth-century scholars who contributed most richly to our understanding of the problem, de Tocqueville and Marx. This being so, anyone who claims to be wholly unbiased in making such a selection is bound to be suspect.

It may be useful to indicate some of the considerations which have entered into the selection that is presented here. I have tried to avoid the extremes of two types of approach. The first is rooted in philosophical speculations on the moral basis of equality, and is a feature of certain European approaches to the problem of class and social inequality. It tends to be expressed in a highly polemical style which makes it difficult to separate sociological questions and issues from philosophical ones.

At the other extreme are a number of recent American

contributions to the subject. The poverty of their approach derives from an obsessive concern for 'methodology' and scientific precision at the expense of sociologically significant problems. Although American scholars have contributed richly to the understanding of specific and limited areas of 'social stratification', their preoccupation with the rigours of scientific method has not always led to fresh insights of a truly fundamental nature.

The contributions selected here deal, on the whole, with sociologically significant problems which are (or can be) discussed in terms of empirically testable propositions. None of them is concerned with problems of methodology as such; it is felt that formal discussions of method do not quite belong to a selection of this kind. Nor are the pieces chosen for this volume concerned directly with normative questions; such questions belong more properly to the domain of social philosophy than to that of sociology. The first four and the last two pieces are general and comparative in nature, while the others are devoted to more concrete empirical problems.

In its origin and development sociology has been largely a product of Western experience. This experience contains much that is of significance to the world as a whole but it must not be forgotten that it is limited in both time and space. A truly comprehensive science of society can emerge only by pooling together the experiences of every type of society whether 'backward' or 'advanced'.

Within the Western world itself one notices certain broad differences between European and American scholars in their approach to the study of social inequality. To put it in somewhat oversimple terms, European scholars tend to be more preoccupied with the problem of class in the narrow Marxian sense of the term while their American counterparts deal more generally with the broader problems of 'social stratification'.[1] Both European and American sociologists have (perhaps understandably) been, so far, concerned essentially with problems of inequality in their own societies. This has led inevitably to certain problems and issues being overstressed and to others being ignored or neglected. The

1. This distinction has been lucidly brought out in Professor Aron's contribution in this volume.

ethnocentricism of the American approach has recently been commented upon by Lenski:

> This is probably the major reason why American theory in the field of stratification seems so strange and irrelevant to many foreign observers. It is adapted to a very special set of conditions which have no counterpart in most societies.[2]

No doubt, the European preoccupation with class consciousness and class conflict appears equally bizarre to many American observers.

Social inequality exists, of course, in non-Western as well as in Western societies. Perhaps we can learn more about it from the experiences of the former because it is here that it exists in its most extreme and manifest forms both as a set of facts and as a system of values. I have tried to make this selection truly comparative in scope by including materials relating to as many types of society as possible.

An attempt at this kind of comprehensiveness within the scope of a relatively small volume faces a special kind of problem. Undoubtedly, the most sophisticated and theoretically insightful studies of social inequality are those which relate to Western societies. Many of these have had to be excluded in order to make room for material from other societies which illustrate new and significant problems of inequality. As indicated earlier, the emphasis here is on significant issues and problems rather than on refined and sophisticated methodology.

This concern with both Western and non-Western societies has led me to seek a balance between the writings of sociologists and of social anthropologists. Unfortunately the two disciplines continue to be divided by an artificial distinction which derives mainly from certain historical experiences in the West. Consequently, the problem of social inequality is not often studied on a truly comparative basis. The social anthropologist, who is more often than not a European or an American, studies inequality in 'other' cultures; the sociologist, again generally an American or a European, studies the same problem in his own culture, and the two rarely communicate. As more and more African and Asian

2. Gerhard E. Lenski, *Power and Privilege, A New Theory of Stratification*, McGraw-Hill, 1966, p. 62.

scholars turn to the study of their own – as well as 'other' – cultures, the distinction between social anthropology and sociology will lose its present meaning. This selection is offered in the hope that such a day is not very distant.

I have sought to achieve another kind of balance, somewhat more delicate and difficult than the first one. One reason why the concept of class is so difficult to handle is its close association with certain political systems and ideologies, Marxism in particular. In its origin and development it has been closely associated with the ideas of Marx and even today the Marxist approach to class has a distinctive quality which marks it out from the approaches of non-Marxists. I have thought it fair to give some representation to the two points of view in at least the theoretical parts of the book.

'Class', 'stratification', 'social inequality' – these phrases are often used interchangeably in everyday language, and indeed there is a good measure of overlap between them even in their technical meanings. It would be difficult to give a single and precise meaning to each of these terms and to insist that others should adhere to it consistently. For terms such as these correspond to fundamental categories of thought and their meanings cannot be contained solely by the demands of sociological analysis.

For instance, the word 'class' is bound to evoke certain meanings among Marxists and anti-Marxists which it would not for those who take a detached view of Marxism. Apart from the problem of differing ideological idioms, there is the question of language in the narrow sense of the term. In French, for example, the term for 'class' seems to refer to something more organic than it generally does in English. Hence in French the terms 'classe' and 'stratification' are often opposed[3] whereas in English the first is generally viewed as a form of the second. This, of course, is partly due to the fact that Marxist literature has played a much greater part in the development of French than of the Anglo-American sociological tradition.

In Anglo-Saxon usage the term 'stratification' has generally a broad and inclusive meaning whereas in French it tends to refer

3. cf. R. Dahrendorf, *Class and Class Conflict in Industrial Society*, London, 1963, p. 76.

specifically to an arrangement of statistical aggregates. Hence, Dumont[4] opposes 'hierarchie' and 'stratification' and rejects the view, commonly adopted by Anglo-American writers, that caste is a form of social stratification. For him, caste is an expression of hierarchy – a consciously organized principle – whereas stratification refers to layers which are constructed by the sociologist on the basis of variable criteria.

The problem of social inequality has two aspects, a distributive and a relational aspect. The first refers to the ways in which different factors such as income, wealth, occupation, education, power, skill, etc., are distributed in the population. The second refers to the ways in which individuals differentiated by these criteria are related to each other within a system of groups and categories. The distributive aspect of social inequality provides only the basis for a proper sociological understanding of how individuals interact with each other in socially significant ways. The emphasis in this selection is on the relational aspects of social inequality. Hence, the pieces chosen here are often qualitative or even impressionistic, for relational problems do not always or easily lend themselves to the kind of quantitative treatment which can be applied to problems of distribution.

I have not attempted to make the selection representative in terms of every region in the world; such attempts have a certain mechanical quality which I have tried to avoid. What I have tried to do is to focus on a limited number of significant themes and to cover on the one hand, different types of societies and, on the other, different modes of stratification.

There are two pieces on modern industrial societies, one dealing with the problem mainly under capitalism and the other under socialism. It is here that some of the most fundamental ideas regarding class and stratification are tested, for while all societies have some form of social inequality, it is beyond question that the most seminal insights into the problem (at least until today) have grown out of studies of Western societies.

Although the richest and the best sociological studies of class and stratification relate to industrial societies, a large proportion of the world's population continues to live by agriculture.

4. Louis Dumont, *Homo hierarchicus*, Paris, 1966.

Introduction

Agrarian modes of production are associated with patterns of inequality which are rather different from those associated with industrial organization. A separate section is devoted to agrarian class relations in view of their importance in the non-Western world.

Colonial rule created new patterns of stratification in many parts of what has now come to be known as the Third World. It imposed new forms of inequality based on distinctions of race. It also introduced new modes of production, new political ideologies and new conceptions of social equality. Some of these have been carried over into the post-colonial phase where the challenges of development and modernization are giving a new character to the entire problem of social stratification.

There is already an overlap when we examine in turn agrarian and ex-colonial societies. The reason for treating them separately is that, in terms of problems, the focus is rather different in the two cases. In the first case, the problem is examined in static terms, and also in relation to a limited universe. In the second, we view it in more dynamic and global terms.

It was believed for a long time that primitive societies were unstratified. A closer look at them has shown that this is an over-simplified view. While concepts of rank and status do exist in primitive societies, they are rather different there from those prevalent in either industrial or agrarian societies. Our interest in stratification in primitive societies is two-fold: to show the truly universal nature of social inequality, and to bring to light forms and bases of inequality which appear somewhat unusual from the viewpoint of 'modern' societies.

I have given separate attention to two specific modes of stratification or, rather, to two idioms through which social inequalities are ordered. One is that based on the ritual concepts of purity and pollution of which caste provides the most characteristic example. The other is based on 'race' which is not only one of the most persistent bases of social discrimination, but one which seems to be growing in importance. Caste and 'race' are again discussed in the two final chapters which are devoted to the problem of social inequality as a value rather than as an existential fact.

Part One
The Nature and Types of Social Inequality

Inequality is not merely a matter of individual abilities and aptitudes; it is above all a social fact. The opportunities an individual has and even his abilities are in part governed by his position in society. While many have talked about 'classless' societies of either the past or the future, these ideas have found very little support in historical experience. Dahrendorf relates the problem of social inequality to the existence of norms and sanctions and to the distribution of power; these are truly universal features of human society. Among the many forms of social inequality, three have received particular attention from sociologists: those which follow from disparities of wealth and income; those which relate to differential prestige or honour; and those which derive from the distribution of power. Runciman, following Max Weber, argues that these three dimensions of inequality are related but not reducible to each other.

1 R. Dahrendorf

On the Origin of Inequality among Men

This essay was initially given as an inaugural lecture in the University of Tübingen and is reprinted from R. Dahrendorf, *Essays in the Theory of Society*, Stanford University Press, 1968, pp. 151–78.

Even in the affluent society, it remains a stubborn and remarkable fact that men are unequally placed. There are children who are ashamed of their parents because they think that a university degree has made them 'better'. There are people who decorate their houses with antennas without having the television sets to go with them, in order to convince their neighbors that they can afford television. There are firms that build their offices with movable walls because the status of their employees is measured in square feet and an office has to be enlarged when its occupant is promoted. There are clerical workers whose ambition it is to achieve a position in which they not only can afford, but are socially permitted to own, a two-tone car. Of course, such differences are no longer directly sustained by the force of legal sanction, which upholds the system of privilege in a caste or estate society. Nevertheless, our society – quite apart from the cruder gradations of property and income, prestige and power – is characterized by a multitude of differences of rank so subtle and yet so penetrating that one cannot but be skeptical of the claim one sometimes hears that a leveling process has caused all inequalities to disappear. It is no longer usual to investigate the anxiety, suffering and hardship that inequalities cause among men – yet there are suicides because of poor examination results, divorces based on 'social' incompatibility, crimes occasioned by a feeling of social inequality. Throughout our society, social inequality is still turning men against men.

These remarks are not meant as a plea for equality. On the contrary, I shall later agree with Kant, who called 'inequality among men' a 'rich source of much that is evil, but also of everything that is good' (1, p. 325). Yet the extreme effects of inequality may give a general idea of the problem that concerns me. Diderot has our sympathy when he states in his article 'Société' in the *Encyclopédie*:

There is no more inequality between the different stations in life than there is among the different characters in a comedy: the end of the play finds all the players once again in the same position, and the brief period for which their play lasted did not and could not convince any two of them that one was really above or below the other (2, p. 208).

But the life of men in society is not merely a comedy, and the hope that all will be equal in death is a feeble consolation for most. The question remains: Why is there inequality among men? Where do its causes lie? Can it be reduced, or even abolished altogether? Or do we have to accept it as a necessary element in the structure of human society?

I shall try to show that historically these were the first questions asked by sociology. By surveying the various attempts to answer them a whole history of sociological thought might be written, and I shall at least give some indication of how this may be so. So far, however, as the problem of inequality itself is concerned, this history has achieved little more than to give it a different name: what was called in the eighteenth century the origin of inequality and in the nineteenth the formation of classes, we describe today as the theory of social stratification – all this even though the original problem has not changed and no satisfactory solution to it has been found. In this essay I shall attempt a new explanation of the old problem, one that in my opinion will take us a few steps beyond the present state of our thinking.

The younger a branch of scholarship is, the more concerned are its historians to pursue its origins back at least as far as Greek antiquity. Historians of sociology are no exception to this rule. But if one regards the problem of inequality as a key to the history of sociology, it can be clearly shown not only that Plato and Aristotle were definitely not sociologists, but also why they were not. It is always awkward to ascribe to an academic discipline a precise date of birth, but this discussion may help us to date the beginnings of sociology with reasonable plausibility.

In 1792, a gentleman by the name of Meiners, described as a

'Royal British Councillor and *rite* teacher of worldly wisdom in Göttingen', wrote some reflections on 'the causes of the inequality of estates among the most prominent European peoples'. His results were not especially original:

> In all times inequality of natures has unfailingly produced inequality of rights. . . . If the negligent, the lazy, the untrained and the ignorant were to enjoy equal rights with those who display the corresponding virtues, this would be as unnatural and unjust as if the child had rights equal to those of the adult, the weak and cowardly woman rights equal to those of the strong and courageous man, the villain the same security and respect as the meritorious citizen (3, p. 41).

Meiners's reflections are a version, highly characteristic of his time, of an ideology that to the present day, and with only minor refinements, is invoked by all societies that are worried about their survival to reassure themselves of the justice of their injustices. By repeating in a simplified form the errors of Aristotle, such societies assert a pre-established harmony of things natural and social, and above all a congruence of natural differences between men and social differences between their positions. It was Aristotle, after all, who said:

> It is thus clear that there are *by nature* free men and slaves, and that servitude is agreeable and just for the latter. . . . Equally, the relation of the male to the female is *by nature* such that one is superior and the other inferior, one dominates and the other is dominated. . . . With the barbarians, of course, the female and the dominated have the same rank. This is because they do not possess a naturally dominating element. . . . This is why the poets say, 'It is just that Greeks rule over barbarians,' because the barbarian and the slave are *by nature* the same (4, p. 1254b, 1252a).

Now this is just the attitude that makes impossible a sociological treatment of the problem, that is, an explanation of inequality in terms of specifically social factors expressed in propositions capable of being empirically tested.

So far, I have talked about social inequality as if it were clear what is meant by this notion. Obviously, this is a somewhat optimistic assumption. The lathe operator and the pipe fitter, the general and the sergeant, the artistically gifted child and the mechanically gifted child, the talented and the untalented, are all pairs of unequals. Yet these inequalities are evidently themselves rather unequal, and have to be distinguished from one another in at least two respects. First, we must distinguish between inequalities of natural capability and those of social position; second, we must distinguish between inequalities that do not involve any evaluative rank order and those that do. If we combine these two approaches, four types of inequality emerge, all of which we shall have to discuss. In relation to the individual there are (*a*) *natural differences of kind* in features, character and interests, and (*b*) *natural differences of rank* in intelligence, talent and strength (leaving open the question of whether such differences do in fact exist). Correspondingly, in relation to society (and in the language of contemporary sociology) there are (*c*) *social differentiation* of positions essentially equal in rank, and (*d*) *social stratification* based on reputation and wealth and expressed in a rank order of social status.[1]

Our interest here is primarily in inequalities of the stratification type. On the question of what these are, or, more technically speaking, how they can be measured, no consensus has so far been reached, nor has a suggestion been offered that would make a consensus possible. I am accordingly making an arbitrary decision here when I distinguish the distributive area of stratification – the explicandum of our theoretical discussion – from nondistributive inequalities such as those of power.[2] According to this distinction, wealth and prestige belong to the area of stratification, even if they are assembled to a considerable extent by one person; property and charisma, by contrast, are nondistributive. How wealth and prestige relate to each other, and especially whether they are mutually convertible and can therefore be

1. The distinction between natural and social inequalities can be found in Rousseau; indeed, it constitutes the core of his argument. 'I perceive two kinds of inequality among men: one I call natural or physical . . . ; the other might be called moral or political' (5, p. 39). The distinction between social stratification and social differentiation, by contrast, has only recently been made unambiguously, for example by Melvin M. Tumin (6) and Walter Buckley (7). Yet this distinction is no less important than the other, as the attempt to explain social stratification in terms of social differentiation shows.

2. For what has here been called 'distributive' and 'nondistributive' one could also use the terms 'intransitive' and 'transitive' (in the grammatical sense). Transitive or nondistributive inequalities are the creators of the more passive intransitive or distributive ones.

reduced to one concept, one single 'currency' of social stratification, is an important technical question that I cannot go into here.[3]

Aristotle was concerned as we are here to examine the origin of the fourth type of inequality, social stratification. However, by trying to explain social stratification – as so many authors of antiquity, the Christian middle ages and modern times did after him – in terms of assumed natural differences of rank between men, he missed precisely that type of analysis which we should to-day describe as sociology. In consequence, his analysis subjects a potentially sociological problem to assumptions that transcend the realm of social fact and defy the test of historical experience. That this attitude helped to delay the birth of sociology by more than twenty centuries is perhaps no great loss, considering the political consequences of so unhistorical an explanation. I believe that Rousseau was right, for all his polemical tone, when he argued that it did not make sense:

to investigate whether there might not be an essential connexion between the two inequalities [the natural and the social]. For it would mean that we must ask whether rulers are necessarily worth more than the ruled, and whether strength of body and mind, wisdom and virtue are always found in the same individuals, and found, moreover, in direct relation to their power or wealth; a question that slaves who think they are being overheard by their masters may find it useful to discuss, but that has no meaning for reasonable and free men in search of the truth (5, p. 39).[4]

3. A possible currency of this kind might be the (structured) 'chances of participation' – or, in Weber's terms, 'life chances' – that we acquire by virtue of our positions.

4. Clearly Aristotle and numerous thinkers between his time and the revolutionary period had important sociological insights; one need only mention the way Aristotle relates social strata to political constitutions in the *Politics*. Nor would it be correct to charge Aristotle with having naïvely asserted the congruence of natural and social inequalities. But Aristotle (to say nothing of Plato) and all others down to the eighteenth century lacked what one might call pervasive 'sociological thinking', i.e. an unwavering sense of the autonomously social (and thus historical) level of reality. Such thinking required a radical break with the undisputed constants of earlier epochs, a break that first became general in the age of the great revolutions. For this reason one may well derive the birth of sociology from the spirit of revolution.

This is Rousseau's argument in his prize essay in 1754 on 'The Origin of Inequality among Men and Whether It Is Legitimated by Natural Laws'. Unlike his earlier essay of 1750 on 'The Moral Consequences of Progress in the Arts and Sciences', this essay was not awarded the prize of the Dijon Academy. I do not know why the judges preferred the essay of 'a certain Abbé Talbert' (as one editor of Rousseau's work describes him); but conceivably they began to feel uneasy about the radical implications of their own question. For the new meaning given by Rousseau and his contemporaries to the question of the origin of inequality involved a revolution in politics as well as intellectual history.

The pivotal point of the Aristotelian argument – if I may use this formula as an abbreviation for all treatments of the problem before the eighteenth century – was the assumption that men are by nature unequal in rank, and that there is therefore a natural rank order among men. This presupposition collapsed in the face of the assumption of natural law that the natural rank of all men is equal. Politically, this meant that together with all other hierarchies, the hierarchies of society also lost their claim to unquestioning respect. If men are equal by nature, then social inequalities cannot be established by nature or God; and if they are not so established, then they are subject to change, and the privileged of today may be the outcasts of tomorrow; it may then even be possible to abolish all inequalities. A straight road leads from such reflections to the Declaration of the Rights of Man and Citizen of 1789: 'Men are born and remain free and equal in rights. Social differences, therefore, can only be based on general utility.'

In terms of intellectual history, the same process meant that the question of the origin of inequality was now phrased in a new and different, i.e. sociological, manner. If men are by nature equal in rank, where do social inequalities come from? If all men are born free and equal in rights, how can we explain that some are rich and others poor, some respected and others ignored, some powerful and others in servitude? Once the question was posed in these terms, only a sociological answer was possible.[5] With good

5. Historically, therefore, one necessary condition of the sociological mode of inquiry into the origin of equality was the assumption of the natural equality (equality of rank) of all men. But here as so often what was

21

reason, then, Werner Sombart and others have seen the beginnings of sociology in the works of those authors who first tried to give a sociological answer to this question – notably the French *philosophes*, the Scottish moral philosophers and political economists, and the thinkers of the German Enlightenment in the second half of the eighteenth century.[6]

The first sociological explanation of the origin of inequality proved disappointing, though for a century it reappeared in a succession of new forms. It consisted in a figure of thought, which may be demonstrated by further reference to Rousseau's prize essay.

As we have seen, Rousseau begins by assuming the natural equality of men. In the style of his time, he then projects this assumption into history and constructs a pre-social original state in which there was complete equality of all, where no one was superior to anyone else in either rank or status. Inequality, he argues, came about as a result of leaving the state of nature; it is a kind of original sin, which he links with the emergence of private property. How private property itself came into existence, Rousseau does not explain; instead, he confines himself to a statement as obscure as it is concrete: 'The first man who fenced in an area and said, "This is mine," and who found people simple enough to believe him, was the real founder of civil society' (5, p. 66).

Not all of Rousseau's contemporaries, even those who shared

---

historically necessary is logically superfluous: once the question of the origin of inequality is posed in a sociological way (i.e. without recourse to natural inequalities), its answer has nothing to do with whether or not men are by nature equal or unequal. Thus the difficult philosophical question of the natural rank of men can be set aside here as irrelevant to the truth or falsity of sociological explanations of social stratification. We rule out only explanations based on the assumed congruence, or tendency to congruence, of the natural and social rank orders.

6. Few historians of sociology have taken up Sombart's reference to the Scottish moral philosophers and their attack on natural law (8); apart from a recently published dissertation (9), only William C. Lehmann has elaborated on it (10, 11). Parallel developments on the Continent are described even more rarely. One can write the history of sociology in many ways, of course; but it seems to me that the origin of inequality would be far from the worst central theme.

most of his assumptions, accepted the one-sidedness of his explanation or his evaluation of the process he described. Adam Ferguson's *History of Civil Society* (1767) and John Millar's *Origin of the Distinction of Ranks* (1771) come quite close to Rousseau in assuming a natural state of equality and ascribing to property the crucial part (Millar) or at least an important part (Ferguson) in destroying this natural state. But both of them regard the fact that men have learned 'to strive for riches and admire distinctions', and thus to differentiate according to income and prestige, not as a curse but as a step toward the civilization of 'civil society' (see 12, vol. 2, pp. 2, 3).

Even further removed from Rousseau the romantic Utopian are Schiller's Jena lectures of 1789, 'On the First Human Society'; the title is a clear, if implicit, reference to Kant's essay on the 'Probable Beginning of Human History', which in turn referred explicitly to Rousseau's essay (see 13, pp. 322, 325). Schiller praises the 'abolition of equality of status' as the step that enabled man to leave the 'tranquil nausea of his paradise' (13, pp. 600–601). But the assumption of an original state of equality, and the explanation of the origin of inequality in terms of private property, remained unchallenged from Rousseau to Lorenzo von Stein and Karl Marx.[7]

7. Obviously these men's arguments were not as simple as this account may suggest. The most unambiguous emphasis on property as a cause of inequality is found in Rousseau, Millar, Stein and Marx. Millar displays a nice historical concreteness on this point: 'The invention of taming and pasturing cattle gives rise to a more remarkable and permanent distinction of ranks. Some persons, by being more industrious or more fortunate than others, are led in a short time to acquire more numerous herds and flocks' (14, p. 204). Property here has a very definite sociological sense which becomes even clearer in Stein (15, p. 275): 'Class formation is that process by which the distribution of property leads to a distribution of spiritual rights, goods, and functions among the individual members of society, such that the attributes of persistence and fixity are transferred from property to social position and function.' This means that property both causes inequality and stabilizes it socially; as Ferguson aptly puts it, 'Possessions descend, and the luster of family grows brighter with age' (12, p. 166).

The other authors mentioned here do not give property quite the same prominence; in varying degrees they invoke the division of labor, the motive of conquest and natural differences in rank between men. Rousseau and Marx are unrivaled in their radical insistence on property as the sole cause of social inequality.

For many writers between 1750 and 1850, and for their public, the explanation of inequality in terms of private property remained politically attractive. A society without private property is at least conceivable; and if the idea of equality is associated with this notion, the abolition of private property may become the supreme goal of political action. Indeed, it can be argued that two great revolutions have been abetted to no small extent by the association of inequality with private property, one by Rousseau's dream of re-establishing the original, natural equality of man, the other by Marx's dream of a communist society. Attractive as this explanation may be to some people, however, and though it represents an undeniable methodological advance over the Aristotelian argument, it does not stand the test of historical experience.

To be sure, private property was never completely abolished in the Soviet Union. Nevertheless, the disappointment of the Webbs and other Socialist visitors in the 1930s, caused by the evident inequalities of income and rank in the Soviet Union, may be taken as an experimental refutation of the thesis of Rousseau and Millar, Ferguson and Schiller, Stein and Marx. In the Soviet Union, in Yugoslavia, in Israel and wherever else private property has been reduced to virtual insignificance, we still find social stratification. Even if such stratification is prevented for a short period from manifesting itself in differences of possessions and income (as in the *kibbutzim* of Israel), the undefinable yet effective force of prestige continues to create a noticeable rank order. If social inequality were really based on private property, the abolition of private property would have to result in the elimination of inequality. Experience in propertyless and quasi-propertyless societies does not confirm this proposition. We may therefore regard it as disproved.[8]

8. The scientific significance of Communism can hardly be overestimated in this context, though it provides yet another example of the human cost of historical experiments. For almost two centuries, property dominated social and political thought: as a source of everything good or evil, as a principle to be retained or abolished. Today we know (though we do not yet have the most rigorous sort of proof) that the abolition of property merely replaces the old classes with new ones, so that from Locke to Lenin the social and political significance of property has been vastly overestimated.

Stein and Marx are only marginal members of the group of writers who, by explaining the origin of stratification in terms of property, contributed to the emergence of sociology. Both Stein and Marx (and, to a lesser extent, Ferguson and several political economists of the late eighteenth century) mention a second factor in addition to property, one that came to dominate the discussion of the formation of classes, as our problem was now called, throughout the second half of the nineteenth century and the beginning of the twentieth. This factor was the division of labor.

As early as the 1870s Engels, in his *Anti-Dühring*, had developed a theory of class formation on the basis of the division of labor. The subsequent discussion, however, is associated pre-eminently with the name of Gustav Schmoller. It began with the famous controversy between Schmoller and Treitschke over Schmoller's essay on 'The Social Question and the Prussian State' – a controversy that is of interest to us here because it raised once again the question of whether a sociological science was possible. Against Schmoller, Treitschke argued (one would be tempted to say a century too late, if this were not characteristic of the whole of German history) for a congruence of natural and social rank orders. Schmoller (with arguments often no less curious) tried to explain the formation of classes by the division of labor.

Schmoller's essays on 'The Facts of the Division of Labor' and 'The Nature of the Division of Labor and the Formation of Classes', published in 1889 and 1890, prompted Karl Bücher's polemical Leipzig inaugural lecture of 1892 on 'The Division of Labor and the Formation of Social Classes', which was later extended and modified in his book *The Emergence of Economy*. This in turn was attacked not only by Schmoller, but by Emile Durkheim in his *Division of Labor in Society*. Durkheim also discussed at some length Georg Simmel's 'On Social Differentiation', which had appeared in 1890 in Schmoller's *Staatswissenschaftliche Forschungen*. Schmoller greeted Durkheim gladly in a review 'as one striving to the same end, although he has not convinced us altogether', and continued to pursue the subject and his thesis. After Schmoller's death in 1917, however, both the subject and his view of it found few friends – only Pontus Fahlbeck and (with reservations) Franz Oppenheimer and Joseph Schumpeter come to mind – before they were forgotten, at which point, of course, the dispute remained unresolved.

Many of the issues that came up in the course of this prolonged debate cannot be discussed here, either because they lead us too far from our subject or because they are merely historical curiosities. Notable among the other issues was Simmel's and Durkheim's discussion of the relation between the division of labor and social integration.[9] Among the historical curiosities is Schmoller's theory of the genetics of special abilities acquired by the progressive division of labor. Bücher rightly attacked this theory repeatedly and violently, without succeeding in forcing out of Schmoller more than very minor concessions. Yet Schmoller's position, especially in his early papers of 1889 and 1890, contains elements of a theory of class formation that has to be taken quite seriously, if only because in a new (but not very different) form it seems to play a certain role in contemporary sociology.

According to Schmoller's theory, class formation (that is, inequality of rank) is based on the fact that occupations are differentiated. However one may wish to explain the division of labor itself – Schmoller explains it in terms of the exchange principle, Bücher in terms of property (and neither regards it as universal) – differentiation precedes the stratification of social positions. 'The emergence of social classes always depends in the first instance on an advance in the division of labor within a people or a nation' (16, p. 74). Or even more clearly: 'The difference in social rank

9. For Simmel and Durkheim, and to some extent for Bücher and even Schmoller, the division of labor was the main concern, and class formation merely one of its aspects. There would certainly be a point in re-examining the origin of inequality of the differentiation type as well as inequality of the stratification type. The main question is whether the division of labor is based on the natural differences among men (between man and woman, adult and child, etc.), or whether it might be explained by purely social factors (such as technical development). As with stratification, one of the problems of the division of labor is whether it is a universal phenomenon, or a historically developed and therefore at least potentially ephemeral one (as Marx as well as Schmoller and Bücher believed). The consequences of the division of labor, too, require a re-examination that goes beyond Durkheim's at many points. I mention these problems to show that in confining ourselves to explanations of class formation by the division of labor, we are considering only a small segment of the sociological debate of the turn of the century.

and property, in prestige and income, is merely a secondary consequence of social differentiation' (see 16, p. 29).

Schmoller later modified his position without disavowing the principles on which it rested (see 17, p. 428 ff.). It must be admitted, however, that the crucial arguments against his views were not made in the literature of the time. To state them, we must remember the distinction between social differentiation and social stratification introduced above.

Since we tend, particularly in modern society, to associate social rank with occupational position, one might be led to suspect that differences of rank are in fact based on the differentiation of occupations. On the contrary, it must be emphasized that the notion of differentiation does not in itself imply any distinctions of rank or value among the differentiated elements. From the point of view of the division of labor (the 'functional organization' of industrial sociology), there is no difference in rank between the director, the typist, the foreman, the pipe fitter and the unskilled laborer of an enterprise: these are all partial activities equally indispensable for the attainment of the goal in question. If in fact we do associate a rank order (or 'scalar organization') with these activities, we do so as an additional act of evaluation, one that is neither caused nor explained by the division of labor; indeed, the same activities may be evaluated quite differently in different societies. What we have, then, is a rank order (i.e. a social stratification) of activities that in functional terms are merely differentiated in kind.[10]

Schmoller seems to have sensed this gap in his argument when, in later editions, he suddenly inserted a 'psychological fact' between the division of labor and the formation of classes: 'the need for human thought and feeling to bring all related phenomena of any kind into a sequence, and estimate and order them according to their value' (17, pp. 428–9). However factual this fact may be, that Schmoller felt compelled to introduce it serves as further evidence that social differentiation and social stratification cannot explain each other without some intermediate agency.

10. One difficult question remains unresolved here: whether there are two different kinds of coordination of partial activities – one 'functional', which merely follows 'inherent necessities' and completes the division of labor, and one 'scalar', which produces a rank order founded on other requirements.

This conclusion played an important part in the third major historical phase of sociological theorizing about the origin of inequality: the American discussion of the theory of social stratification. Since Talcott Parsons first published his 'Analytical Approach to the Theory of Social Stratification' in 1940, there has been an unceasing debate over the so-called 'functional' theory of social stratification. Almost all major American sociologists have taken part in this debate, which – unknown though it still is on the Continent – represents one of the more significant contributions of American sociology towards our understanding of social structures.

The chief immediate effect of Parsons's essay of 1940 was to acquaint American sociologists with the idea of a theory of social stratification. The largely conceptual paper published by Parson's disciple Kingsley Davis in 1942 was also mainly preparatory in character. The discussion proper did not begin until 1945, when Davis and Wilbert E. Moore published 'Some Principles of Stratification'. Both Rousseau and his successors and Schmoller and his adherents had regarded inequality as a historical phenomenon. For both, since there had once been a period of equality, the elimination of inequality was conceivable. Davis and Moore, by contrast, saw inequality as a functional necessity in all human societies – i.e. as indispensable for the maintenance of any social structure whatever – and hence as impossible to eliminate.

Their argument, at least in its weaknesses, is not altogether dissimilar to Schmoller's. It runs as follows. There are in every society different social positions. These positions – e.g. occupations – are not equally pleasant, nor are they equally important or difficult. In order to guarantee the complete and frictionless allocation of all positions, certain rewards have to be associated with them – namely, the very rewards that constitute the criteria of social stratification. In all societies, the importance of different positions to the society and the market value of the required qualifications determine the unequal distribution of income, prestige and power. Inequality is necessary because without it the differentiated (occupational) positions of societies cannot be adequately filled.

Several other writers, among them Marion J. Levy and Bernard Barber, have adopted this theory more or less without modification. But it has been subjected to severe criticism, and despite several thoughtful replies by the original authors, some of the criticisms seem to be gaining ground. The most persistent critic, Melvin M. Tumin, has presented two main arguments against Davis and Moore (in two essays published in 1953 and 1955). The first is that the notion of the 'functional importance' of positions is extremely imprecise, and that it probably implies the very differentiation of value that it allegedly explains. The second is that two of the assumptions made by Davis and Moore – that of a harmonious congruence between stratification and the distribution of talent, and that of differential motivation by unequal incentives – are theoretically problematical and empirically uncertain.

This second argument was bolstered in 1955 by Richard Schwartz, whose analysis of two Israeli communities showed that it is in fact possible to fill positions adequately without an unequal distribution of social rewards (18). Buckley charged Davis and Moore in 1958 with confusing differentiation and stratification; unfortunately, however, his legitimate objection to the evaluative undertones of the notion of 'functional importance' led in the end to an unpromising terminological dispute. Since then, criticism of the functional theory of stratification has taken two forms. Some critics have followed Dennis Wrong, who in 1959 took up Tumin's suggestion that Davis and Moore had underestimated the 'dysfunctions' of social stratification, i.e. the disruptive consequences of social inequality (19); the conservative character of the functional theory has been emphasized even more clearly by Gerhard Lenski (20). Other critics have raised methodological objections, questioning the value of a discussion of sociological universals that ignores variations observed in the workings of real societies.[11]

But the significance of the American debate on stratification is

11. The origin of inequality has been only one of several subjects of dispute in the American debate on stratification. Davis and Moore, for example, after their first few pages, turn to the empirical problems of the effect and variability of stratification. Their critics do much the same thing. But the dispute was ignited by the 'functional explanation of inequality': its substantive justification, its scientific fruitfulness and its political significance. The dispute, which still continues, may be seen as a commentary on the subterranean conflicts in American sociology.

only partly to be found in its subject matter. In this respect, its main conclusion would seem to be that social inequality has many functions and dysfunctions (that is, many consequences for the structure of societies), but that there can be no satisfactory functional explanation of the origin of inequality. This is because every such explanation is bound either to have recourse to dubious assumptions about human nature or to commit the *petitio principii* error of explanation in terms of the object to be explained. Yet this discussion, like its historical predecessors, has at several points produced valuable propositions, some of them mere remarks made in passing. With the help of these propositions, let us now attempt to formulate a theory of social stratification that is theoretically satisfactory and, above all, empirically fruitful.[12]

The very first contribution to the American debate on stratification, the essay by Parsons, contained an idea which, although untenable in Parsons's form, may still advance our understanding of the problem. Parsons tries to derive the necessity of a differentiated rank order from the existence of the concept of evaluation and its significance for social systems. The effort to formulate an ontological proof of stratification is more surprising than convincing – as Parsons himself seems to have felt, for in the revised version of his essay, published in 1953, he relates the

12. The concentration of my historical account of discussions of inequality on three epochs and positions – property in the eighteenth century, division of labor in the nineteenth and function in the twentieth – rests on my conviction that these are the most important stages in the discussion of the subject. But historically this account involves some questionable simplifications. As early as 1922, Fahlbeck (23, pp. 13–15) distinguished four explanations of inequality: (*a*) 'differences in estate are exclusively the work of war and conquest in large things, force and perfidy in little ones'; (*b*) 'in property and its differential distribution' can be found 'the real reason for all social differences'; (*c*) 'the origin and raison d'être of classes' can be traced to 'the connexions with the general economic factors of nature, capital, and labor'; and (*d*) 'classes are a fruit of the division of labor'. (Fahlbeck favors the last.) To these we should have to add at least the natural-differences explanation and the functional explanation. All six notions found support, at times side by side in the same works, and all six would have to be taken into account in a reasonably complete historical account of the problem. It is another question whether such an account would advance our knowledge.

existence of a concept of evaluation to the mere probability, not the necessity, of inequality.[13] In fact, Parsons's thesis contains little more than the suggestion, formulated much more simply by Barber, that men tend to evaluate themselves and the things of their world differently (21, p. 2). This suggestion in turn refers back to Schmoller's 'psychological assumption' of a human tendency to produce evaluative rank orders, but it also refers – and here the relation between evaluation and stratification begins to be sociologically relevant – to Durkheim's famous proposition that 'every society is a moral community'. Durkheim rightly remarks that 'the state of nature of the eighteenth-century philosophers is, if not immoral, at least amoral' (22, p. 394). The idea of the social contract is nothing but the idea of the institution of compulsory social norms backed by sanctions. It is at this point that the possibility arises of connecting the concept of human society with the problem of the origin of inequality – a possibility that is occasionally hinted at in the literature but that has so far gone unrealized.[14]

Human society always means that people's behavior is being removed from the randomness of chance and regulated by established and inescapable expectations. The compulsory character of these expectations or norms[15] is based on the operation of sanctions, i.e. of rewards or punishments for conformist or deviant behavior. If every society is in this sense a moral community, it

13. Parsons 1940 (24, p. 843): 'If both human individuals as units and moral evaluation are essential to social systems, it follows that these individuals *will be* evaluated as units.' And 1953 (25, p. 387): 'Given the process of evaluation, *the probability is* that it will serve to differentiate entities in a rank order of some kind.' (My emphases.) In both cases, as so often at those points of Parsons's work where classification is less important than conceptual imagination and rigor of statement, his argument is remarkably weak.

14. An attempt in this direction has recently been made by Lenski, but his approach and the one offered here differ significantly in their para-theoretical and methodological presuppositions.

15. Since expectations, as constituent parts of roles, are always related to concrete social positions, whereas norms are general in their formulation and their claim to validity, the 'or' in the phrase 'expectations or norms' may at first seem misleading. Actually, this is just a compressed way of expressing the idea that role expectations are nothing but concretized social norms ('institutions').

follows that there must always be at least that inequality of rank which results from the necessity of sanctioning behavior according to whether it does or does not conform to established norms. Under whatever aspect given historical societies may introduce additional distinctions between their members, whatever symbols they may declare to be outward signs of inequality, and whatever may be the precise content of their social norms, the hard core of social inequality can always be found in the fact that men as the incumbents of social roles are subject, according to how their roles relate to the dominant expectational principles of society, to sanctions designed to enforce these principles.[16]

Let me try to illustrate what I mean by some examples which, however difficult they may seem, are equally relevant. If the ladies of a neighborhood are expected to exchange secrets and scandals with their neighbors, this norm will lead at the very least to a distinction between those held in high regard (who really enjoy gossip, and offer tea and cakes as well), those with average prestige and the outsiders (who, for whatever reasons, take no part in the gossiping). If, in a factory, high individual output is expected from the workers and rewarded by piecework rates, there will be some who take home a relatively high paycheck and others who take home a relatively low one. If the citizens (or better, perhaps, subjects) of a state are expected to defend its official ideology as frequently and convincingly as possible, this will lead to a distinction between those who get ahead (becoming, say, civil servants or party secretaries); the mere followers, who lead a quiet but somewhat anxious existence; and those who pay with their liberty or even their lives for their deviant behavior.

16. A similar idea may be found at one point in the American discussion of stratification – as distinguished, perhaps, from Othmar Spann's biology-based argument (26, p. 293), 'The law of stratification of society is the ordering of value strata', which might seem superficially similar – in a passing remark by Tumin (6, p. 392). 'What does seem to be unavoidable,' Tumin says, 'is that differential prestige shall be given to those in any society who conform to the normative order as against those who deviate from that order in a way judged immoral and detrimental. On the assumption that the continuity of a society depends on the continuity and stability of its normative order, some such distinction between conformists and deviants seems inescapable.' It seems to me that the assumption of a 'continuity and stability of the normative order' is quite superfluous; it shows how closely Tumin remains tied to the functional approach.

One might think that individual, not social, inequalities are in fact established by the distinction between those who for essentially personal reasons (as we must initially assume, and have assumed in the examples) are either unprepared for or incapable of conformism and those who punctiliously fulfill every norm. For example, social stratification is always a rank order in terms of prestige and not esteem, i.e. a rank order of positions (worker, woman, resident of a certain area, etc.), which can be thought of independently of their individual incumbents. By contrast, attitudes toward norms as governed by sanctions seem to be attitudes of individuals. There might therefore seem to be a link missing between the sanctioning of individual behavior and the inequality of social positions. This missing link is, however, contained in the notion of social norm as we have used it so far.

It appears plausible to assume that the number of values capable of regulating human behavior is unlimited. Our imagination permits the construction of an infinite number of customs and laws. Norms, i.e. socially established values, are therefore always a selection from the universe of possible established values. At this point, however, we should remember that the selection of norms always involves discrimination, not only against persons holding sociologically random moral convictions, but also against social positions that may debar their incumbents from conformity with established values.

Thus if gossip among neighbors becomes a norm, the professional woman necessarily becomes an outsider who cannot compete in prestige with ordinary housewives. If piecework rates are in force in a factory, the older worker is at a disadvantage by comparison with the younger ones, the woman by comparison with men. If it becomes the duty of the citizen to defend the ideology of the state, those who went to school before the establishment of this state cannot compete with those born into it. Professional woman, old man, young man and child of a given state are all social positions, which may be thought of independently of their individual human incumbents. Since every society discriminates in this sense against certain positions (and thereby all their incumbents, actual and potential), and since, moreover, every society uses sanctions to make such discrimination effective, social norms and sanctions are the basis not only of ephemeral individual rankings but also of lasting structures of social positions.

The origin of inequality is thus to be found in the existence in all human societies of norms of behavior to which sanctions are attached. What we normally call the law, i.e. the system of laws and penalties, does not in ordinary usage comprise the whole range of the sociological notions of norm and sanction. If, however, we take the law in its broadest sense as the epitome of all norms and sanctions, including those not codified, we may say that the law is both a necessary and a sufficient condition of social inequality. There is inequality because there is law; if there is law, there must also be inequality among men.

This is, of course, equally true in societies where equality before the law is recognized as a constitutional principle. If I may be allowed a somewhat flippant formulation, which is nevertheless seriously meant, my proposed explanation of inequality means in the case of our own society that all men are equal *before* the law but they are no longer equal *after* it: i.e. after they have, as we put it, 'come in contact with' the law. So long as norms do not exist, and in so far as they do not effectively act on people ('before the law'), there is no social stratification; once there are norms that impose inescapable requirements on people's behavior and once their actual behavior is measured in terms of these norms ('after the law'), a rank order of social status is bound to emerge.

Important though it is to emphasize that by norms and sanctions we also mean laws and penalties in the sense of positive law, the introduction of the legal system as an illustrative *pars pro toto* can itself be very misleading. Ordinarily, it is only the idea of punishment that we associate with legal norms as the guarantee of their compulsory character.[17] The force of legal sanctions produces the distinction between the lawbreaker and those who succeed in never coming into conflict with any legal rule. Conformism in this sense is at best rewarded with the absence of penalties.

17. Possibly this is a vulgar interpretation of the law, in the sense that legal norms (which are after all only a special case of social norms) probably have their validity guaranteed by positive as well as negative sanctions. It may be suspected, however, that negative sanctions are preponderant to the extent to which norms are compulsory – and since most legal norms (almost by definition) are compulsory to a particularly great extent, behavior conforming to legal norms is generally not rewarded.

Certainly, this crude division between 'conformists' and 'deviants' constitutes an element of social inequality, and it should be possible in principle to use legal norms to demonstrate the relation between legal sanctions and social stratification. But an argument along these lines would limit both concepts – sanction and stratification – to a rather feeble residual meaning.

It is by no means necessary (although customary in ordinary language) to conceive of sanctions solely as penalties. For the present argument, at least, it is important to recognize positive sanctions (rewards) as both equal in kind and similar in function to negative sanctions (punishments). Only if we regard reward and punishment, incentive and threat, as related instruments for maintaining social norms do we begin to see that applying social norms to human behavior in the form of sanctions necessarily creates a system of inequality of rank, and that social stratification is therefore an immediate result of the control of social behavior by positive and negative sanctions. Apart from their immediate task of enforcing the normative patterns of social behavior, sanctions always create, almost as a by-product, a rank order of distributive status, whether this is measured in terms of prestige, or wealth, or both.

The presuppositions of this explanation are obvious. Using eighteenth-century concepts, one might describe them in terms of the social contract (*pacte d'association*) and the contract of government (*pacte de gouvernement*). The explanation sketched here presupposes (*a*) that every society is a moral community, and therefore recognizes norms that regulate the conduct of its members; (*b*) that these norms require sanctions to enforce them by rewarding conformity and penalizing deviance.

It may perhaps be argued that by relating social stratification to these presuppositions we have not solved our problem but relegated its solution to a different level. Indeed, it might seem necessary from both a philosophical and a sociological point of view to ask some further questions. Where do the norms that regulate social behavior come from? Under what conditions do these norms change in historical societies? Why must their compulsory character be enforced by sanctions? Is this in fact the case in all historical societies? I think, however, that whatever the answers to these questions may be, it has been helpful to reduce social stratification to the existence of social norms backed by sanctions, since this explanation shows the derivative nature of the problem of inequality. In addition, the derivation suggested here has the advantage of leading back to presuppositions (the existence of norms and the necessity of sanctions) that may be regarded as axiomatic, at least in the context of sociological theory, and therefore do not require further analysis for the time being.

To sum up, the origin of social inequality lies neither in human nature nor in a historically dubious conception of private property. It lies rather in certain features of all human societies, which are (or can be seen as) necessary to them. Although the differentiation of social positions – the division of labor, or more generally the multiplicity of roles – may be one such universal feature of all societies, it lacks the element of evaluation necessary to explain distinctions of rank. Evaluative differentiation, the ordering of social positions and their incumbent scales of prestige or income, is effected only by the sanctioning of social behavior in terms of normative expectations. Because there are norms and because sanctions are necessary to enforce conformity of human conduct, there has to be inequality of rank among men.

Social stratification is a very real element of our everyday lives, much more so than this highly abstract and indeed seemingly inconsequential discussion would suggest. It is necessary, then, to make clear the empirical relevance of these reflections, or at least to indicate what follows from this kind of analysis for our knowledge of society. Such a clarification is all the more necessary since the preceding discussion is informed, however remotely, by a view of sociology as an empirical science, a science in which observation can decide the truth or falsity of statements. What, then, do our considerations imply for sociological analysis?

First, let us consider its conceptual implications. Social stratification, as I have used the term, is above all a system of distributive status, i.e. a system of differential distribution of desired and scarce things. Honor and wealth, or, as we say today, prestige and income, may be the most general means of effecting such a differentiation of rank, but there is no reason to assume that it could not be effected by entirely different criteria.[18] As far as legitimate power is concerned, however, it has only one aspect that can be seen as affecting social stratification, namely patronage, or the distribution of power as a reward for certain deeds or virtues. Thus to explain differences of rank in terms of the necessity of sanctions is not to explain the power structure of societies;[19] it is rather to explain stratification in terms of the social structure of power and authority (using these terms to express Weber's distinction between *Macht* and *Herrschaft*). If the explanation of inequality offered here is correct, power and power structures logically precede the structures of social stratification.[20]

It is hard to imagine a society whose system of norms and sanctions functions without an authority structure to sustain it. Time

18. Honor and wealth (or prestige and income) are general in the sense that they epitomize the ideal and the material differences in rank among men.

19. Thus the theory advanced here does not explain the origin of power and of inequalities in the distribution of power. That the origin of power also requires explanation, at least in a para-theoretical context, is evident from the discussion of the universality of historicity of power (see below). What an explanation of inequalities of power might look like is hard to say; Heinrich Popitz suggests that the social corollaries of the succession of generations are responsible for such inequalities.

20. This conclusion implies a substantial revision of my previously published views. For a long time I was convinced that there was a strict logical equivalence between the analysis of social classes and constraint theory, and between the analysis of social stratification and integration theory. The considerations developed in the present essay changed my mind. I have now come to believe that stratification is merely a consequence of the structure of power, integration a special case of constraint, and thus the structural–functional approach a subset of a broader approach. The assumption that constraint theory and integration theory are two approaches of equal rank, i.e. two different perspectives on the same material, is not so much false as superfluous; we get the same result by assuming that stratification follows from power, integration from constraint, stability from change. Since the latter assumption is the simpler one, it is to be preferred.

This conclusion may also be seen as opposing the 'synthesis' of 'conservative' and 'radical' theories of stratification proposed by Lenski (20). It seems to me that this synthesis is in fact merely a superficial compromise, which is superseded at important points by Lenski himself: 'The distribution of rewards in a society is a function of the distribution of power, not of system needs' (20, p. 63).

and again, anthropologists have told us of 'tribes without rulers', and sociologists of societies that regulate themselves without power or authority. But in opposition to such fantasies, I incline with Weber to describe 'every order that is not based on the personal, free agreement of all involved' (i.e. every order that does not rest on the voluntary consensus of all its members) as 'imposed', i.e. based on authority and subordination (27, ch. 13, p. 27). Since a *volonté de tous* seems possible only in flights of fancy, we have to assume that a third fundamental category of sociological analysis belongs alongside the two concepts of norm and sanction: that of institutionalized power. Society *means* that norms regulate human conduct; this regulation is guaranteed by the incentive or threat of sanctions; the possibility of imposing sanctions is the abstract core of all power.

I am inclined to believe that all other categories of sociological analysis may be derived from the unequal but closely related trinity of norm, sanction and power.[21] At any rate, this is true of social stratification, which therefore belongs on a lower level of generality than power. To reveal the explosiveness of this analysis we need only turn it into an empirical proposition: the system of inequality that we call social stratification is only a secondary consequence of the social structure of power.

The establishment of norms in a society means that conformity is rewarded and deviance punished. The sanctioning of conformity and deviance in this sense means that the ruling groups of society have thrown their power behind the maintenance of norms. In the last analysis, established norms are nothing but ruling norms, i.e. norms defended by the sanctioning agencies of society and those who control them. This means that the person

21. This is a large claim, which would justify at least an essay of its own. For our present purposes only two remarks need be added. First, the three categories are obviously disparate. Sanction is primarily a kind of intermediate concept (between norm and power), although as such it is quite decisive. Norm has to be understood as anterior to power, just as the social contract is anterior to the contract of government (this may help as a standard of orientation). Second, we must ask whether the 'elementary category' of social role can also be derived from the trinity norm–sanction–power. I tend to think it can, at least in so far as roles are complexes of norms concretized into expectations. Beyond that, however, the question is open.

who will be most favorably placed in society is the person who best succeeds in adapting himself to the ruling norms; conversely, it means that the established or ruling values of a society may be studied in their purest form by looking at its upper class. Anyone whose place in the coordinate system of social positions and roles makes him unable to conform punctiliously to his society's expectations must not be surprised if the higher grades of prestige and income remain closed to him and go to others who find it easier to conform. In this sense, every society honors the conformity that sustains it, i.e. sustains its ruling groups; but by the same token every society also produces within itself the resistance that brings it down.

Naturally, the basic equating of conformist or deviant behavior with high or low status is deflected and complicated in historical societies by many secondary factors. (In general, it must be emphasized that the explanation of inequality proposed here has no immediate extension to the history of inequality or the philosophy behind it.) Among other things, the ascriptive character of the criteria determining social status in a given epoch (such as nobility or property) may bring about a kind of stratification lag: that is, status structures may lag behind changes in norms and power relations, so that the upper class of a bygone epoch may retain its status position for a while under new conditions. Yet normally we do not have to wait long for such processes as the '*déclassement* of the nobility' or the 'loss of function of property' which have occurred in several contemporary societies.

There are good reasons to think that our own society is tending toward a period of 'meritocracy' as predicted by Michael Young, i.e. rule by the possessors of diplomas and other tickets of admission to the upper reaches of society issued by the educational system. If this is so, the hypothesis of stratification lag would suggest that in due course the members of the traditional upper strata (the nobility, the inheritors of wealth and property) will have to bestir themselves to obtain diplomas and academic titles in order to keep their position; for the ruling groups of every society have a tendency to try to adapt the existing system of social inequality to the established norms and values, i.e. their own. Nevertheless, despite this basic tendency we can never expect historical societies to exhibit full congruence between the scales of stratification and the structures of power.[22]

The image of society that follows from this exceedingly general and abstract analysis is in two respects non-Utopian and thereby anti-Utopian as well.[23] On the one hand, it has none of the explicit or concealed romanticism of a revolutionary Utopia à la Rousseau or Marx. If it is true that inequalities among men follow from the very concept of societies as moral communities, then there cannot be, in the world of our experience, a society of absolute equals. Of course, equality before the law, equal suffrage, equal chances of education and other concrete equalities are not only possible but in many countries real. But the idea of a society in which all distinctions of rank between men are abolished transcends what is sociologically possible and has a place only in the sphere of poetic imagination. Wherever political programs promise societies without class or strata, a harmonious community of comrades who are all equals in rank, the reduction of all inequalities to functional differences, and the like, we have reason to be suspicious, if only because political promises are often merely a thin veil for the threat of terror and constraint. Wherever ruling groups or their ideologists try to tell us that in their society all men are equal, we can rely on George Orwell's suspicion that 'some are more equal than others'.

The approach put forward here is in yet another sense a path out of Utopia. If we survey the explanations of inequality in recent American sociology – and this holds for Parsons and Barber as it

22. The variability of historical patterns of stratification is so great that any abstract and general analysis of the kind offered here is bound to mislead. The criteria, forms, and symbols of stratification vary, as does their meaning for human behavior, and in every historical epoch we find manifold superimpositions. The question of what form stratification took in the earliest known societies is entirely open. This is but one of the many limitations of the present analysis.

23. The following para-theoretical discussion is *inter alia* a criticism of Lenski's oversimple dichotomy between 'conservative' and 'radical' theories of stratification. Our approach is 'radical' in assuming the dominant force of power structures, but 'conservative' in its suspicion that the unequal distribution of power and status cannot be abolished. Other combinations are conceivable.

does for Davis and Moore – we find that they betray a view of society from which there is no road leading to an understanding of the historical quality of social structures. In a less obvious sense this is also true, I think, of Rousseau and Marx; but it is more easily demonstrable by reference to recent sociological theory.[24] The American functionalists tell us that we ought to look at societies as entities functioning without friction, and that inequality among men (since it happens to exist) abets this functioning. This point of view, however useful in other ways, may then lead to conclusions like the following by Barber: 'Men have a sense of justice fulfilled and of virtue rewarded when they feel that they are fairly ranked as superior and inferior by the value standards of their own moral community' (7, p. 7). Even Barber's subsequent treatment of the 'dysfunctions' of stratification cannot wipe out the impression that the society he is thinking of does not need history any more because everything has been settled in the best possible way already: everybody, wherever he stands, is content with his place in society, and a common value system unites all men in a big, happy family.

It seems to me that whereas an instrument of this kind may enable us to understand Plato's Republic, it does not describe any real society in history. Possibly social inequality has some importance for the integration of societies. But another consequence of its operation seems rather more interesting. If the analysis proposed here proves useful, inequality is closely related to the social constraint that grows out of sanctions and structures of power. This would mean that the system of stratification, like sanctions and structures of institutionalized power, always tends to its own abolition. The assumption that those who are less favorably placed in society will strive to impose a system of norms that promises them a better rank is certainly more plausible and fruitful than the assumption that the poor in reputation and wealth will love their society for its justice.

Since the 'value system' of a society is universal only in the

24. The assumption that history follows a predetermined and recognizable plan is static, at least in the sense in which the development of an organism into an entelechy lacks the historical dimension of openness into the future. For this reason, and because of the static-Utopian notion of an ultimate state necessarily connected with such a conception, a lack of historicity might also be imputed to Rousseau and Marx.

sense that it applies to everyone (it is in fact merely dominant), and since, therefore, the system of social stratification is only a measure of conformity in the behavior of social groups, inequality becomes the dynamic impulse that serves to keep social structures alive. Inequality always implies the gain of one group at the expense of others; thus every system of social stratification generates protest against its principles and bears the seeds of its own suppression. Since human society without inequality is not realistically possible and the complete abolition of inequality is therefore ruled out, the intrinsic explosiveness of every system of social stratification confirms the general view that there cannot be an ideal, perfectly just, and therefore non-historical human society.

This is the place to recall once again Kant's critical rejoinder to Rousseau, that inequality is a 'rich source of much that is evil, but also of everything that is good'. There is certainly reason to regret that children are ashamed of their parents, that people are anxious and poor, that they suffer and are made unhappy, and many other consequences of inequality. There are also many good reasons to strive against the historical and therefore, in an ultimate sense, arbitrary forces that erect insuperable barriers of caste or estate between men. The very existence of social inequality, however, is an impetus toward liberty because it guarantees a society's ongoing dynamic, historical quality. The idea of a perfectly egalitarian society is not only unrealistic; it is terrible. Utopia is not the home of freedom, the forever imperfect scheme for an uncertain future; it is the home of total terror or absolute boredom.[25]

25. These last paragraphs contain in highly abridged form – and in part imply – two arguments. One is that the attempt to realize a Utopia, i.e. a society beyond concrete realization, must lead to totalitarianism, because only by terror can the appearance of paradise gained (of the classless society, the people's community) be created. The other is that within certain limits defined by the equality of citizenship, inequalities of social status, considered as a medium of human development, are a condition of a free society.

References

1. I. KANT. *Populäre Schriften* (edited by P. Menzer), Reimer, Berlin, 1911.
2. D. DIDEROT, *Encyclopédie, ou Dictionnaire raisonné* etc., new edition, Lausanne, 1786.
3. C. MEINERS. *Geschichte der Ungleichheit der Stände unter den vornehmsten Europäischen Völkern*, Hannover, 1792.
4. ARISTOTLE, *Politics*.
5. J. J. ROUSSEAU. *Discours sur l'origine de l'inégalité parmi les hommes*, in *Du contrat social* etc., new edition, Garnier Fréres, Paris, n.d.
6. M. M. TUMIN. 'Some principles of stratification: a critical analysis', *American Sociological Review*, vol. 18 (1953), no. 4.
7. W. BUCKLEY. 'Social stratification and the functional theory of social differentiation', *American Sociological Review*, vol. 23 (1958), no. 4.
8. W. SOMBART. 'Die Anfänge der Soziologie', *Erinnerungsgabe für Max Weber*, edited by M. Palyi, Leipzig, München, 1923.
9. H. H. JOGLUND. *Ursprünge und Grundlagen der Soziologie dei Adam Ferguson*, Dunker and Humblot, Berlin, 1959.
10. W. C. LEHMANN. *Adam Ferguson and the Beginnings of Modern Sociology*, Columbia University Press, New York, 1930.
11. W. C. LEHMANN. 'John Millar, Historical Sociologist', *British Journal of Sociology*, vol. 3 (1952), no. 1.
12. A. FERGUSON. *An Essay on the History of Civil Society*, London, 1783.
13. F. VON SCHILLER 'Etwas über die erste Menschengesellschaft nach dem Leitfaden der mosaischen Urkunde' *Sämmtliche Werke* (edited by Goedeke), vol. 6, Cotta, Stuttgart, 1872.
14. J. MILLER. *The Origin of the Distinction of Ranks*, Edinburgh, 1771.
15. L. VON STEIN. *Die Gesellschaftslehre*, 1852.
16. G. SCHMOLLER. 'Das Wesen der Arbeitsteilung und die soziale Klassenbildung', *Jahrbuch für Gesetzgebung, Verwaltung, und Volkswirtschaft*, vol. 14 (1890).
17. G. SCHMOLLER. *Grundriss der allgemeinen Volkswirtschaftslehre*, Duncker and Humblot, Liepzig, München, 1920.
18. R. SCHWARTZ, 'Functional alternatives to inequality', *American Sociological Review*, vol. 20 (1955). no. 4.
19. D. WRONG. 'The functional theory of stratification: some neglected considerations', *American Sociological Review*, vol. 24 (1959), no. 6.
20. G. LENSKI. *Power and Privilege: A Theory of Social Stratification*, McGraw-Hill, New York, 1966.
21. B. BARBER. *Social Stratification*, Harcourt, Brace, New York, 1965.
22. E. DURKHEIM. *De la division du travail social*, Presses Universitaires de France, Paris, 1960.
23. P. FAHLBECK. *Die klassen und die Gesellschaft*, G. Fischer, Jena, 1922.

24. T. PARSONS. 'An analytical approach to the theory of social stratification', *American Journal of Sociology*, vol. 45 (1940).
25. T. PARSONS. *Essays in Sociological Theory* (revised edition), Glencoe, Free Press, 1954.
26. O. SPANN. *Der wahre Staat*, Quelle and Meyer, Leipzig, 1921.
27. M. WEBER. *Wirtschaft und Gesellschaft*, Mohr (Siebeck), Tübingen, 1956.

2 W. G. Runciman

The Three Dimensions of Social Inequality

Excerpt from W. G. Runciman, *Relative Deprivation and Social Justice*, Routledge & Kegan Paul, 1966, pp. 36–52.

What exactly should be meant by 'social inequality'? Few of the many writers about it have been greatly concerned with niceties of terminology, for the various differences which can exist between groups or classes in wealth, or rank, or privilege have been readily visible and easy to describe since Aristotle and before. In post-industrial Europe, the obvious question has been how far the proletariat (whether or not referred to by this term) could or ought to advance towards a condition of equality with the strata of society above it. Some writers, like de Tocqueville or J. S. Mill or Alfred Marshall, have thought that European society was without doubt advancing towards a greater equality:

> Eight centuries ago [wrote Mill in 1830] society was divided into barons and serfs. . . . At every succeeding epoch, this inequality of condition is found to have somewhat abated; every century has done something considerable towards lowering the powerful and raising the low.[1]

Others, and most notably Marx, have argued that inequality was steadily widening. But whatever disagreement there might be about the consequences of industrialization, the question itself has always been obvious enough. Few observers of the evident differences between the rich and the poor have felt the need to define a rigorous and comprehensive theoretical framework, within which the various kinds of social inequality should be classified. But social inequalities are diverse and intricate, and some sort of categorization is a necessary prerequisite to any clear discussion of

1. J. S. Mill, 'Tocqueville on Democracy in America, vol. I' in *Essays on Politics and Culture*, ed. Gertrude Himmelfarb, New York, 1963, p. 175.

them. If social inequalities, of any kind, are to be either evaluated or explained, they must be first of all distinguished by reference to the numbers of separate dimensions in which the members of societies are collectively ranked above or below one another – that is, the meaning to be given to 'social stratification' as such.

The classification which results from putting the question in this form is not a new one. Sometimes it is phrased as the dis-distinction between 'economic', 'social' and 'political' equality. Alternatively, it can be phrased as the distinction between equality of 'class', 'status' and 'power'. But although it is a familiar distinction, it is almost always obscured or overridden by others. It is seldom, if ever, used to provide the fundamental classification under which all the others[2] ought at the outset to be subsumed. Any classification, of course, is legitimate if it answers to the purpose at hand. But if there are three, and only three, basic dimensions in which societies are stratified – class, status and power – then it necessarily follows that all social inequalities (in the sense opposed to individual inequalities such as height or weight) are inequalities of one or other of these three, and only three, kinds. It is, perhaps, self-evident that inequalities of class, status and power need not always coincide. But surprising as it seems, there is as far as I know no major writer on social inequality who has explicitly formulated and consistently retained the tripartite distinction. Indeed, I would go so far as to say that every one of the best-known discussions of inequality, from Aristotle to Rousseau to de Tocqueville to Tawney, has been confused by the neglect of it.

It does, however, raise difficulties of both terminology and substance. The terms class, status and power, as used in this sense, are generally credited to Max Weber. But it is not entirely clear what he meant by them, and even if a three-dimensional model is correct, the three are not terms of the same logical kind. It will, therefore, be convenient to recapitulate the distinction in ap-

2. For example, the useful distinction between 'civil', 'political' and 'social' equality drawn by T. H. Marshall, *Citizenship and Social Class*, Cambridge, 1950; or the five-fold distinction made by Lord Bryce, *The American Commonwealth*, 2nd edn, New York, 1910, vol. 2, chapt. 113; or the different five-fold distinction made by Giovanni Sartori, *Democratic Theory*, Detroit, 1962, p. 340.

proximately Weber's terms.[3] How far this represents a view with which Weber himself would have agreed does not matter very much. What does matter is that the distinction should be sufficiently well drawn to make clear what it means to argue that both the relation between inequality and relative deprivation and the implications of social justice for this relation are different in each of the three dimensions of social inequality.

A person's 'class'-situation, in Weber's sense, is the location which he shares with those who are similarly placed in the processes of production, distribution and exchange. This is close to the Marxist definition of class, and should be taken to cover not merely the possession or lack of capital, but also opportunities for any accretion of economic advantage under the conditions of the commodity and labour markets. Under the heading, therefore, of inequality of class we must consider not only differences of income between workers in different occupations, but also such differences as opportunities for upward mobility, advantages in kind, provisions for retirement and security of employment. In addition, there falls under the heading of class-situation what David Lockwood has called 'work-situation'. 'Work-situation', as distinct from 'market-situation', is defined as 'the set of social relationships in which the individual is involved by virtue of his position in the division of labour'.[4] What this means is that manual workers, as a distinct stratum in the economic system, need to be seen not only as venders whose location in the processes of the market habitually separates them, as workers, from those engaged in clerical or managerial tasks. Class-situation, therefore, is itself a complex phenomenon which embraces aspects of a person's economic situation in society which need not be in strict correlation with each other. They all, however, reflect inequalities directly derived from the productive system, so that to speak of a person's 'class' is to speak of his approximate, shared location in the economic hierarchy as opposed to the hierarchies of prestige or of power.

3. This account derives chiefly from the relevant passages translated in H. H. Gerth and C. Wright Mills (eds.), *From Max Weber: Essays in Sociology*, Oxford University Press, 1947.

4. David Lockwood, *The Blackcoated Worker*, Oxford University Press, 1958, p. 15.

'Status', by contrast, is concerned with social estimation and prestige, and although it is closely related to class it is not synonymous with it. Whether people recognize each other as social, as opposed to economic, equals is apt to depend on whether they share the same class-situation. But this is not necessarily so, as can be easily demonstrated by comparing, for instance, a curate and a bookmaker, or (an example of Orwell's) a naval commander and his grocer. Distinctions of status separate from class are visible among both non-manual and manual workers and their families. Within the same profession and therefore class, doctors or lawyers will belong in different status-groups according to social origin or secondary education or manner of speech. Among manual workers who are all operatives in the same factory, some will assume superior status in the neighbourhood where they live on the basis of a greater exclusiveness or respectability in social contacts and mode of life.[5] Just as habits and norms divide the middle from the upper-middle status-groups, so they divide the 'respectable' working-class status-groups from the 'rough'; even such apparently random factors as family size may be determinant.[6] There is always some sort of relation between the hierarchies of class and status, but status derives from a different aspect of economic behaviour from that which determines class location itself. As Weber emphasizes, status is generally determined by style of consumption rather than source or amount of income. The *nouveau riche* is the most familiar example. He may well be better placed in the economic hierarchy than the impoverished aristocrats whose social recognition he solicits; but until he has successfully modelled his manners and style of life upon theirs, they do not accept him as their equal. Status, like class, can be exceedingly complex. In different societies a man's status may depend not merely on his style of life but on such factors as his race or his age or his religious beliefs, and the problem of 'status-crystallization' . . . depends precisely on this fact. In addition, there may not be complete agreement in any society as to what entitles a person to high or low status.

5. If documentation is thought necessary, see the description given in the study of a Liverpool housing estate in *Neighbourhood and Community*, Liverpool, 1954, pp. 42 ff.

6. See L. Kuper (ed.), *Living in Towns*, London, 1953, p. 78.

Surveys have shown that there is a remarkable unanimity among industrialized countries on the prestige ranking of different occupations;[7] but there may well be groups within all societies who do not share the commonly accepted gradings, and by whom some attributes are quite differently ranked.[8] Thus several qualifications may have to be made in assigning to either a group or a single person a place in the prestige hierarchy of his society. But such placings must be subsumed under the general headings of status, as distinct from class, however much overlap or discrepancy may appear.

Inequality of status, therefore, covers those differences in social attributes and styles of life which are accorded higher or lower prestige. It is in this sense, not the sense of enonomic class, that the United States is sometimes spoken of as 'classless' or 'egalitarian'; inequalities of class are as wide as in Europe, but, as every European visitor to America has noticed, people in an inferior class-situation feel far less unequal in status. 'There is no rank in America,' wrote Bryce in 1893; 'that is to say, no external and recognized stamp, marking one man as entitled to any social privileges or to deference and respect from others.'[9] In Britain, by contrast, distinctions of status are deep-rooted, pervasive and readily visible. Status is manifested in such attributes as education, accent, style of dress and (sometimes independently of class-situation) type of job. Inequality of status, not class, is at issue when a clerical worker looks down on an artisan because he works with his hands or a middle-class father does not want his son to marry a working-class girl. Very often, relative deprivation of status rather than of class lies at the root of what is termed 'class-consciousness'. Although inequalities of all three kinds are complementary aspects of the same situation, this does not make them identical with each other.

It is, therefore, perfectly possible to claim or desire a greater equality of class but not of status, or of status but not of class. The difference can be readily illustrated by taking the two to their

7. See particularly A. Inkeles and Peter H. Rossi, 'National comparisons of occupational prestige', *American Journal of Sociology*, vol. 61 (1956), pp. 329–39.

8. As found by Michael Young and Peter Willmott, 'Social grading by manual workers', *British Journal of Sociology*, vol. 7 (1956), pp. 337–45.

9. op. cit. vol. 2, p. 813.

extremes. It is possible to envisage two kinds of egalitarian Utopias (leaving aside, for the moment, egalitarianism of power). In the first, all economic differentials are abolished, so that a university professor or a minister of state is no more highly rewarded than a labourer; but there still exist graded status-groups whose members rate each other as social equals in a recognized hierarchy of esteem. In the second kind of Utopia, every man treats every other as a social equal, whatever individual differences in character and aptitude may remain; but economic differentials are still permitted, and rewards, although not determining status, are themselves determined by criteria which yield considerable variations. Perhaps neither Utopia could in practice be realized. But they serve to illustrate that the demands for equality of class and of status need not be synonymous. Such loosely used phrases as 'social equality' or 'a classless society' may cover either or both of them.

In the same way, inequality of power need not be coterminous with inequality of status or even of class, although the connexion between class-situation and power-situation is usually demonstrable enough. Just as it is possible to want to equalize rewards without equalizing status, or vice versa, so it is possible to want to increase or diminish inequality of power independently of either status or class. The holders of power in a society need not be the most highly rewarded of its citizens, or even the most highly esteemed, and the demands of the relatively powerless may be independent of grievances of either class or status. It is true that trade unions, which are the most obvious example of a power-group or stratum, are normally concerned with the attainment of power in order to redress economic inequalities. It is also true that the demand for political equality in the sense of the franchise has almost always been tied both to economic interests and to the demand for social recognition for an underprivileged class. But it is possible to demand universal suffrage or equality before the law or workers' control of industry irrespective of demanding equality of class or status. The wish for a greater say in the decisions to which one's group will be required to submit may be an entirely independent motive. To the extent that power is a separate dimension of stratification from class and status, it must be a separate dimension of social inequality.

Political-cum-legal equality – what the Greeks called *isonomia* – is often distinguished from other kinds; but power is seldom explicitly treated as a dimension of stratification analogous to status and class. There is no equivalent terminology for power. We speak of a 'low-status' occupation, but not of a 'low-power' one; we speak of the 'middle class', but never of the 'middle power-stratum'. Weber himself does not use an equivalent word to *Klassen* and *Stände* when he talks about power: indeed, he is usually concerned with the relative power of classes and status-strata more than with the power hierarchy on its own. He does sometimes speak of 'politically oriented corporate groups', but, even if the phrase is accurate, it is much too cumbrous for ordinary use. In any case, when discussing stratification and inequality we need a word with the overtones of 'stratum' rather than 'group' or 'faction'. It must cover not only 'parties' in the usual sense but also pressure-groups, or trade unions, or any other collectivity whose potential for coercion enables us to place its members at a common level in the hierarchy of power. It might be argued that there is a second good reason for the deficiency of vocabulary since power may be of many different kinds, and those who hold it in varying degrees may not feel the least common identity as a social group. But this problem arises equally in the analysis of class and status: Marx's discussion of the French peasantry is the most celebrated of many statements of it. Social inequalities and the attitudes to them must as far as possible be equivalently analysed in each of the three dimensions of social stratification, irrespective of the separate issue of how far the members of a particular category are conscious of their common location.[10]

But although the tripartite distinction may not have been as clearly followed in discussion of inequality as one might expect, this does not mean that the importance of power in the social hierarchy has gone unrecognized. It has even been suggested, for instance, that in advanced industrial societies 'class' should be taken to mean 'conflict groups that are generated by the differential distribution of authority in imperatively co-ordinated

10. To a few writers, however, 'classes' are by definition self-conscious 'action-groups', and on this view it presumably follows that social inequalities are not necessarily differences of 'class' (or status or power).

associations'.[11] It might be preferable, for the sake of clarity, to rephrase this as the suggestion that stratification by power is more important than stratification by class, rather than as a redefinition of 'class'. But a strong case can be made for saying that in advanced industrial societies the genesis of 'class conflict' is to be looked for in the distribution of authority rather than economic benefits. The inequality of power inherent in industrial relations is similarly brought out by G. D. H. Cole in his comment that:

employers and workmen may be, in the eyes of the law, equal parties to a civil contract; but they are never equal parties in fact. The worker, under contract, is bound to serve his employer; the employer is entitled to order the workman about. The relation between them is thus essentially unequal.[12]

A wide variety of writers have argued that equality is unattainable precisely because whatever form a society takes there will have to be some men who are giving orders and others who are following them. To choose only a trivial example, some cogent remarks to this effect can be found in the mouth of Dick Deadeye in Gilbert and Sullivan's *H.M.S. Pinafore*. There is nothing very novel in the emphasis on either status or power as against economic class. What is difficult is to retain the tripartite distinction throughout all discussion of social stratification and the feelings of relative deprivation to which it gives rise.

The problem of terminology can be met only by laying down a chosen procedure and following it as consistently as possible. The lack of generally accepted practice is largely due to the variety of overtones which the term 'class' has acquired in English. We speak of a 'middle-class' house, or education, or way of speaking, when status rather than class is meant. We use the term 'ruling class' to talk about the holders of power. The phrase 'social class'

11. Ralf Dahrendorf, *Class and Class Conflict in an Industrial Society*, Stanford, 1959, p. 204.

12. G. D. H. Cole, *British Trade Unionism Today*, London, 1939, p. 86; cf., e.g. R. H. Tawney, *Equality*, Allen and Unwin, 1952, pp. 65–6, or Allan Flanders, *The Fawley Productivity Agreements*, Faber, 1964, p. 235: 'To use a political analogy, management represents the government of industry, and the unions, at their most effective, never more than a permanent opposition.'

may cover either or both of class and status. Furthermore, both 'class' and 'status' often carry a still broader sense: 'class' can be a virtual synonym for 'category' and 'status' for 'role'. Nor has the situation been helped by the diversity of jargon among academic writers; the sociological literature contains every kind of possible phrase, including both 'class status' and 'status class'. The practice which I shall accordingly follow is this: I shall use 'class' and 'status' in the sense which I have roughly defined and which derives from Weber; I shall use 'stratum' as the general term for a group or category of people who can be collectively ranked in any one, or all, of the three dimensions of social inequality; and I shall use 'stratification' as the corresponding abstract noun. I shall, however, use the phrases 'working class' and 'middle class' as synonyms for the manual and non-manual strata respectively (postponing for the moment the further difficulties of the manual/non-manual distinction). I shall also use 'working-class' and 'middle-class' as the corresponding adjectives, without in either case tying the meaning to class, status or power except to such extent as is made clear by the context.

This procedure is neither very elegant nor wholly unambiguous, but it is the best that can be done. The matter is further complicated by the use of survey material in which people are asked questions about 'class' which are neither phrased nor answered in terms of Weber's distinction. As a result, what people say has to be translated out of their own words and into the words of the investigator. There is, however, no objection in principle to this. It is true that whatever theoretical or terminological framework is used by the academic investigator, his subjects will not necessarily think in terms of it; but the framework will not be right or wrong solely for that reason.

At the same time, this is not to say that people's own views of the question can be disregarded by the investigator. In the first place, people's own pictures of how their society is stratified play an important part in their feelings, or lack of feelings, of relative deprivation. In the second, stratification by status depends by definition on the prestige which people assign to their own and other groups; people may be wrong about 'subjective' status in the sense that their own prestige is not what they think it is, but

53

the status-structure of their society is in fact determined solely by the feelings of its members. It is, therefore, just as important to know how stratification is seen by people themselves as to establish an 'objective' framework for assessing their views in terms of the relation between inequality and grievance.

There is some useful material on 'subjective' stratification from Britain,[13] as well as some from the United States,[14] Germany,[15] French Switzerland[16] and Australia.[17] On the basis of these studies, the pictures of Western industrial society which its inhabitants have can in principle be classified in terms of class, status and power models (or mixed models incorporating elements of all three). Although different terminologies have been used by the different investigators as well as by the different respondents whom they have interviewed, the distinction still holds good. A pure power model is not found very often; it is the type of model used by people who see society in terms of 'us' and 'them', where 'them' means those seen to be in authority, such as the government and the bosses, rather than the rich or the socially esteemed. A status model is the type where society is seen as arranged in a graded hierarchy of prestige; users of status models tend to see the social hierarchy as composed of more numerous and overlapping 'classes' (that is, status-strata) than the users of power or class models. A class model, finally, is a model based on distinctions of job or income, and particularly on the economic aspects of a person's job. In a status model also, occupation may play an important role. But in a status model, the social aspect is more significant than the economic. The prestige of a job, or the style of life that goes with it, or the educational qualifications which it requires, are what matter for the hierarchy of status. In a

13. F. M. Martin, 'Some subjective aspects of social stratification', in D. V. Glass (ed.), *Social Mobility in Britain*, Routledge, 1954, chapt. 3; Elizabeth Bott, *Family and Social Network*, Tavistock, 1957, chapt. 6.

14. In particular, R. Centers, *The Psychology of Social Class*, Princeton, 1949; but see also, e.g. J. G. Manis and B. N. Meltzer, 'Attitudes of textile workers to class structure', *American Journal of Sociology*, vol. 60 (1954), pp. 30–35.

15. H. Popitz *et al.*, *Das Gesellschaftsbild des Arbeiters*, 2nd edn, Tübingen, 1961.

16. A. Willener, *Images de la Societé et Classes Sociales*, Berne, 1957.

17. O. A. Oeser and S. B. Hammond, *Social Structure and Personality in a City*, Routledge, 1954, chapts. 21 and 22.

power model, by contrast, the authority invested in certain occupational positions is their most important feature; and in a class model, the significance of occupations is the wealth or security of tenure which will accrue from them. In either a pure model or a combination of the three society may in principle be seen as divided into any number of separate strata. But in practice, the users of class models seem seldom to envisage more than two or, at the most, three strata; only the users of status models may be aware of a slightly more complex multiplicity of levels.

It is obvious that many people will operate with a mixture of these models. Moreover, they may apply a different model in a different context or they may have no explicit views on the matter at all. But not the least interesting result of these studies is to show how rarely this is so. There are bound to be a few respondents whose pictures of society are so anomalous or unclear that any categorization would be illegitimate. In addition, there are always a few who resolutely refuse to avow any acceptance of the term 'class' at all. But in general, the studies carried out afford strong evidence that in advanced industrial societies the majority of people do have an explicit picture of their social hierarchy and that most of these pictures fall into one or other of a relatively few distinguishable categories.[18] The 'subjective' evidence cannot by itself show how systems of stratification ought best to be classified; but it does provide further support for the validity of the tripartite distinction between class, status and power.

The most difficult question, however, is not how many dimensions of stratification there are, but where the dividing-line should be drawn within each. The dividing-line around which this study is organized is that between the manual and non-manual strata, defined in terms of occupation or, in the case of married women, husband's occupation. But this division, although widely used, could be argued to be no more significant for social inequality than others, and it is in any case difficult to define exactly. The Registrar-General uses it but he does not give a criterion for it, and he deliberately conflates class and status: his two classifications by 'social class' and 'socio-economic group' are explicitly based on considerations of 'standing within the community' and

18. See particularly the tables shown in Willener, op. cit., p. 161, and Popitz, op. cit., p. 233.

on the correlation of occupational position with similarities of 'social, cultural and recreational standards and behaviour'.[19] No single criterion is satisfactory; and whatever definition is used, there will be some difficult borderline cases. But despite the difficulty of precise demarcation, the manual/non-manual division can be defined and applied in such a way that the number of borderline cases is small. I have therefore relegated the problem of applying it to an appendix,[20] where it is discussed with detailed reference to the analysis of the survey. It is, however, necessary to give some justification for adopting it in the first place as the principal line of demarcation, however widely it may be recognized and used.

It can, indeed, be attacked from either of two opposite viewpoints. On one view, deriving from Marx, the dichotomy is not between manual and non-manual workers but between the capitalists and the propertyless; on the opposite view, deriving from the alleged *embourgeoisement* of the working class, the line is, if anywhere, between skilled and unskilled, since many manual workers have become so prosperous as not to be ranked as proletarians, but rather as members of a newly emergent 'middle class'. Either of these two criticisms can be supported by the observation that many manual workers now earn as much as or more than many white-collar workers. On either argument, some manual and some non-manual workers, even if they should still be assigned to different status-strata, nevertheless belong to the same economic class; to the Marxist, all clerical workers are below the proletarian line; to the anti-Marxist, many manual workers are above it. Both these arguments, however, are outweighed by other aspects of the structure of inequalities which still divide the manual from the non-manual worker in class as well as status. To argue that this remains the fundamental distinction is not to deny that a partial breakdown of it may be taking place. But the breakdown, if that is what it is, cannot be claimed to have gone so far that the two categories have merged, whether on one side of the line or the other. It is therefore necessary to look at the changes which are taking place initially in terms of the manual/non-

19. *Classification of Occupations 1960*, H.M.S.O., pp. 10–11.

20. See Appendix 3, 'The manual/non-manual distinction' [not included in this edition].

manual distinction, even if the conclusion to which this leads is that the distinction is not as significant as it once was.

This is not to say that the divisions to be drawn within the two strata are not for some purposes as significant as those between them. In the hierarchy of class, there is obviously a difference between craftsmen and labourers, just as there is between the lowest-paid clerical workers and the possessors of land or capital or highly marketable professional skills. In the hierarchy of status, the difference between the middle and the upper strata may be as wide or wider than that between the artisan and the clerk: the members of the upper stratum may no more often treat as equals those differently brought up from themselves, than the lower stratum of white-collar workers will treat the skilled manual workers with whom they might have shared a common schooling. In the hierarchy of power, indeed, it is hardest to show that the manual/non-manual division is fundamental. The lower-paid white-collar worker is in general as much the recipient of orders as the manual worker, and may have no more influence than the member of a strong trade union on the processes of decision by which his working life is governed; it is only the tendency of the non-manual stratum not to form trade unions, and to identify its political interests with the strata opposed to labour which shows the division to be important in the dimension of power, as well as status and class. If, however, one looks in broad terms at the social structure of an advanced industrial society such as Britain, it is difficult not to see the biggest single division as that between the two out of three people the head of whose household works with his hands, and the one out of three the head of whose household does not.

Of the reasons why manual and non-manual workers should still be assigned to separate strata, one of the most important is 'work-situation' in Lockwood's sense. Although manual and clerical workers can be described with equal truth as virtually propertyless, and although their level of wages and salaries overlaps to an increasing extent, they are nevertheless engaged, as a result of their different location in the processes of production, in fundamentally different work. It is not only different in its externals – the white collar as against the calloused hands, or the desk instead of the machine. It is different in terms of the relation between employer and employee. The clerical worker may be less one of 'them' than the manual worker thinks him, but he is still closer to 'them', both literally and metaphorically, than the manual worker is. This may not have been so in the days when a 'factory' consisted of a handful of craftsmen who were all on personal terms with the head of the firm; and it may not be so in the future when both manual and clerical work have become completely automated. But in the mid-twentieth century, the division between 'works' and 'staff' is basic to large-scale industry, and it is this division which places the clerical worker on one side and the manual worker on the other. Moreover, the non-manual worker's work-situation is a determinant of his place in the status hierarchy also; he is associated with the employers by being associated with that part of the productive process where authority is exercised and decisions taken. This still does not make his own location in the power hierarchy of society any higher than that of the manual worker; this is always a function of unionization more than of location in the productive process. But in conditions of work the white-collar worker is on the other side of a distinctive line from the manual worker, and this is both a significant aspect of his class-situation and also one of the determinants of his status.

The class-situation of the non-manual worker is different in other respects also. Even if his salary, particularly at the early stages of his career, is below what is earned by many manual workers, he has the prospect of both a greater security of tenure and a greater increment in reward. By and large, the non-manual worker's income can be expected to rise steadily with length of service and experience, whereas a manual worker may well reach his maximum earning power in his twenties. There are exceptions to this, notably in the steel industry, where a manual worker's earnings will increase markedly as a result of promotion within the range of manual work. But this is rare. The great majority of manual jobs are such that there is no premium on experience, and increasing age, particularly if coupled with ill-health, will be a greater disadvantage than it will ever be in non-manual work. The premium on experience may become a disadvantage when unemployment is severe, because a man whose job in one firm has been taken away will find his experience no recommendation to any prospective employer except the one who has just declared him redundant. But as we shall see . . . even when unemployment in Britain has been widespread its incidence has been a good deal lower among non-manual than manual workers. Moreover, greater economic advantages are enjoyed by non-manual workers in such things as holidays, allowances and provisions for retirement, and apart from all these the manual worker is likely to have to work considerably longer hours than the clerical worker in order to equal him in income. Thus neither the partial equivalence of earnings between the manual and non-manual class, nor their common propertylessness, should be allowed to outweigh the distinction in class-situation between them.

The argument for continuing to treat the manual/non-manual division as basic is further supported by the evidence on subjective attitudes to stratification, even though, as I have said, this does not make it necessarily correct. In spite of the additional divisions or subdivisions also cited by respondents, the relevant studies seem to bear out the significance in most people's minds of this central division. Willener, though explicitly more cautious than Centers about placing too much emphasis on a manual/non-manual dichotomy,[21] still notes how often responses are given in terms of either 'middle class' or 'working class'. There are many people who will place themselves in either the 'middle' or 'working' class without exactly meaning by this the manual or non-manual stratum; but this is still the commonest criterion given. Martin found that among a sample drawn in Greenwich and Hertford in 1950 four out of five respondents explicitly assigned themselves to the 'working' or 'middle' class when asked first 'How many social classes would you say there are in this country?', second 'Can you name them?', and then 'Which of these classes do you belong to?'[22] Popitz suggests that the manual/non-manual distinction may be considerably reinforced by the belief of manual workers that it is only they who really 'work';[23] in other words, what they see clerical workers doing seems to them not only easier (in the English term, 'cushier') than what they do themselves, but it is also harder for them to see its

21. op. cit., p. 216.
22. op. cit., pp. 54–5.
23. op. cit., pp. 237 ff.

relation to the actual production of goods. Zweig, writing about London in 1946–7, called the difference in mentality, attitude and behaviour between the two 'perhaps the most outstanding single fact' brought to light by his inquiry.[24] In England, further evidence may be adduced from the popular image of the two major political parties, particularly the Labour Party. To most Englishmen, the Labour Party is the party of the working class; and the working class means those who work with their hands.

In the same way, the evidence for subjective attitudes to stratification reinforces the argument for treating the manual/non-manual line as fundamental in the hierarchy of status. Evidence about self-rated 'class' is likely to be relevant here, precisely because the distinction between class and status is explicit in very few people's minds; attitudes about status expressed in terms of 'class' can preserve the manual/non-manual distinction even when rewards are more or less equal. There is not yet sufficient evidence to dispute Lockwood's assertion, in his discussion of the status-situation of the clerical worker, that 'there are many indications that the division between manual and non-manual work is still a factor of enduring significance in the determination of class-consciousness, despite changes in the relative economic position of the two groups'.[25] This seems, moreover, to be true on both sides of the line. Not only do manual workers often seem contemptuous of the lower-middle class,[26] but it is often the members of the lower-middle class who are most anxious to distinguish themselves in prestige and social contacts from manual workers. Willmott and Young, studying the London suburb of Woodford in 1959, concluded that a greater equivalence of incomes, houses and styles of life had the effect of reinforcing the endeavours of the middle class to preserve the status barrier between themselves and manual workers.[27] The equivalence of incomes makes it possible in principle for working-class families to adopt a style of life similar to that of middle-class families whose earnings are the same; the assimilation in style of dress which has to some extent

24. F. Zweig, *Labour, Life and Poverty*, London, 1948, p. 88.

25. *The Blackcoated Worker*, p. 131.

26. Martin, op. cit., p. 61; and cf., e.g., Zweig, *The British Worker*, London, 1952, p. 206.

27. Peter Willmott and Michael Young, *Family and Class in a London Suburb*, Routledge, 1960, p. 122.

taken place since the Second World War is one manifestation of this.[28] But the visible differences in manners, education and leisure are still there; and the division at places of work between 'staff' and 'works' still continues to reinforce the disincentive for those on either side of the line to treat each other as status equals.

If manual and clerical workers were all to treat each other as equals, ask each other with equal frequency into each others' houses as friends, and so on, then differences in styles of dress or speech or leisure, however visible, would cease to constitute barriers of status. But no one can seriously suppose that this has yet happened in Britain; and therefore the differences which remain in styles of dress and the rest can be legitimately described as 'objective' status differences. It is also true that gradations of status may be so subtle that it becomes impossible to draw a line between one subdivision and the next. There have always been intricate subdivisions within the manual as well as the non-manual stratum: the 'aristocrats of labour' of the Victorian period were aristocrats of status as well as class, and some middle-class differentiations of status in terms of schooling, or accent, or family are particularly difficult to pin down. No hard and fast line can be drawn within the hierarchy of status to distinguish the 'respectable' working class from the 'rough', or the 'U' middle class from the 'non-U', although both these distinctions have a meaning. But one of the strongest arguments for drawing the principal line between manual and non-manual workers is the well-attested difference in the traditional values and ethos of the two strata – a difference which at once derives from, and helps to preserve, the other differences of which I have been speaking.

This difference can be put in one way by saying that working-class norms are 'collectivist', and middle-class norms 'individualist';[29] this is one reason why the relative deprivations felt by working-class people are more likely to be what I have called 'fraternalistic' and those felt by middle-class people 'egoistic'.

28. See, e.g., the remark of a middle-aged East End workman that 'In my days, you could tell a workman by his dress, even on a Sunday, but you can't now', quoted by Zweig, *The British Worker*, p. 164; and cf. Mark Abrams, *The Changing Pattern of Consumer Spending*, London, 1959, for evidence on the assimilation of styles of life.

29. J. H. Goldthorpe and David Lockwood, 'Affluence and the British class structure', *Sociological Review*, n.s. vol. 11 (1963), pp. 146–8.

The 'collectivistic' norms extend over a wide area of attitudes and behaviour, including not merely attitudes to the social structure. For Britain, they are vividly described in Hoggart's *Uses of Literacy*.[30] They embody a whole different attitude to life from that in which the middle-class child is reared, and they are reinforced throughout adult life by the differences in both work-situation and market-situation which separate the manual from the non-manual stratum. They are not, of course, universally shared by manual workers and their families. But they are sufficiently strong and widespread to reinforce very considerably the barriers of status which divide the two strata. Even where a manual and a non-manual family may be earning as much as each other the difference in outlook is likely to be enough to sustain the mutual distrust described in Woodford by Willmott and Young. Quite apart, moreover, from the wish of the middle class not to accept manual workers as social equals, the 'collectivist' attitudes of the working class may lead its members not to have any wish to be so treated. Some convincing evidence for this is provided by investigations carried out in the United States.[31] Even in a country where manual incomes are higher and status-differences less than in Britain, it seems that prosperity need not assimilate manual workers to non-manual in either personal contacts or social norms.

The claim that the working and middle class were becoming steadily fused was quite often made in the 1930s, and increasingly so during the 1940s and 1950s. But it must for all the reasons which I have given be heavily qualified. It has, indeed, come under effective attack, notably in the work of Lockwood.[32] It is un-

30. Richard Hoggart, *The Uses of Literacy*, Penguin, 1957.

31. See particularly A. Kornhauser *et al.*, *How Labor Votes*, New York, 1956, ch. 7, and Bennett M. Berger, *Working-class Suburb*, Berkeley, California, 1960; and cf., e.g. R. A. Dahl, *Who Governs?*, New Haven, 1961, pp. 232–3.

32. As well as *The Blackcoated Worker*, see 'The New Working Class', *Archives Européennes de Sociologie*, vol. 1 (1960), pp. 248–59, and Goldthorpe and Lockwood, op. cit. For an attempt to relate some of the evidence of the present study to Goldthorpe and Lockwood's model of *embourgeoisement*, see W. G. Runciman, '*Embourgeoisement*, self-rated class and party preference', *Sociological Review*, n.s. vol. 12 (1964), pp. 137–54. For references to statements of the *embourgeoisement* thesis, see the footnotes to the papers by Goldthorpe and Lockwood and by myself.

questionable that the difference between the manual and non-manual strata was in many respects wider in 1918 than 1962; the changes which occurred between these two dates will in part be documented elsewhere. But they are not such as to shift the most important dividing-line in the British social structure, whether considered in the light of inequalities of status or of class. The principal question, therefore, in examining the relation between inequality and grievance, is how far the relative deprivations felt by the members of the manual stratum are proportionate to its position of inequality by comparison with the non-manual.

This is true also in the dimension of power. Power raises difficulties of its own, and I shall say less about it than the other two. But any discussion of the relation between inequality and grievance would be incomplete without some reference to it. Not only are the implications of social justice different for power as against class and status. In addition, it is impossible to understand the radicalism, or lack of it, of the British working class without understanding something of how both its power-situation and its members' own view of its power-situation have altered since 1918. I shall not explore this in any detail, since it leads almost at once into the separate and specialized field of industrial sociology. In a country where universal suffrage and equality before the law are established and where there is a strong left-wing party explicitly formed to represent the working-class interest, inequalities of power are perceived and resented mainly in the relations between employer and employee. This complex topic lies outside the scope of this book, and the sample survey does not attempt to deal with it. I shall, however, suggest that the relation between inequality and grievance is different in this dimension of inequality also. In each dimension, the relation between inequality and grievance can only be settled by asking separately what are the inequalities to which manual workers and their families are subject, and whether the relative deprivations which they feel are proportionate to them. Only then can the further question be asked whether the relative deprivations felt in each dimension accord with the demands of social justice.

Part Two
Different Conceptions of Class

For many, the term 'class' has become a synonym for social inequality. Yet there are few words in the entire vocabulary of sociology to which so many different meanings have been attached. The concept of class owes much to the ideas of Marx; here we examine contributions by two European authors (one from the West, the other from the East), whose attitudes to Marxism are very different. Aron contrasts the American concept of class with the French (or European); the first he finds to be nominalist and the second to be realist. Ossowski makes a different kind of contrast; he opposes the hierarchical view of class to the dichotomous view. Historically, the dichotomous view has been closely associated with a realist position, and the hierarchical view with a nominalist one.

3 R. Aron

Two Definitions of Class

R. Aron, *La Lutte de Classes*, Gallimard, Paris, 1964, pp. 57–73. Translated by A. Béteille.

I tried to explain earlier in my last lecture how Marx's doctrine of class comprises two aspects. The first – positive and almost empirical – defines class as a social ensemble characterized by its place in the process of production; this place is determined at one and the same time by its technical role and by its relation to the means of production; further, this social ensemble acquires consciousness of itself, discovers its unity in relation to other ensembles and enters into conflict with them. This definition, with certain reservations, is acceptable to others besides Marxists. What constitutes the distinctiveness of Marx's doctrine is its second aspect, its philosophy of history, centred on the notion of class according to which the whole society should be defined by its ruling class which controls the means of production and dominates and exploits the others. Between these two aspects a middle way is provided by an interpretation of the development of capitalist society. In effect, if, along with the development of this society, the different social groups tend to be polarized around the two principal classes, the conflict between the bourgeoisie and the proletariat is the essential thing, and everything is reduced to a choice between the former and the latter.

Today I would like to leave aside altogether the philosophy of history, and to take as my point of departure the sociological definition of class, without intending to add my own to all the others which you can find in the books devoted to the subject. In this context I would advise you to read, for example, the course on the concept of social class which has been published by my colleague, Mr Gurvitch, in which you will find an enumeration and analysis of the different definitions that have been formulated. I believe, in fact, that every new definition ends almost inevitably in creating additional ambiguities; the real problem in the definition of the concept is to determine what follows from a convention and, as such, does not lend itself to discussion and what, on the other hand, represents affirmations pertaining to reality and is, consequently, susceptible to being discussed, demonstrated or refuted. In the controversies concerning class, my aim is to distinguish questions of terminology which do not relate to the true or the false but only to what is convenient or inconvenient, suitable or unsuitable, from what constitutes the real problem, to be solved in one way or another by the different theorists, i.e. what concerns facts and, consequently, ought to be either true or false.

In order to attempt this distinction, which is not without its difficulties, I shall begin with a question which is often asked and to which I already referred in my last lecture: are social classes distinctive of modern industrial societies or does one find them in all known societies? The Marxists would reply that they exist in all historically recorded societies; so would Schumpeter; but other sociologists like Mr Gurvitch argue that social classes exist only in contemporary societies where economic activities predominate, and where industrialization progressively transforms the totality of existence. I wish to see how much, in these two theories, derives from terminology and how much from facts. Where do the sociologists disagree on terminology and where do they diverge in their manner of conceiving societies in general and ours in particular?

According to the Marxist conception, all societies are divided into social classes because the infrastructure is always constituted by the means and the relations of production, i.e. the régime of property and the technical organization of work taken together. In each society there is a dominant class which is the owner of the means of production; in each, one encounters discrimination between the dominating and the dominated, the exploiters and the exploited. Schumpeter's response is the same, but the reasons adduced are different. His essential idea is the *fundamental heterogeneity of each human society*. Individuals are unequally endowed, they fulfil different functions or exercise different trades; in each society a certain type of human or social quality is necessary for occupying superior positions.

Everywhere, then, there are men who are at the top, who rule and dominate, and these men or, rather the families to which they belong, do not remain there indefinitely; some fall and others rise. This social circulation is found in all societies because everywhere we find heterogeneity defined at the same time by the unequal qualities of individuals, and by the diversity of aptitudes which assure promotion and success, according to the climate of the times. Whereas, according to Marx, there have always been classes because until the present there has always been private ownership of the means of production, according to Schumpeter, this fact is due to the heterogeneity of men and to social mobility.

Those who deny the universality of social classes in all historical epochs define them in a more precise and limiting way. Mr Gurvitch would say that it is proper to distinguish, for instance, between *caste*, *order* and *class*. Of these three notions, the first denotes a closed group, characterized by the occupation of its members and the impossibility of entering or leaving it; these two characteristics are not present in modern social classes. Likewise, in France there existed formerly essential legal inequalities between members of different *orders*; a nobleman was born as such, he enjoyed prerogatives and privileges and he was subject to a different law from what applied to the commoners, the bourgeois, the peasants or the artisans; personal status differed from one order to another. Now, social classes are neither closed like castes nor rigorously defined by law like orders; if you define classes by non-discrimination of legal status, obviously you will not find them in all societies. *Social class is one among the modalities of group differentiation encountered in all societies*; this differentiation presents specific characters in each type of society. If you choose a vague definition (e.g. 'groups hierarchically arranged within a global society'), you will find classes in all known societies. But, again, if you decide to consider only the characters presented by these groups in modern societies, then social classes will not be there in all societies.

Is this to say that the dispute is purely and simply verbal? It would be oversimple to imagine that these questions of terminology do not conceal sociological, historical or philosophical problems. Why, according to the Marxists, can one establish the same phenomenon everywhere and for all periods? It is because, for them, the basis, the principle of all known societies is, in the last analysis, the same. At least in its usual interpretation, Marxism implies that the infrastructure determines or conditions society; in other words, the economic factor must have been dominant in the past as it is today. When one believes that the fundamental structure of all societies is the same, one defines classes in such a fashion that they are found in all societies. By contrast, the concept, as it is defined by Mr Gurvitch, suggests or presupposes that the dominant factor differs from one society to another.

Beyond this, the real problem is formulated in the following question: up to what point is the structural or organizational principle of all societies the same? This question evidently leads to another: up to what point can social classes disappear in the society of the future? If you define classes with reference to private ownership of the means of production, nothing is easier than to make the former vanish by hoping to suppress the latter. By contrast, if you explain the existence of classes by the unequal talents of individuals and the rise and fall of families, you will affirm on the same evidence that the phenomenon will persist. For the moment, I do not wish to carry the argument further. I will simply say that, through an arbitrary choice, I will consider in what follows only social groups in modern industrial societies in their characteristic features (except where the contrary is expressly indicated).

Let us go back to the limiting definition of social class; we are very far from finding one on which all are agreed. To continue the same kind of analysis, i.e. to distinguish between disputes over words and over facts, I will present two definitions which I have taken over from two sociologists, an American and a Frenchman. Here is the first:

The term class denotes an ensemble, a conglomeration of persons within society, possessing approximately the same status. The class system, or the system of social stratification, is the system of classes in their internal and external relations. The class system is not identical with the structure of power, i.e. with the network of relations in which conduct is influenced by command and constraint. Nor is it identical with the property system in which the use of material objects and the returns from them are reserved for those with specific qualifications (property rights). The class system is not identical with the occupational system. The class system is the totality of relations constituted by expressions of deference, accorded to individuals, roles and institutions in the light of their place in the systems of power, property and occupation. Deference is an expression of respect or honor associated with sentiments of inequality or inferiority. By a logical extension, sentiments showing lack of respect or esteem, or showing contempt or superiority are also included in this conception of deference.

This passage puts the accent on the social status of each individual in terms of the esteem or respect accorded to him by the others. Simultaneously, it suggests that it is legitimate to distinguish between the systems of power, occupation and property. Finally, it implies that the status of each individual is, so to say, the synthetic product of multiple factors. Each person enjoys a certain position of esteem or prestige which results from the totality of situations in which he exists, and each situation can be analysed from three points of view: in relation to property, occupation and power. Is a definition of this kind true or false? To begin with, let us admit that the question posed in this way is without meaning: the problem is to know if a definition is acceptable, if it can be applied to real facts which it is able to isolate or identify, and if the propositions which follow from it are true. Let us examine these conditions. Does the passage which I have just quoted apply to any real fact? Unquestionably: roughly, one can say that different individuals in a society have greater or lesser prestige in relation to their fellow-men, a social status which can be described as position in society or level in a hierarchy of prestige or esteem. The phenomenon is perhaps not easy to identify, the place which each person has in the esteem of the other members may vary according to the milieu, it has not been demonstrated that the different occupations are equally esteemed or despised by all; in spite of these obstacles, one can say that the phenomenon is real even though it is badly defined. Moreover, the hierarchy of prestige is not the same when one considers occupation, income and power. You can think of a man who is very rich but has little prestige (consider the gangster chief) or, again, someone whose occupation as such does not confer high prestige – a teacher, for example – but who on his own account and by his personal qualities gains respect and admiration. Finally, power does not necessarily imply a very high degree of prestige: a union secretary may have real authority over many of his fellows without being highly esteemed by all the members of society. Whatever be the case, one may admit that the relations of property, occupation and power should not be confused with the sum total of social considerations.

If these propositions are acceptable, so is the definition; in other words, we have here a real phenomenon. You may decide by convention to speak of 'social classes' when referring to the different groups within the total society, each comprising men having analogous prestige status. How far are these groups clearly defined? Does one know precisely to which one each individual belongs? These questions do arise, but since the phenomenon is real, you are free to define class in this way.

Let us now take the more complicated definition given by a French sociologist:

Social classes are specific groupings of very vast span, representing macrocosms of subordinate groupings, macrocosms whose unity is based on their suprafunctionality, their resistance to penetration by the global society, their radical incompatibility with each other, their extended structuring, implying a predominant collective conscience and specific cultural products. These groupings, which appear only in industrialized global societies, where technical models and economic functions are particularly important, have the following traits in addition: they are *de facto* groupings, open, dispersed, permanent, unorganized and possess only conditional constraint.

Here we are dealing with a more complex, a more difficult definition; it brings together a large number of criteria which we shall examine. Let us begin with the simplest, which will be acceptable to all and which serves, so to say, to demarcate the phenomenon. *Social classes are de facto groupings*; in fact, one belongs to a class without doing anything specific to join it. I will concede readily that one chooses one's football club, but not one's class. To say that social classes are *open groupings* signifies that one can enter or leave them with equal facility, at least when one has the material means to do so. Not everybody can enter a religious order or a State educational institution; by contrast, no one is debarred from becoming a member of a social class. Thus, compared to groups which impose special conditions, classes are open groupings. It is equally incontestable that they are *dispersed*, differing, for example, from a group composed of students gathered together in a lecture theatre at the Sorbonne: here you are all condemned to listen to me. By contrast, one has never seen the working class at one glance; the group is too large for all its members to be gathered together. *Permanent* groupings? Well and good! If I am a bourgeois, I remain one, at least until I enter another class of which I shall remain a permanent member. *Unorganized?* Yes. Political parties require an organization of power, a staff, a group of militants, a constitution – all the things which a class as such lacks, for if the party can be called the organization of a class, it still remains distinct from the latter. The formula, *possessing only conditional constraint* signifies that a social class cannot, in a general way, impose upon its members to do this or that. The army, the police, the State or even groups of a more peaceable kind possess means of coercion. A class can exercise pressure on its members, but in a limited or conditional manner. The expression, *macrocosm of specific groupings* indicates the evident fact that the whole of a class can be divided into a plurality of lower order groups: workers are dispersed in a large number of enterprises, and the workers in each of these constitute a specific element integrated into the macrocosm of the working class; or, again, a class may be divided according to the branches of an industry or according to the levels of skill.

The attribute of *suprafunctionality* can also be accepted once one knows the meaning given to the term. A unifunctional grouping is a sports club, for example, which has a single objective: to devote itself to a particular objective, namely, sports. One would call multifunctional, local or kinship groupings, and, in general, those which have multiple objectives. Nation and class would be called suprafunctional to the extent that they are defined neither by one nor by several activities, but embrace the whole of existence.

Up to this point we are dealing with an acceptable definition because it is confined to a number of easily visible attributes of the phenomenon. By contrast, when we come to formulas like *resistance to penetration by the global society* or *radical incompatibility between classes which are highly structured*, it is no longer a question of denotative criteria which an examination of the reality would suffice to confirm but of propositions of fact which are amenable to discussion. The first of these two formulations implies that each social class has a particular way of thinking, of living, of placing itself in relation to the other classes and the global society. I do not say that this proposition is false, but that it is not evident. It is possible that it applies to certain classes and not to others, that not all of them have specific and distinctive ways of thinking and being. In other words, some of the criteria in the definition form part of a *theory* of social classes: they cannot be determined in advance of research but after it; they imply that the different classes each have their structure, their way of life, their consciousness and that each is a real totality which is conscious of itself as such. It is not evident that this is so, because it is precisely here that the object of controversy between the theorists lies.

In order to draw the conclusions from these two analyses let us now try to confront the two definitions, the one in terms of *prestige status* and the other of the *real totality*, because they mark the two possible directions in which the theory of social classes may develop. The American sociologist places the accent on the deference accorded to each, and considers that this psycho-social phenomenon constitutes the characteristic trait of the ensemble, which one calls social class. The second definition insists not on these interpersonal relations of esteem or contempt, but on the collective reality, which is constituted by social class, and on the growth of consciousness which accompanies it. Now that we have indicated these two directions, where do the contradictions lie over facts and over words?

The two definitions admit certain propositions in common. Both of them suppose that in actual societies there are multiple discriminations. The members of a society are differentiated from each other in regard to property or the relation to property, by the occupations they perform, by the means to which they have recourse for earning their livelihood, by their prestige status in society. Moreover, both definitions admit implicitly that in modern societies this discrimination of individuals is particularly complex because social classes are not legally recognized. In the societies of the *ancien régime* each knew with certitude to which order or *estate* he belonged; today one knows this so little that one of the favourite pastimes of sociologists is to conduct opinion polls inquiring about the class to which people think they belong. One would like to know what proportion of the population considers itself to belong to the working class or the middle or upper middle class or to the bourgeoisie. The words employed differ from one society to another in spite of the similarities in social structure. From the inquiries one notices, for instance, that Americans believe more readily that they belong to the middle class and the French to the working class. This phenomenon is partly linked to what I would call the 'prestige status' of the word employed; in a country where Marxist influence is strong as in France, it is sometimes a title of honour to belong to the working class; in a country that is anti-Marxist in its ideology like the United States, the term 'working class' does not have the same glamour. The replies given by individuals do not, then, always reflect the reality, but here a difficulty arises. The idea which individuals form of the class to which they belong is a part of the reality one seeks to study. It would be simple to distinguish, on the one hand, the real situation of the individual and, on the other, the idea which he has of it. But his idea of it is a part of the reality one studies. In what sense can one say that someone belongs to a group to which he does not profess to belong? The difficulty is well known: does the material situation of the individual or the consciousness which he forms of it constitute the *essential reality*? And, once again we reach the two directions of analysis or definition which I tried to disentangle.

The first tendency, that of the American sociologist, is *nominalist*. The systems of class and of stratification are not distinguished. A class is not a real ensemble, but a conglomeration of individuals. Individuals are differentiated from each other by multiple criteria and social status or class is only one among several discriminations determined essentially by psychological phenomena. Each is in the class which is imposed by the idea which others have of the position he occupies. Each has a status which is defined by the esteem of others. A definition of this kind regards the psychology of individuals, with all the contradictions it may allow for, as the essence of the phenomenon. (The consciousness that each has of his status does not always coincide with the consciousness of others.)

The second tendency is *realist*. It considers social class as a real ensemble defined at one and the same time by material facts and by the collective consciousness which individuals form of it. According to this realist tendency, one establishes a distinction between strata and classes. One distinguishes different *strata*, i.e. different hierarchical layers whether within a social class or in the total society, without the layers or strata constituting a collective unity. According to this conception, the essence of class is the collective unity which is real and conscious of itself. Class is a historical reality, it has a collective consciousness, it seeks to achieve specific tasks, to employ the expression which figured in the definition which I presented to you.

Inevitably, the nominalist school recognizes social classes in all societies. In effect, if class simply presupposes a scale of prestige, there have always been hierarchies of prestige in all known societies, and it is extremely probable that these will always be there. It is difficult to conceive of a complex society where the different groups will recognize each other reciprocally on a plane of equality. If, on the other hand, social class is a real totality, conscious of itself, if the essence of these totalities is their conflict, one can in theory imagine a transformation of the character of classes, and if not the disappearance, at least the transformation of their conflict.

The two definitions are thus opposed on several planes, philosophical, political, scientific. At the very outset, one places the accent on individuals and interpersonal relations, whereas the other adheres to collective realities, which brings us back to the antinomy between those who believe in the reality of the whole and those who hold to that of individuals.

This philosophical opposition more or less conceals another which is political. The American sociologist postulates the permanence of social stratification in all societies and tends to reduce the importance of the phenomenon of classes and their conflicts. In effect, if one is given simply an assemblage of persons who have a comparable social status or prestige, the limits between classes are unclear, one passes easily from one to the other, the groups recognize their interchangeability, but have no reason to find themselves in a permanent state of conflict. Above all, the conflict for power does not take place between classes; because for this to be so, one must define class in such a manner as to allow it to seize power. Now, if you relate it simply to prestige status, power will always be held by the upper classes, the workers will never be able to exercise it. The realist definition, on the contrary, suggests the importance and the significance of class conflict and relates it to the conflict for power. Finally, scientific controversies are implicit between the two conceptions: the realist accuses the nominalist of allowing the essential, i.e. the collective phenomenon, to escape; he in turn suffers from the reproach of inventing a collective reality which does not exist, or hardly exists, or exists unequally.

I have shown you up to which point the different definitions of social class are linked to philosophical conceptions, to political preferences and to scientific interpretations. How are the ambiguities to be resolved? We will not do this today, and till the next lecture I will leave you at the extreme point in the confusion. To add further to it, before we find a way out, I would like to put forward the idea which I shall try to define more rigorously when we return to it: sociologists continue to dispute over words and definitions, not out of ill will, but because they are confronted by a reality which by its nature is complex and ambiguous. If there are so many ways of conceiving of class, and if it appears that the more one speaks about it, the less one knows what it is, the reason is partly that they *really* are indeterminate. The ambiguity is there in our science because, to begin with, it is there in reality.

Let us briefly validate this proposition: you may ask, what constitutes the reality of a group, let us say the working class; you have a choice between diverse phenomena: *the situation* of the worker in the labour market *vis-à-vis* the directors of industry or those who pay his wages, *the manner* in which the worker thinks, feels and reacts to his work, to the industry or to the rest of society; in brief, you can successively consider the situation, the attitude or conduct, the state of consciousness, the acquisition of consciousness and the judgement which the surrounding milieu makes on the group itself. These different aspects are not created by the sociologist, they are there in reality. I have simplified the analysis even so, because each of these elements can be defined by multiple criteria which are difficult to apprehend. The unity of groupings may be of fact, of situation, or of conduct: these three kinds of unity do not clearly determine each other. People can think in the same fashion without being conscious of their unity; some consider that they form a unity although they are different in many respects. There never is complete unity of either situation or attitude or state of consciousness or acquisition of consciousness. Inevitably, when the sociologist tries to comprehend reality, he is condemned to interpret it. Perhaps it is just as well that this is so: to the extent that the sociologist is not satisfied with observing reality, he modifies it. One would never have thought of social classes as one does today if Marx had not thought of them, perhaps before they existed.

4 S. Ossowski

Old Notions and New Problems: Interpretations of
Social Structure in Modern Society

S. Ossowski, 'Old notions and new problems: interpretations of social
structure in modern society', *Transactions of the Third World Congress of
Sociology*, International Sociological Association, London, 1956, pp. 18–25.

Class Structure and Social Stratification

In the *Programme of the Third World Congress of Sociology*,
Section III, we find two terms which seem to be used as
synonyms: 'class structure' and 'class stratification'. Such
interpretation of these terms is suggested not only by the text
of the programme but also by the name of the chairman of Sub-
section I, who wrote some time ago in his study of class conflict:
'We are discussing a particular kind of group, whose nature is
indicated by the phrase: *social stratification*. The groups, that is
to say, lie one above the other in layers.'[1]

This is, however, not the only way of interpreting class
structure. Class structure was not reduced to social stratification in Madison's conception of class structure at the end
of the eighteenth century, nor in Stalin's view of the non-
antagonistic class structure of Soviet society in the middle of the
twentieth.

In order to get a clear apprehension of the sphere of problems
involved in the discussion about changes in class structure, a
classification of the main types of interpretation of class structure
will, perhaps, be useful; I mean a classification which would be
independent of the current distinction of 'objective' and 'subjective' notions of class (as, e.g. Marx's distinction of '*die
Klasse an sich*' and '*die Klasse für sich*' or Centers's distinction
between 'class – as a "sociopsychological phenomenon" – and
"stratum" ').

An interesting proposition has been presented in a concise

1. T. H. Marshall, 'The nature of class conflict', in *Class Conflict and
Social Stratification*, Le Play House, 1938, p. 97.

recent study by Alain Touraine,[2] where Centers's notion of stratum ('*le strate*') is opposed to the notion of class, conceived rather in conformity with the Marxist tradition. But the problem of different visions of class structure seems more complicated.

Classes as Components of a System

In spite of all the ambiguities of the term 'social class', it seems that there are certain common assumptions in all different theories of social class. One of these assumptions takes for granted that classes are components *of a system* of two or several groups of the same kind, forming together a society. It means that any definition of any social class must imply relations of this class to other groups of the same system: to explain, e.g. who is a proletarian in the Marxist sense of the word we must take into account his relation to the capitalist; the notion of the middle class implies again the notions of the lower and the upper classes. Such an implication constitutes a basic difference between a class and a professional group. When we treat a professional group as a component of a *system* of basic groups in a social structure it becomes for us a social class without ceasing to be a professional group from another point of view (for example, agriculturists, priests or warriors in a feudal system).

Main Ways of Conceiving Class Structure

There are two kinds of relations which enable us to speak about a system of social classes: *relations of order* and *relations of dependence*. We have correspondingly two types of schemes of class structure: schemes based on relations of order and schemes based on relations of dependence.

Schemes of gradation

Class division is conceived in the first case as a division according to the degree of a quality treated as a criterion of class participation, e.g. according to the amount of income. This scheme of

2. *Rapport sur la préparation en France de l'enquête internationale sur la stratification et la mobilité sociales*, I.S.A. mimeographed papers, vol. 1, 1953.

class structure may be called *the scheme of gradation*. An asymmetrical transitive relation determines the place of each class in this scheme. Let us take as examples the Warner six-class scheme, or schemes connected with the term 'stratum' of some authors, like Centers and Touraine, or the old distinction of the upper, the middle and the lower classes.

Within the schemes of gradations we can distinguish the scheme of *simple gradation*, where people are ranked according to one objective criterion, and the scheme of *synthetic gradation*, where the class position is determined by the inter-relation of several criteria which have no common gauge. Only in the first case have we to do with an objective ranking: any scale established as the result of a synthesis of two or several objective scales (where a lower position on one scale can be compensated by a higher position on the other) is not an objective scale if particular criteria, as for example, wealth and education, are incommensurable. The ranking based on several criteria, for example the ranking which is the subject matter of Warner's study, can be treated only as an expression of attitudes of a given social environment. This important difference has not usually been taken into account by those who speak about ranking the strata from the point of view of 'one or several objective criteria'.

Schemes based on relation of dependence

If we understand by a class system a system of relations of dependence, we characterize particular classes by different attributes. We have to do with two kinds of dependence in different conceptions of class structure: with a one-sided dependence and with a mutual one.

One-sided dependence in a system of social relations is understood usually as a subjection to somebody's power. *Mutual dependence* in a class system may have two different aspects. In the first one it appears as an 'organic' dependence: classes constitute a system, since each one has its particular functions in the life of society; so in Adam Smith's scheme one of the three fundamental classes has to furnish land, the second, capital, the third, labour. In the second aspect, the mutual dependence of social classes consists in a negative correlation of interests: successes of one class are failures of the other. We find such a view also in

Adam Smith's work, and more explicitly in Madison's articles if we look for Marx's predecessors.

Two schemes based on relation of dependence are to be distinguished in connexion with the two kinds of dependence in social relations to which we have referred.

The first one is a dychotomic scheme, where two classes are terms of an asymmetrical relation: I mean the relation of one-sided dependence. These classes are characterized by attributes mutually opposed: dominating – dominated, exploiting – exploited, propertied – nonpropertied, working – idle or leisure class. Let us call such a scheme of class structure a *dychotomic scheme of one-sided dependence*. This one-sided dependence, however, may be interpreted, from another point of view, as a mutual dependence of antagonistic interests. Antagonism is, of course, a symmetrical relation.

Simple schemes may be combined into composite ones. The classical Marxist three-or-four class scheme of social structure in capitalist society is formed by the crossing of three dychotomic divisions based on different criteria: (*a*) those who possess and those who do not possess the means of production, (*b*) those who work and those who do not work, (*c*) those who employ hired labour and those who do not.

The second main scheme of class dependence may be called the *functional scheme*. Society is here divided into classes bound together by some relation of mutual dependence, conceived in its 'organic' aspect (which does not exclude, however, some negative correlation interests). They are characterized by different, but not by contradictory attributes. This is the case in the medieval idea of society as composed of those who pray, those who defend and those who work, or in Adam Smith's three-classes scheme, or in the Stalinian scheme of non-antagonistic classes (see diagram opposite).

Different Visions of the Same Society

The same society can be classified according to different schemes. From legendary Agrippa, from Aristotle to Herbert Spencer and Durkheim, from St Clement of Alexandria to modern papal encyclicals, to Oxford Movement declarations and fascist manifestos, the defenders of the existing order endeavoured to represent it as based on mutual dependence resulting from the division of tasks equally useful for the whole society, while the oppressed classes did perceive the same social reality in a dychotomic asymmetrical scheme.

Classification of Types of Interpretation of Class Structure

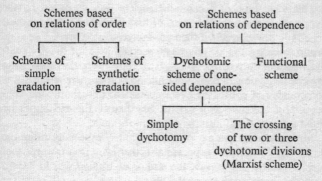

Through visions of the social structure, visions characteristic of particular classes or particular environments, we approach most vital social problems. An aspect of social structure, more or less universally accepted in a given environment, can be an important element of the social situation.

The Ideal Type of Capitalist Society and its Impact on Actual Interpretations of Class Structure

The three main schemes of social structure we have tried to discern seem to represent very general aspects of class society, since the examples cover thousands of years. Nevertheless the various historical forms of social organization suggest one scheme rather than another; and the criteria of interhuman dependence have been conceived differently in different epochs.

The modern theories of social class began to develop in a period when a new ideal type of society was taking shape in the social mind of Western Europe. The concept of social structure as a system of interhuman dependencies corresponded strictly, in that ideal type, to the concept of economic gradation. In other words, the scale of wealth had to be the only regulator of social position. All power was expected to result from the possession of wealth. Political power had to perform only a stabilizing function in the system of interhuman dependencies, and was not to have any place in the image of the social structure in its constitutive lines.

This ideal type of a capitalist society was suggested by the dynamics of real social changes of that time. The importance of economic power reached then an unprecedented level. The state began to be treated as 'an executive committee' of the dominating class not only by the Marxists: a conviction, that those who govern the state can be bought like any other merchandise, was sometimes not concealed by businessmen; and the liberal conception of the state as a passive guardian of the existing order fitted also very well into the Marxian formula.

Moreover, the people of that period – especially after the American Civil War – expected a further evolution towards that ideal type. In this respect, the author of *Capital* was in accord with the representatives of the liberal bourgeoisie, although for them the goal of this evolution had to be the highest form of civilized social organization, and for him – the last phase of capitalist society.

History did not follow that way. Lenin was already obliged to introduce some important corrections into the Marxian predictions, and liberal writers became aware with dismay that the line of progress was broken and that 'the course of civilization took an unexpected turn'.[3] This 'unexpected turn' separates the civilization of classical capitalism – when the conceptual frame of sociology, as a new science, was formed – from the civilization of world wars, of big monopolies, of new socialist states and social planning on an unprecedented scale.

Social Changes and Interference of Two Denotations of a Term

One of the fundamental postulates of the ideal type of society we have spoken of was that history in its main lines had been a result

3. F. A. Hayek, *La route de la servitude*, Paris, Librairie de Médicis, p. 15.

of innumerable individual spontaneous actions. This opinion, shared also by the socialists,[4] was reflected in the nineteenth-century conception of social class as a group shaped spontaneously by the independent actions of individuals.

It has been associated with a new term. Sieyès, in 1789, spoke about *estates* in French society; for Babeuf, six years later, France was divided only into *classes*. The word 'class', in the sense of social class, was used occasionally in the eighteenth century, but it was only after the French Revolution that it gradually became a *term*, which soon gained citizenship in most of the European languages. Even Adam Smith in his distinction of the three main classes of the society still employed the word 'orders', and not the term 'classes', which his disciples employed. The new term became so strongly connected with the social structures of nineteenth-century bourgeois democracy that not long ago P. Sorokin, in his explanation of the meaning of that term, regarded as one of the peculiarities of its designate that class is a group 'characteristic of the western society of the eighteenth, nineteenth and twentieth centuries'.[5]

Although the *term 'class'* in capitalist society has been opposed to such terms as 'estate' or 'caste', at the same time in certain contexts it has taken the place of the older terms, 'order' and 'estate', in their most general sense, as names of basic groups in any class society. Its connotation, influenced by the opposition of the new order to feudal society, led to confusion in some general theories of social development and in some analyses of pre-capitalist societies. Today – in the absence of a more general term – there is some analogous trouble in connexion with social structure of 'post-capitalist' societies too, where changes in social structure are included in the plans of state activity.

Classes and Organizations in Social Structure

The view that it is the free activity of spontaneous forces that ultimately shapes social life has led to the thesis that the classes,

4. cf., e.g. F. Engels, *Ludwig Feuerbach und der Ausgang der Klassischen Deutschen Philosophie*, ch. 6.

5. P. Sorokin, *Society, Culture and Personality*, Harper and Brothers, 1947, p. 271.

as non-organized groups, have a dominant role in the social structure, conceived as a system of interhuman dependencies. But the functions of large organizations in the structure of society have changed very much since the time of Marx and J. S. Mill. It is enough to mention the role of state organizations in the socialist countries, the role of the capitalist state in war economy, the continuous increase in the number of state, communal and trade union employees, the prospects opened up by the discovery of new sources of energy which surely cannot be entrusted to the play of spontaneous activities. Already before the last war some aspects of the social structure connected with the old idea of social class collided with new experiences of powerful organizations in the capitalist countries: the influence of huge monopolies on the life of society, struggles of antagonistic working-class organizations propagating different class ideologies in the name of the same class, the penetration of the monoparty organizations into the social structure in the fascist states. While the fact that humanitarian or national slogans frequently mask a class interest was known long ago, new experiences revealed that it is no less possible to mask the interests of an organization by class slogans.

The history of the twentieth century has taught us in this way that the relation between social classes and social organizations is more complicated than might be supposed from the patterns of social structure, and social dynamics inherited from former generations.

The Marxist Criterion of Class in the Present World

The Marxian conception of social class, as defined by its relation to the means of production, succeeded in disclosing a very essential criterion in the epoch when private ownership of the means of production seemed to be the almost only durable way of exploitation of other people's labour, and to determine entirely the whole system of interhuman subjection in the Western world.

This conception, however, seems today much less adequate, even in regard to the capitalist countries. It is not only because we have had occasion to get acquainted with fascist methods of compulsion on a mass scale, and not only because of the expansion of the planning functions of the state or because of the development of such institutions as social assistance (health service) in post-war England, in which the communist rule 'to everybody according to his needs' seems to be realized. It is also because of the changes in the occupational structure of society. In the United States, for example, the middle class, in the Marxist sense (small independent producers), declined during the last century in accordance with Marx's prediction. But at the same time a new middle class has arisen which once constituted only an insignificant margin, and which does not fit in the classical Marxist notion. Our opinion then as to the fulfilment of Marx's prediction about the fate of the 'middle class' depends on the interpretation of that term which, in Marx's time, did not provoke any such trouble.

On the other side, the birth and development of socialist states has shown that the abolition of private ownership of the means of production has not, as yet, put an end to economic inequality or class division. The inadequacy of the classical Marxist–Leninist conception of class in regard to socialist society has found its expression in Stalin's notion of 'non-antagonistic classes' in the U.S.S.R.

Two Interpretations of Classlessness

At the beginning of this paper we pointed to interpretations of 'class structure' where this term did not imply class stratification. Nevertheless the social importance of the modern notion of class is connected with the postulates of democracy and with the struggle of the oppressed for equality.

Democratic slogans, which guided people in their attempts to overthrow the feudal order, became later a common possession of new classes in their struggles with one another. The defenders of the new social order had to cope with the postulate of equality. A new problem of interpretation then appeared: in what sense has 'classless society' to be demanded by those who accept the ideas of the French and the American Revolutions? 'Classlessness' did not mean the same for the representatives of bourgeois democracy and for Marx or Bakunin. It did not mean for those democrats the economic equality demanded by the founders of the *Conjuration des Égaux*. Since the new class structure was so much less rigid and visible than the social order of the *ancien régime*, Guizot could affirm that there were no more social classes in French society, and the same was proclaimed by the school manuals of the Third Republic. Social structure in the United States is now sometimes interpreted as a *continuum* of social positions without any class divisions. The term 'classlessness' was applied to American society in some post-war discussions, and this 'classlessness' did not mean the sort of equality which de Tocqueville attributed to American society a hundred years ago.

The problem is not limited to the capitalist countries. The existence of classes in the U.S.S.R. is accepted by communist social science; but the existence of class stratification is denied, as it is supposed that even considerable inequalities of income cannot constitute a basis for class stratification if private property of the means of production does not exist. The class structure of that country is not interpreted there in conformity with the scheme of gradation, although the tendency toward levelling all revenues ('*uravnilovka*') has been strongly combated. The scheme of gradation, however, is applied to the social structure of the U.S.S.R. by the representatives of the Western non-communist milieux; we can easily find examples in American sociological and political reviews.

Hence a further question: How denotations of two terms: 'egalitarian society' and 'society without class stratification' are to be related? Under what conditions should even a considerable economic inequality not be interpreted as a symptom of class division?

Conclusion

Taking as a point of departure the more or less perennial aspects of class society, I have tried, within the narrow limits of this paper, to show some problems suggested by the inadequacy of the inherited nineteenth-century ideas of social structure in our new world. These problems, as we have seen, arise when we take into consideration the interrelationship of spontaneous and planned processes in the changing society, the relation of social classes and social organizations, the distinction of the means of production and the means of compulsion, or when we have to do with the interrelation of two denotations of the term 'class' and with different interpretations of the term 'classlessness'.

Among new social conditions on the world scale, the most important, from this point of view, is perhaps the coexistence of socialist and capitalist states. We need, I think, a new frame of notions to compare, by means of the same conceptual categories, changes of social structures in socialist and in capitalist countries; we need a frame of notions both wide enough to enable us to unveil similarities disguised under different names, different interpretations and different appearances, and subtle enough to shed light on essential particularities and contrasts.

Part Three
Classes and Strata in Industrial Society

It was with the systematic study of European society that the concept
of class developed into a tool of sociological analysis. The industrial
mode of production has brought about numerous changes in the
societies of Europe and America. For many, the essential question is
whether these changes have led to a lessening of social inequality (as
de Tocqueville had predicted) or to a polarization of economic and
political opportunities (as Marx had prophesied). Dahrendorf
examines the changes that have come about in industrial societies
(mainly of the capitalist type) since the time of Marx; his conclusion
is that class differences have become less and not more conspicuous.
Wesolowski examines the recent changes in Polish society; he argues
that classes in the orthodox sense have ceased to exist in socialist
society and have been replaced by what are better described as strata.

5 R. Dahrendorf

Changes in the Class Structure of Industrial Societies

Excerpt from R. Dahrendorf, *Class and Class Conflict in Industrial Society*, Routledge & Kegan Paul, 1963, pp. 41–64.

Ownership and Control, or the Decomposition of Capital

Marx was right in seeking the root of social change in capitalist society in the sphere of industrial production, but the direction these changes took turned out to be directly contrary to Marx's expectations. With respect to capital, he had, in his later years at least, a vision of what was going to happen, as his brief and somewhat puzzled analysis of joint-stock companies shows. Joint-stock companies were legally recognized in Germany, England, France and the United States in the second half of the nineteenth century. Laws often indicate the conclusion of social developments, and indeed early forms of joint-stock companies can be traced back at least to the commercial companies and trade societies of the seventeenth century. But it was in the nineteenth and early twentieth centuries that this type of enterprise first gained wide recognition and expanded into all branches of economic activity. Today, more than two-thirds of all companies in advanced industrial societies are joint-stock companies, and their property exceeds four-fifths of the total property in economic enterprises. The enterprise owned and run by an individual, or even a family, has long ceased to be the dominant pattern of economic organization. Moreover, the stock of companies is dispersed fairly widely. Three per cent of the adult population of the Federal Republic of Germany, and approximately 8 per cent of that of the United States, own one or more shares of joint-stock companies. Probably the proportion in other countries is somewhere between these extremes.[1] For purposes of the present

1. For the data presented or implied in this paragraph, and in this section in general, see, among other sources, A. A. Berle and G. C. Means, *The*

analysis, we may add to joint-stock companies the co-operative enterprises and those owned by the state, which command an ever-increasing proportion of the national wealth in contemporary societies. All these together, and their growth in the last decade, leave little doubt about the significance of this change.

It is not surprising that sociologists should have shared, from an early date, the interest of lawyers and economists in these new and rapidly expanding types of organization. There is, moreover, on the whole an astonishing degree of consensus among sociologists on the implications of joint-stock companies for the structure of industrial enterprises, and for the wider structure of society. If one wants to distinguish between points of view, one might contrast a rather more radical with a somewhat conservative interpretation of this phenomenon. Marx was, in this sense, the founder of the radical school; surprisingly enough, however, most of his later adherents took the more conservative view.

According to the radical view, joint-stock companies involve a complete break with earlier capitalist traditions. By separating what has come to be called ownership and control, they give rise to a new group of managers who are utterly different from their capitalist predecessors. Thus for Marx, the joint-stock company involves a complete alienation of capital 'from the real producers, and its opposition as alien property to all individuals really participating in production, from the manager down to the last day-laborer.'[2] In other words, by separating ownership and control, the joint-stock company reduces the distance between manager and worker, while at the same time removing the owners altogether from the sphere of production, and thereby isolating their function as exploiters of others. It is merely a step from this kind of analysis to the thesis that, as Renner has it, the 'capitalists

Modern Corporation and Private Property, Macmillan, 1932; Hargreaves Parkinson, *Ownership of Industry*, London, 1951; F. Rosensteil, 'Der amerikanische "Volkskapitalismus"', *Frankfurter Allgemeine Seitung* 11 November 1956; Karl Schwantag, 'Aktiengesellschaft: (II) AG in wirtschaftlicher Hinsicht', in *Handwörterbuch der Sozialwissenschaften*, vol. 1, Stuttgart, Tübingen and Göttingen, 1956; and Elisabeth Noelle and E. P. Neumann, *Jarbuch der öffentlichen Meinung, 1947 bis 1955*, Allensbach, 1956.

2. Karl Marx, *Das Kapital*, new edn, Berlin, 1953, vol. 3, p. 478.

without function' yield to the 'functionaries without capital', and that this new ruling group of industry bears little resemblance to the old 'full capitalists'.[3] Burnham, Geiger, Sering and others followed Marx (and Renner) in this radical interpretation of the social effects of joint-stock companies.

The conservative view, on the other hand, holds that the consequences of the apparent separation of ownership and control have been vastly overrated. It is argued that in fact owners and controllers, that is, stockholders and managers, are a fairly homogeneous group. There are often direct connexions between them, and where this is not the case, their outlook is sufficiently similar to justify insisting on the old assumption of a homogeneous class of capitalists opposed to an equally homogeneous class of laborers. This view is not often heard in the West nowadays, although traces of it are evident in the work of C. Wright Mills.[4] It may be added that this conservative view is clearly contrary to Marx's own analysis.

We cannot here exhaust the complex subject of ownership and control, but it seems desirable not to leave the subject without considering which of these two views seems more plausible and appropriate. There can be little doubt that the social structure of joint-stock companies as well as co-operative and state-owned enterprises differs from that of the classical capitalist enterprise, and that therefore a transition from the latter to the former is a process of social change. However, what type of change are we dealing with in this problem? Is it a change involving the transference of certain rights and duties attached to social positions from an old to a new group? Or is it a change that involves some rearrangement of the positions endowed with rights and duties themselves? These questions are not quite as rhetorical as they may sound. In fact, I would claim that the separation of ownership and control involved both a change in the structure of social positions, and a change in the recruitment of personnel to these positions. But it is evident that, in the first place, joint-stock companies differ from capitalist enterprises in the structure of

3. Karl Renner, *Wandlungen der modernen Gesellschaft: zwei Abhanlungen über die Probleme der Nachkriegszeit*, Vienna, 1953, pp. 182, 198.

4. C. W. Mills, *The New Men of Power*, New York, 1954; *The Power Elite*, Oxford University Press, 1956.

their leading positions. In the sphere with which we are here concerned, the process of transition from capitalist enterprises to joint-stock companies can be described as a process of role differentiation. The roles of owner and manager, originally combined in the position of the capitalist, have been separated and distributed over two positions, those of stockholder and executive.[5]

At the very least, this process of differentiation means that two physical entities occupy the positions formerly occupied by one. But this is not all. Apart from its manifest effects, the separation of ownership and control has a number of latent effects of even greater importance; that is, it seems clear that the resulting positions, those of stockholder and executive, differ not only with respect to the obvious rights and duties of their incumbents, but also in other respects. Generally, the 'capitalist without function' is indeed, as Marx emphasized, alienated from production, that is, largely removed from the enterprise whose stock he owns. He does not participate in the day-to-day life of the enterprise, and above all he does not have a defined place in the formal hierarchy of authority in the enterprise. The 'functionary without capital', on the other hand, has this place, although he typically has no property in the enterprise which he runs.[6]

From the point of view of the social structure of industrial enterprises, this means a significant change in the basis of legitimacy of entrepreneurial authority. The old-style capitalist exercised authority because he owned the instruments of production. The exercise of authority was part and parcel of his property

5. In a more extensive analysis, it would have to be recognized that this process of differentiation involved not only two, but at least three, roles and positions: the third being that of investor or 'finance capitalist' (Hilferding). Renner would add even more:

'Three capitalist character masks have stepped into the place of the one full capitalist: the producer owning the capital of production in the mask of the entrepreneur, the commercial capitalist in the character mask of the businessman, and the financial capitalist' (op. cit., p. 175).

6. In 1935, members of management in 155 of the 200 largest American corporations had on the average no more than 1·74 per cent of the ordinary shares of their enterprises. Cf. National Resources Committee, 'The Structure of Controls', in Reinhard Bendix and S. M. Lipset (eds.), *Class, Status and Power: A Reader in Social Stratification*, Free Press, 1953, p. 135.

rights, as indeed property may always be regarded from one point of view as simply an institutionalized form of authority over others. By contrast to this legitimation by property, the authority of the manager resembles in many ways that of the heads of political institutions. It is true that even for the manager property has not ceased to function as a basis of authority. The right of the manager to command and expect obedience accrues in part from the property rights delegated to him by the shareholders, acting either as a group or through an elected board of directors. But besides these delegated property rights, the manager, by virtue of his more immediate contact with the participants of production, has to seek a second, and often more important, basis of legitimacy for his authority, namely, some kind of consensus among those who are bound to obey his commands. Typically, this consensus merely takes the form of an absence of dissensus. However, the manager, unlike the 'full capitalist', can ill afford to exercise his authority in direct and deliberate contravention to the wishes and interests of his subordinates. The mechanisms by which manual and clerical workers who object to a member of top management can make their interests felt are complex and largely unregulated.[7] But there are such mechanisms, and managers have ways and means to forestall their being brought to bear. In this sense, the 'human relations' movement is nothing but a symptom of the changing basis of legitimacy of entrepreneurial authority once ownership and control are separated.[8]

7. They extend from direct pressure aimed at forcing the manager to resign or change his attitudes to indirect means of disturbing the operation of the enterprise which may result in the manager's being reprimanded or deposed by the directors, who, in this case, act in a sense on behalf of the employees.

8. Bendix has impressively demonstrated that this change was accompanied by a change in 'managerial ideologies', i.e. in attempts to justify theoretically the authority of the entrepreneur. Cf. Reinhard Bendix, *Work and Authority in Industry: Ideologies of Management in the Course of Industrialization*, Wiley, 1956. He asserts an ideological change from basing unlimited authority on the interests of a ruling class to presuming, on the part of modern management, an identity of interests among all participants of production. Bendix's argument lends considerable support to my thesis that the separation of ownership and control involved a change in the basis of legitimacy of authority.

With the differentiation of capitalist roles, the composition of the entrepreneurial class – if it is a class – changes too. This is probably a gradual development, but one that is far advanced in most of the highly industrialized societies today. If we follow Bendix[9] in distinguishing capitalists, heirs and bureaucrats as three types of entrepreneurs, it is evident that three significantly different patterns of recruitment correspond to these types. The capitalist in this sense is a man who owns and manages an enterprise which he has founded himself. From having been perhaps a skilled craftsman or a shopkeeper at the beginning of his career, he has built up, 'from scratch', a sizeable firm or factory and one that continues to grow in scope, size and production. The heir, by contrast, is born into the ownership of an enterprise, and apart from perhaps a few years' experience in some of its departments he has known nothing but the property he has inherited. Both the capitalist and the heir are owner-managers.

For mere managers, however, there are two typical patterns of recruitment, and both of them differ radically from those of capitalists and heirs. One of these patterns is the bureaucratic career. In the early joint-stock companies in particular, executives were often chosen from among the firm's leading employees, both technical and clerical. They had worked their way up from the ranks. More recently, a different pattern has gained increasing importance. Today, a majority of top management officials in industrial enterprises have acquired their positions on the strength of some specialized education, and of university degrees. Lawyers, economists and engineers often enter management almost immediately after they have completed their education, and gradually rise to the top positions. There can be little doubt that both these patterns of recruitment – but in particular the latter – distinguish managerial groups significantly from those of old-style owner-managers, as well as new-style mere owners. Their social background and experience place these groups into different fields of reference, and it seems at least likely that the group of professionally trained managers 'increasingly develops its own functionally determined character traits and modes of thought'.[10] For this is, in our context, the crucial effect of the

9. Bendix, op. cit., p. 228.
10. Paul Sering, *Jenseits des Kapitalismus*, Nürnberg, 1947, p. 205.

separation of ownership and control in industry: that it produces two sets of roles the incumbents of which increasingly move apart in their outlook on and attitudes toward society in general and toward the enterprise in particular. Their reference groups differ, and different reference groups make for different values. Among classical capitalists, the 'organization man' is an unthinkable absurdity. Yet the manager is 'not the individualist but the man who works through others for others'.[11] Never has the imputation of a profit motive been further from the real motives of men than it is for modern bureaucratic managers.[12] Economically, managers are interested in such things as rentability, efficiency and productivity. But all these are indissolubly linked with the imponderables of what has been called the social 'climate of the enterprise' (*Betriebsklima*). The manager shares with the capitalist two important social reference groups: his peers and his subordinates. But his attitude toward these differs considerably from that of the capitalist (as does, consequently, the attitude expected from him by his peers). For him, to be successful means to be liked, and to be liked means, in many ways, to be alike. The manager is an involuntary ruler, and his attitudes betray his feelings.

Before concluding this analysis it would perhaps be well to point out briefly what it does not mean or imply. Despite many differences, there are without doubt considerable similarities in the positions, roles and attitudes of both the capitalist and the manager. Both are entrepreneurial roles, and both are therefore subject to certain expectations which no social context can remove. Moreover, there are numerous personal and social ties between owners and managers in all industrial societies. If anything, the unpropertied managers are more active in political affairs, both as individuals and through their associations and lobbies. Also, while the joint-stock company has conquered the sphere of industrial production (that is, of secondary industries),

11. W. H. Whyte, *The Organization Man*, Doubleday, 1957, p. 21.
12. Which is not to say that this 'imputation' may not be useful as an assumption in economic theory. There is no need for theoretical assumptions to be altogether realistic. However, it may be advisable even for economists to try and extend their models by including in their assumptions some of the social factors characteristic of entrepreneurial roles.

it is still of only minor importance in the tertiary industries of trade and commerce and in the services. Thus, the separation of ownership and control is not as fundamental a change as, say, the industrial revolution. But it is a change, and one with very definite, if restricted, implications for class structure and conflict.

There is little reason to follow Marx and describe the condition of separation of ownership and control as a transitional form of historical development. It is no more transitional than any other stage of history, and it has already proven quite a vital pattern of social and economic structure. But I think that we can follow Marx in his radical interpretation of this phenomenon. The separation of ownership and control has replaced one group by two whose positions, roles and outlooks are far from identical. In taking this view, one does of course agree with Marx against himself. For it follows from this that the homogeneous capitalist class predicted by Marx has in fact not developed. Capital – and thereby capitalism – has dissolved and given way, in the economic sphere, to a plurality of partly agreed, partly competing and partly, simply, different groups. The effect of this development on class conflict is threefold: first, the replacement of capitalists by managers involves a change in the composition of the groups participating in conflict; second, and as a consequence of this change in recruitment and composition, there is a change in the nature of the issues that cause conflicts, for the interests of the functionaries without capital differ from those of full-blown capitalists, and so therefore do the interests of labor *vis-à-vis* their new opponents; and third, the decomposition of capital involves a change in the patterns of conflict. One might question whether this new conflict, in which labor is no longer opposed to a homogeneous capitalist class, can still be described as a class conflict at all. In any case, it is different from the division of the whole society into two great and homogeneous hostile camps with which Marx was concerned. While I would follow the radical view of the separation of ownership and control in industry to this point, there is one thing to be said in favor of the conservative view. Changes in the composition of conflict groups, of the issues and of patterns of conflict do not imply the abolition of conflict or even of the specific conflict between management and labor in industry. Despite the effects of the decomposition of capital on class structure, we have no reason to believe that antagonisms and clashes of interest have now been banned from industrial enterprises.

Skill and Stratification, or the Decomposition of Labor

While Marx had at least a premonition of things to come with respect to capital, he remained unaware of developments affecting the unity and homogeneity of labor. Yet in this respect, too, the sphere of production which loomed so large in Marx's analyses became the starting point of changes that clearly refute his predictions. The working class of today, far from being a homogeneous group of equally unskilled and impoverished people, is in fact a stratum differentiated by numerous subtle and not-so-subtle distinctions. Here, too, history has dissolved one position, or role, and has substituted for it a plurality of roles that are endowed with diverging and often conflicting expectations.

In trying to derive his prediction of the growing homogeneity of labor from the assumption that the technical development of industry would tend to abolish all differences of skill and qualification, Marx was a genuine child of his century. Only the earliest political economists had believed that the division of labor in manufacturing would make for an 'increase of dexterity in every particular workman'[13] by allowing him to refine the 'skill acquired by frequent repetition of the same process'.[14] Already in the following generation, social scientists were quite unanimous in believing that the processes of industrial production 'effect a substitution of labor comparatively unskilled, for that which is more skilled',[15] and that the division of labor had reached a phase 'in which we have seen the skill of the worker decrease at the rate at which industry becomes more perfect'.[16] Marx was only too glad to adopt this view which tallied so well with his general theories of class structure:

13. Adam Smith, *An Inquiry into the Nature and Causes of the Wealth of Nations*, new edn, New York, 1937, p. 7.

14. Charles Babbage, *On the Economy of Machinery and Manufactures*, London, 1832, p. 134.

15. Andrew Ure, *The Philosophy of Manufacturers*, London, 1835, p. 30.

16. P. J. Proudhon, *Système des contradictions économiques, ou Philosophie de la misère*, 3rd edn, Paris, 1867, p. 153.

The interests and life situations of the proletariat are more and more equalized, since the machinery increasingly obliterates the differences of labor and depresses the wage almost everywhere to an equally low level.[17]

The hierarchy of specialized workmen that characterizes manufacture is replaced, in the automatic factory, by a tendency to equalize and reduce to one and the same level every kind of work that has to be done.[18]

Indeed, so far as we can tell from available evidence, there was, up to the end of the nineteenth century, a tendency for most industrial workers to become unskilled, that is, to be reduced to the same low level of skill. But since then, two new patterns have emerged which are closely related on the one hand to technical innovations in production, on the other hand to a new philosophy of industrial organization as symbolized by the works of F. W. Taylor[19] and H. Fayol.[20] First, there emerged, around the turn of the century, a new category of workers which today is usually described as semiskilled. As early as 1905, Max Weber referred to the growing importance of 'the semiskilled workers trained directly on the job'.[21] By the 1930s, the theory had become almost commonplace that 'there is a tendency for all manual laborers to become semiskilled machine minders, and for highly skilled as well as unskilled workers to become relatively less important'.[22] The semiskilled differ from the unskilled not so much in the technical qualifications required from them for their work, as in certain less easily defined extrafunctional skills which relate to their capacity to accept responsibility, to adapt to difficult conditions, and to perform a job intelligently. These extrafunctional skills are acquired not by formal training (although many semiskilled workers receive this also), but by experience on

17. Karl Marx, *Manifest der kommunistischen Partei*, new edn, Berlin, 1953, p. 17.

18. Karl Marx, *Das Kapital*, new edn, Berlin, 1953, vol. 1, p. 490.

19. F. W. Taylor, 'The Principles of Scientific Management', *Scientific Management*, Harper, 1947.

20. Henri Fayol, *Administration industrielle et générale*, Paris, 1916.

21. Max Weber, 'Der Sozialismus' in *Gesammelte Aufsätze zur Soziologie und Sozialpolitik*, Tübingen, 1924, p. 502.

22. A. M. Carr-Saunders and D. C. Jones, *A Survey of the Social Structure of England and Wales*, 2nd edn, Oxford, 1937, p. 61.

the job; yet these 'skills of responsibility' constitute a clear line of demarcation between those who have them and the unskilled who lack both training and experience. Apart from the semi-skilled, there appeared, more recently, a new and ever-growing demand for highly skilled workers of the engineer type in industry. Carr-Saunders and Jones, in their statement above, still expected the simultaneous reduction of unskilled as well as skilled labor. Today we know – as Friedmann,[23] Geiger,[24] Moore[25] and others have pointed out – that the second half of this expectation has not come true. Increasingly complex machines require increasingly qualified designers, builders, maintenance and repair men, and even minders, so that Drucker extrapolates only slightly when he says:

> Within the working class a new shift from unskilled to skilled labor has begun – reversing the trend of the last fifty years. The unskilled worker is actually an engineering imperfection, as unskilled work, at least in theory, can always be done better, faster and cheaper by machines.[26]

Because of changing classifications, it is a little difficult to document this development statistically. As for the unskilled, a slight decrease in their proportion can be shown for England where, in 1951, they amounted to 12·5 per cent of the occupied male population, as against 16·5 per cent in 1931. In the United States, an even sharper decrease has been noted, from 36 per cent of the labor force in 1910 to just over 28 per cent in 1930 and, further, to less than 20 per cent in 1950.[27] But statistics are here neither very reliable nor even indispensable evidence. Analysis of industrial conditions suggests quite clearly that within the labor force of advanced industry we have to distinguish at least three skill groups: a growing stratum of highly skilled workmen who increasingly merge with both engineers and

23. Georges Friedmann, *Zukunft der Arbeit*, Cologne, 1953.

24. Theodor Geiger, *Die Klassengesellschaft im Schmelztiegel*, Cologne and Hagen, 1949.

25. W. E. Moore, *Industrial Relations and the Social Order*, New York, 1947.

26. P. F. Drucker, *The New Society: The Anatomy of the Industrial Order*, Harper, 1950, pp. 42–3.

27. See Theodore Caplow, *The Sociology of Work*, McGraw, 1954, p. 299.

white-collar employees, a relatively stable stratum of semiskilled workers with a high degree of diffuse as well as specific industrial experience, and a dwindling stratum of totally unskilled laborers who are characteristically either newcomers to industry (beginners, former agricultural laborers, immigrants) or semi-unemployables. It appears, furthermore, that these three groups differ not only in their level of skill, but also in other attributes and determinants of social status. The semiskilled almost invariably earn a higher wage than the unskilled, whereas the skilled are often salaried and thereby participate in white-collar status. The hierarchy of skill corresponds exactly to the hierarchy of responsibility and delegated authority within the working class. From numerous studies it would seem beyond doubt that it also correlates with the hierarchy of prestige, at the top of which we find the skilled man whose prolonged training, salary and security convey special status, and at the bottom of which stands the unskilled man who is, according to a recent German investigation into workers' opinions, merely 'working' without having an 'occupation' proper.[28] Here as elsewhere Marx was evidently mistaken:

Everywhere, the working class differentiates itself more and more, on the one hand into occupational groups, on the other hand into three large categories with different, if not contradictory, interests: the skilled craftsmen, the unskilled laborers, and the semiskilled specialist workers.[29]

In trying to assess the consequences of this development, it is well to remember that, for Marx, the increasing uniformity of the working class was an indispensable condition of that intensification of the class struggle which was to lead, eventually, to its climax in a revolution. The underlying argument of what for Marx became a prediction appears quite plausible. For there to

28. See Heinz B. Kluth, 'Arbeiterjugend – Begriff und Wirklichkeit', in Helmut Schelsky (ed.), *Arbeiterjugend – gestern und heute*, Heidelberg, 1955, p. 67.

29. André Philip, *La démocratie industrielle*, Paris, 1955. In argument and evidence the preceding account is based on two more elaborate studies of mine, one of unskilled labor (*Unskilled Labour in British Industry*, Ph.D. Thesis, London, 1956), and one of skill and social stratification ('Industrielle Fertigkeiten und soziale Schichtung', *Kölner Zeitschrift für Soziologie und Sozialpsychologie*, vol. 8, no. 4, 1956). For further references as well as data I must refer to these studies.

be a revolution, the conflicts within a society have to become extremely intense. For conflicts to be intense, one would indeed expect its participants to be highly unified and homogeneous groups. But neither capital nor labor has developed along these lines. Capital has dissolved into at least two, in many ways distinct, elements, and so has labor. The proletarian, the impoverished slave of industry who is indistinguishable from his peers in terms of his work, his skill, his wage and his prestige, has left the scene. What is more, it appears that by now he has been followed by his less depraved, but equally alienated successor, the worker. In modern industry, 'the worker' has become precisely the kind of abstraction which Marx quite justly resented so much. In his place, we find a plurality of status and skill groups whose interests often diverge. Demands of the skilled for security may injure the semiskilled; wage claims of the semiskilled may raise objections by the skilled; and any interest on the part of the unskilled is bound to set their more highly skilled fellow-workmen worrying about differentials.

Again, as in the case of capital, it does not follow from the decomposition of labor that there is no bond left that unites most workers – at least for specific goals; nor does it follow that industrial conflict has lost its edge. But here, too, a change of the issues and, above all, of the patterns of conflict is indicated. As with the capitalist class, it has become doubtful whether speaking of the working class still makes much sense. Probably Marx would have agreed that class 'is a force that unites into groups people who differ from one another, by over-riding the differences between them',[30] but he certainly did not expect the differences to be so great, and the uniting force so precarious as it has turned out to be in the case both of capital and of labor.

The 'New Middle Class'

Along with the decomposition of both capital and labor a new stratum emerged within, as well as outside, the industry of modern societies, which was, so to speak, born decomposed. Since Lederer and Marschak first published their essay on this group, and coined for it the name 'new middle class' (*neuer*

30. T. H. Marshall, *Citizenship and Social Class*, Cambridge, 1950, p. 114.

Mittelstand), so much has been written by sociologists about the origin, development, position and function of white-collar or black-coated employees that whatever one says is bound to be repetitive. However, only one conclusion is borne out quite clearly by all these studies of salaried employees in industry, trade, commerce and public administration: that there is no word in any modern language to describe this group that is no group, class that is no class and stratum that is no stratum. To be sure, there have been attempts to describe it. In fact, we are here in the comparatively fortunate position of having to decide between two or, perhaps, three conflicting theories. But none of these attempts has been free of innumerable qualifications to the effect that it is impossible to generalize. Although the following brief discussion will not distinguish itself in this respect, it could not be avoided in an account of social changes of the past century that have a bearing on the problem of class.

By the time Marx died, about one out of every twenty members of the labor force was in what might roughly be described a clerical occupation; today, it is one out of every five and, in the tertiary industries, one out of every three. More accurate figures of size and growth of the 'new middle class' could be given,[31] but even these are surprisingly precise in view of the fact that it is virtually impossible to delimit the 'group' which they count. For, technically, the 'occupational salad' (Mills) of salaried employees includes post-office clerks as well as senior executives, shop supervisors as well as hospital doctors, typists as well as prime ministers. Presumably, a 'middle class' is located somewhere between at least two other classes, one above it and one below it. Yet the 'new middle class' has stubbornly resisted all attempts to define its upper and lower limits. In fact, it is obvious

31. For data used in the following section, see, apart from the early work by Emil Lederer and Jakob Marschak, 'Der neue Mittelstand', in *Grundriss der Sozialökonomik*, Section 9, Part I, Tübingen, 1926, above all the following studies: David Lockwood, *The Blackcoated Worker*, Allen and Unwin, 1958; Theodor Geiger, *Die Soziale Schichtung des deutschen Volkes*, Stuttgart, 1932; Fritz Croner, *Die Angestellten in der modernen Gesellschaft*, Frankfurt a.M and Vienna, 1954; Roy Lewis and Angus Maude, *The English Middle Classes*, London, 1949; and C. W. Mills, *White Collar, The American Middle Classes*, Oxford University Press, 1951. Some interesting figures are given by Reinhard Bendix, op. cit., p. 214.

that the questions where salaried employees begin to be members of an upper stratum or ruling class and where they 'really' still belong in the working class cannot in general be answered. Our questions will have to be rather more specific.

If one is, as we are, concerned not with patterns of social stratification but with lines of conflict, then one thing is certain: however we may choose to delimit the aggregate of salaried employees, they are not a 'middle class', because from the point of view of a theory of conflict there can be no such entity as a middle class. Evident as it is, this statement is bound to be misunderstood – but, then, much of this study is an attempt to elucidate it. It is true that in terms of prestige and income many salaried employees occupy a position somewhere between the very wealthy and the very poor, somewhere in the middle of the scale of social stratification. But in a situation of conflict, whether defined in a Marxian way or in some other way, this kind of intermediate position just does not exist, or, at least, exists only as a negative position of nonparticipation. This point might be illuminated by a slightly misleading example: an election in which there is a choice between two parties; while it is possible to abstain, only those who make up their minds one way or the other participate actively in the contest. Similarly, our problem here is to determine in which way the so-called new middle class has made up its mind or is likely to make up its mind. And the answer we shall give corresponds – to remain within the metaphor for a moment – to the findings of Bonham in England[32] and von der Heydte in Germany,[33] according to which two-thirds of the 'new middle class' tend to vote for conservative, and one-third for radical parties.

I have claimed above that there are two or, perhaps, three competing theories about the position of the 'new middle class'. From the point of view of our problem, these are soon reduced to what at best amounts to two and a half theories. For the third theory I had in mind is in fact little more than a description, and an inconclusive one at that. It is embodied in Crozier's 'working hypothesis' of an empirical investigation conducted in France:

32. John Bonham, *The Middle Class Vote*, London, 1954.

33. F. A. von der Heydte and Karl Sacherl, *Soziologie der deutschen Parteien*, Munich, 1955.

The situation of the salaried employee is one that makes possible an identification with the world of the ruling class and promises considerable rewards if this succeeds. But at the same time it is a working-class situation and therefore suffers from most of those limitations to which all other workers are subjected – limited income as well as lack of autonomy and a position of subordination.[34]

Statements of this kind are as frequent as they are useless for purposes of conflict analysis. We can therefore dismiss at the outset any theory that confines itself to statements with clauses like 'partly this . . . partly that' or 'on the one hand this . . . on the other hand that'.

There are two theories which do not suffer from this indecision, and they are directly contradictory. According to the first of these, the 'new middle class' constitutes in fact an extension of the old, capitalist or bourgeois, ruling class, and is in this sense part of the ruling class. Croner – who, apart from Renner,[35] Bendix[36] and others, recently espoused this theory – argues that 'the explanation of the special social position of salaried employees can be found in the fact that their work tasks have once been entrepreneurial tasks'.[37] This statement is meant by Croner both in a historical and in a structural sense. Historically, most clerical occupations were differentiated out of the leading positions in industry, commerce and the state. Structurally they are, according to this view, characterized by the exercise of delegated authority – delegated, that is, from the real seat of authority in social organizations, from, in other words, their leading positions. In contrast to this view, Geiger, C. Wright Mills and others claim that the 'new middle class' is, if not exactly an extension of the proletariat, at any rate closer to the working class than to the ruling class, whether capitalist or managerial:

Objectively, . . . the structural position of the white-collar mass is becoming more and more similar to that of the wage-workers. Both are, of course, propertyless, and their incomes draw closer and closer

34. Michel Crozier, 'Le rôle des employés et des petits fonctionnaires dans la structure sociale française contemporaine' in *Transactions of the Third World Congress of Sociology*, vol. 3, London, 1956, pp. 311–12.

35. Renner, op. cit.

36. Bendix, op. cit., chapt. 4.

37. Croner, op. cit., p. 36.

together. All the factors of their status position, which have enabled white-collar workers to set themselves apart from wage-workers, are now subject to definite decline.[38]

Mills does not say so, but he would probably have no quarrel with Geiger's conclusion that 'from the point of view of class structure in Marx's sense the salaried employee is undoubtedly closer to the worker than to any other figure of modern society'.[39]

The two views are clearly in conflict and it seems desirable to come to a decision as to their relative merits.[40] Fortunate as it is, from a methodological point of view, to have to decide between two conflicting theories, our situation here does not, upon closer inspection, turn out to be quite so simple. In fact, Mills may well be right when he suspects that because of the vastly different 'definitions' of the 'new middle class' the two theories not only may peacefully co-exist but even both be correct.[41] Clearly the theory that salaried employees have delegated authority and are therefore part of the ruling class cannot have meant the office boy, the salesgirl or even the skilled worker who has been granted the status symbol of a salary; equally clearly, the theory that salaried employees resemble the working class does not apply to senior executives, higher civil servants and professional people. However, there is more than a question of definition involved in this difficulty.

Instead of asking which of two apparently conflicting theories applies to the 'new middle class', we can, so to speak, reverse our question and ask whether there is any criterion that would allow

38. Mills, 1951, op. cit., p. 297.
39. Geiger, 1949, op. cit., p. 167.
40. C. Wright Mills, in his very balanced account of views about the 'new middle class', 1951, op. cit., chapt. 13, enumerates four competing theories (pp. 290 ff.). To the two mentioned he adds the theories that (i) the middle class is destined to be the ruling class of the future, and (ii) the growth of the 'new middle class' operates as a force to stabilize the old, and eventually to abolish all class conflicts. The latter view will be discussed at a later stage, since it presupposes some consideration of the significance of social conflict in general. As to the former view, it simply betrays an unpardonable confusion of terms on the part of the authors Mills refers to. It seems obvious that so long as the middle class is a middle class there must be a class above it, and once it is the ruling class it is no longer the middle class.
41. Mills, 1951, op. cit., pp. 291 ff.

us to distinguish between those sectors of the 'new middle class' to which one theory applies, and those to which the other theory applies. I think that there is such a criterion, and that its application provides at least a preliminary solution to our wider problem of the effects of the growth of a 'new middle class' on class structure and class conflict. It seems to me that a fairly clear as well as significant line can be drawn between salaried employees who occupy positions that are part of a bureaucratic hierarchy, and salaried employees in positions that are not. The occupations of the post-office clerk, the accountant and, of course, the senior executive are rungs on a ladder of bureaucratic positions; those of the salesgirl and the craftsman are not. There may be barriers in bureaucratic hierarchies which are insurmountable for people who started in low positions; salaried employees outside such hierarchies may earn more than those within, and they may also change occupations and enter upon a bureaucratic career; but these and similar facts are irrelevant to the distinction between bureaucrats and white-collar workers proposed here. Despite these facts I suggest that the ruling-class theory applies without exception to the social position of bureaucrats, and the working-class theory equally generally to the social position of white-collar workers.

There is, in other words, one section of the 'new middle class' the condition of which, from the point of view of class conflict, closely resembles that of industrial workers. This section includes many of the salaried employees in the tertiary industries, in shops and restaurants, in cinemas, and in commercial firms, as well as those highly skilled workers and foremen who have acquired salaried status. It is hard to estimate, from available evidence, the numerical size of this group, but it probably does not at present exceed one-third of the whole 'new middle class' – although it may do so in the future, since the introduction of office machinery tends to reduce the number of bureaucrats while increasing the demand for salaried office technicians.[42] Although some white-collar workers earn rather more than

42. It is still too early to make any definite statements about this important development, which Bahrdt described as the 'industrialization of bureaucracy' . . . but the automation of office work is sure to have consequences for the class structure of contemporary societies.

industrial workers, and most of them enjoy a somewhat higher prestige, their class situation appears sufficiently similar to that of workers to expect them to act alike. In general, it is among white-collar workers that one would expect trade unions as well as radical political parties to be successful.

The bureaucrats, on the other hand, share, if often in a minor way, the requisites of a ruling class. Although many of them earn less than white-collar and even industrial workers, they participate in the exercise of authority and thereby occupy a position *vis-à-vis* rather than inside the working class. The otherwise surprising fact that many salaried employees identify themselves with the interests, attitudes and styles of life of the higher-ups can be accounted for in these terms. For the bureaucrats, the supreme social reality is their career that provides, at least in theory, a direct link between every one of them and the top positions which may be described as the ultimate seat of authority. It would be false to say that the bureaucrats are a ruling class, but in any case they are part of it, and one would therefore expect them to act accordingly in industrial, social and political conflicts.

The decomposition of labor and capital has been the result of social developments that have occurred since Marx, but the 'new middle class' was born decomposed. It neither has been nor is it ever likely to be a class in any sense of this term. But while there is no 'new middle class', there are, of course, white-collar workers and bureaucrats, and the growth of these groups is one of the striking features of historical development in the past century. What is their effect on class structure and class conflict, if it is not that of adding a new class to the older ones Marx described? It follows from our analysis that the emergence of salaried employees means in the first place an extension of the older classes of bourgeoisie and proletariat. The bureaucrats add to the bourgeoisie, as the white-collar workers add to the proletariat. Both classes have become, by these extensions, even more complex and heterogeneous than their decomposition has made them in any case. By gaining new elements, their unity has become a highly doubtful and precarious feature. White-collar workers, like industrial workers, have neither property nor authority, yet they display many social characteristics that are quite unlike those of the old working class. Similarly, bureaucrats differ from the older ruling class despite their share in the exercise of authority. Even more than the decomposition of capital and labor, these facts make it highly doubtful whether the concept of class is still applicable to the conflict groups of post-capitalist societies. In any case, the participants, issues and patterns of conflict have changed, and the pleasing simplicity of Marx's view of society has become a nonsensical construction. If ever there have been two large, homogeneous, polarized and identically situated social classses, these have certainly ceased to exist today, so that an unmodified Marxian theory is bound to fail in explaining the structure and conflicts of advanced industrial societies.

Social Mobility

The decomposition of capital and labor as well as their extension by sections of the 'new middle class' are phenomena which have an obvious and direct bearing on class structure. But they are neither the only changes that have occurred since Marx nor, perhaps, the most significant ones from the point of view of class. Apart from such political and economic forces as totalitarianism and socialism, it was in particular the institutionalization of the two great social forces of mobility and equality that has steered class structures and conflicts in directions unforeseen by Marx. Marx was not, in fact, unaware of the importance of these forces. In explaining the absence of stable classes in the United States in terms of what he called the 'exchange between classes',[43] he anticipated the cardinal thesis of Sombart's brilliant essay, *Why is there no Socialism in the United States?*[44] But for Marx, mobility was a symptom of short-lived transitional periods of history, that is, of either the emergence or the impending break-down of a society. Today, we would tend to take the opposite view. Social mobility has become one of the crucial elements of the structure of industrial societies, and one would be tempted to predict its 'breakdown' if the process of mobility were ever

43. cf. Karl Marx, *Der 18. Brumaire des Louis Bonaparte*, new edn, Berlin, 1946.

44. Werner Sombart, *Warum gibt es in den Vereinigten Staaten keinen Sozialismus?*, Tübingen, 1906.

seriously impeded. Marx believed that the strength of a ruling class documents itself in its ability to absorb the ablest elements of other classes. In a manner of speaking, this is permanently the case in advanced industrial societies, yet we should hesitate to infer from a steady increase in the upward mobility of the talented that the present ruling class is particularly strong or homogeneous.

Social mobility represents one of the most studied and, at the same time, least understood areas of sociological inquiry. Today, we know a great deal about social mobility in various countries, and yet we do not really know what we know. Not only do we not have any satisfactory answer to the question about the causes and consequences of social mobility that was recently put by Lipset and Zetterberg,[45] but we cannot even be sure about the so-called facts of the case. The evidence we have is most conclusive with respect to mobility between generations, although even here generalizations rest on extrapolation as much as on interpretation. It appears that in countries like the United States, Great Britain and Germany the rate of intergeneration mobility is generally fairly high. Only in the highest and, in some countries, in the lowest ranges of the occupational scale do we still find a considerable amount of self-recruitment. Moreover, the rate of mobility seems to correspond roughly to the degree of industrialization in a country. It is higher in Britain than in France, higher in the United States than in Italy. This correlation between industrial development and social mobility seems to hold also in the historical dimension. For Britain and Germany, investigations suggest a considerable increase in mobility rates over the last three generations.[46]

45. S. M. Lipset and H. L. Zetterberg, 'A theory of social mobility' in *Transactions of the Third World Congress of Sociology*, vol. 3, London, 1956, p. 158.

46. The first of these generalizations is really little more than a guess based on the interpretation of mobility studies by Glass and others in Britain (D. V. Glass, ed., *Social Mobility in Britain*, Routledge, 1954), Bolte in Germany (K. M. Bolte, 'Ein Beitrag zur Problematic der sozialen Mobilität', *Kölner Zeitschrift fur Soziologie und Sozialpsychologie*, vol. 8, no. 1, 1956; *Sozialer Aufstieg und Abstieg. Eine Untersuchung über Berufsprestige und Berufsmobilität*, Stuttgart, 1959), Rogoff in the United States (Natalie Rogoff, *Recent Trends in Occupational Mobility*, Free Press, 1953), the Japan Sociological Society (*Social Mobility in Japan*. Mimeographed for the Third World Congress of Sociology, 1956), and the data included in the

However, even if these generalizations are taken as suggestions rather than conclusions, they have a high degree of verisimilitude. For with respect to intergeneration mobility we have at our disposal another kind of evidence which, although not quantitative, is quite conclusive. When Marx wrote his books, he assumed that the position an individual occupies in society is determined by his family origin and the position of his parents. The sons of workers have no other choice but to become workers themselves, and the sons of capitalists stay in the class of their fathers. At the time, this assumption was probably not far from the truth. But since then a new pattern of role allocation has become institutionalized in industrial societies. Today, the allocation of social positions is increasingly the task of the educational system. Even a hundred years ago, 'the attendance of a certain type of school meant a confirmation of a certain social status or rank, and not its acquisition'.[47] Today, the school has become the 'first and thereby decisive point of social placement with respect to future social security, social rank and the extent of future consumption chances'.[48] In post-capitalist society, it is:

---

article by Lipset and Zetterberg (op. cit.). Some comparative data have been brought together in this article also, as well as in the volume edited by Glass (op. cit., p. 263). Historical studies of mobility suffer from the fact that they have to rely on people's memories; some tentative findings have been presented by Mukherjee (in Glass, op. cit., p. 284) and Bolte (K. M. Bolte, 'Some aspects of social mobility in Western Germany', in *Transactions of the Third World Congress of Sociology*, vol. 3, London, 1956). Despite my qualifications, this evidence is not, after all, unimpressive. However, all the studies mentioned do not really stand up to a thorough methodological inspection. This is almost obvious in comparative analyses based on vastly different occupational classifications which nobody so far has taken the trouble to reclassify. But it is also true for studies in one country. They have usually employed the index of association for measuring mobility rates, and, as Professor John W. Tukey has pointed out to me, this index is neither formally sound nor empirically useful. Formally, the index of association would have to be weighted by the size of status categories to be of any use at all. Empirically, it fails to describe the most important aspect of social mobility: the existence of barriers between strata. These and other objections to existing studies make great caution imperative in the use of their findings.

47. Helmut Schelsky, *Soziologische Bemerkungen zur Rolle der Schule in unserer Gesellschaftsverfassung*, unpublished, 1956, p. 3.

the process of socialization itself, especially as found in the educational system, that is serving as the proving ground for ability and hence the selective agency for placing people in different statuses according to their capacities.[49]

To be sure, there still are numerous obstacles and barriers in the way of complete equality of educational opportunity, but it is the stubborn tendency of modern societies to institutionalize inter-generation mobility by making a person's social position dependent on his educational achievement. Where this is the case, no social stratum, group or class can remain completely stable for more than one generation. Social mobility, which, for Marx, was the exception that confirmed the rule of class closure, is built into the structure of post-capitalist society and has therefore become a factor to be reckoned with in all analyses of conflict and change.

There are forms of mobility other than that between genera-tions, but about these we know even less. Thomas's study of intrageneration mobility in Britain[50] suggests a truly extra-ordinary degree of exchange between occupational groups. According to this study, there is not in contemporary Britain a single status category the majority of the members of which have never been in higher or lower strata.[51] But while it seems probable that there is a considerable amount of movement between occupations in various spheres of work, findings like those of Thomas's would require a more thorough analysis than the data published so far would permit. There are sure to be even higher barriers for intrageneration mobility than for mobility between generations, so that all we can infer from what patchy data we have is what anybody living in a modern society can observe for himself: in post-capitalist societies there is a great deal of movement, upwards and downwards as well as on one social level, between generations as well as within them, so that the individual who stays at his place of birth, and in the occupa-tion of his father throughout his life has become a rare exception.

48. ibid., p. 6.

49. Kingsley Davis, *Human Society*, Macmillan, 1949, p. 219.

50. G. Thomas, 'Labour mobility in Great Britain 1945–49', *Report No. 134 of the Social Survey*, London, n.d.

51. ibid., p. 30.

When Marx dealt with the 'exchange between classes' in the United States, he assumed that a high degree of exchange would be detrimental to the formation of powerful classes, and therefore inconducive to the fomentation of violent conflicts. This assumption is plausible. A class composed of individuals whose social position is not an inherited and inescapable fate, but merely one of a plurality of social roles, is not likely to be as powerful a historical force as the closed class Marx had in mind. Where mobility within and between generations is a regular occurrence, and therefore a legitimate expectation of many people, conflict groups are not likely to have either the permanence or the dead seriousness of caste-like classes composed of hopelessly alienated men. And as the instability of classes grows, the intensity of class conflict is bound to diminish. Instead of advancing their claims as members of homogeneous groups, people are more likely to compete with each other as individuals for a place in the sun. Where such competition is not possible, or not successful, group conflicts assume a somewhat milder and looser character than class struggles of a Marxian type. Again, the question arises whether such conflict groups of mobile individuals can still be described as classes. In any case, the institutionalization of social mobility through both the educational and the occupational systems contradicts quite clearly the prediction of a continuous increase in the intensity of class conflicts.

In a study of the effects of social mobility on group relations, Janowitz arrived at two interesting conclusions:

One, social mobility generally has been found to have disruptive implications for the structure of primary group relations and on related social psychological states, and thereby to carry socially maladjustive consequences. . . . Second [with respect to the consequences of social mobility for secondary group structures], markedly different order of inferences can be made. Upward social mobility, especially in the middle class, tends to orient and incorporate mobile groups into many types of secondary structures with relative effectiveness. On the other hand, . . . downward mobility does not produce effective involvement in secondary group structures in pursuit of self-interest.[52]

52. Morris Janowitz, 'Some consequences of social mobility in the United States', *Transactions of the Third World Congress of Sociology*, vol. 3, London, 1956, p. 193.

This finding (which evidently applies to intergeneration mobility only) is a welcome reminder of the fact that although mobility diminishes the coherence of groups as well as the intensity of class conflict, it does not eliminate either. While civil wars and revolutions may be unlikely in a highly mobile society, there is no *a priori* reason to believe that conflicts of interests will not find their expression in other ways. Marx's theory of class fails to account for such other types of conflict, and it will be our task in this study to find an approach that accounts for group conflicts in mobile as well as in relatively immobile industrial societies.

Equality in Theory and Practice

In the preceding sections two of the three predictions that Marx made about the future development of classes in capitalist society have been discussed in the light of the social history of the last decades. We have seen that neither of them has come true. Contrary to Marx's expectations, the increasing differentiation as well as homogeneity of classes was checked by the decomposition of labor and capital, the emergence of white-collar workers and bureaucrats, and the institutionalization of social mobility. But none of Marx's hopes – for such they were – has been refuted more dramatically in social development than his prediction that the class situations of bourgeoisie and proletariat would tend toward extremes of wealth and poverty, possession and deprivation. Here, too, Marx had a simple theory. He believed in a direct and unfailing correlation between the extremity of class situations and the intensity of class conflict. It is quite possible that this theory contains an element of truth, but if it does, then the remarkable spread of social equality in the past century has rendered class struggles and revolutionary changes utterly impossible.

T. H. Marshall has shown that much of modern social history can be understood in terms of what he calls the 'war' between 'citizenship rights' (which, by definition, are equal rights) and the 'capitalist class system'.[53] In successive periods, three types of citizenship rights have been adopted by most industrial societies, and they have increasingly affected the processes of

53. Marshall, op. cit.

class differentiation and class conflict. The first of these rights, that of the generalization of legal equality, was still quite compatible with class conflict and even with class war. Indeed, Marx used his most mocking and cynical style when he referred to legal equality in capitalist society:

Liberty! For buyers and sellers of a commodity, e.g. labor power, are determined by their free will alone. They enter into contracts as free, legally equal persons. . . . Equality! For they are related merely as owners of commodities, and exchange equivalent for equivalent. Property! For everybody controls merely what is his.[54]

But Marx overlooked what de Tocqueville (whose work he probably knew) had observed before him, namely, that equality is a highly dynamic force, and that men, once they are equal in some respects, 'must come in the end to be equal upon all'.[55]

A considerable step toward complete equality was taken when citizenship rights were, in the nineteenth century, extended to the political sphere. Universal suffrage and the right to form political parties and associations involved the removal of political conflicts from the factory floor and the street to negotiating bodies and parliaments. On a different level, it opened up the possibility for Marx's followers to convert their master's theories into political realities – but it is as well that they did not fail as miserably in this process as Marx did himself. By virtue of freedom of association and political equality, the early trade-union movement as well as socialist parties grown out of it achieved considerable success in improving the lot of the working class, although this progress was still restricted by many an obstacle:

Civil rights gave legal powers whose use was drastically curtailed by class prejudice and lack of economic opportunity. Political rights gave potential power whose exercise demanded experience, organization, and a change of ideas as to the proper functions of Government.[56]

Only when, in our own century, legal and political citizenship rights were supplemented by certain social rights, did the process

54. Karl Marx, *Das Kapital*, new edn, Berlin, 1953, vol. 1, p. 184.
55. Alexis de Tocqueville, in Bradley, ed., *Democracy in America*, New York, 1945, p. 55.
56. Marshall, op. cit., p. 46.

118

of equalization of status really reach a point where the differences and antagonisms of class are affected.

The social rights of citizenship which are widely recognized in contemporary societies include old-age pensions, unemployment benefits, public health insurance and legal aid, as well as a minimum wage and, indeed, a minimum standard of living. 'Equal participation in the material and intellectual comforts of civilization ... is the undisputed basic material right of our social constitution.'[57] Where established rights guarantee this kind of equality for every citizen, conflicts and differences of class are, at the very least, no longer based on inequalities of status in a strict sense of this term. From the point of view of legal privileges and deprivations, every citizen of advanced industrial societies has an equal status, and what social differences there are arise on the undisputed basis of this fundamental equality. The 'absolute' privilege of the bourgeoisie, and the equally 'absolute' alienation of the proletariat which Marx with a characteristic Hegelian figure of thought predicted, has not only not come true, but, by institutionalizing certain citizenship rights, post-capitalist society has developed a type of social structure that excludes both 'absolute' and many milder forms of privilege and deprivation. If equality before the law was for most people in the early phases of capitalist society but a cynical fiction, the extended citizenship rights of post-capitalist society represent a reality that forcefully counteracts all remaining forms of social inequality and differentiation.

This is *a fortiori* the case, since along with the spread of citizenship rights, the social situation of people became increasingly similar. The completeness of this levelling tendency can be, and has been, exaggerated. There are of course even to-day considerable differences in income, prestige, spending habits and styles of life. But as a tendency the process of levelling social differences cannot be denied. By the simultaneous rise of the real wages of workers and the taxation of top earnings, a redistribution of incomes has taken place – a redistribution that some believe today has gone so far as to remove every incentive for work requiring special training or skill. Many of the technical comforts and status symbols of modern life are increasingly

57. Schelsky, 1956, op. cit., p. 5.

available to everybody. The mass-produced commodities of the 'culture industry'[58] unite distant people and areas in nearly identical leisure-time activities. Schelsky gives voice to the impression of many when he summarizes this development as a process of 'social levelling with predominantly petty-bourgeois or middle-class patterns of behavior and ideals'.[59]

Social stratification and class structure are two distinct aspects of social organization, but they both refer to inequalities in the social life of individuals. If, therefore, the legal and social status of people undergoes a process of levelling which apparently tends toward complete equality of status, the concepts of social stratification and class structure tend to lose their meaning. In so far as social stratification is concerned, there is evidence and argument to contest this inference. For one thing there is some doubt as to whether one can really extrapolate from developments of the past century and infer a further levelling of socioeconomic status. For another thing, it seems far more likely from the point of view of a functioning social structure that there is a certain minimum of inequalities which will not be touched by egalitarian trends under any condition.[60] With respect to class structure, the answer is not as simple. There can be little doubt that the equalization of status resulting from social developments of the past century has contributed greatly to changing the issues and diminishing the intensity of class conflict. By way of extrapolation – fairly wild extrapolation, I may say – some authors have visualized a state in which there are no classes and no class conflicts, because there is simply nothing to quarrel about. I do

58. Max Horkheimer and T. W. Adorno, *Dialektik der Aufklärung*, Amsterdam, 1947.

59. Helmut Schelsky, *Wandlungen der deutschen Familie in der Gegenwart*, 3rd edn, Stuttgart, 1955. There is a host of literature on problems of equality and social class. Apart from the works of Marshall and Schelsky ... see especially, R. H. Tawney, *Religion and the Rise of Capitalism*, London, 1926 and T. B. Bottomore, *Classes in Modern Society*, Allen and Unwin, 1955.

60. The argument of Davis and Moore (Kingsley Davis and W. E. Moore, 'Some principles of stratification' in Logan Wilson and W. L. Kolb, *Sociological Analysis*, New York, 1949) to this effect is not, in my opinion, wholly convincing, but many of the considerations relevant to the problem of the function of inequality have come out in their argument and the controversy following it.

not think that such a state is ever likely to occur. But in order to substantiate this opinion, it is necessary to explore the structural limits of equality, that is, to find the points at which even the most fanatic egalitarian comes up against insurmountable realities of social structure. One of these is surely the variety of human desires, ideas and interests, the elimination of which is neither desirable nor likely. But while this is important, it is not as such an element of social structure. I shall suggest in this study that the fundamental inequality of social structure, and the lasting determinant of social conflict, is the inequality of power and authority which inevitably accompanies social organization. But this is an anticipation about which much more will have to be said. In so far as the theory and practice of equality in post-capitalist societies are concerned, it seems certain that they have changed the issues and patterns of class conflict, and possible that they have rendered the concept of class inapplicable, but they have not removed all significant inequalities, and they have not therefore, eliminated the causes of social conflict.

6 W. Wesolowski

The Notions of Strata and Class in Socialist Society

W.Wesolowski, 'Les notions de strates et de classe dans la société socialiste', *Sociologie du Travail*, vol. 9 (1967), pp. 144–64. Translated by A. Béteille.

The social stratification of socialist societies is a subject of lively discussion among Polish sociologists and economists. Apart from the findings of empirical research concerning particular strata and classes (conceived, according to the traditional scheme, as the working class, the stratum of the intelligentsia and the class of small peasants), several articles have recently appeared which set forth new theories on the structure of class or of social stratification in socialist society.[1] Polish scientists are not the only ones to show an interest in these problems. A similar tendency may be observed in other socialist countries.[2] The present article is intended to be a contribution to the contemporary discussion. It deals with three problems:

1. the Marxist theory of class structure and of the conditions of socialist society;

2. the nature of social stratification in socialist society;

3. the basis for contradictions of interests in this type of society.

The ideas sketched below constitute a preliminary inquiry rather than a definitive solution.

1. cf. B. Minc, 'Classes and strata in socialist society', *Polytika* nos. 39, 42, 46, 1961. J. Wiatr, 'Social stratification and egalitarian tendencies', *Kultura i spoleczenstwo*, no. 2, 1962. B. Galeski, 'Some problems of social structure in the light of surveys in rural communities', *Studia Socjologiczne*, no. 1, 1963. B. Minc, 'Social stratification in socialist society', *Kultura i spoleczenstwo*, no. 3, 1963. W. Wesolowski, 'The process of disappearance of class differences', *Studia Socjologiczne*, no. 2, 1964. S. Widerszpil, 'An interpretation of transformations of social structure in people's Poland', *Newe Drogi*, no. 1, 1963.

2. cf. P. N. Fiedosijew, *From Socialism to Communism*, Moscow, 1962. *Sociology in the U.S.S.R.*, vol. 1, Moscow, 1965. *Socjologija* Nos. 1–2, 1966, Belgrade: special number of the Yugoslav sociological journal devoted to problems of 'Socialism and Transformations in the Class Structure.'

W. Wesolowsk

I. Socialist Society and the Marxist Theory of Classes

The Marxist theory of class structure establishes first of all the existence of two mutually antagonistic groups engaged in the process of production. These are what one calls the 'basic classes'. They are distinguished from each other by their relations to the means of production. One of these classes owns the means of production; the other is deprived of these although it is the one which operates them. This relationship determines the nature of the first as the exploiting class and of the second as the exploited class.

This brief résumé leads to the proposition, now a commonplace, that the proletarian revolution abolishes the class structure thus conceived. The socialization of the means of production and of capitalist property signifies the elimination of one of the elements of the antagonistic relationship between capital and labour. Consequently, it signifies the disappearance of the basic relationship of the class which is typical of capitalist society. Deprived of their 'opposed role', the workers cease to be a class in the traditional sense of the term. This is due to the fact that the exploitation of the means of production by the owners, the essential characteristic by which they constituted a class in capitalist society, has disappeared. In the Marxian sense, they are no longer a 'true class', but rather an 'ex-class'.

We have deliberately simplified the preceding propositions in order to draw a fundamental distinction. When the workers free themselves from their 'Siamese twin', they lose the principal characteristic of their social position, but they are not thereby automatically deprived of their other characteristics. Because of these survivals we continue to call them 'workers', but not 'the working class' in the Marxian sense of the term. Perhaps it would be convenient to call them 'the stratum of workers'. The workers continue to be tied to a certain type of production (industrial production) and a specific type of work (manual work). They possess specific social and cultural attributes. In other words, the workers occupy a given place in the social division of labour; they have a specific income, education, mode of life, political attitude and numerous other social qualities or attributes.

We have here before us one of the typical features of the Marxian theory of classes, a feature which is none the less not always clearly apprehended. In this theory, one of the attributes and one of the social relations following from it – the monopoly of the means of production on the one hand and the deprivation from these on the other – are considered as the basis of the complex structure of the attributes of class.

The attributes of class create a sort of specific hierarchy and a causal chain of inter-relations. There is one constellation of attributes pertaining to the capitalists and another, and a different one, to the workers. The ownership of the means of production places control over the process of production in the hands of the capitalist and gives him a privileged position as regards the distribution of incomes accruing from production. The worker executes commands in course of the process of production, and suffers discrimination in the distribution of the income derived from production. From the combination of these elements follow other attributes which determine the social positions of capitalists and workers. These can be defined as an inequality in the possibilities of obtaining and profiting from diverse values such as education, health and the enjoyment of cultural values. It is on the basis of all these attributes of social position that different modes of life, different mentalities and dissimilar political attitudes are constituted.

It is true that some of these attributes have been strongly underlined by Marx, whereas others have only been mentioned. It is also true that in the writings of several later Marxists some have been neglected or forgotten. But they were present in the thoughts of Marx.

Moreover, one ought to note that the causal relations do not resemble a uniform linear chain. For example, the relationship to the means of production forms class consciousness by determining level of income and status in the social organization of work. The amount of income acts upon class consciousness in terms of the possibilities it represents and in terms of social prestige. There is besides an interaction between some of these attributes.

A simplified scheme of relations between the attributes of class is presented below: According to the point of view adopted, some among them may be diversely defined and envisaged in different combinations in the course of analysis, and the details of this are not definitive. What concerns us here is to illustrate the general idea that Marx has taken account of a certain number of attributes and of their relationships. The enumeration of these shows that the difference between Marxists and non-Marxists who study social stratification is not so much a difference of choice within the totality of attributes but rather one of perspective in approaching this totality. One may call the Marxist approach 'deterministic' and that of the non-Marxists 'operational'. The Marxists regard the whole structure of attributes as being linked from bottom to top. The majority of non-Marxists divide all the members of a given community into 'prestige classes' and they

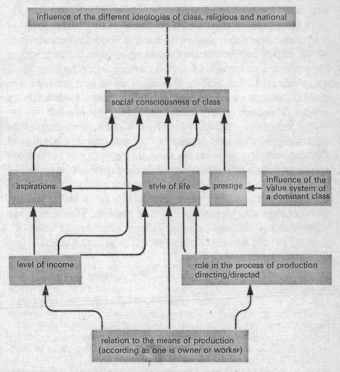

Figure 1 Scheme of relations between the attributes of class

are less interested in the underlying structure of the other attributes.[3]

One has to insist on the fact that *the relationship to the means of production has been considered by Marx as the decisive criterion in the differentiation of classes because it determines a certain number of social attributes.* We will here call them, according to convention, attributes of social position (or status). One set of attributes refers to the contradictory nature of the relations between antagonistic classes, and the other indicates differences of degree between them. The first type represents oppositions such as 'manual' and 'non-manual', 'governing' and 'governed'; the second represents people of 'higher economic level', 'middle economic level' and 'lower economic level' (or of 'high', 'middle' and 'low' levels of education).

The attributes of class which are found at the 'higher level' of the scheme relate to classes in their totality and not necessarily to all the individuals in a class. For example, there are members of the proletariat who, due to certain circumstances, have acquired a superior education. But the chances of access to it are unequally divided between workers and capitalists taken collectively as groups. The same remark would apply to styles of life.[4]

The influence of attributes external to our scheme on prestige and class consciousness requires to be specified. The prestige of the members of a class results from the 'application' of a given system of values to their objective characteristics. This system of values is linked to the ideology of the dominant class. Thus, according to the value system appropriate to capitalist society, workers have low and capitalists high prestige. This is why our scheme shows prestige as being influenced from the 'outside', that is, by the dominant ideology. In a similar fashion, class

3. There are other differences between the two approaches, but it is equally useful to consider the similarities. This point has been developed in our Introduction to the Polish edition of the book by C. W. Mills: *White Collar*, cf. *Beale kolnierzyki: Amerykanskie klasy srednie*, Warsaw, 1965.

4. The present tendency in the capitalist countries is that the government has a certain influence on the status attributes of the working class by introducing social legislation, by providing scholarships, by fixing minimum wages, etc. This leads to a weakening of the direct dependence of these attributes of status on the means of production, although the two basic classes (capitalists and workers) continue to differ radically in the same way.

consciousness is formed by the ideologies of class which are propagated by political parties in open competition with each other, as are also propagated national, religious and other ideologies by different organizations and institutions, which maintain relations with the ideologies of a class that are sometimes overt and often covert. These influences are also indicated in the scheme.

We see then that the determining role of the relation to the means of production – the fundamental element in the whole structure – may be modified and its effect weakened by some influence having its origin outside the entire structure. Nevertheless, in the long run, this role is never eliminated.

Capitalist society is not composed exclusively of the 'fundamental classes', capitalists and workers, but also of other classes and strata. These strata are equally a 'heritage' of socialist society. In general, for Marxists, the question relates to the 'stratum of the intelligentsia' (understood as the broad group of non-manual workers) and the stratum of small agriculturists.

These strata possess well-defined attributes of social position, similar in their nature to those comprised in our scheme. From the viewpoint of these attributes, the positions of workers, 'employees'[5] and small agriculturists are comparable.

The process of the socialist transformation of agriculture may be of long or short duration and may also take different forms. We will leave this question aside. One may say, nevertheless, that transformations in the class structure inherited from the capitalists lead on the one hand towards an equalization in the relation to the means of production of former small agriculturists, workers and the intelligentsia; and, on the other, to a disappearance of the decisive role of the relation to the means of production in the determination of the other attributes of status (income, prestige, life expectancy, etc.).

The relationship to the means of production is the same for all citizens. And if there appear differences in income, nature of work, prestige, opportunities and political attitudes, these are not determined by this relationship.

5. The word 'employé' has a more restricted meaning in French than in English. It refers generally to the lower ranks of white-collar workers. The meaning adopted here is more clearly explained in the author's note 11. [Ed.]

II. The Process of Disintegration of the Attributes of Class

The attributes of status, devoid of the determining influence of the relation to the means of production, retain an 'autonomous' existence in the socialist régime. Thus, even though classes (in the Marxian sense of the term) disappear in a developed socialist society, there remain social differentiations which may be characterized as social stratification.[6]

This stratification may be conceived in a two-fold way. The first conception refers to income, occupation or prestige as criteria for the diverse dimensions of stratification. This represents a fairly simple theoretical concept which lends itself easily to research. It will allow the application of a simplified conception of this multidimensional stratification to an investigation of socialist society. Each characteristic will lead to a subject of independent research and its magnitude will be the basis of distinguishing the individual levels of stratification.

The second conception is more complex, but it allows in turn a better grasp of social structures and processes. This is the multi-dimensional approach properly so called.

One should remember that for Marx, classes differed in terms of a certain number of attributes interlinked with each other. The bourgeoisie enjoy a higher income, a higher level of education and higher prestige. The workers have a low income, a low level of education and low prestige. The petite bourgeoisie have an intermediate income, enjoy medium prestige and their level of education is higher than that of the workers but lower than that of the bourgeoisie. This conception of class has appeared not only in Marx but also among many non-Marxist theoreticians.

Here then arises a question of exceptional importance: up to what point is there congruence between certain attributes in the strata of a socialist country? Is there, for example, a correspondence between income on the one hand and education and prestige

6. Until now we have used the terms 'characteristics of class' or 'attributes of class'. From now onwards, we shall speak rather of 'characteristics of status', or 'attributes of status' since the 'relationship to the means of production' ceases to play a part. The attributes of social position on the 'higher levels' of our scheme are normally associated with the term 'status' or 'social status'.

on the other? This is the problem of 'status crystallization' in Lenski's terminology.[7]

The process of revolutionary transformation leads to a certain disintegration or 'decomposition' of the attributes of status. The character of work, the amount of income, the level of education and the degree of prestige tend to be dissociated. There are groups with a low level of education but with high income, or others with a high economic level but low prestige, etc. This is a result of transformations in the economic system and in the ideology. There are many examples of this 'process of disintegration' in Poland. The theoretical significance that this represents is neglected by sociologists and economists.

The processes of the disintegration of the attributes of status are intermixed with others by which certain differences are levelled. Some of these decompositions may be viewed as processes leading to equalization. If, for example, a specialized worker earns as much as a doctor, this may be viewed as an equalization of their social position in one zone of difference (income) whereas a difference in another zone (education) is maintained. The same observation applies, for example, to the equalization of the level of income of a turner and an engineer. But other processes can also be seen to appear. When a turner earns more than an engineer or when a miner enjoys greater prestige than an advocate, the disintegration of the attributes of status exceeds the limits of equalization of levels and leads to a dislocation which is more profound or 'more distended'. Certain groups begin to be distinguished from each other as being, in terms of certain attributes, in an inverse relationship to that in which they were in the preceding socio-economic system.

The disintegration of the attributes of status may henceforward take two forms. One is the equalization of 'levels' of certain attributes pertaining to certain former classes or particular strata. The other illustrates the case where one class goes beyond another with regard to some of these attributes.

By way of example we present below some data concerning the

7. G. Lenski, 'Status crystallization. A non-vertical dimension of social status', *The American Sociological Review*, no. 4 (1954); see also L. Broom, 'Social differentiation and stratification' in R. K. Merton *et al.* (eds.), *Sociology Today*, Harper, 1959.

disintegration of three attributes of status in contemporary Poland. These are: the nature of work, the amount of income and the degree of prestige.

In pre-War Poland nearly all non-manual workers earned more than manual workers. (The mean salary of a non-manual worker was more than twice that of a manual worker.) Table 1 represents the comparative wage structure of the two groups today.[8]

It is true that the Table shows a higher percentage of manual workers among those with low wages and, conversely, a larger number of non-manual workers among those with higher salaries. Nevertheless, the two other phenomena indicated in the Table are no less important: a high percentage of workers, both manual

Table 1

Distribution of Different Categories of Workers by Income Classes in 1963

Income class	Manual workers		Non-manual workers	
701–800	10·7		1·3	
801–1000	7·2		5·4	
1001–1200	8·7	66·9	9·1	59·2
1201–1500	15·6		17·1	
1501–2000	24·7		26·3	
2001–2500	15·9		16·3	
2501–3000	8·5	33·1	10·4	40·8
3000+	8·7		14·1	

and non-manual, earn the same amount (from 1200 to 2000 zlotys per month). This bears witness to an equalization of income. In addition, there are a large number of manual workers who earn more than the non-manual workers. Among manual workers, 33·1 per cent earn more than 2000 zlotys whereas 59·2 per cent of non-manual workers earn less. Here we perceive the course of disintegration of two attributes, the nature of work and the amount of income.

An inquiry on occupational prestige in Poland today suggests the disintegration of another pair of attributes: nature of work

8. *Poland in Figures 1944–1964*, Warsaw, 1965, p. 104.

and social prestige. Table 2 illustrates the hierarchy of occupational prestige among the people of Warsaw. It indicates that certain manual occupations enjoy a higher prestige than other, non-manual occupations. Thus, skilled manual workers occupy a higher position in the hierarchy of prestige than office workers and other non-manual categories. By contrast, a sociologist wrote of the corresponding situation before the War: 'It is probable that nowhere outside Poland is the gulf so great between non-manual work of even the most subordinate kind and manual work of even the most essential kind.'[9]

A partial variance between income and prestige is at once evident. For example, the wages of nurses and teachers are today relatively low. A teacher earns between 1500 and 2000 zlotys per month and a nurse, around 1500. But these occupations occupy a higher place on the scale of prestige than that of the turner who

Table 2

Evaluation of Employment and Occupation According to Social Prestige[10]

Rank	Employment or occupation	Score
1	University professor	1·22
2	Doctor	1·44
3	Teacher	1·71
4	Engineer	1·78
5	Pilot	1·83
6	Lawyer	1·97
7	Agricultural expert (with University diploma)	1·97
8	Minister	2·07
9	Journalist	2·13
10	Skilled steel worker	2·18
11	Skilled worker (machine)	2·27
12	Priest	2·35
13	Nurse	2·38
14	Foreman	2·53
15	Accountant	2·54
16	Tailor	2·70

9. W. Wesolowski, 'Hierarchies of professions and of positions', *Studia Socjologiczne*, no. 2 (1961), p. 101.

10. S. Rychlinski, 'Social strata', *Przeglad Socjologiczny*, vol. 8, p. 180.

Rank	Employment or occupation	Score
17	Metal worker	2·73
18	Office superintendent	2·77
19	Farmer	2·78
20	Officer	2·79
21	Small trader	3·01
22	Railwayman	3·18
23	Policeman	3·21
24	Office worker	3·43
25	Secretary	3·50
26	Salesman	3·59
27	Construction worker	3·95
28	Charwoman	4·08
29	Agricultural worker	4·16

reaches 3000 to 4000 zlotys or of the tradesman whose income is even higher.

Table 3

Evaluation of Occupational Groups According to Remuneration and Social Prestige[11]

	Remuneration		Prestige	
Occupational group	Rank	Score	Rank	Score
Private entrepreneurs	1	1·81	3	2·81
Higher staff and liberal professions	2	2·35	1	1·74
Skilled workers	3	2·40	2	2·33
'Employees'[12]	4	3·10	4	3·17
Specialized workers	5	4·12	5	4·06

The members of society are naturally conscious of this process of dissociation. In the inquiries cited above, the informants were asked to evaluate the same occupations according to the criteria of income and prestige. The hierarchies did not correspond with each other. Each occupation was assigned to one place on the economic scale and to another on the scale of prestige. This is given in condensed form in Table 3.

11. ibid., p. 4. In this table, all non-manual workers are divided into two groups described as 'higher staff or liberal professions' and 'employees'. The reason for this distinction is that professors, doctors, teachers, lawyers, engineers and journalists are evidently on a different level of the hierarchy from nurses, accountants, office superintendents and office workers.

12. See Note 11 above.

One will also note that a certain decomposition of the attributes of status in some categories of manual and non-manual workers has been established in certain contemporary capitalist societies. But the extent of this is much more limited than in socialist societies.

III. The Contradiction of Interests in Socialist Society

The problem of interests, and more particularly of contradictions of interest, plays an important role in the Marxist theory of social structure. In discussing transformations of the class structure in socialist society, we will limit ourselves to the domain of social interests. The problems implicit in this are extremely complex. Up to the present they have been studied rarely, or rather, superficially, by Marxist researchers. We do not aspire here to treat this difficult problem in depth, but simply to make certain preliminary suggestions with regard to the types of problems that ought to be in the forefront of all discussions concerning contradictions of interests between strata in a socialist society.

First of all, certain distinctive traits showing the contrast between capitalist and socialist societies ought to be isolated. This has to be done in order to help in comprehending some of the specific features of socialist society.

According to Marx, the capitalist mode of production is characterized by the presence of two social classes of which one appropriates the products of the other's work. The capitalist class appropriates the surplus value which is the fruit of the workers' labour. This kind of class relationship is tied to the distribution of goods according to the 'principle of distribution based on property'. When this principle is in operation a person does not need to work in order to take his share in the distribution of economic goods or even to enjoy the privileges of this distribution.

The 'principle of distribution based on property' ceases to operate with the abolition of the capitalist ownership of the means of production. This signifies at the same time the end of conflicts of class interest typical of capitalist societies (i.e. between the class of capitalists and the working class).

In socialist society, the place left vacant by the principle of property is filled by the principle 'to each according to his work'. Thus the share of the individual in the division of the social product is determined by the quality and the quantity of his work. This principle is not entirely new. In capitalist society also it applies to individuals without capital, i.e. to persons who live by their own work. With the abolition of interest on capital under socialism, the principle of distribution according to work attains universal validity. In socialist society there is only one sole criterion which determines the share of the individual in the social product: the quantity and quality of the work accomplished.

Let us examine some questions relating to the formula 'to each according to his work'. The problems of social stratification are linked to that part of the formula which postulates that wages are a function of the quality of work, that is, that they are a function of the level of skill and education necessary for carrying out a given job. There is a very clear difference at this level between a specialized worker, for example, and a university professor.

It is necessary to clarify the situation we have in mind when we talk about what creates 'contradiction of interests'. One ought to remember that Marx had a very broad conception of the 'contradiction of interests'. He had described not only the contradictions of interests between classes but also those which exist between two workers canvassing for the same job. Following this approach, we are inclined to look for a contradiction of interests wherever there is scarcity of goods (or, more generally, of values) desired by all and where their distribution is necessarily such that any increase for one group inevitably reduces the share of the other.[13]

1. *Two types of conflicts deriving from the unequal distribution of goods*. If we consider the formula 'to each according to his work' and the definition proposed of the 'contradiction of interests', we arrive at the conclusion that the unequal distribution of

13. We have omitted here the question of the unity of interests in socialist society. This important problem has been the subject of our contribution to *Classes, Strata and Power*, Warsaw, 1966, cf. ch. 4. The need for a relativist point of view in regard to the treatment of interests is discussed in 'Ruling class and social elite', *The Polish Sociological Bulletin*, no. 1 1965).

goods among socio-professional groups (or strata) can take two forms. The first appears when the unequal distribution of goods is conditioned by the application of the principle 'to each according to his work'; the second, when it is due to factors other than the application of this principle or to inadequacies in its application. In both the cases we will be faced by an objective contradiction of interests. But there exists none the less a significant difference between the two situations.

The principle 'to each according to his work' is considered as the basic principle of distribution in socialist society, but it is not always strictly applied. In the first place, economists have not until now studied the precise methods of evaluating the quality of work in relation to the level of skill involved (and other factors, as for example, the degree of responsibility and risk). The measures which exist are largely intuitive. So long as precise means of evaluation are not available, it is extremely difficult to say in what measure the wages of a porter and a nurse, for example, or of a civil servant and of a factory director, or of a turner and of a university professor and the whole wage system in general conform to the principle 'to each according to his work'.

Two problems have to be taken into consideration at this point. One of these relates to the degree to which the objective contradiction of interests would be compatible with a socialist system. One could say that a deviation from the socialist principle of distribution would end in 'overpayment' of some and 'underpayment' of others as returns for their work. Consequently, the contradictions of interests in socialist countries can result in something resembling antagonistic contradiction, since overpayment and underpayment may be viewed as a particular form of the 'exploitation' of some people by others (in spite of the social ownership of the means of production).

Again, there is a psychological aspect to the contradiction of interests in socialism. The 'employees' (in Poland) are less sensitive to inequality in wages than to the relative level of wages paid in different types of occupations. There is a general sentiment that a 'just' and 'equitable' wage is that which conforms to the principle 'to each according to his work'. People are on their guard in case others encroach upon what is their due. These results suggest that the practice of 'overpayment or of underpayment' may end not only in quasi-exploitation but also in increased dissatisfaction. It appears that the objective contradiction of interests implied in the unequal distribution of goods following from the application of the principle 'to each according to his work', does not arouse such strong tendencies towards the creation of conflicts as the defects in its application.

The term 'contradictions of interests' is used here to signify an objective state of things. The term 'conflict of interests' is conceived as reflecting the subjective interpretation of a state of affairs, that is, the interests of the subject. As these are two different phenomena, we have felt the need to use two different terms.

2. *The limitation of the principle 'to each according to his work'.* We will now turn to certain supplementary factors which influence the system of wages. If the principle 'to each according to his work' does not find systematic application, it is not solely because of a lack of precise measures. There are other formulae which are considered to be an integral part of the socialist credo, and which are therefore translated into the world of practice.

Thus we can find instances of 'overpayment' and 'underpayment' which are compatible with the principles of socialism in spite of their evident discrepancy with the model formula of remuneration.

One form of deviation from this formula is the high remuneration of less qualified workers and the low remuneration of highly qualified workers. The restrictions imposed on very high salaries, just like the law of minimum wages are all evidence of deviations from the principle 'to each according to his work'. And, none the less, both these phenomena seem to exist in socialist society.[14]

A second deviation consists in providing advantages to workers employed in high investment industries situated far from urban and industrial centres. Such industries require large amounts of manpower but manpower is not sufficiently mobile. A worker has his home, his family, his friends and the company of his choice; he is attached to his domicile. In agreeing to go to work in a distant place or in a newly constructed factory, he will perhaps be

14. L. Morecka, 'Wages in the socialist economy' in O. Lange, *Zagadnienia ekonomii politycznej socjalizmu* (1960).

forced to undergo a reconversion, to live without his family in a workers' hostel and to adapt himself to a new milieu which still lacks all the attractions of urban life. The relatively higher wage conferred on workers employed under such conditions ought to be considered as a sort of compensation for the unfavourable conditions of life and work which they have accepted. Such a wage may be considered as the normal wage multiplied by a factor representing the supplementary social and psychological cost imposed on the worker. As opposed to the purely 'economic' wage, this kind of wage may be called the 'socio-economic' wage.[15] In addition to the work as such, this wage takes into account a certain number of privations suffered by the worker.

We have defined some of the deviations from the principle 'to each according to his work', caused by the operation of other principles which are also in accordance with the ideas of socialism. But the mechanism of social life today being a highly complicated affair, it is not possible for the average man to follow all its intricacies in everyday life. There is a tendency among men to adopt criteria of judgement based on simple facts or on simplified formulae which strike their imagination and satisfy their moral sense. And it is for this reason that it seems that any deviation from the formula 'to each according to his work' (whether or not it is justified by social or economic reasons, or whether it is an unjust imposition of privilege, or a result of the absence of an objective measure of the quality of work) leads to the same increasing consciousness of conflicts of interest in socialist society. The consciousness of conflict may be linked to two causes: to the objective contradictions of interests which come into play when one applies the socialist principle 'to each according to his work'; and, on the other hand, to distortions of this principle. To ascertain which of these motivates the consciousness of conflicts, one will have to await future empirical studies.

There are yet other hypotheses which deserve to be treated empirically. For example, there are probably two factors which create or simply aggravate the consciousness of conflicts. The one could be defined in terms of the 'burden of the past', and the other as 'anticipation of the future'.

15. Z. Morecka, 'Economic or socio-economic wages?', *Zycie Gospodarcze*, nos. 8, 9 (1958).

The 'burden of the past' is felt among members of those groups which had higher incomes in the past (in the capitalist system). Such persons never cease to ask why a worker earns so much and a doctor so little. Conversely, the members of groups which were formerly oppressed tend to 'anticipate the future' (that is, the principle postulated for communism, 'to each according to his needs'), and to ask why a charwoman earns so little and the head of an enterprise so much.

Further, there seems to exist a 'natural' tendency towards the emergence of consciousness of conflicts among members of economic groups at the extremes. Consequently, even in the socialist system, certain persons (above all, those earning less) tend to speak of the 'rich' and the 'poor', of the 'privileged' and the 'common people'. This is inderstandable if we consider that the judgements of men are relative to their economic position.

3. *Contradictions of interests and the state.* In socialist society the unequal distribution of goods in high demand is made through the mechanism of governmental decisions. The general system of wages and the income of the individual citizen are determined by the government. Contradictions of interests may emerge here at two levels: that of contradictions between groups with different incomes, and of contradictions between these groups and the 'general regulator' represented by the government (in the broad sense of the term).

Objective contradictions between the interests of groups which partake of different degrees of the national product exist, whatever be the mechanism of distribution. In the case of the market mechanism, the government also acts as a regulatory factor in maintaining market relations, or by direct intervention in market relations (that is, by fixing a minimum wage, or by intervening in collective agreements). Such is the situation under capitalism today.

In the socialist system, the government assumes the role of direct regulator. This explains a special psychological situation. People with insufficient incomes tend to blame the government (as the regulator of incomes) rather than the more favoured groups. This tendency is much less frequent and much less explicit in the capitalist system. There, contradictions of interests are conceived rather as contradictions between different social groups. This difference between the two systems is extremely important for all discussions of conflicts of interests.

Equipped with the concepts of 'overpayment' and 'underpayment' as well as the distinction between the objective contradictions of interests and conflicts subjectively perceived, we can now attempt to deepen the theoretical complexity of the situation created by the direct regulatory function of the State.

Let us consider a certain number of possibilities: In determining the system of wages, the government can act in any one of the following ways: (a) applying fully the principle 'to each according to his work'; (b) applying this principle with certain deviations in favour of highly skilled persons; (c) applying this principle with deviations in favour of the unskilled strata. If we consider the obvious failings in the wage systems of the different socialist countries, it appears probable that these three alternatives do in fact all exist.

In the first case the government acts as a 'just' and 'impartial' regulator of wages. The highly skilled are paid more in line with the socialist principle of remuneration.

But the contradiction of interests set up in this case between different social and occupational groups (or strata) is a direct consequence of government policy. This fact in itself can give birth to a consciousness of conflict among the poorly paid and their resentment will be directed against the State (the government). There is an objective contradiction between the interests of each social and occupational group, but at the same time, there is, among the poorly paid, a consciousness of conflict directed against the government. Here we find a 'transfer' of the consciousness of conflict to the detriment of the 'general regulator'.

It is evident that this type of contradiction of intergroup interests is inevitable in socialism.

The situations described above (under points b and c) are of another nature. Here the government 'overpays' or 'underpays' certain social and occupational groups (or entire strata). This may well result in the satisfaction of some, but at the same time it may cause an aggravation in the consciousness of conflict among others. The tendencies which create conflict are born out of the 'partiality' of the government; the resulting contradictions transgress the socialist system of remunerations. The consciousness of conflict is more exacerbated in face of such discrimination when the 'underpayment' affects those who are unskilled and hence more handicapped. In practice perhaps it is the contrary which takes place. In Poland, for example, if there is an 'overpaid' group, it is the less skilled. For society as a whole this appears to have the effect of reducing the consciousness of conflicts.

Finally, another possibility appears in the situation where the group responsible for the elaboration of the wage system (which is to say, the political directors of the country in general) is itself 'overpaid'. Whereas in the preceding examples, the directors as a group did not appear *vis-à-vis* other groups (or some among them) in a position of contradictory interests of the non-socialist type, this last case illustrates precisely such a contradiction. This is a fertile field in which the consciousness of conflict may arise in a brutal form.

The situations mentioned above are purely theoretical. They derive from a broad and specific interpretation of the contradictions of interests, and of the conception of 'overpayment' and 'underpayment'. In order to employ these conceptions in empirical research we ought first to discover objective measures of the social value of different types of work. These measures should take into account not only the 'purely economic' value of work, but also other factors of a 'socio-economic' nature. Although it is perhaps not easy to discover such measures, one cannot conceive of any other way of effectively studying the objective contradictions of interests existing in socialism.

4. *Contradictions of interests concerning non-economic goods.* Together with an unequal distribution of income we find in socialist society an unequal distribution of many other values. The distribution of income implies the distribution of certain other goods, given the partial convertibility of these values. In a situation where a large gamut of non-economic (i.e. cultural) values can be bought in the market, the acquisition of other goods is determined by the distribution of income. We can, consequently, feel fully justified in centring our attention on the dis-

tribution of income. While fully a characteristic of capitalist society, this also applies largely to socialist society. But a distinctive feature of socialist society is the weakened inter-relationship between the amount of income and participation in other values. In effect, *being distributed through different channels, non-economic goods are subject to extremely important contradictions of interests.* Among these non-economic values we find education, certain goods in the domain of what is called cultural consumption (e.g. vacations at reduced rates), social security and many others.

Let us take the example of education. It is free in socialist society and provided through a network of State schools. But in reality it is provided unequally and there are mechanisms which determine in advance its further distribution (in the next generation). These two facts are a source of contradictions of interests concerning education as a social value.

Let us take the relatively simple case of the frequent inequalities in the level of education. Some persons are more cultivated, others less, and education is a value which is highly in demand in the population. This demand is created by two factors: the inherent value of education and the advantages of education as an instrument giving access to other values. Education is one of the determinants through which the individual partakes in other values such as income, prestige, stability of employment and political influence.

Greater attention should be given to the instrumental role of education in socialist society. In all industrial societies the individual level of education is an essential component of occupational qualifications, and these form the basis of the general status of the individual. In capitalist society, however, this interdependence hardly applies to the members of the capitalist class. Their status and possibilities are principally determined by the amount of capital at their disposal rather than by education. Education here represents only an additional premium enabling the capitalist to undertake certain activities.

In socialist society the position of each and everyone is largely determined by his occupational status, and the latter depends greatly on his education (and on skills following from this education). And because there is a direct bond between occupation on the one hand and income and social prestige on the other,

141

education represents an important instrument for obtaining other values.

We have already alluded to the instrumental role of education within a generation, but it is present also between the generations. Education is the principal instrument which serves to define the future occupational position of a young man making his entry into adult social life. One should not lose sight of the fact that in societies where education is not free, the level of education attained by a young person depends largely on the income of his parents: his own future income is in turn determined by his education. As a consequence, status is subjected to a 'hereditary' tendency (the system of scholarships can partially modify this tendency).

In socialist society, where education is free at all levels, the inter-relation between the parents' income and their children's opportunities in education is reduced enormously. This reflects the fact that the instrumental and intergenerational role of income is reduced and that of education is enhanced in socialist society.

But as yet there does not at all exist an abundance of secondary and higher educational institutions in the socialist countries. As a consequence, there is ground for contradictions of interests between the social strata in regard to the criteria providing access to secondary and higher educational institutions. This contradiction concerns the operation of the channels by which education, as a factor which is instrumental and 'autonomous' with regard to income, is distributed.

The specific social conditions underlying this contradiction are linked to inequalities in the general intellectual development of children of workers and peasants on the one hand, and of the intelligentsia on the other. This comes out at the time of entrance examinations to the university and other institutions of higher learning, and also at the time of similar examinations in secondary schools.

The culturally differentiated conditions of individual homes accounts for differences in the initial levels of children of different social strata. Hence, workers and peasants accept the preferential system of access to schools, a system in which supplementary points are awarded to their children to compensate for their social milieu. This system acts against the chances of admission of the children of the intelligentsia. This is why the culturally privileged prefer a system of selection based exclusively on the results of examinations testing pure ability. The latter system tends naturally to reduce the chances of the children of workers and peasants.

In a situation of free education the lack of equilibrium between supply and demand in the matter of education is the source of contradictions of interests regarding the principles of selection.

5. *The cumulative and non-cumulative distribution of values.* The distribution of values in capitalist society is, to a high degree, cumulative: high income, great political influence, high level of education and high prestige are always combined in the same individuals whereas others suffer from insufficiencies in these areas. Thus, there is high congruence of the attributes of status in capitalist society, above all when one considers the two 'fundamental classes' in the Marxian sense.

In socialist society we observe a decomposition of the attributes of social status resulting from the non-cumulative distribution of the values generally desired. Income, education, political influence and prestige are distributed more independently of each other. The effect of this phenomenon in the realm of interests is enormous.

Two general hypotheses may be put forward here in this perspective:

(*a*) The cumulative distribution of values and, its consequence, the congruence in the attributes of status, both favour the development of fairly well-defined social strata or classes.

(*b*) The same phenomena end in an aggravation of the contradictions of objective interests between groups (strata) in creating parallel and related spheres of inequality.

These two hypotheses lead to another general proposition: the contradictions of objective interests and the subjective consciousness of conflicts tend to diminish in socialist society relatively to capitalist society.

IV. Two Tendencies

Our insistence on the decomposition of the attributes of status in socialist society was due to the relative novelty of the phenomenon which is often neglected or forgotten by sociologists. It would be wrong, however, to forget the congruences of these attributes. These congruences may be either a heritage of the past or the result of the socialist mechanisms of proper distribution. In fact, there are good reasons for looking into the sources of congruence in the attributes of status.

The principle 'to each according to his work' leads towards a synchronization of at least some of the attributes of status.

One may suppose that certain significant decompositions observed in Poland were caused, among other things, by the denial and omission of this principle under the pressure of an egalitarian ideology as well as of certain economic necessities (dearth of manpower in certain occupations).

The principle 'to each according to his work' contributes to the synchronization of the attributes of status in so far as it regulates income according to the 'quality' of work and, thus, according to education and the professional qualifications which follow. Formal education (i.e. the school) has a decisive influence on occupational skills in highly developed industrial societies. The application of the principle 'to each according to his work' tends to increase the congruence between education and income. There is a similar tendency towards congruence between income and position in the structures of power or of direction. The same synchronizing tendency is reinforced by the fact that prestige depends on education.

At the same time, an opposite tendency is at work. Certain tendencies towards the decomposition of status are created by those deliberate distortions of the principle 'to each according to his work' which aim at increasing the incomes of those who are less qualified. The result of this is a contradiction between qualifications (low) and income (medium). Similar effects are produced by deviations from this principle, such as limiting the salaries of highly qualified persons.

In a general way, the scale of qualifications seems to be broader than the scale of incomes. This 'levelling' of income towards a median position ends in a decomposition of the attributes of status, a decomposition which takes the form of 'levelling' rather than 'overstepping'. One of the attributes of status in a certain social and occupational group or in an entire stratum is raised while all the others remain stationary. This kind of decomposition is probably the one most in operation.

It is easier to observe such a 'partial decomposition' of the attributes of status when it is placed in the context of the broad spectrum of status attributes. Let us take prestige for example. There are groups of highly qualified persons in Poland who enjoy great prestige, but receive only a moderate salary (e.g. doctors and young researchers). There are occupations which require moderate qualifications, provide a low income and enjoy moderate prestige, for example nursing. In the first case qualification and prestige are uniformly high, whereas income is lower, towards the 'middle' of the scale. In the latter case, qualification and prestige are on a par, whereas income shows a 'lag'. The two cases demonstrate the partial decomposition of the attributes of status and both demonstrate a greater congruence between prestige and qualifications than between prestige and income. They also provide certain indices which permit us to suggest the autonomization of prestige in relation to the other attributes of status.[16]

We thus find in socialist societies two opposite tendencies in the domain of the distribution of values representing the important attributes of status (education, income, social prestige). Each tendency is linked to a different socialist principle. One tendency (congruence in the attributes of status) is linked to the principle 'to each according to his work'. The other tendency is associated with egalitarian ideals and leads to the decomposition (at least partial) of the attributes of status.

16. The nature of social prestige appears to transform itself gradually in socialist society as compared to the situation in capitalist society. It becomes subject to a greater autonomization in relation to certain attributes of objective status (income, power, etc.). We do not have space here to discuss this problem at greater length.

Part Four
Stratification in Agrarian Systems

Agrarian societies have their own characteristic modes of stratification which differ from those of industrial societies. In general, social inequalities here are more sharply defined and more readily visible. The characteristic relations are between landowners on the one hand and their tenants or labourers on the other. Agrarian societies are marked by a tendency towards 'cumulative inequalities'; the landowner enjoys a high position not only economically but also socially and politically. Dore's study examines the social position of a landowning family within the context of tenancy relations in pre-war Japan. Wolf gives an account, first, of a coffee plantation or hacienda and, then, of the main agricultural classes in Manicaboa which is a barrio or administrative division within the municipality of San José in Puerto Rico. In Dore's account we get a picture of 'traditional' agrarian relations; the set-up in San José is more dynamic and a part of a more highly commercialized system.

7 R. P. Dore

The Tenancy System in Pre-War Japan

Excerpt from R. P. Dore, *Land Reform in Japan*, Oxford University Press, 1959, pp. 23–44.

'Economic bondage which has enslaved the Japanese farmer to centuries of feudal oppression.' Such were the words used by General MacArthur, in his memorandum to the Japanese Government on 9 December 1945, to describe the system which he instructed it to reform. How, in fact, did this system work in practice? Who were the landlords? And what were their relations with their tenants?

Exact data on the types and size of landholdings before the reform are unfortunately lacking, but as a broad estimate it would appear that in mid-1947 about 18 per cent of the total tenanted land was owned by absentee landlords, another 24 per cent by non-farmers living in the same village or town as their land-holding or in a neighbouring village or small town, and the remaining 58 per cent by men who were farmers themselves. At the beginning of the war the proportion owned by absentee land-lords may have been somewhat larger.[1]

Absentee Landlords

These three main categories cover, of course, a wide variety of different types. Absentee landlords, in the sense used here (non-farming landlords not resident in or near the village in which the

1. These figures are the subject of much dispute and the present estimates can claim no final authority. They are calculated from data provided by (a) the 1941 *Denbata shoyū jōkyō chōsa*, a Ministry survey of landownership (see Nōchi Kaikaku Kiroku Iinkai, ed: *Nōchi Kaikaku Temmatsu Gaiyō*, 1951, *NKTG*, p. 782); (b) Nōrinshō, Nōchikyoku, Nōchika, *Nōchi-tō Kaihō Jisseki Chōsa*, 1956, pp. 16–17 (1950 estimates of the 1945 state of affairs provided by Land Committee secretaries); (c) the 1 August 1947 Agricultural Census (see *NKTG*, pp. 605, 786).

land is held) include two main categories. (Absentee landlord for the purpose of the land-reform legislation meant all landowners not resident in *the same* village and included, therefore, the further category of farming landlords whose holding of leased-out land extended into neighbouring villages.) In the first place there were the sons of farming families who had left their native village for jobs elsewhere but retained the family land after the death of their parents. The 20 per cent of absentee landowners resident in Tokyo and Osaka at the time of the 1941 survey[2] were probably mostly in this category. (It included, incidentally, many of the officials and professors of agricultural economics who helped in the drafting of the Land Reform Bill.) Fairly big landlords with a history of generations and a proper sense of family pride often avoided educating their eldest sons on principle, in order that the ancestors should not be betrayed by an abandonment of the status they had achieved for the family in the village. Lesser landlords and the more prosperous owner-cultivators had fewer familistic scruples about giving their sons the chance to make good in other directions. And even in a bigger landlord family it was difficult for fond parents, who had the necessary resources, to refuse the chance of higher education to an eager child, particularly given the traditional Japanese emphasis on the noble virtue of learning as such. And once the son had a university degree and had acquired town ways the chances of his returning to his ancestral duties were small. 'An educated child turns up his nose at the privy at home' as one local proverb has it. Sometimes, even if the *de jure* heir, the eldest son, left the village, a less intelligent or less ambitious younger son would stay as *de facto* heir and continue the farming family. Sometimes the family would leave the village altogether with the death of the parents. Nevertheless landlords' sons who migrated to the towns did not entirely lose their roots in the village: apart from the income value of keeping the land, it was still a family duty to keep in touch with the village where the family graves were, to make occasional visits to see that they were properly cared for and possibly to ensure that after one's death one's ashes, or a part of them, should be sent to lie with the ancestors. Land so retained was generally placed in the hands of a tenant family-retainer who

2. *NKTG*, p. 603.

cultivated some of it himself and supervised the letting out of the rest to other tenants.

The second main type of absentee landlord was the merchant or money-lender from a near-by town who had acquired land as a result of commercial or financial operations. Such, for instance, was the draper of a country town in Akita who acquired some 30 *chō*** in the Meiji period. His method was simple, according to village legend. He would send his travellers around the villages with rolls of cloth. The farmers' reluctance to buy would be countered by the bland offer to leave it with them in case they felt like using it before he came round next time – with, of course, no obligation to purchase. Very often by the time he came again they had used it and had not the ready money to pay for it. The matter was easily settled by a credit note at a very high rate of interest, and after a year or two the transaction was completed by the transfer of a *tan* of land. Fertilizer merchants and rice merchants and pawnbrokers probably predominated in this category.

Also counted among the absentee landlords were various minor categories – schoolteachers transferred from their native village to other schools, younger sons of poor farmers who had made money in some other occupation and bought land in their native village to retire to in their old age, members of the town middle class who had invested their savings in land for the income returns to be derived – including, of course, the widows and orphans who are traditionally cited by the opponents of any attack on property as its principal victims.

Village Landlords

Non-cultivating landlords resident in the village were also heterogeneous. One major category comprised the large-scale landowners whose income from rents was sufficient to allow them to 'wear white socks': the gentlemen landowners who devoted themselves to politics, to the supervision of their tenants, to financial speculation and money-lending activities, or to private hobbies. There were others, including many with much smaller holdings, who had some other primary source of income: officials

* 1 *chō* = 10 *tan* = 2·45 acres [Ed.].

of the village office and Agricultural Association, schoolteachers, technical advisers, doctors, shopkeepers, millers or priests. Some of them had acquired their land during their own lifetimes, many of them were the sons of small landlords or richer cultivators who had received a middle-school education, returned to their villages in a salaried post and eventually gave up cultivation of their family land, putting it out to tenants.

How many such landlords there were it is difficult to determine. Simply by subtracting from the number of owners of leased land shown in the 1941 land Census the number of *farm households* owning leased land, one arrives at a figure of nearly a million for the 'absentee' and 'non-cultivating resident' categories combined, but this figure is slightly inflated by the fact that an owner with land in two administrative areas appears in the statistics as two owners. With this important proviso, then, one may add that only about a quarter of this million owners had more than 3 *chō* of land.[3] A further relevant figure, perhaps, is that of the 1930 population Census, in which 46,000 people reported agricultural rents as their main source of income.[4]

Owners of tenanted land who were themselves farmers (a category responsible for more than half the total tenancy) again covered a wide range. At one end of the scale might be, say, the owner of 1 *chō* who was employed in the village office and used his Sundays and the women of his household to cultivate a third of it while tenants rented the rest, or the middling farmer who cultivated 1·5 *chō* and let out 0·2 *chō* to relatives until such time as his eldest son should be old enough to work on the farm. At the other end stood the owner of some hundred *chō* who farmed a couple of them himself to provide home-grown vegetables and rice, or from a notion that he should set an example of diligence to his tenants and not allow the womenfolk of his family to grow effete. As Table 1(a) shows, more than a fifth of the total number of farmers owned some tenanted land. The majority were cultivators of a more-than-average size of holding who supplemented their income by leasing a small amount of additional land. As is shown by Table 1(b), 80 per cent of these cultivating owners of tenanted land leased less than 1 *chō* to

3. Tōbata Seiichi, *Tochi o meguru Jinushi to Nōmin*, 1947, p. 28.
4. ibid., p. 30.

Table 1(a)

Farm Households by Area Cultivated and Area Leased to Tenants (including Hokkaido), 1947

No. of households ('000)

No. of chō cultivated	Land leased out									Total	
	No land		−0·49 chō		−0·99 chō		1·0 chō+				
	No.	%	No.	%	No.	%	No.	%	%	No.	%
−0·49	2032	(83)	299	(12)	62	(3)	59	(2)	(100)	2452	(41)
0·5–0·99	1434	(78)	260	(14)	78	(4)	62	(3)	(100)	1834	(31)
1·0–1·49	661	(71)	158	(17)	50	(5)	56	(6)	(100)	925	(16)
1·5–1·99	242	(66)	63	(17)	24	(7)	35	(10)	(100)	364	(6)
2·0–2·99	132	(63)	34	(16)	16	(8)	28	(13)	(100)	210	(4)
3·0–4·99	51	(69)	7	(9)	5	(6)	11	(15)	(100)	74	(1)
5·0+	40	(81)	2	(4)	1	(2)	6	(12)	(100)	49	(1)
Total	4592	(78)	823	(14)	237	(4)	257	(4)	(100)	5909	(100)

Source: 1 August 1947 Census (*NKTG*, p. 607).

Table 1(b)

Cultivating Owners of Tenanted Land and Area of Leased Land by Size of Leased Holding (excluding Hokkaido), 1947

	Size of leased holding (chō)								
	−0·49		0·5−0·99		1·0−4·9		5+		Total	
	No.	%	No.	%	No.	%	No.	%	No.	%
No. of owners ('000)*	813	(63·3)	230	(18·0)	212	(16·5)	28	(2·2)	1·284	(100)
Area of land leased ('000 chō)†	167	(15·7)	173	(16·2)	470	(44·0)	256	(24·0)	1·067	(100)

* According to 1 August 1947 Census (*NKTG*, p. 604).
† Estimates of Namiki Masayoshi, 'Nōchi Kaikaku ni yoru Kaihō Nōchi Menseki ni tsuite', *Nōgyō Sōgō Kenkyū*, vol. **2**, no. 3, pp. 62–3.

tenants, less, that is, than the size of one average farm. A good many were both landlords and tenants. The Japanese village settlement is a concentrated cluster of dwellings with the surrounding land divided into plots of an average size of only about 0·06 *chō*.[5] After centuries of land exchange, sale and purchase, the holdings of an individual farmer are often scattered widely over a large area. Hence, frequently, for sheer convenience of cultivation farmers let out some of their own more distant plots and themselves cultivated as tenants more conveniently situated plots of other farmers.

Many of these farming owners of tenanted land, then, could hardly be called 'landlords' in the proper sense of the term, and indeed many of them with only small plots of leased land were left unaffected by the land reform. The term 'peasant-landlord' has been suggested for their counterparts in Southern China,[6] but sharp lines of division are difficult to draw and throughout this chapter the term 'landlord' (or 'landowner') will be used as a simple translation of the Japanese word *jinushi*, i.e. anyone who leases any amount of agricultural land to tenant cultivators.

The smaller of these cultivating landlords were economically and culturally little differentiated from their fellow-villagers, and how much land one had to have to exercise a dominating influence on one's village depended on the district and the general size of holdings in it. But probably not many with less than 5 *chō* held a social position of the sort suggested by the word 'landlord' in English. In terms of income, a holding of about 6½ *chō* of land of average quality would, in 1936, have been necessary to secure the same income from rents as the salary of an urban civil servant or teacher.[7] As Table 1(b) shows, only 2 per cent (some 28,000) of the total number of cultivating landlords had more than 5 *chō*, though, according to the estimates of that table, the proportion of the total tenanted area (in the hands of *cultivating*

5. For rice land only in 1920 (Sakurai Takeo, *Nihon Nōhon-shugi*, 1935, p. 181).

6. H. S. Chen, *Landlord and Peasant in China*, Oxford, 1936.

7. Assuming an average 1·03 *koku* rent per *tan* (Kangyō Ginkō survey, Ogura Buichi, *Tochi Rippō no Shiteki Kōsatsu*, 1951, p. 623) and a 30 yen per *koku* price (Jiji Shimpōsha, *Jiji Nenkan 1937*, p. 234). The average civil servant and the average teacher were estimated by government surveys to have monthly wages of 155 and 156 yen respectively (ibid. p. 417).

landlords) which they owned was about 24 per cent. About a quarter of a million farmers owned 68 per cent of the total of these village-landlord holdings, in more than 1 *chō* lots, bigger, that is, than the size of an average farm unit.

The vast majority of the really large landowners – the nearly 3000 who owned more than 50 *chō*, including the 4 giants with over 1000 – were, whether themselves farming or not, resident in the same prefecture as their landholding. (More than a third of these 3000 were, however, Hokkaido landlords; and in Hokkaido, where the whole scale of agriculture is bigger ... the ownership of 50 *chō* is less impressive than in the rest of Japan.) A survey of the occupations of landlords in 1924 covered 3000 holdings of more than 50 *chō*; 96 per cent of them were in the names of private individuals, and only 4 per cent were held by limited companies and other bodies such as temples or shrines. Of these private owners 94 per cent were then living inside the prefecture in which they held land, and a third had some occupation other than agriculture – 14 per cent were merchants, 5 per cent brewers of *sake* or *shōyū*, 5 per cent money-lenders and 5 per cent officials, businessmen, doctors, lawyers, etc. The remaining two-thirds were made up of 29 per cent who were themselves culti-vating more than a third of a *chō* of land, while the other 36 per cent found being a landlord a full-time occupation.[8]

Within certain limits tenancy was fairly widely distributed throughout the country. The proportion of tenanted land, for instance – 46 per cent for the whole country in 1941 – varied as between prefectures only within the limits of 33 per cent (Naga-saki) and 59 per cent (Kagawa);[9] though generally speaking there was a greater concentration of tenancy in the north, and it was here (the Tōhoku and Hokuriku districts) that the larger holdings were to be found, and here too that the more 'familistic', 'pater-nalistic' or 'feudalistic' landlords were concentrated.

8. Nōshōmushō, Nōmukyoku, *Go-jitchōbu ijō no kōchi o shoyū suru dai-jinushi ni kansuru chōsa*, 1925, quoted *NKTG*, p. 807. The original data from which this compilation was made are to be found in Nōgyō Hattatsu-shi Chōsakai (ed.), *Nihon Nōgyō Hattatsu-shi*, vol. 7 (1955), pp. 715–74.

9. *NKTG*, p. 653

The Paternalistic Landlord

What tenancy meant in practice in these areas can best be illustrated by an account of the growth and activities of one of these latter paternalistic landlord families in the Yamagata village,[10] situated in the broad coastal rice plain of Shōnai.

The village was one in which the average holding cultivated per family was large – over 2 *chō*, or more than twice the average for Japan and half as much again as the average for the prefecture. This was a result, in part, of the fact that the feudal ruler of this district in Tokugawa times and later the landlords did their best to prevent any division of holdings by forbidding the establishment of cadet-branch families. But although holdings were relatively large, ownership was highly concentrated; 39 per cent of the farmers in the village were wholly, and another 50 per cent were partly tenants, while a mere 7 per cent of the number of families owned 62 per cent of the land.[11] Of these, far and away the biggest owner was the Otaki family which at the time of the land reform held some 180 *chō* of land (150 *chō* of it rice land) distributed among 170 tenants. Not all the tenants were exclusively theirs. The majority also rented land from some other landlord as well. But of the forty-five houses in the hamlet[12] where Otaki himself lived, forty cultivated some of his land.

The Otakis were already large landowners by the time of the Meiji Restoration. Then they had about 100 *chō*, mostly acquired at the end of the Tokugawa period by money-lending and the cumulative process by which the small man, who can just not withstand a crop failure, is swallowed up by the bigger man, who

10. See Preface (to Dore's book), p. 11. Tōgō-mura before the war is described (though with an astonishing coyness about tenancy conditions) in Nishigori Hideo (ed.), *Shōnai Tadokoro no Nōgyō, Nōson oyobi Seikatsu*, 1936.

11. Sekisetsu Chihō Nōson Keizai Chōsa-sho, *Shōnai Chihō Beisaku Nōson Chōsa*, 1937, p. 43.

12. Here and henceforth 'hamlet' is used as a translation of *buraku*, the concentrated settlement which was often a separate administrative unit in the Tokugawa period and still is the most important social unit. 'Village' will be kept as a translation of the modern administrative unit, the *mura*, which covered in most cases from ten to twenty such 'hamlets' until the recent amalgamations, which have made them considerably larger.

can more than just survive. In their case their success apparently owed nothing to the possession of a privileged official position. The headmanship of the village belonged hereditarily to another related family which, however, had fallen on hard times, and it is possible that the headman's power was in fact exercised by the head of the Otaki family, and that the opportunities for profit in the position of intermediary between the tax-paying peasant and the tax-demanding officials were a partial explanation of their growing wealth.

Their accumulation of land proceeded rapidly in the Meiji period. The head of the family at the time, a man of no more than a 'temple-school', three Rs education, had a keen head for business and let no opportunities slip. An old family retainer has memories of this 'master before the master before last' trudging five miles through the snow to the neighbouring town to borrow money from a banker relative, the object being to 'help out' a peasant who had come with the tearful request that Otaki should rescue him from financial difficulties by buying a piece of his land. They grew rich, but they did not let it go to their heads. Unlike the landlords of neighbouring districts, they did not ape town manners. The master, said the retainer, 'did not keep a mistress. He did not buy a bowler hat. Nor did he grow a moustache.' He did not build a lavishly expensive garden. He grew dwarf trees as a hobby, but he tended them himself. He wore 'long clothes' – the mark of a leisured gentleman – only for weddings and funerals. He did not fritter away his money by playing politics. The family mixed barley with its rice to set an example of frugality to its tenants. The 'master-before-last' spent a short time at a university in Tokyo studying agriculture, but otherwise none of the family received more than a middle-school education, and until about a generation ago sons were sent for a period to complete their education as living-in workers in the house of another landlord or prosperous farmer – a practice common, too, among old commercial families in Japan. (The theory is that parents are inevitably too lenient to their own children and a period of 'eating someone else's rice' is a necessary means of character training. As the proverb has it: 'If you love your child send him on a journey.') Spare savings were invested in safe securities and in forest land. The only incursion into commercial ventures was the financing of a silk-reeling factory within the village, which was combined with efforts to encourage the tenants to develop sericulture as a subsidiary source of income. The factory went bankrupt in the silk depression after the First World War, and this taught the family the desirability of sticking to its last. Division of its landed property was scrupulously avoided. The only younger son produced in three generations was set up as a fertilizer merchant in a near-by town.

They were, then, not only in, but of, the village. They accepted peasant values and found the source of their pride not in dissociating themselves from the peasant class, but in exhibiting the peasant values in their heightened and ideal form; they eschewed risks and extravagances and devoted themselves to keeping intact, and if possible increasing, the property of the ancestors.

They had the reputation of being tolerably 'good landlords'. At a time when the moustachioed, bowler-hatted, mistress-keeping landlords of neighbouring districts were suffering from the assaults of peasant unions, hardly a breath of revolt stirred among their tenants. Unlike many landlords of the paternalistic type, however, the Otakis left nothing to chance. From 1893 onwards tenancy contracts, which had hitherto been verbal, were put in writing. A contract of the time reads as follows:

To Otaki Saburoemon:
[Description and Designation of the land . . . rent . . . surcharge. . . .]

I hereby certify that, from this year and for such time as the relationship between us shall last, I have undertaken tenancy of the above land. I undertake to deliver, by 31 December each year, at such place as you shall direct, the above rent and surcharge[13] in selected rice,[14] carefully and conscientiously baled.

13. The surcharge (*kuchimai*) dates from the Tokugawa period and is found generally throughout the country. Bales which were transported to the central markets inevitably suffered some wastage from theft and leakages. In order that they should contain the standard amount of rice when they arrived, they had to start with a little more than the standard. It was one of the facts offered as evidence of the Otakis' benevolence that they demanded a surcharge of only 2 per cent compared with the 4 per cent of many local landlords.

14. At this time, at the height of the landlords' power and when the landlords were responsible for about half the rice sold to the markets, new and strict quality standards for rice delivered in rents were being imposed throughout the country, in some cases at the expense of tenant riots.

159

I beg that in years of bad harvest through natural causes you will, on inspection of the crop, make such reduction in rent as seems to you fit. In the case, however, of a fall in yields resulting from my own bad management and affecting myself alone, I undertake to ask for no reduction in rent. I shall, of course, make no attempt to sell the right of tenancy, nor be indolent in cultivation of the land, nor engage in any other unjust conduct. In the event that I should break contract, irrespective of whether I am resident in the village or not, the guarantor will pay full compensation. In such circumstance, or, indeed, at any other time, I undertake to raise no single word of complaint should you, as your convenience makes necessary, decide to terminate my tenancy. In sign whereof and for future reference.

Tenant................................

Guarantor ....

These, with some alterations of form, but not of substance, were the terms of the contract binding the Otaki tenants at the time of the land reform. The landlord had, if he chose to exercise it, complete power, if not of life and death, at least of livelihood or no livelihood over his tenants. But there were certain social pressures, certain standards of fair conduct which limited his ability to exercise this power too arbitrarily. And, moreover, he had no economic motive for doing so. As long as the rents were being paid he was satisfied. When the tenant defaulted, the debt was marked against him and compounded at 10 per cent per annum. If he was an incompetent farmer or was hampered by illness or lack of family labour, his debts mounted. After a few years there was no difficulty at all in finding an energetic and efficient tenant who was willing to take over the land and a part at least of the debt burden attached to it. In form this was a voluntary private arrangement between the parties concerned; but the landlord's manager or the tenant in chief acted as go-between.

These tenancy contracts, though in form contracts between individuals, were in fact arrangements between families. Most villages showed a great stability in terms of the family units composing them, and on the death of the house-head the eldest son who succeeded him took over, as a matter of course, the tenancy arrangements of his father. In this village, in fact, it was common for an eldest son to take over his father's given name when he succeeded him. Thus, the head of the Otaki family was always called Saburoemon.

The landlord was an exalted being – the respect language of the original tenancy contract, the flavour of which cannot easily be rendered in translation, strengthens the impression of respectful humility on the part of the tenant and lofty superiority on that of the landlord. He did not deal with his tenants directly, but through a three-tiered chain of control. First, there was his manager (*bantō*). The man who acted as such since the end of the last century was of very humble origin. He had entered the Otaki household as a living-in labourer hired for a few bales of rice a year, and had shown the intelligence and forcefulness of character which made him eminently suited for the job. He was the devoted family retainer, wholly identified with his master's interests, considered and treated as part of the family, though of definitely inferior status – he always ate his meals in the kitchen, and still does, though since the death of the former house-head and during the minority of his son he is the effective master of the household. He was a power feared, if not respected, in the village. He himself told the story of how, in his youth, his marriage go-between had taken him aside to offer him a friendly word of advice. He ought to know, said the go-between, that he was being much criticized in the village. People said he was getting above himself. 'People are quite right,' he had replied, 'I am above myself. As Horii Tomegoro I am a plain and humble man. But as manager and representative of Otaki Suburoemon, owner of 4000 bales' worth of land, I behave as such and with appropriate dignity. I have to be arrogant.'

Secondly, in all hamlets in which the Otakis held land, except that in which they themselves lived (where the manager exercised direct control), sub-managers (*shihainin*) were appointed to look after their interests. These were generally men who owned the greater part of the land they cultivated and were consequently of a slightly superior economic status to most of the tenants.

Below them were the tenants in chief (*kosaku-gashira*). These were appointed in each hamlet in which Otaki tenants were living and through them all requests and complaints by the tenants had to be channelled. They were appointed from among the most prosperous and the most loyal of the tenants. They were, in so far

161

as conflicts of interest were grudgingly admitted to exist in the situation, 'on the tenants' side'. But the whole tendency was to blur and conceal the existence of such conflicts of interest in a veil of loyalty and paternalistic devotion, and the ambiguities of their position were sufficient for some of them to derive minor profit from it – just as the village headmen of the Tokugawa period profited from their ambiguous position between the feudal authorities and the peasants. It was no accident that the three tenants in chief in Otaki's own hamlet all acquired some additional land of their own during the ten years before the land reform.

The most important function of this chain of command was the negotiation of rent reductions. Rents were, as the contract shows, fixed in terms of rice. (They were commonly referred to as *nengu*, the word used in the Tokugawa period for dues paid to the feudal lord – an incidental indication that the Meiji Restoration did not greatly change the social structure of the countryside.) The fixed rates amounted to about half of an average crop; but it was regular practice to fix them at a higher rate than the landlord actually expected to get in order that he could exhibit his benevolence annually by granting reductions. According to the manager, the amount collected was generally about 10 per cent below the level of fixed rents. The reduction would be assessed for their respective hamlets by the manager and the sub-managers after inspection of the crops, and communicated to the tenants in chief. Tenants who thought their reduction insufficient could appeal through the tenants in chief and the original assessment would be reconsidered – though rarely substantially reduced. The reductions granted by Otaki in the hamlets in which his land predominated set the standard for the reductions granted by other landlords with land in the same hamlet, and he similarly accepted the lead of other landlords in hamlets where his land represented a smaller proportion. As a survey of tenancy practices in 1927 remarks, the regular granting of rent reductions was so widespread that although tenancy agreements generally specified a fixed rental in kind, in substance they nevertheless amounted to a modified form of share-cropping with fixed ceilings. In some districts, indeed, in years of particularly bad harvests, the equal division of the crop between landlord and tenant was the regular means of making reductions.

The tenant had the responsibility for maintaining the land and irrigation ditches in good repair, but there were no regular provisions for compensating him for improvements should the land be taken from him. New irrigation works or large-scale repairs would be financed by the landlord, the labour being provided by the tenants. As the contract indicates, tenants had to bear the cost of threshing and hulling the rent rice and of transporting it to the landlord's granary or to a commercial warehouse. (This often meant several four- or five-mile journeys by hand-drawn or oxen-drawn sled.) Tenants also provided their own seed, fertilizer and implements. To this extent they were formally independent entrepreneurs. On the other hand, they had to ask the landlord's permission to grow anything other than the accustomed crop on the land, and the landlord was severe in his strictures on what he considered to be inefficient cultivation.

The Otakis were not, however, 'progressive landlords'. . . . Apart from keeping a few model fields and their encouragement of silkworm rearing at the time of their abortive silk-reeling-factory experiment, they took few positive measures to educate their tenants into higher productivity. They played safe; devoting their energies to preventing any reduction in their income, rather than either to increasing it or to improving the lot of their tenants. Their interference was mostly negative. Thus, for instance, tenants were threatened with dispossession if they used too much fertilizer. If luck held, more fertilizer meant a better crop. But it also meant rice plants more sensitive to damage from winds and early frosts, and hence the possibility of a worse-than-ever crop failure. Custom prevented the increase of rent in good years, but it demanded a reduction in bad ones proportionate to the extent of the damage. They therefore preferred a none too heavily fertilized, safe mediocrity of yields and scolded the tenants for their reckless cupidity. Likewise they would have nothing to do with schemes for extensive re-drainage and re-irrigation. In the first place the expense would be great (though from 1899 onwards some government assistance was available). Secondly, the exact resurveying necessary would reveal the fact that (the surveyors at the time of the compilation of the early Meiji registers having been thoroughly wined and dined by the landowners) plots of land were sometimes as much as 20–30 per cent larger than their registered area. This, as well as involving them in extra taxes, would arouse alarm among the tenants in whom centuries of exploitation had bred the belief that all change engineered from above must necessarily be for their disadvantage. And in this case they would have good grounds for alarm, since generally they paid rents assessed on the *registered* area of their land and it was notorious that where such schemes had been carried through the same rents were demanded from a smaller plot exactly its nominal area. Productivity would undoubtedly be increased by such a scheme, and possibly at a profit to the landlord. But the Otakis preferred to avoid trouble, and indeed the fact that the disputes and riots which they escaped were common in near-by districts, where landlords had carried out such land-replanning schemes, is perhaps a proof of their wisdom.

It was on their careful avoidance of anything that might arouse the resentment of all the tenants at once, and on their granting of reasonable rent reduction, that the Otakis' reputation for being tolerably good landlords rested. Benevolence was also displayed in other ways. There were, after all, plenty of opportunities for a display of such benevolence. The gap in living standards between the landlord and the tenants was naturally very great. For all that the landlord, too, mixed barley with his rice, he always had rice to mix it with, and plenty of fish made his diet rather different from that of the tenants who subsisted mainly on rice, millets, sweet potatoes, vegetables and bean-pastes in various forms. Tenants could rarely afford bicycles or radios before the war, and few took a newspaper (only 5 per cent in this village according to a survey in 1932). The landlord's house, with the majestic sweep of its closely thatched roof, its three entrances and its large reception rooms covered with close-woven *tatami* mats and capable of seating fifty people for a wedding feast, contrasted with the tiny two- or three-roomed houses of the tenants, often with only wooden floors and coarse rush mats reserved for visitors to sit on. The grounds of the landlord's house contained four large store-houses and granaries; only a few of the better-off tenants had even one. And there were many factors in the situation of the tenant living at about subsistence level which helped to prevent him from rising above it. Insufficient nutrition and illness dulled his working efficiency. He often had not enough money to pay for fertilizers. He therefore had to borrow money at high (15–25 per cent) interest from the landlord or from the fertilizer merchant, and the harvest, when it came, left him little better off than before by the time he had paid not only his rent but his fertilizer debts as well.

The pressing need for ready cash generally forced him to sell off his marketable surplus of rice immediately after the harvest when the price was lowest. A survey in this district in 1937 showed that tenants disposed of 62 per cent of the total amount of rice they marketed before the end of January, whereas landlords, who could afford to hold off for better prices, had sold only 32 per cent by that time.[15] A government survey for the whole country for the years 1925–9 showed similar results.[16] Sometimes tenants were forced to sell after the harvest not only their marketable surplus but also rice needed for home consumption as well, either in the vague hope that something would turn up before the next summer, or in order to benefit from a possible small price differential between the rice they sold and the foreign rice they later had to buy. A survey in 1930–31 of a widely distributed sample of nearly 500 farm households found that 32 per cent had during the year to buy some rice, and 15 per cent to buy more than six months' supply.[17]

The tenant in such a situation was often dependent on the favours of the landlord for survival. The Otakis sometimes made loans of money or of rice at rates of interest somewhat lower than the normal market rates. Regularly at the midsummer Bon festival they made a gift of two *to* of rice (enough to last a family of five for about ten days) to twenty of the most indigent tenant families who had by then run through their yearly stock. The annual completion of rice payments was celebrated by a feast at which enough rice-wine was provided for each of the tenants to drink himself into a pleasant stupor. They lent tenants the crockery and utensils for weddings and funerals. They provided the equipment and a part of the expenses for the hamlet festival, though the master himself took part only perfunctorily and

15. Sekisetsu . . . Chōsasho, *Shonai Nōson Chōsa*, pp. 27–8.

16. Seiichi Tobata, 'Japanese rice control', in W. L. Holland (ed.), *Commodity Control in the Pacific Area*, Stanford, 1935, p. 163.

17. ibid., p. 164.

ceremonially, leaving the villagers to merrymaking unrestrained by his presence.

The landlord was referred to by the tenants as *oyakata* ('father', 'the old man'), but the paternalism which this acknowledged was paternalism within the context of traditional Japanese family institutions, with the accent on authority rather than affection. Status distinctions were maintained with a rigidity all the more surprising when one recalls that the master and his tenants had for six years of their young lives sat side by side in the same primary school. Tenants used respect language when addressing the landlords and removed any covering on their heads; the landlord when calling them by name omitted the normally polite *san* suffix used between equals. The landlord's house had three entrances; one used only by the master and distinguished guests; the middle one used by less distinguished guests – village officials, the technician of the Agricultural Association, etc.; and the lower one used by women of the household, servants and tenants. A tenant in chief who had business with the master would go no further than the wooden-floored corridor adjoining his room, make a low bow which the landlord answered with a slight nod and remain in the formal kneeling position throughout the interview which the landlord conducted at a distance from his seat by the brazier in the centre of the room. ('X was mayor for a short time a couple of years ago,' said the local extension officer recently. 'Poor bumbling old X, mayor! And not more than ten years ago I have seen him kowtowing in Otaki's corridor and hissing respect like a steam engine!')

The distinction between tenants and servants was not, indeed, altogether a clear one. When there were festivities at the landlord's house – a wedding or a funeral – women from the tenant families in Otaki's own hamlet would act as additional servants – for no agreed wage, though a gift of food might be made later. Likewise, the men would act as labourers when the Otaki house was to be rethatched, and they might be expected, every once in a while, to put in a day's work on the smallish holding which Otaki himself cultivated.

Within certain limits the landlord exercised a paternal authority over the private lives of his tenants. If one was in trouble with the police, he would secure his release and undertake to administer a severe scolding himself. Tenants in chief, or the tenants in his own hamlet most completely dependent on him, would consult him as to the suitability of the match when they contemplated marrying one of their children. He might use his influence to place a younger son or a daughter in some job in the local town. One occasion on which he had, of necessity, to be consulted was when a farmer proposed to establish a 'branch family', for if a younger son were to be set up in a separate household in the village, either the main stem-family's land would have to be divided or he would have to be granted tenancy on other land. The Otakis almost always refused permission for such arrangements. One family with 2 *chō* of tenanted land was much less likely to get into difficulties and default on its rent payments than two families with 1 *chō* each. On one occasion when the establishment of a branch family was permitted in special circumstances (the tenant acted as local sub-manager for a landlord relative of the Otakis) the master decided how much land should be apportioned to the main and how much to the branch family.

None of the Otakis held any official position in the village, though they could have had the mayoralty at any time for the asking. To men of their wealth, however, it was a despised, rather than a coveted, honour. As the source of more than half the village taxes, their consent was, in any case, obtained before any substantial item of expenditure was decided. In national politics – and particularly after 1925 when universal suffrage gave the tenants the vote – they were wooed by local candidates of all the major parties. The last of the line, in the days before the war, gave his support to the Seiyukai candidate and instructed his tenants accordingly. The predominant group among the smaller landlords who made up the village council had Minseito connexions. Nevertheless, the mayor was a Seiyukai man, out of deference to Otaki and in order to secure co-ordination of the two major channels of influence on the higher levels of administration – that which the mayor could exercise by virtue of his office, and that guaranteed by Otaki's wealth and vote-getting potential. This was necessary for the efficient extraction of central-government grants-in-aid and subsidies.

Variations in Tenancy Practices

The Otaki family described above was typical of the traditionally oriented, paternalistic landowner, though, living in a district where small, medium and large landowners held interlocking estates, Otaki did not exercise such a monopolistic control over his tenants as some landlords, nor was his paternalism reinforced by extended kinship ties as it was in some villages where the landlord was also the head of the main family of which his tenants were subordinate branches. At the same time the scale of his holding was sufficiently large for something to be lost in the personal relationship between the landlord and the tenant. The contractual impersonality of the written tenancy agreement is an indication of this and something of a rarity. A survey of 1921 found that only 30 per cent of tenancy agreements were formalized in writing,[18] and, although that proportion was increased by the tenancy disputes of the years that followed, it was still not much above 30 per cent in a renewed survey of 1936.[19]

Nevertheless, many features of the Otakis' relations with their tenants were almost universal. Nearly all tenants were tenants at will, though in some districts traditional rights of permanent tenancy were customarily recognized and after 1896 given some measure of legal recognition. In these cases the tenant could sell the right of tenancy, and demand compensation if the landlord wished to dispossess him. Also, in some cases, the tenant was given a certain security by the specification of the term of contract – but almost never for more than five years, in the case of rice land, ten years in the case of mulberry fields and twenty years in the case of orchards and tea gardens.[20] At the same time custom and the pressure of village opinion often operated to protect the tenant from arbitrary dispossession; and sub-tenancy, or the private transfer of land between tenants often amounting in practice to the sale of tenancy rights, were often winked at.

Tenancy contracts were almost always for specific individual plots of land, though in one district of Shimane Prefecture there

18. *NKTG*, p. 43.
19. Ogura, *Tochi Rippō*, p. 619.
20. *NKTG*, p. 39.

was a particular form of tenancy – *kabu-kosaku* or 'whole-lot tenancy' – whereby the tenant leased a complete farm unit, including the dwelling house in which even the paper of the partition walls bore the landlord's crest.[21] In certain northern districts where forms of medieval serfdom continued into the modern era and the 'family-servant' character of the tenant was most marked, the landlord provided seed, tools and fertilizer which the tenants requited by labour service on the landlords' land at times most convenient to the landlord, which were, necessarily, often the times most inconvenient to themselves.

Rents for rice land were almost always in kind until the war years, and in the rare cases where money was paid instead – chiefly where the landlord was an absentee – it was usually in the form of a money commutation of a rice rent: that is to say it was the calculated value of a fixed amount of rice at current market prices. In a survey of 1943, fixed money payments for rice land were found in less than 1 per cent of cases. Money commutation of a fixed rent in rice was paid in some 12 per cent of cases: some increase, largely due to war-time legislation, over the pre-war 4 per cent. Elsewhere the rent was paid in kind.[22]

Produce rents were almost always in terms of fixed amounts, though in a small number of cases (less than 1 per cent, according to the 1943 survey) share-cropping was also found, the usual proportions being 50:50. It was common in such cases for the sheaves or the threshed grain to be divided into two heaps, the landlord having the right to decide which would be his.

For upland fields money rents were more common and were becoming increasingly so. In 1943, for ordinary upland fields, 57 per cent of rents were in fixed money terms and only 30 per cent actually paid in produce, either in rice (even if it was not grown on the field) or in wheat or beans.[23] In some districts – such as Yamanashi – rents for upland fields were paid in labour – at so many man-days per *tan*.

Rent rates generally amounted to something over half of an average crop and year-by-year reductions were common. Although

21. Nosei Chōsakai: *Shimane-ken ni okeru Kabu-kosaku-seido to Tanabe-ke (Tatara) no Kōsei narabi ni Nōchi Kaikaku no Eikyō*, 1952.

22. *NKTG*, p. 487.

23. ibid.

there was no great difference, the rent exactions of absentee landlords tended, if anything, to be slightly less than those of resident landlords. (And the tenants tended to be on bigger holdings and more secure in their tenure – the absentee landlord had a greater need for stability on his holding and less opportunity to press every advantage for profit.)

From at least 1920 onwards there was a slight tendency for rates to decline, both absolutely and, even more, relatively to production. Two surveys of 1921 and 1936 support the findings of the Industrial Bank's annual survey in showing reductions in rents *actually paid* of 5 per cent in the case of single-cropped and 7 per cent in the case of double-cropped land between these two years. Since productivity was also growing, the relative value of the rent decreased even further – *actual* rents represented 51 per cent of the crop for single-cropped and 55 per cent of the crop for double-cropped land in 1921, and 46 and 50 per cent respectively in 1936. The absolute decrease was due partly to a reduction in rent *rates* (contracted rates were found to have declined by 3–4 per cent), and partly to an increase in year-by-year reductions – both, primarily, the result of the activities of tenant unions at this time.[24] An indication of the size of these year-by-year reductions may be given by the findings of these same surveys. In 1921 average rents actually paid amounted to 94 per cent of the specified rent for single-cropped and 95 per cent for double-cropped land, while in 1936 the proportions were 91 and 92 per cent respectively.[25] The degree of bad harvest necessary to provoke a reduction varied, but surveys noted that in the more paternalistic north even a small reduction in crop of only 10–15 per cent would be recognized as requiring a reduction in rent, while in the more impersonally contractual districts around Tokyo the landlord would be reluctant to recognize even a fall of 50 per cent as any of his business.[26] In most cases the reduction was decided by simple inspection; in some cases by precise measurement of sample plots. The officials of the Homma family – the biggest landowners in Japan – had a method which showed their awareness of the value of a display of generosity. A lathe

24. Ogura, *Tochi Rippō*, p. 621, and *NKTG*, p. 40.
25. *NKTG*, p. 43.
26. ibid.

frame of a fixed size was dropped haphazardly on the field to measure the amount to be cut for the sample. Inevitably some clumps were partly inside and partly outside the frame. (Rice is planted not evenly over the whole field but in rows of small clumps.) Before cutting, the manager first went round the edges ostentatiously pushing *outside* the frame those clumps which were caught partly within it.

8 E. R. Wolf

The Hacienda System and Agricultural Classes in San José, Puerto Rico

Excerpt from E. R. Wolf, 'San José, subcultures of a "traditional" coffee municipality', in J. H. Steward *et al.* (eds.), *The People of Puerto Rico*, University of Illinois Press, 1956, pp. 190–95, 200–203.

The Rise of the Hacienda System

The development of cash crop production

During the first part of the nineteenth century we begin to witness the initial changes . . . away from the production of crops for the satisfaction of immediate consumption needs to the production of one major crop for the world market in exchange for money or its equivalents. The shift was gradual. It did not affect many small farmers until a much later period. During the second decade of the century, however, a Spanish nobleman received a land grant in San José. He planted some cane and some rice on his holding. But at the same time he began to plant large areas in nothing but coffee. In 1832, an outside observer, Pedro Tomás de Córdoba, could discern the coming trend and advise the people of San José to increase their production of coffee with an eye to the future.[1] 'Coffee is the only crop of any use to them,' he said, 'due to the high costs of transportation.' By 1836, San José exported 220 cwt of coffee and 150 cwt of tobacco. During the same year the influx of commodities into the municipality was still negligible, and money extremely scarce. Fourteen years later, however, the importance of coffee was clearly established. In 1850 a Spaniard, highly placed in the government of the island, decided to invest capital in the establishment of a coffee credit and marketing firm in San José. Twenty-five years later coffee began to boom. With the boom came an acceleration of the changes initiated fifty years earlier. San José offered much unused land for the extension of coffee plantings. In this it contrasted with other parts of the

1. Pedro Tomás de Córdoba, *Memorias geográficas, históricas, económicas y estadisticas de la Isla de Puerto Rico*, San Juan, 1931–3, vol. 2, pp. 123–6.

highland area, which had been more densely settled in the past and where the introduction of coffee had to be superimposed on a more tenacious earlier pattern. San José, with its few subsistence farms, must have seemed like a frontier area to the men interested in increasing the production of coffee. To this day, this difference in earlier settlement is reflected in the larger average size of farms in the San José area when compared to most other parts of the western highlands.

Availability of land was not enough, however. Additional conditions had to be established if coffee production was to grow. First, the acreage planted to coffee had to increase. Second, workers had to be found to work the larger plantations. Third, credit had to be pumped into the system to finance the extension of coffee acreage, to pay the workers and to finance the growers during the unproductive period of their investment as well as during the hiatus between harvest and harvest.

The preceding culture pattern was oriented mainly to the immediate satisfaction of a restricted number of cultural wants. Coffee production, on the other hand, implied the postponement of consumption both during the period in which the shrubs were reaching maturity and then from harvest to harvest. Land was plentiful. Workers would be difficult to find where land could be easily acquired and some degree of self-sufficiency was assured. As long as fields could be cleared and squatters' rights were recognized, no worker would voluntarily exchange the independent role of a self-sufficient producer for that of a dependent laborer. Finally, the preceding pattern functioned without capital. The change toward postponement of consumption, toward formation of a labor pool and toward the introduction of capital had to come from outside. This involved the application of economic and political force where the older pattern would not give way voluntarily. It involved manipulation of the indigenous pattern to meet the new demands.

The innovators needed about $20,000 to start a coffee estate of 100 *cuerdas*.* Dinwiddie[2] computed the cost of such a *finca* as $23,500. He counted $40 for each *cuerda* of land; $2500 for

* A *cuerda* is 0·97 of an acre [Ed.].

2. William Dinwiddie, 'Our new possessions – Puerto Rico: sugar culture', *Harper's Weekly*, vol. 43 (1899), no. 2, p. 200.

buildings, including quarters for the planter; $300 for clearing and planting; $2000 for weeding; $1500 for 'incidental expenses'; and $8000 for processing machinery.

Land could be obtained in a number of ways. It could be obtained in a land grant. It could be bought. It could be acquired through a challenge of squatters' rights. It could be acquired by force. And it could be received in the course of credit transactions.

As early as 1821, the government of the island began the distribution of virgin land to poor citizens of the municipality, so they could 'make them produce, and contribute to the upkeep of the Treasury and the municipality'.[3] This available territory could also be granted as a reward to favored and loyal supporters of the government's policies as well as in efforts to bolster governmental resources. In 1873 almost 5000 *cuerdas* of land were distributed in San José, and another 1000 in 1880. A sample contract shows that the ultimate rights of tenure were retained by the state. If within one year one-tenth of the land granted was not under cultivation, the property reverted to the Crown. Within ten years half the land had to be under crops. In return for such grants the recipients were sometimes required to pay nominal fees. In one such transaction the recipient paid $50 for 250 *cuerdas*, or one dollar for each five *cuerdas* of land. Inspection was lax, and very often the standards of the contract were not met. Since land was still plentiful and population scarce, squatters were often welcomed on such property since they increased its value and expanded the area under cultivation. Often unused and low in value, land passed frequently from hand to hand, until the holders of the title or the settlers on the property bore no relationship to the original recipient of the grant.

Buying land outright was thus a second way in which land could be acquired. The man who bought the same 250 *cuerdas* mentioned above from the original recipient of the grant paid $625, or $2.50 per *cuerda*. His grandson sold the property again in 1876 for $2000, or $8.00 per *cuerda*. In 1948 some of this land was valued at $200 or $300 per *cuerda*. Some land close to the town valued in 1948 at $800 to $1000 per *cuerda*, sold in 1870 for $50 a *cuerda*. Another property, valued in 1948 at $300 to $400

3. San José, Municipal Archives, *Junta de Repartimiento de Terrenos Baldíos*, 1873, pp. 7–9.

per *cuerda*, sold in the 1880s at $1.00 for every two *cuerdas*. Land was thus fairly cheap, and any man with a little capital could acquire safe title through purchase.

A third way of getting land into one's possession was to challenge squatters' rights. These rights were invariably customary rights, and no written documents attested to their origin. A man who knew how to manipulate the legal system and knew how to read and write could easily receive a title to land which someone else had cleared and cultivated.

A fourth way to obtain land was through force. This usually took the form of collusion with the police authorities of the island, the dreaded *guardia civil*. This procedure is illustrated in the words of an eighty-five-year-old man who witnessed some of the consequent evictions:

A Mallorcan would come to the barracks of the Civil Guard. He would go to the chief of the Guard who was also a Spaniard, and he would ask him for two guards. He would say: 'Look, they are robbing my taro and taniers, they are cutting down my coffee shrubs, they are slashing the ankle joints of my cattle.' These stories were all lies, because they were untrue. But he would leave with the two policemen. The people would come to get their purchases at the hacienda store, for in those times people bought most of their things at the hacienda stores. And the Mallorcan would say: 'Look, this man with the blue shirt, he is the one who is bothering me.' The two guards would then walk up to the man and ask: 'Do you own property?' The man would reply: 'I own some twenty *cuerdas*. They yield enough coffee for the needs of my own family. I raise a few little plants to feed my family. I live in peace, although I must work hard and they pay me little. But here I live in peace, the owner of my own house.' Then the guards would say: 'If you want to continue to live in peace, you must sell your farm, or we shall clap you in jail.' So the poor man had to sell his land to the rich owner at one-fourth of its value.

A fifth way to obtain land was through the extension of credit, with land offered as a security in the transaction. This was without doubt the most important mechanism of acquiring the land needed in coffee production:

The coffee industry of Puerto Rico was built upon a credit system which was well-known in Louisiana as the system of 'advances'. The farmer would arrange with a city merchant [a coffee exporter] to furnish the necessary credit to make his crop. This credit was secured by means of a mortgage on the plantation at a very high rate of interest. Furthermore, this credit was not given in cash, but most of it in supplies. This meant a second profit on the same investment. The farmer would open a 'despacho de peones' [hacienda store] ... in his plantation, and pay the wages to his laborers in orders at his store. When the crop was harvested it had to be taken to the creditor merchant who would set a price on it ... thereby a third profit was made on the same crop loan.[4]

We have seen that the people in Manicaboa were acquainted with the notion that cash crop commodities could be exchanged for goods they needed. From this it was but a short step to the accept-ance of a system of credit in which they pledged their cash crop production in the future for commodities received now. What they did not understand was interest. Most of them were illiterate and did not know how to keep books. They believed in the bind-ing quality of the spoken word and in the force of customary law. The creditor merchants, who dominated the coffee industry in the second half of the nineteenth century, however, belonged to a new and different culture. Most of them were Spaniards who had learned the notion of interest in their home-country. They were fully literate and kept close accounts. What counted for them was a man's signature on the written page, the written contract. An old informant described the meeting of these two cultures in the following words:

People came here from all over Spain: Asturians, Mallorcans, Canary Islanders, Galicians. Men who owned neither shirts nor pants. But a few years later each one of them sat on a hoard of 30,000 pesos. You can't deny that they were hard-working people. But it was a misery to witness the way they treated the sons of Puerto Rico. For this reason God has seen fit to punish Spain and to let her tumble from her high place. ... They laid hold of the riches of this country from their seats behind the tradesman's counter. If a man came and bought the codfish or the fatback he needed, they charged him 25 per cent interest. And if he couldn't pay, they charged interests on the interests. We all took credit this way: the N. family, the G. family, the M. family, my own father. They didn't understand anything about those things. And afterwards the Spaniards came, and they took the farms from the poor people who could not pay.

4. Puerto Rico Government, *Annual Report of the Governor of Puerto Rico*, Washington, 1925, p. 512.

Not all the farmers lost their holdings. But to those who realized what credit meant to them and grasped its consequences in terms of capitalist economics, it meant one of two things. If they became coffee producers, they could compete with the growing hacienda system as long as they performed the operations of production and processing by hand. This meant an intensification of labor and a closer marshalling of the available resources of family labor. It also meant a curtailing of their standards of consumption. If the credit system threatened them with loss of house and home, then the answer was to restrict the amount of credit to cover bare necessities. On the other hand, they had the alternative of balancing their ownership of land with wage labor at the newly developing hacienda. This alternative meant that they received goods in payment for extra work performed on land which belonged to somebody else. Such payments made them more independent of credit. It also provided them with commodities they could not hope to obtain with such regularity if they tightened their belt and stuck to their farms without performing outside wage labor. At the same time it tied them to the hacienda system. Both alternatives were products of the new cultural context. The credit system meant restricted consumption for many, wage labor for others. In time, both alternatives became part of the established way of life of the small farmers.

The economic conflict between large growers who specialized in the production of coffee and the small farmers, between the creditor merchants and the victims of the credit system, gave rise to a cultural conflict. An old small holder opined:

Those Spaniards were worse than the Devil. They wanted to become the lords of the earth around here. They gave credit to the farmer during the year until the harvest came around. They chalked up more than the goods were worth. Then they took the farms away. That's the way it was. They had soldiers all over the countryside. One day a Spaniard called on the soldiers to hunt down a Puerto Rican. He said the man had stolen something from his farm. They hunted down the man, and killed him with the butts of their rifles. They wanted to kill us, these people, so they could take over the farms and the land.

The new conditions created a new cultural stereotype. After this, any large landowner and creditor merchant who fitted its description was called a 'Spaniard'. Not all the new large land-owners and creditor merchants were Spaniards by birth. But if they were 'bad', like Don C.Z., 'they were so bad they could have been Spaniards'. If they were stingy, they fell into this category. 'There is a man on the hill,' an informant said. 'He is just like a Spaniard. He has a lot of money but he doesn't spend any of it. He is all skin and bones himself, and his sons are all exceedingly thin. But he sells all his vegetables, and he sells all his milk and will not give them any of it.' Under this stereotype Spaniards are described as 'very hard-working, hard-bitten, much like Americans'. They 'work too hard for a dollar'. They 'are very stingy', 'as hard as the elbow'. 'They rob people's money, but then they just sit on it. They don't spend it.' They 'came here to make money and then go back to Spain with it'. They 'are very individualistic. Nobody can tell them what to do. They don't take other people into considera-tion.' They 'don't give the workers subsistence plots on which to grow things to eat'. They 'are clannish'. They 'don't like to marry Puerto Rican women. They don't like to mix with the sons of the country.' They are 'they', *ellos*, members of the outgroup, adversaries of the *hijos del país*, 'the sons of the country'.

From these descriptions and adjectives emerges the contrasting stereotype, the picture of the ideal Puerto Rican. Unlike the Spaniards, 'he is easy-going'. Puerto Ricans 'work hard, but they don't just work for the sake of work'. They 'are considerate of others'. They 'are shrewd and make money. But if they have money, they don't sit on it. They are free with it.' They 'are always hospitable, free with their belongings'. If they own land, they 'always let their workers have subsistence plots'. This stereotype is in turn charged with the value which people put on co-operativeness, hospitality, the use of money for purposes of con-sumption, personal and shared, and for reciprocal social relation-ships. These are the ideal norms of behavior for a 'son of the country'. If a large landowner or a creditor merchant fits this picture, he is then said to be 'not like a Spaniard at all'. Don Pancho is thus adjudged 'so good that it is hard to believe that he is indeed a Spaniard'.

The Spaniards, in turn, judge the Puerto Ricans with whom they have to deal through the eyes of their own accumulative capitalist culture. They think of them as 'really a bunch of

Andalusians'. They 'don't like to work'. They 'have too many holidays'. They 'don't know how to save. If a peasant gets any money on Saturday, he hasn't got any left on Monday. He drinks it away. He plays it away. He is a real *Andaluz*.' They 'like to drink and gamble. Just take the sung devotion to the saints. Just an excuse for a *fiesta*. People always come away drunk.' 'A Mallorcan will grow all kinds of vegetables: peppers, tomatoes, and so on. Not just taro and sweet potatoes. But they grow nothing else, so they can just cut them off with a machete. They are so lazy.'

The cultural conflict implicit in these generalizations grew sharper as more and more people lost their land and were forced to exchange the status of independent and sovereign farm owners with the status of dependent workers working on someone else's land. The municipal census of 1871 listed 1660 working owners. In 1892, or twenty-one years later, there were only 555 farm units in all of San José. We may assume that some 1000 individuals shifted to wage labor during the period. Whether eager to obtain the commodities given to them as payment at the hacienda stores, or whether attempting to supplement their income from their own farms, they set the precedent by which a man sold his labor power to obtain needed goods.

At the same time, the increasing prosperity of the coffee area brought streams of migrants from the coast. During the years from 1871 to 1897, San José more than doubled its population.

To ensure a steady supply of labor, the legal and political authorities enforced strict vagrancy laws. Until July of 1873 an insular statute required every able-bodied adult, who owned no property beyond the labor of his arms, to find employment for wages, and it ensured compliance through a system of work books and inspections. After 1873, some of these rulings were continued formally or informally on the municipal level. In San José a register was kept of all petty misdemeanors, and the men whose names appeared on the register were drafted for work whenever the judge or the mayor found it necessary.

Political and legal force were undoubtedly of importance in re-shaping the older cultural pattern. The credit system appears, however, to have been the most active factor in loosening the bonds of the semisubsistence pattern in the barrio. We have

179

pointed out that the notion of interest was introduced along with the idea of credit. It thus forced people to accumulate capital above and beyond the level of barter exchange. At the same time it guaranteed a steady stream of commodities to the rural area, because it granted its loans mainly in the form of goods. This introduced the other incentive to wage labor into a community which had previously functioned on the basis of a minimum of purchased goods mediated through money as tokens to be used in barter. Now people began to obtain these tokens through sale of their labor power. Wage labor replaced the neighborhood exchange labor team as the predominant way of obtaining labor.

Credit tied the rural community firmly to the town, which served as a point of concentration for the goods that came in from the countryside. It gathered quantities of produce and sold them in a market with which the rural farmers had no acquaintance. It funnelled credit into the rural area. Credit made the new way of life possible. The division of functions between town and country emerged as basic to the new coffee culture.

The new way of life had two major poles. Its urban pole was the creditor merchant, its rural pole the hacienda.

The hacienda

Hacienda La Gorra in Manicaboa represents the new rural way of life in its most typical form. At present the hacienda comprises about 690 *cuerdas*. Roughly 400 *cuerdas* were acquired through purchase of two land grants from their original owners. A little more than 100 *cuerdas* were bought from small owners surrounding the holding. The provenience of 150 *cuerdas* remains uncertain. Most of the hacienda terrain lies in the area of best coffee production. . . . It is surrounded on all sides by small holdings, some of which are owned by descendants of the original owners of the lands now held by the hacienda.

The location of the main land grants purchased by the original owner determined the organization of the hacienda into two parts for purposes of administration and processing. One grant comprised land lying to either side of the Hacienda Trail. The other consisted of terrain sloping down to the Río Josco. Each part is equipped with coffee-processing machinery. These processing plants have a characteristic appearance when seen from a plane.

The concrete drying floors show up as light gray rectangles surrounded by sheds and houses, the whole enclosed by the dark area of coffee plantings and shade trees. Each processing plant contains a gasoline-driven hulling machine, concrete washing tanks, concrete drying platforms and storage barns. . . . La Gorra does not own a steam-driven and steam-heated drying drum, and it lacks the automatic labor-saving device which passes the berries through the hulling machine for a second hulling. This shows that the capitalization of this hacienda does not place it among the largest productive units among Puerto Rican coffee farms. Yet its machinery is valued at some $9000 to $10,000.

To the right of one of the processing plants stands the hacienda house, a large one-story structure of wood with a galvanized corrugated-iron roof. It contains four large rooms, a kitchen, a bathroom and servants' quarters. It is simply furnished with articles imported from Spain.

In the days when the hacienda system was established in the barrio, three structures adjoined the living quarters of the owner. These have now been torn down. The first was the hacienda store (*el despacho de peones*), which was owned by the landlord. Each two weeks or once a month his mules and men would haul up the needed provisions from town. Throughout the week the hacienda workers and the outside people who had performed labor for wages bought these goods on credit. On Saturdays a line would then form at the store. The workers would pass through the store and obtain the commodities they needed for the week-end, and then step in front of a cubicle at the end of the store where the hacienda owner sat behind a small counter. There he checked their weekly purchases against their accumulated wages. If the sum of their wages exceeded the value of their purchases, he would pay them the difference in cash. On some haciendas the workers were paid in special tokens redeemable only at the hacienda store. Hacienda La Gorra, however, always made it a practice to pay out the small differences in cash. If a man had used up more commodities than his wages were worth, the hacienda owner wrote down the sum he owed in labor and waved the man on. The workers were thus able to obtain consumption credit throughout the year, *whether they worked or not*. The owner of the hacienda, on the other hand, ensured himself of a steady supply of labor. Many men never accumulated enough wages to make up for their debts and were under obligation to work to make these differences good.

The other two wooden structures next to the hacienda store housed a butcher shop and a bakery respectively. Both were also the property of the hacienda owner. Here he sold fresh meat and bread to all comers. His own workers could buy these delicacies on credit, if they wished. The stores were, however, open to all the people of the barrio who could pay for the bread and meat in cash. These two small business ventures were thus competitive, whereas the hacienda store was not. This became clear when a butcher in a neighboring barrio flooded Manicaboa with fresh meat and put Hacienda La Gorra out of the meat business. The hacienda store, however, had a certain market as long as the special system of labor prevailed. Through it, the hacienda substituted a mode of payment-in-goods for cash wages.

Scattered through the coffee patches, and away from the central plant and living quarters of the owner, lay the huts of the workers. On some haciendas attempts were made to place resident workers into unitary structures (*cuarteles*), each family occupying a cubicle. These attempts were fiercely resented by the workers as violations of their customary settlement pattern, and they were usually abandoned. According to the traditional unwritten contractual agreement, which came to define conditions of labor on Puerto Rican coffee haciendas, each worker received a separate hut. These huts were wooden one-room structures, roofed with palm-leaf thatch. With the hut came a one-*cuerda* or two-*cuerda* plot on which the worker could grow subsistence crops for his own use on the basis of a share arrangement. Half of the subsistence crops he raised on his subsistence plot (*tala*) had to go to the hacienda owner. In actual practice, the hacienda owners on La Gorra required from their workers only as much as they could use for their own consumption, which left more than half in the hands of the tenants.

To provide for its transportation needs, the hacienda owned more than a dozen mules and several horses. They were never corralled but left to pasture freely. During this period no road led from San José up into the rural hinterland. It took a day's fast ride on horseback to get to town, and the mule-trains loaded with produce were three to four days under way, coming or going.

The workers were called *agregados*, or resident laborers. The word *agregarse* means to 'settle close to'. At Hacienda La Gorra, as on most other coffee haciendas in Puerto Rico, the *agregados* received subsistence plots and houses on the terrain of the hacienda, which enabled them to 'settle' as part of the permanent labor supply of the farm. At the same time they received the right of share cropping the subsistence plot. There was no share cropping of coffee, however, all work in coffee being paid in wages. Coffee represented too great an investment for the hacienda owner to share its produce with any worker. Nevertheless, this arrangement does not derive from the nature of the crop alone. Share cropping in coffee has been practiced under conditions of scarce labor supply even in the plantation area of Brazil. If scarcity of labor supply represents one of the conditions for the appearance of share cropping in coffee production, it is interesting to note that labor was relatively scarce during the development phase of the Puerto Rican coffee industry. Perhaps we may explain the absence of share cropping during this phase by the desire of the newly established hacienda owners to get maximum returns on their recently invested capital.

To the people who did the work on his farm, the hacienda owner was a person of enormous importance. He became their adviser in many matters of life which required money or mediation with political or legal authorities. Knowledge of his moods and his personal characteristics became a requirement for all the households in the barrio, for they facilitated dealings with the man whose descendants still call themselves 'the kings of Manicaboa'. The founder of the hacienda, though of Spanish descent, was himself a second-generation Puerto Rican. A member of the Spanish upper-class club, the Casino in San Juan, he yet knew how to deal with the country people who worked for him. His motto was that 'when you understand the country people, you can get anything out of them'. We shall see later how these hierarchical relationships, between landowner and dependent workers, gave rise to a set of cultural norms and ideals which served to regulate conduct between people of such unequal statuses. These norms guided behavior in recurring situations, constituting a mechanism for the settlement of recurring conflicts.

The authority of the hacienda owner was supplemented, and occasionally checked, on the barrio level by the presence a short way above the hacienda of a civil guard post, and a barrio commissioner. The civil guard policed the rural area. They would always walk in twos, clad in their wide black capes and peaked hats. They had the right of entry into any house, under any pretext, and according to an old informant, 'used to walk about to make sure that the cultivable land was planted. Then they would demand that people grow such and such crops in such and such a place'. For a while the hacienda owner was himself commissioner of the barrio. The commissioner acted as the mayor's representative in the rural area. 'Being commissioner of the barrio was like being mayor of the barrio.' He called the people to donate free labor to repair trails and roads, certified official papers, settled quarrels and so on. Later, another landowner, living closer to the river, took over the position.

The development of the coffee industry caused the establishment of units similar to Hacienda La Gorra in most parts of the Puerto Rican highland area. All such units were organized for the purpose of obtaining profits on invested capital. This capital was obtained through a credit system which united the functions of producers' credit and consumers' credit. All devoted themselves to the production of one major cash crop for the export market and employed processing machinery and extensive rather than intensive means of cultivation. The initial capital outlay required for the purchase of processing machinery and land and the sums required for payment of a large labor force were obviously beyond the ability of the small grower. Yet the capitalization required for the average Puerto Rican coffee hacienda was not comparable to the scale of capital characteristic of modern corporate organization. Since such haciendas were often founded by wealthy families or backed by the financial resources of such families, we may simply label this type of economic enterprise a 'family-type hacienda'.

In essence, the hacienda constituted a social system for stabilizing the necessary labor supply. We have seen that coffee requires much labor at unequal intervals throughout the year, and that labor, not machinery, constitutes the limiting factor in production. The large producer must, therefore, be continuously concerned about the quantity of labor at his disposal, and make the massing of the labor supply a primary consideration.

The labor on the hacienda was bound through the use of perquisites, and through purchases at the hacienda store. Several factors combined to make this form of control the most efficient. Subsistence farming in the preceding stage of development made people accept goods rather than straight wages. Land was still relatively plentiful and easily acquired. The extension of credit, therefore, served to draw the worker away from farming on his own behalf into dependence on the large unit. Population was still relatively scarce in terms of needed supply of labor. The provision of perquisites thus attracted workers. Finally, the farm owner also received his credit in goods. This was due to a low rate of accumulation and a scarcity of credit on the island. The provision of credit in goods afforded the creditor merchant added profit.

The Hierarchy of Ownership

Life and expectations of the people in Manicaboa are tied closely to the land and its products. Land is the basic means of production in an agricultural society. In Puerto Rico, land has been held privately since the middle of the eighteenth century. If the society specializes in the production of cash crops, inequalities in the amount and quality of land held mean inequalities in the ability to turn produce into money. In the course of our historical analysis, we have noted some of the factors which led to inequalities of wealth within the rural segment of the coffee culture.

In our discussion of the behavior and ideal norms of the people of Manicaboa, we shall speak of five major groupings. These groupings are: the agricultural workers, the small holders, the small farmers, the middle farmers and the large landowners. In the course of our presentation, we shall refer to these groupings as classes.

In our discussion of Manicaboa we shall . . . attempt to avoid hard-and-fast fixed criteria by which to draw sharp distinctions. We do not, for example, differentiate the agricultural worker from the man who owns a small plot but also does wage labor alongside the landless workers for the greater part of the year. Many agricultural workers of today are, in fact, the sons of landowners of yesterday. Thus, thirteen of eighteen landless workers in Limones come from landowning families, three from landless families, while the origin of two is unknown. In a sample of twenty-nine landowners in Manicaboa Altura, nine heads of families who own land today come from parents who were formerly landless.

The classes distinguished here resulted from three major and inter-related historical processes: first, the concentration and fragmentation of landownership; second, the development of wage labor; third, the increase of specialized cash crops at the expense of subsistence crops.

In our historical section we have noted the tremendous decline in the number of landowners which followed the concentration of land in large holdings during the rise of the coffee culture. In 1948 there were, according to data supplied by the Agricultural Adjustment Administration, ten farms of more than one hundred *cuerdas* in Manicaboa. These ten farms represent 3·8 per cent of all the farms of the barrio. Nine of them own 50 per cent of all the coffee land in Manicaboa, while 250 small farms own the other 50 per cent. These ten farms also own 44 per cent of all the land in the barrio.

Concentration of land in these ten large estates has been accompanied, however, by increased fragmentation of land owned by the remainder of the population. Later, we shall attempt to assess some of the factors responsible for this change. In 1948, 250 farms in Manicaboa were less than one hundred *cuerdas*; 55·34 per cent of all the farms in the barrio, or 145 of the total 262 farms, were less than ten *cuerdas*, and together they owned only 9 per cent of the land; 28·24 per cent, or seventy-four of the 262 farms, ranged between ten and thirty *cuerdas*, and together held 17 per cent of the land; 12·24 per cent, or thirty-two of the 262 farms, ranged from thirty to one hundred *cuerdas*, and held 25 per cent of all the land. The farms may be divided into four rough groupings, which have cultural significance: first, those of less than ten *cuerdas*; second, ten to thirty *cuerdas*; third, thirty to one hundred *cuerdas*; and fourth, more than one hundred *cuerdas*. We do not at all imply that these groups are sharply separable, for example, that a man who owns thirty-one *cuerdas* is of necessity a different type of man than a man who owns twenty-nine and a half *cuerdas*. We shall show, however, that the way of life within each group tends to be distinctive.

We have seen that acceptance of wage labor has emerged in the course of cultural development. The same process which produced a decline in the number of independent landowners conditioned the growth of a group of people who depended upon wages to meet their subsistency needs. Today, three kinds of people fall into this category. The first are represented by the estimated 250 to 300 agricultural workers of Manicaboa, the second by the owners of less than ten *cuerdas* of land and the third by the owners of between ten and thirty *cuerdas* of land. The second and third groups depend on wages for additional income. The smallholders usually do wage labor in order to supplement the resources derived from their insufficient property. The small farmers, or owners of ten to thirty *cuerdas*, often send members of their families to work elsewhere and appropriate their cash earnings. Both groups, moreover, make every effort not to employ wage labor, unless their own family labor force proves insufficient. All of the fifteen landowners who hold less than thirty-five *cuerdas* in the neighborhood of Limones customarily work their land with family labor. By contrast, the farmers holding between thirty and one hundred *cuerdas*, like the large landowners, employ laborers and pay them cash wages.

The third historical process affecting class groupings is the shift from the production of subsistence crops to the production of a cash crop. We have seen how this change was first effected on a large scale on the large farms, while the smaller farms followed suit. We have also noted that farming in Manicaboa was never wholly subsistence farming, but that some cash crop was always sold to meet certain daily needs. People in Manicaboa differ today in the extent to which the sale of cash crops permits capital accumulation after they have met subsistence needs. In crude terms, the people who sell cash crops principally in order to eat we shall call peasants. The people who run their farms as business enterprises for accumulation of cash or credit we shall call farmers. This is a cultural definition of the peasant depending upon what the particular culture defines as its minimum standard of living, and not an absolute definition. As Greaves has pointed out, it is necessary to distinguish 'several forms of peasant production in the various tropical countries, each form indicating a different degree of subsistence culture and capitalization'.[5]

In our discussion we shall make the possession of about thirty *cuerdas* roughly coterminous with the point at which monetary accumulation beyond the culturally defined subsistence needs becomes possible. Peasantry thus designates landowners holding less than thirty *cuerdas*. We hope to show that the norms of behavior and ideals of the peasantry tend to dominate the character of the barrio. In Puerto Rican parlance, these two hundred odd households would be called *jíbaros*, or rural, backward, unsophisticated folk. We shall use the term 'peasant' rather than *jíbaro* which has been used to designate agricultural workers and small holders as well as small farmers. It can be used by the people of one neighborhood for the people of another neighborhood. Thus the people of the Altura in Manicaboa call the people of Limones *jíbaros*. The agricultural workers of the sugar coast call the highland folk *jíbaros*. Yet they are themselves labelled *jíbaros* by the people of the towns. Residents of San Juan may even refer laughingly to the inhabitants of the country as *jíbaros*, in the sense of the English word 'hick'. *Jíbaro* is thus a term which denotes a degree of backwardness relative to the cultural position of the speaker. Its meaning tends to change, as the position of the speaker changes.

Summarizing our definitions, we shall deal with the following groupings or classes:

1. *The peasantry*. The peasantry is composed of persons owning less than ten *cuerdas* (small holders) and persons owning between ten and thirty *cuerdas* (small farmers). Peasants rely upon members of their own families to till their holdings and employ wage labor only rarely, but often supplement their income by performing wage labor elsewhere. They grow cash crops to satisfy a culturally defined standard of living and are unable to accumulate capital beyond this limit.

5. Ira C. Greaves, *Modern Production among Backward Peoples*, London, 1935, p. 193.

2. *The middle farmers.* The middle farmers own between thirty and one hundred *cuerdas* of land, rely on wage labor and accumulate capital beyond subsistence needs.

3. *The agricultural workers.* The agricultural workers are landless, though differing in degree of access to land. They meet their subsistence needs through the sale of their labor power.

4. *The hacienda owner.* The hacienda represents the largest productive enterprise in the barrio, specializes in the production of cash crops, employs wage labor on a large scale and manifests a high rate of capital accumulation relative to the other farms in the barrio.

In Manicaboa, as elsewhere, differences in wealth produce differences in prestige. A large set of different symbols enables people to measure the economic standing of their neighbors. If a man owns a pig or chickens, if he has a bedspread, if his wife rides on a horse or a mule, if she carries things on her hip or on her head, if they eat bananas dry or with milk – all are symbols which define social status. When a person is clearly of higher social status than another, he is addressed as *Usted* by his inferior. 'I say *Usted* to you because I respect you more. I say *tu* to Dona T., because we associate each day in our work.' Such criteria are merely derivative, however, of a basic one: access to land. People in the barrio rank each other not only by whether they do or do not own land but also by the degree to which they are able to use land. A wage worker who has access to a subsistence plot through customary arrangements with a landowner tends to rank higher in the social scale than a wage worker who must support himself entirely by the sale of his labor power. A man who owns a small plot, be it ever so humble, ranks higher than a wage worker who is provided with a subsistence plot by a landowner. This is true even in cases where a worker may be materially better off than the owner of a small splinter of land. Such criteria of ranking are the products of cultural experience. They depend on what the culture defines as an adequate income rather than on an absolute sum of money earned during the year. The criteria refer to steadiness and regularity of the flow of income, cash or goods. Amount and regularity, in turn, are not measured solely by what the individual family needs to eat, but include their notion of hospitality to their fellow men. A wage worker is an 'unfortunate' man (*un infeliz*), because the sharp seasonal variation in earnings may force him to sell his chickens and his lone pig during the period of lowered income. A peasant, on the other hand, and even a wage worker with a subsistence plot (*tala*) can attempt to eke out an existence during the same bitter months, and conserve their precious capital investment.

Another corollary of this scale of values is that people are more concerned about access to land, *per se*, than about legal titles of ownership. Most of the properties in Manicaboa are not formally listed in the insular Register of Property. On a more intangible basis, most farms are in debt, and the titles of ownership lie in some bank outside the confines of San José, or in the strong box of a creditor merchant or moneylender in town. However, as long as the land cannot be exploited profitably except under existing conditions of peasant tenure, these conditions will tend to persist, and the *de facto* user of the land will continue to be the nominal owner of his property. Thus ownership implies to the peasant in Manicaboa the free use of his land, rather than the free and un-hindered right to dispose either of the land or of its produce on the open market. When people say of a man that he 'owns' land (*tiene finca*), they actually say that he 'has' land, and they mean that he has use of land. Land on which he stands with both his feet is his by a claim superior to all paper claims. One of the worst crimes in their eyes is to dispossess a man in a case where the creditor merchant himself cannot make effective use of the property. The laws enacted by the Popular Democratic party in 1940, calculated to protect the peasants against seizures by creditors, undoubtedly constitute one of the effective bases for peasant support of P.P.D. government and of the present governor of the island, Luis Muñoz Marín.

Part Five
Colonialism and the Emergent Countries

For many countries the most significant experience of the last
hundred years has been that of colonial rule. Colonialism introduced
new forms of stratification into the traditional societies of Africa and
Asia. It also created conditions for the transformation of these
societies and the emergence of new classes and strata within them.
Wertheim examines how Dutch rule in Indonesia created a new
system of stratification in which racial cleavages at first played a
predominant part. It also witnessed the emergence of new classes and
strata which came into conflict both with the traditional elements in
their own society and with the colonial rulers. Worsley discusses in
more general terms the emergence of a bourgeoisie and a petty
bourgeoisie in the ex-colonial countries of Africa and Asia, and
discusses their links with the past, and also their prospects for the
future.

9 W. F. Wertheim

Indonesian Society in Transition: the Changing Status System

Excerpt from W. F. Wertheim, *Indonesian Society in Transition*, W. van Hoeve Ltd, The Hague, Bandung, 1956, pp. 132–52.

I. The Status System in the Old Native Society

It is not possible to speak of a single original Indonesian status system. There are sharp divergencies according to whether the community is organized predominantly on a genealogical or a territorial basis. The former type is mostly associated with *ladang* cultivation, while the latter is found chiefly among peoples practising agriculture on irrigated rice fields. The structure is dependent in large measure, too, on the extent to which village communities are overshadowed by a feudal or princely super-structure.

Within the Javanese *desa*, a person's social standing was connected particularly with his relationship to the land. The fully qualified member of the village, the 'nuclear villager', was a man who owned farmland as well as his own compound and house. His position often stemmed from an ancestor who was one of the founders of the *desa*, a genealogical element within the territorial structure. The man who owned a compound and a house, but no farmland, fell into the second rank. One who possessed only a house in another man's compound was classed in still a lower category. In the lowest category of all we find those who merely shared another man's dwelling.[1] In communities organized on more genealogical lines social prestige was determined by other factors, such as the clan to which one belonged and the rank held inside the clan by virtue of one's family relationships.

As a rule the position of the chief in the small communities, both territorial and genealogical, was not one of authoritarian

[1] B. ter Haar, *Adat Law in Indonesia*, New York, 1948, pp. 71 ff.

command but rather one of *primus inter pares*.[2] A certain measure of democracy is inherent to the primitive Indonesian social structure. Important decisions are not made by a single leader with discretionary powers but by a council of elders or a meeting of the nuclear villagers.

Above the village communities were the principalities, bound together by princely authority. A great social gulf divided the noble families from the common man, both in the inland-states and in the coastal principalities. There was also a slave class, usually small in numbers, on which the ordinary freeman could, in his turn, look down. Slavery was, in general, the result of war, debt or an offence against the *adat* (customary law). In the agricultural areas the nobility represented only a small percentage of the population, far removed socially from the great mass of the peasants. The nobility lived on the labour of the peasants and the slaves. The status system was maintained by a rather strict endogamy which made it, in particular, a mortal sin for a noblewoman to marry a commoner or, worse still, a slave. The nobility left all heavy manual labour to the ordinary freeman and the slaves, limiting its activities to those forms of occupation in keeping with its status (hunting, jousting, war and the more delicate handicrafts). Different modes of social intercourse and manners of speech symbolized the great distinction between the classes. Where Hinduism prevailed, social stratification even assumed the character of a caste system. There was also a high degree of differentiation inside the ranks of the nobility, depending upon the purity of one's line of descent.[3]

Social subdivision was far advanced in the harbour principalities also. There was a wide gulf between the ruling noble families, closely associated with a numerically small class of rich patricians

2. Alb. C. Kruyt, 'The influence of Western civilisation on the inhabitants of Poso (Central Celebes)', in B. Schrieke (ed.), *The Effect of Western Influence on Native Civilisations in the Malay Archipelago*, Batavia, 1929, pp. 1 ff.; F. H. van Naerssen, *Culture Contacts and Social Conflicts in Indonesia*, New York, 1947, p. 6.

3. cf., for example, H. J. Friedericy, 'De standen bij de Boegineezen en Makassaren' (Social classes among the Buginese and the people of Macassar), in *Bijdragen tot de Taal-, Land- en Volkenkunde van Nederlandsch-Indië* (Contributions to the Philology, Geography, and Ethnology of the Netherlands Indies), vol. 90 (1933), pp. 447 ff.

of predominantly foreign origin, and the broad mass of town dwellers, composed of pedlars, artisans and slaves. The small traders grouped in the foreign wards of the coastal towns seldom showed the traits associated with the free bourgeoisie in the commercial cities of Western Europe. There were few traces to be found of an urban democracy. Both the towns and the areas surrounding them were as a rule completely dominated by the ruling noble families.[4]

Naturally there were many factors which cut across this system of social strata. In the countryside particularly, elders often enjoyed a traditional authority over the young. The social and economic functions of the women differed from those of the men; on the whole their status was inferior. Notwithstanding local differences their social position was, however, favourable as compared with the rights of women in many other Asian countries. In agriculture, where women fulfilled an important economic function, their position was by no means subordinate.

Unusual abilities, ascribed to magical powers, also conferred on their possessor a special social status. In the countryside, for example, the medicine man and the smith were usually regarded as being endowed with magical powers. In the towns, too, certain professions gave special status, which often passed from father to son along with the profession itself. Qualifications, mostly of an intellectual character, such as the art of writing or knowledge of the religious scriptures, lent distinction and often brought partial exemption from manual labour. Greater proximity to princely circles and work closely related to the care of the prince's person could also provide enhanced status. On the other hand, remoteness from the centres of princely authority was sometimes associated with greater freedom and independence.[5]

Religion, of course, affected social prestige. Despite a large degree of tolerance and hospitality in most harbour principalities with regard to merchants of different religions, those who held the same creed as the ruler were generally more trusted and more favoured than the others. Thus, the scale of preference

4. J. C. van Leur, *Indonesian Trade and Society. Essays in Asian Social and Economic History*, Selected studies on Indonesia by Dutch scholars, vol. 1, The Hague, Bandung, 1955, pp. 66, 92, 137 ff., 204 ff.

5. F. H. van Naerssen, op. cit., p. 8.

varied greatly according to the creed prevalent in an Indonesian state.

These subordinate strands in the web do not, however, substantially blur the primary pattern of the old Indonesian status system.

II. The Rise of a New Status System Based on Race

As early as the seventeenth and eighteenth centuries a status system had grown up in the enclaves controlled by the East India Company, which differed substantially from the old Indonesian pattern. In Batavia the Dutch employees of the Company formed the uppermost social layer; below them came the free citizens, among whom the Christians (Dutch, mestizos and enfranchised Christian slaves, in that order) occupied the most privileged positions; after these came the Chinese; and the Indonesian population, a large number of them slaves, formed the lowest layer.[6] Although this structure seemed opposed to that in the majority of Indonesian harbour principalities, there were also certain resemblances, for in Batavia, too, foreign traders and artisans lived together in separate wards under their own chieftains, while those who shared the religion of the rulers, or at least did not profess the Islamic religion – which the rulers of Batavia regarded as a hostile faith – enjoyed a privileged position and a certain measure of confidence.

This status system in Batavia formed the starting point for the colonial society of nineteenth-century Java. When colonial dominion spread over the entire island, penetrating, during the culture system period, even into the rural areas, it was inevitable that the old Indonesian prestige scale should be replaced by a new one.

As in the British colonial empire, it was no longer the religion of the settlers that provided the criterion for social prestige, but race. The extension of the white man's power over the coloured races in the nineteenth century was accompanied everywhere by a marked rise in the social standing of the whites and high social regard for all outward characteristics, such as language, dress and skin colour, which symbolized white race. Thus in a large part of the world the colour line became the cornerstone of the colonial

6. F. de Haan, *Oud Batavia* (Old Batavia), Bandung, 1935, pp. 349 ff.

social structure. In the nineteenth-century Java, too, came under the spell of the colour line. But since in every colonial area the social pattern showed certain distinctive characteristics,[7] we must examine more closely the particular forms this pattern assumed in Java.

About 1850 the colonial stratification based on race had assumed a fixed form in Java, which was reflected in the laws. The Europeans formed the ruling stratum, resembling a caste. In contrast with the situation in the British colonies, people of mixed blood belonged to this upper stratum if they descended from a white man in the male line and were either legitimate or recognized by the father.

Over against this upper layer stood the Indonesians, referred to as the 'Inlanders' (natives) and representing the subject stratum. The gulf between the two layers was practically unbridgeable. Apart from one or two exceptional cases, transfer from the lower to the upper stratum was impossible. Discrimination was made on a racial basis in almost all departments of justice and social life. Only the 'Inlanders' were subject to compulsory service for public works and forced labour on the government plantations. Discrimination was found everywhere in the fields of government and justice, eligibility for official positions and teaching. The native mother of a natural child of a European father had no rights of guardianship after the death of the latter. Her permission was not required before the child married.[8] A person's position depended

7. See R. Kennedy, 'The colonial crisis and the future', in R. Linton (ed.), *The Science of Man in the World Crisis*, New York, 1945, pp. 308, 320 ff.

8. See articles 40 and 354 of the Civil Code of 1848:

Art. 40. Illegitimate children, legally acknowledged by the father, are not allowed to marry, when under age, without the consent of their father. In default of the father the consent of the mother is required.

If the mother belongs to the native population or to those legally assimilated with natives, the consent of the Court of Justice has to be secured; in that case the provisions of the preceding article are applicable.

Art. 354. In default of the father, or in case the latter is not able to exercise the guardianship, the Court of Justice also provides for the guardianship of illegitimate children who are legally acknowledged by Europeans or by persons assimilated with Europeans, and whose mothers belong to the native or assimilated population.

not on what he was himself but on the population group to which he belonged. Punitive measures were framed to ensure that the colour line should not be overstepped – it was forbidden to dress otherwise than in the manner customary in one's own population group.[9] The colonial rulers even succeeded in large measure in forcing the Indonesians themselves to accept the system of values based on race. The members of the colonial ruling class were from their birth, or from the moment of their disembarkation on the shores of the Indies, conditioned to this pattern of behaviour and imbued with all the stereotypes connected with it.

There were many kinds of differentiation within each 'caste'. Thus for a long time Dutch officials enjoyed high social prestige. On the other hand the 'colonials', the Dutch professional soldiers, although part of the ruling stratum, had relatively low social standing. After private capital was admitted into Java, private individuals gradually increased not only in number but also in social prestige, while on the plantations the planters gained a patriarchal power and a social esteem which often equalled that of the Indonesian *pryayis* – members of the Javanese nobility.[10]

More important still was the fact that though half-castes were counted in the European group, their social position within the group was determined by a prestige scale closely related to the colonial value system: a scale based on the colour of their skin and other characteristics reflecting the degree of relationship to the white race. The darker the skin, the more 'Indian' the speech, clothing and manners, the lower the social standing. Although the colour line was drawn along the division between '*Inlander*' and 'half-caste', there was no question of equality between white man and half-blood. The entire social life was so imbued by colour-consciousness – though certainly less so than in India – that many Indo-Europeans (then usually known as '*Sinjos*'; later, besides the term 'Indo-Europeans', the term 'Indos' came into use) were kept fully occupied by the effort to demonstrate as close a

9. See, for example, art. 2 No. 6 of the Penal Police Ordinance in *Staatsblad* (State Journal), 1872, No. 111. See also Gouw Giok Siong, *Segi-segi hukum peraturan perkawinan tjampuran* (Legal aspects of the regulation on mixed marriages), Jakarta, 1955, ch. 1.

10. See D. H. Burger, 'Structuurveranderingen in de Javaanse samen-leving' (Structural changes in Javanese society), in *Indonesië*, vol. 3 (1949/50), p. 104.

relationship as possible with the white race and to dissociate themselves as far as possible from the '*Inlanders*'. Like corresponding groups in the other colonies, they were typical marginal men.

Just as in the days of the Company, many of these *Indos* filled clerical posts. For the Dutch, they represented a loyal and trustworthy group, even though they sometimes had every reason to complain of the treatment they experienced at the hands of the white men. And as they were able, from 1850 onwards, to profit increasingly from Dutch schooling, by degrees they began to regard themselves as the bearers *par excellence* of Dutch culture.

Among the '*Inlanders*' a great part of the original status system was preserved. The Javanese nobility was brought into the framework of the Western government apparatus. After a short period in which an unsuccessful effort was made to introduce more democratic ideas into Javanese society, this nobility was reinstalled in its former authority during the period of the culture system, partly as a result of lessons learned in the Java War of 1825–30. Its position was even reinforced in so far as the function of the regent was declared hereditary.[11] Colonial stratification based on race was merely superimposed on the original Indonesian class system.

All the same, the colonial régime did bring about structural changes in Javanese society. Slavery was abolished – although for some time afterwards Indonesians continued to look down on the descendants of slaves. The culture system had marked effects on the internal structure of the Javanese *desa*. Compulsory labour on government plantations often imposed so severe a burden that the members of the village were compelled to share the burden equally and to break through the dividing line separating 'nuclear villagers' from those of second rank. Sugar cultivation, either under the culture system or after the introduction of private plantations, also had an equalizing effect on native land ownership, through the fiction of communal ownership, whereby it was assumed that the land belonged to the *desa* as a whole, the individual peasant having merely a right of use. This assumption had

11. See B. Schrieke, *Indonesian Sociological Studies. Selected Writings*, Part I. Selected studies on Indonesia by Dutch scholars, vol. 2, The Hague, Bandung, 1955, p. 188.

definite advantages from the point of view of the government and the plantation owners, since for purposes of supervision and irrigation it was much easier to deal with compact blocks of land than with tiny holdings. On the other hand, the status of the village chief was raised above that which he had enjoyed under the customary law (*adat*). From being a *primus inter pares* he became an authority, and at the same time a tool of the central government.[12]

Another point deserves attention. In contrast to the Western prestige system, a scale of values was preserved which to a certain extent embodied a protest against the colonial system: a prestige scale based on religion. According to this scale, the Islamic scribe, the *haji* (pilgrim returned from Mecca) and the Arab *Sayyid* (descendant of the Prophet) were men of high standing, whereas white men were merely '*kafirs*', that is, unbelievers.

Finally, mention should be made of a third social stratum besides the *Europeans* and the *Inlanders*, namely the *Foreign Orientals*, composed of the Chinese and the Arabs; they occupied an intermediate position between the Europeans and the Indonesians. In Java they formed in the main a middle class of independent merchants and artisans. In their function of professional traders, the Chinese were held in little esteem by the Indonesian nobility and peasant class. But in the colonial estimation they were, within certain limits, very useful and usually fairly loyal intermediaries between the white man and the Indonesian population, with greater affinity to the former than the native people.

The above sketch typifies the general situation in Java up to the end of the nineteenth century. The Surakarta (Solo) and Jogjakarta Principalities, too, where an Indonesian princely authority was recognized – though more in name than in fact – came more and more under the influence of the new colonial values, although the resistânce put up by the original Indonesian class system was naturally more marked here, as was the social and economic

12. See, for example, Alb. C. Kruyt in B. Schrieke (ed.), *The Effect of Western Influence on Native Civilisations in the Malay Archipelago*, pp. 4 ff.; D. H. Burger, *De ontsluiting van Java's binnenland voor het wereldverkeer* (The opening of the interior of Java to world trade), Wageningen, 1939, pp. 128 ff.

differentiation within the native community.[13] The relatively simple, static pattern of ancient Indonesia was replaced by a new pattern on colonial principles, one which was also fairly stable and simple in nature.

III. The Decay of the Colonial Status System in the Twentieth Century

About 1900 the Netherlands succeeded in establishing its dominion over the whole archipelago. The colonial stratification according to race, prevalent in Java, was thus spread to the Outer Islands. Simultaneously, however, there were dynamic developments in the twentieth century which cut across this rigid pattern and increased social mobility.

In the Outer Islands it was mainly money that made a breach in the old native status system. It was primarily the Indonesian city traders who revolted against tradition and the power of the clan. In many parts of the Outer Islands the indigenous population's dislike of professional trading was less marked than in Java, so that the status system based on ethnic groups, which left trade to the Foreign Oriental, did not exert anything like the same influence on the social pattern as it did in Java. The cultivation of market crops in the country areas also created a certain economic individualism which revolted against traditional bonds and against the authority of the *adat* chiefs. The material prosperity achieved by many a farmer and trader caused them to strive after a social prestige which would equal that enjoyed by the *adat* chiefs and to demand for themselves a *ius connubii* (right to marriage) within the chieftain class.[14]

The agrarian unrest which began to make itself evident in the

13. See the interesting articles by H. J. van Mook, 'Koeta Gedé' and 'Nieuw Koeta Gedé' (New Kuta Gedé), in *Koloniaal Tijdschrift*, Colonial Journal, vol. 15 (1926), pp. 353 ff. and 561 ff.

14. cf., for example, B. Schrieke, *Indonesian Sociological Studies. Selected Writings*, Part I, pp. 138 ff. In the unpublished part of his Sumatra's West-coast Report Schrieke describes how the rising 'middle class' challenged the traditional privileges of the aristocracy, in matters of precedence at festivities and of marriage. In 1925 the first marriages between 'middle-class' men and girls from the nobility were concluded in Silungkang.

Outer Islands in the twenties (as in the communist rising of January 1927 in Menangkabau) was not simply the effect of the impoverishment of some of the farmers as a result of the mobilization of landed property, but was due also to opposition on the part of the newly-rich farmers to the traditional social structure.[15] Moreover, in so far as the interests of native planters came into conflict with those of the Western entrepreneurs – which happened in the case of rubber cultivation in the crisis years – this agrarian resistance took on a nationalist tint as well, a tendency strengthened by the fact that the government usually acted as a protector, not only of the traditional authority of the chiefs, but also of the Western plantations. In certain areas, such as the Hulu Sungei (South East Borneo), where the feudal *adat* rule had been pushed aside at the time of the 'pacification', as hostile to the Dutch, individualism made further advances and, apart from religious criteria, which had great social significance in this area especially, material welfare represented the chief criterion in determining social prestige – more so than in the '*adat* areas'.[16]

Education, too, had a dynamic influence in the Outer Islands, although less than in Java.[17] There was little employment in the *ladang* and rubber districts for intellectuals or near-intellectuals. The towns, too, were much smaller than in Java. Thus the majority of those with a more Western type of education flocked to Java during and after their study. Hence they formed less of a social problem in the Outer Islands than in Java. The significance of education as a dynamic influence is, therefore, better studied on the latter island.

From 1900 onwards there was increasing professional differentiation to be observed in Java also. The expansion of a money economy and increased contact with the West gave rise to numerous new jobs, e.g. for mechanics, chauffeurs, engine drivers and overseers. A new group emerged, rising to some extent above the mass of the population owing to technical ability. More Indonesians applied themselves to trade than formerly, first as

15. See B. Schrieke, op. cit., p. 131.

16. See J. Mallinckrodt, *Het adatrecht van Borneo* (The *adat* law of Borneo), Leiden, 1928, vol. 2, pp. 154 ff., 181.

17. See Schrieke's contribution in B. Schrieke (ed.), *The Effect of Western Influence on Native Civilisations in the Malay Archipelago*, pp. 241 ff.

retailers, later as middlemen. The impression conveyed by Kahin[18] that the Indonesian commercial class did not increase in numbers and was, up to the Second World War, steadily being eliminated by Chinese competition, seems to me debatable, even for Java and for the pre-depression period. It is not confirmed by what statistical material is available. According to the *Onderzoek naar de mindere welvaart der Inlandsche bevolking op Java en Madoera*[19] in 1905 there were 385,472 independent traders without supplementary income from agriculture, or 560,390 independent traders including those in possession of a farm. A rather restricted number of Indonesians in the service of other tradesmen might be added, but it is difficult to assess their number correctly, as they are included in the 1905 investigation within a larger number of people working in trade, industry and transport combined. In the 1930 census of Netherlands India[20] there were 908,940 'Natives' who mentioned trade as their chief occupation. Since peasants, male or female, who supplemented their income with trading activities often gave the latter as their chief occupation,[21] it seems fair to compare the 1930 figure with the higher figure of 1905. As the 1930 data include people working for others, the category is broader than the independent traders listed in 1905. But the 1930 Census conveys the impression that Indonesians working in the trade for others were still rather few, as the great majority of those occupied in trade were engaged in retaining food and tobacco, which points towards petty independent trade. Moreover, it is commonly known that Chinese shopkeepers mostly employed Chinese personnel, which excludes the possibility that a very large number of Indonesians were working for Chinese. The comparison between the group of traders in 1905 and in 1930 shows, besides a considerable absolute progress, that an increased percentage of the total population of Java and Madura was occupied in trading in 1930. For in 1905

18. George McT. Kahin, *Nationalism and Revolution in Indonesia*, Ithaca, 1952, pp. 27 ff.

19. *Onderzoek naar de mindere welvaart der Inlandsche bevolking op Java en Madoera* (Investigation into the diminished welfare of the native population of Java and Madura), Batavia, 1905–14, vol. 6a, Appendix I.

20. *Census of 1930 in Netherlands India*, Batavia, 1933–6, vol. 8, p. 126, Table 19.

21. *Census of 1930 in Netherlands India*, vol. 8, p. 56.

1·87 per cent of the total population (thirty million) were traders as against 2·27 per cent of the total population (forty million) in 1930.[22] A different picture might emerge if those employed by others were deducted. But an actual decrease in the percentage engaged in trade, as assumed by Kahin, has still to be demonstrated.

Later developments during the depression of the thirties also suggest that even before 1930 an incipient native middle class was beginning to emerge, breaking through the old traditional order of society and exerting an individualistic influence. The plantations, too, jerked the peasant out of his old environment and brought him into contact with the Western world, in which process growing acquaintance with the Western way of life and movie shows on pay-day played an important part.

In Java, however, the influence of these factors is completely overshadowed by the way in which education changed the traditional structure of society. Its effect was felt even in the simplest forms of teaching in the *desa*. However elementary the teaching of the three Rs might be, the fact that the children had to recognize the authority of the teacher, besides that of their parents, had its effect on the traditional scale of social prestige, and in particular on the authority of the elders; for the teacher's authority was exerted in a field in which the parents were quite ignorant, even as compared with their younger children. The effect was even more strongly marked when the child's education enabled him to find employment outside the confines of Indonesian agriculture which brought with it social prestige, and material prosperity, far beyond anything he could have achieved at home.

Quite apart from the nature of the instruction given – and as a rule it came into sharp conflict with the traditional native conceptions – the mere fact of its existence made a breach in the agrarian structure. However much the schools might try to adapt their instruction to the agrarian scene, even those who received a predominantly agricultural or technical training were readily inclined to seek work in the towns, where they could achieve

22. A modest increase, especially between 1913 and 1920, is also indicated by the *Verslag van den economischen toestand der inlandsche bevolking*, 1924 (Report on the economic condition of the native population, 1924), Weltevreden, 1926, vol. 1, pp. 177 ff.

greater social prestige.[23] This was because in the Indonesian community a social premium was attached to more or less intellectual work, and as few people could both read and write, those who possessed these skills could command relatively high incomes. The clerk was held in higher esteem than the skilled farmer, and could even perhaps achieve a higher standard of living.[24]

Thus education created a new class of intellectuals and near-intellectuals who occupied a special position in society. In a certain sense this had an individualizing effect, as the money economy also had in the Outer Islands. The social prestige and the comparative material prosperity attached to an 'intellectual' position were so attractive that many simple people endured the greatest sacrifices in order to afford their children the advantages of a reasonably good education.[25] The individual's effort to rise in the social scale did not express itself, in this society, in a struggle for profit from trade or from an independent profession, but in a struggle to obtain an official appointment by means of diplomas.[26] And since a knowledge of Dutch in particular was a passport to jobs barred to the many, knowledge of the language became involved in the assessment of social prestige.

Traditional bonds played a role in the effort to scrape together enough money to enable a child to study, for several members of the family contributed to finance his schooling, while the whole family tried to profit by it, not only through the successful candidate's enhanced social prestige, but also by his enlarged income. Notwithstanding this, the chase after diplomas had a strongly individualizing effect.

Thus education created a whole class of Indonesians with a

23. See, for example, J. S. Furnivall, *Colonial Policy and Practice. A Comparative Study of Burma and Netherlands India*, Cambridge, 1948, p. 381.

24. J. van Gelderen, *Voorlezingen over tropisch-koloniale staathuishoudkunde* (Lectures on political economy in the colonial tropics), Haarlem, 1927, p. 68.

25. See C. Hooykaas, 'Voldoet de A.M.S. nog?' (Does the A.M.S. still satisfy?), in *Koloniale Studïen* (Colonial Studies), vol. 24 (1940), p. 24. Takdir Alisjahbana, 'De botsing van Oost en West' (The clash between East and West), in *Sticusa Jaarboek* (Yearbook of the Foundation for Cultural Co-operation between the Netherlands, Indonesia, Surinam and the Netherlands Antilles), 1950, p. 58.

26. D. H. Burger, 'Structuurveranderingen in de Javaanse samenleving', loc. cit., p. 105

certain amount of Western education, and the existence of this class had as dynamic an effect on the status system of Java as rubber cultivation had on that of the Outer Islands.

First, the presence of this class affected the social value system within the Indonesian society in the narrow sense of the word. Whereas in the past people had looked up only to the traditional chiefs and religious leaders, they now began to rank the authority of the new spiritual leaders, the intellectuals, above that of the regents and the *kyahis* (Moslem religious teachers). It was the Western-trained schoolteacher who first and foremost personified this new prestige. But it was modern corporate life which first made it clear how deeply the traditional structure had been affected. The enormous growth of *Sarekat Islam* at about the time of the First World War demonstrated that the masses no longer submitted to traditional authority but were prepared to follow the leadership of union chiefs originating from the intellectual group.[27]

Just as the *nouveaux riches* in Menangkabau and elsewhere in the Outer Islands had demanded the *ius connubii* with the *adat* chiefs, so the most prosperous of the new intellectuals in Java, many of them of Sumatran origin, demanded entry into the circles of the higher Javanese nobility.[28] Together with the old ruling aristocracy, these intellectuals were to form a class of 'new *pryayis*' which would become the uppermost layer in Indonesian society.[29]

But it was not only in the traditional Javanese social order that the existence of a class of Indonesian intellectuals and near-intellectuals made a breach. It also broke through the nineteenth-century colonial stratification based on race. Western education gave the Indonesians a chance to fill posts which had previously been reserved for the European 'caste'. In this manner the foundations of the colonial status system gradually collapsed. Here, as

27. See P. A. A. Djajadiningrat, *Herinneringen van Pangeran Aria Achmad Djajadiningrat* (Memoirs of Pangeran Aria Achmad Djajadiningrat), Amsterdam, Batavia, 1936, pp. 284 ff.

28. D. H. Burger, 'Structuurveranderingen in de Javaanse samenleving', loc. cit., p. 105.

29. I. J. Brugmans and Soenario, 'Enkele gegevens van sociale aard' (Some data of social order), in *Verslag van de Commissie tot bestudeering van staatsrechtelijke hervormingen* (Report of the Commission for the study of political reforms), New York, 1944, vol. 1, p. 72.

elsewhere, education acted like dynamite on the colonial caste system.[30]

The great tension in Indonesia in the years before the Second World War was associated to a significant degree with the order in which various groups came into contact with education. Expansion of the apparatus of government and of Western business during the second half of the nineteenth century had brought a need for personnel trained in administration and conversant with the Dutch language. The obvious remedy was to draw, in the first instance, on those groups who had already had some contact with Dutch culture. Thus the Indo-Europeans were the first to profit from the opportunities provided for education. Among the Indonesians, the children of chiefs and the Ambonese and Menadonese Christians were the first to gain access on a large scale to the increased facilities for education.

It was only after 1900 that education was opened to a larger number of Indonesians. The demand for trained personnel continued to increase. Indonesians were being appointed to functions which had previously been the privilege of Europeans. Probably not only for reasons of justice but also in order to prevent lower paid Indonesian personnel from ousting the Europeans, equal pay for equal work for Indonesians and Europeans alike was adopted as a principle after 1913.[31] However, for appointments demanding higher education which for the most part could, for the time being, be filled only by Indo-Europeans, special scales of salary were fixed, adjusted to the Indo-Europeans' higher standard of living; whereas the highest appointments, which were largely filled by personnel brought into the country from abroad, were accorded salaries relatively much higher than the others, in order to attract staff to the tropics. In this way the privileged position of the European upper stratum was preserved for as long as possible. But the progress in education brought jobs of increasing importance within the reach of Indonesians, with the result that the extra remuneration attached to the higher appointments tended

30. cf. R. Kennedy, op. cit., p. 311: 'Education would be dynamite for the rigid caste systems of colonies.'

31. See *Javasche Courant* (Java Journal), 12–8, 1913, No. 67; Paul W. van der Veur, 'The Eurasians of Indonesia: castaways of colonialism', in *Pacific Affairs*, vol. 27 (1954), p. 125.

gradually to disappear and the number of typically 'European' posts declined considerably. Especially during the depression of the thirties 'Indianization' of the administrative service made headway at a remarkable pace.[32]

Table 1

Percentage of Administrative Personnel According to Population Group in 1938 Compared with 1928 [1]

	1938			1928		
	Euro-peans	Indo-nesians	Foreign Orientals	Euro-peans	Indo-nesians	Foreign Orientals
Technical staff	77·14	20·12	2·74	84·77	14·38	0·85
Administrative techn. staff	55·81	41·98	2·21	77·06	22·28	0·66
Financial staff	67·08	30·46	2·46	80·45	18·80	0·75
Administrative staff	65·18	32·16	2·66	93·66	5·10	1·24
Controlling staff	83·97	15·68	0·35	92·46	7·33	0·21

1. Adapted from I. J. Brugmans and Soenario, op. cit., vol. 1, p. 56.

Table 2

Percentage of Government Personnel in Different Ranks According to Population Group in 1938 [1]

Population Group	Lower personnel	Lower medium personnel	Higher medium personnel	Higher personnel
Europeans	0·6	33·3	57·6	92·2
Indonesians	98·9	60·6	38·0	6·4
Indonesians assimilated to Europeans	0·2	3·4	2·0	0·5
Foreign Orientals	0·3	2·7	2·3	0·8
Total	100·0	100·0	100·0	100·0

1. Adapted from I. J. Brugmans and Soenario, ibid.

32. See the articles on Indianization in *Koloniale Studiën* (Colonial Studies), vol. 16 (1932), part 1: J. H. Boeke, 'Indianisation', pp. 243 ff.; D. M. G. Koch, 'De vakbeweging en de Indianiseering' (The trade union movement and the Indianization), pp. 348 ff.

Education on the Western model, with Dutch as the medium of instruction, had produced a cultural affinity between large groups of Indonesians and Europeans who had grown up in Indonesia. Did this bring them closer together socially, too? On the contrary, as the barriers of race became weaker, the tension grew. Despite the growth of an Indonesian middle class of officials, clerks and traders, the differentiation of incomes still largely coincided with the division according to race, with the average earnings of Europeans at the top, those of the Chinese in between and those of Indonesians at the bottom. Indonesians who had enjoyed some education no longer accepted the colonial stratification according to race as a matter of course. Legal and social discrimination decreased, but what still remained rankled all the more. Social demarcation lines were beginning to become fluid. Hence many groups of people sprang up who were no longer content with their social status, while others sensed a threat to their own comparatively favourable position. Economic and social competition developed between adjacent groups, which became all the keener the closer they approached each other culturally.

Intensified competition in a society, in which owing to the dominant economic system there were more applicants than vacancies, caused the members of the bourgeoisie to join forces to achieve group solidarity. And what could be more natural in a society whose cornerstone was the colour line, than that such a fusion should be sought along the existing racial divisions?

Thus, around 1920, the Indo-Europeans joined together in the Indo-European Union (*Indo-Europeesch Verbond*) to protect themselves against the rising class of Westernized Indonesians. Their main object was to maintain the social privileges they had already gained for themselves. They fostered an artificial feeling of superiority towards the *Inlanders* and strove to create a still greater distance between the latter and themselves, while emphasizing their own European character. What, in the nineteenth century, had been largely the reflection of a social reality now became segregation maintained by artificial means. It was fear that caused them to entrench themselves behind the racial barriers more solidly than ever before.

On the other hand, a tendency to greater unity appeared also mong the Indonesians. This was accompanied by a heightened national consciousness and a diminished respect for the Dutch language as a social factor, as well as for appointments in the Dutch government service and for assimilation into Dutch circles. The use of the *Bahasa Indonesia*, a modernized form of Malay, and the wearing of the *kopiah*, a black fez, became symbolic of national consciousness. The true nationalist was a non-cooperator; he no longer aspired to a job in the government service. Indonesian women with self-respect cared less and less for employment as housekeeper-concubines in the service of unmarried European men. Eventually, after 1930, even marriage with a European, apparently, had less attraction for an Indonesian woman than before.[33] Thus a new scale of values gradually projected itself across the old colonial scale. Together with education, this new scale of values affected the position of women and the young. In the capacity of Westernized intellectuals and fellow-fighters in the nationalist struggle, the womenfolk and the young could often win for themselves a social prestige which conflicted with traditional Indonesian ideas. In this sense, too, Western education, from which many young girls also profited, had a revolutionizing influence on Indonesian society.

In the years of crisis the competitive struggle became more intense. The Indo-Europeans had to follow courses of still higher education in order to keep up to the European level. They competed at this level with the whites who came to Indonesia from abroad in much smaller numbers from 1930 onwards. On the other hand, a growing number of Indo-Europeans failed to keep up the struggle and fell away, entering the *kampong*, the poor native quarter of the city. Unemployment in the crisis years reduced many *Indos* to a condition of material distress.

A similar process could be seen in the world of trade. The Chinese no longer retained the monopoly in this field. A growing body of Indonesian traders, some of them organized on co-operative lines, began to threaten their position from below. As

33. A. van Marle, 'De groep der Europeanen in Nederlands Indië. Iets over ontstaan en groei' (The European group in the Netherlands Indies. Something about origin and growth), in *Indonesië*, vol. 5 (1951–2), p. 507. Gouw Giok Siong, op. cit., pp. 31–2, ascribes the decrease of mixed marriages between Indonesian women and European men during the depression to economic factors. However, marriages with Chinese women showed, at the same time, an increasing tendency!

Cator put it: 'In East Java and in the Preanger Regencies there is . . . an undeniable decrease of the Chinese share in trade', and (for the Preanger Regencies and Palembang): 'Native intermediate traders begin to oust the Chinese.'[34] In the field of industrial enterprise the trend was still more pronounced. According to Sitsen's booklet, written in wartime, during the last ten years, contrary to the trends some decades earlier, 'in Djokjakarta and Solo the Chinese *batik* producers were almost all pushed out by the Indonesian contractors, as in Pekalongan also'.[35] For the rest, it should be remembered that in many regions of the Outer Islands native trade had always competed successfully with Chinese enterprise. In some regions, such as Menangkabau and Hulu Sungei,[36] the latter have hardly been able to get a foothold. Kahin's arguments to the effect that the Chinese were ousting the Indonesians from trade until the Second World War[37] cannot, therefore, be regarded as conclusive.

Moreover, in the crisis period the Chinese middlemen got into still greater difficulty, owing to the attempts by Japanese importers to eliminate the Chinese intermediate trade. They, too, were obliged either to organize themselves into larger concerns to withstand Indonesian competition from below, or to seek employment in industry or government service – occupations in which they had shown little interest in the past.[38] Chinese intellectuals began to compete with *Indos* and Indonesians for the higher posts in the administration. On the other hand many Chinese declined into the ranks of the proletariat, which was no longer limited to the *Singkehs*, the Chinese brought in from overseas. The Chinese, too, sought salvation in a greater degree of

34. W. J. Cator, *The Economic Position of the Chinese in the Netherlands Indies*, Oxford, 1936, pp. 74 ff.

35. P. H. W. Sitsen, *Industrial Development of the Netherlands Indies*, New York, 1942, pp. 21 ff.

36. See M. Joustra, *Minangkabau. Overzicht van land, geschiedenis en volk* (Menangkabau. Survey of country, history and people), Leiden, 1921, p. 83; R. Broersma, *Handel en bedrijf in Zuiden Oost-Borneo* (Commerce and Industry in South and East Borneo), The Hague, 1927, p. 119.

37. G. McT. Kahin, op. cit., pp. 27 ff.

38. See Liem Twan Djie, *De distribueerende tusschenhandel der Chineezen op Java* (The distributive intermediate trade of the Chinese in Java), The Hague, 1947, pp. 66 ff. See also Tables 1 and 2 above, showing a remarkable increase of the Foriegn Orientals in government service.

solidarity. In their case, too, this increased segregation from the Indonesians was artificial, in view of the increasing cultural similarity between the two groups. This was reflected in the fact that the Indonesian Chinese had usually forgotten the Chinese language, the more prosperous of them using Dutch, the less well-to-do an Indonesian language, either a local one or Chinese Malay.

Thus, even before the war, the special position occupied by the Europeans and Chinese, like that of the feudal nobility, had become considerably less stable. There was a strong tendency in the direction of a new status system based on individual prosperity and individual intellectual abilities; but this development was still largely held in check by the remnants of both the feudal and the colonial structure.

10 P. Worsley

Social Class in Emergent Countries: Bourgeoisie and
Petty Bourgeoisie

Excerpt from Peter Worsley, *The Third World*, Weidenfeld and Nicolson, London, 1964, pp. 130–51.

The countries which had fallen under European occupation by
the nineteenth century were ... frequently quite advanced economically and in general cultural level. Under European domination,
however, what indigenous industry there was rapidly went to
the wall. But where the wealthier classes in the traditional order
of things were able – and permitted – to adapt themselves to
participation in the new world-market economy, traditional
wealth could be invested in the new sectors of the economy, and
gave rise to a new class of indigenous capitalists.

Japan was perhaps the most striking case: here the ruling
classes in an agrarian feudal society – though one which possessed
a significant urban and commercial sector even before the arrival
of Commodore Perry – were able to come to terms with modern
capitalism by investing heavily in the new industrial economy
which was rapidly constructed after the Meiji Restoration. The
result was a peculiarly centralized and concentrated pattern of
political control and economic ownership, in which indigenous
finance–capital was closely interlinked with industrial enterprise,
but where older feudal–paternalist traditions persisted, and
affected relations between management and workers. From this
launching-platform, Japan successfully built up a modern
capitalist economy.

Indian economic development also displayed many of the
features found in Japanese development, whether the capital
involved was British or Indian. One of its outstanding characteristics was the early development of the joint-stock company under
'managing agents', who began as traders, and later became
organizers and managers of industry:

It was mainly through their agency that European capital and skill found their way to India. They used these in the organization of industrial undertakings and the development of India's resources which paid for the increasing import of foreign manufactures. . . . The whole system was in fact integrated with the imperialist economy. . . . The managing agency system introduced a degree of administrative control and financial integration in business which had never existed before. It preserved the legal and functional independence of each of the concerns opened up by a pioneering managing agency firm, and yet the firm exercised an overall control by putting up most of the capital in the concerns so floated.[1]

Factory industry grew phenomenally from the 1880s onwards; so did the joint-stock companies. Initially, the capital was predominantly British. Even in 1949, nearly a half of India's total capital investment (Rs. 596 crores) was foreign; until this century, the proportion of Indian capital was relatively insignificant. In 1911,

a group of 15 Managing Agents controlled and managed 189 industrial units . . ., 93 of which were controlled and managed by the 'Big Five' Managing Agency Houses of Calcutta, viz. Messrs. Andrew Yule, Bird, Shaw Wallace, Duncan and Begg, Dunlop and Company, all of which were foreign owned and operated. With the exceptions of Tatas, there was no Indian Managing house which controlled or managed more than five industrial units.[2]

But from that time onwards, especially after the large-scale repatriation of British capital in the 1930s due to the depression and to political instability, the number of Indian directors grew rapidly, particularly in cotton textiles (Gujaratis and Marwaris), in steel (Parsis – the Tata family) and in sugar (Marwaris and Punjabis).

The pattern of Indian capitalism, then, was peculiarly centralized and rationalized from the beginning: the emergence of a small number of big enterprises operating in various industrial fields and closely linked with finance-capital was not the end-

1. B. B. Misra, *The Indian Middle Classes*, Oxford University Press, 1961, p. 229

2. ibid., p. 249. I draw heavily on his chapter on 'Economic development' here.

product of a long period of *laissez-faire* competition between small firms. Indian capitalism began quite differently:

> Historically, the expansion of business in India had proceeded from the top downwards, not from the bottom upwards. An Indian plutocracy had even earlier formed a separate caste by itself, and those who carried on business under them did so as their servile agents, not as free merchants. A managing agency firm, Indian or European, similarly held the bulk interest in the several industrial units whose administration it controlled by a system of multiple directorships. Capital remained concentrated under both. Indeed the directors of Indian industries were ... members of the upper rather than the middle classes; for the industrial power of the country was in the hands of a few persons only ... about 100 persons held as many as 1700 directorships of important concerns; 860 of these were held by thirty persons, and only ten of those thirty held between them as many as 400 directorships.[3]

We will consider the wider significance of modernization, economic and political, 'from the top downwards', later. It has left those societies which have achieved independence without military and political revolution, and without radical change in the ownership of land and industry, with a very distinctive legacy in terms of popular predisposition to leave social initiatives to government and to external forces which they commonly see as something alien and external to their village world. To energize such populations, and to transform society without initiating disruptive social revolution, is the problem that non-revolutionary governments are continuously faced with.

Indian capitalism was able to develop quite rapidly as a 'compradore' junior partner of British business. It ran into major opposition, however, when it began to challenge British industry directly. Under free trade, the battle went to the strongest – British industry. For many decades, too, the new Indian capitalist class had to fight restrictive policies imposed by the British government which hindered the free development of Indian-owned industry. Indian capitalists fought unavailingly for years for government assistance in fostering indigenous industry. Only during the two World Wars did they get it. For these reasons, Indian capitalism came into conflict with the alien Government. India's most famous capitalist enterprise, the Tata steel firm, has

3. ibid., pp. 251–2.

long been a major source of strength to Congress (and today a Tata combines his direction of the great private empire with responsibility for the State-owned India Airways). Indigenous capital thus divested itself of its original compradore associations. After Independence, it was able to build a new image of itself as a major *Indian* contributor to national development and prosperity in an economy still half controlled by foreigners.

In consequence, class opposition to Indian capitalism could be fairly easily muted or deflected by skilful appeals to national solidarity. Indonesian capitalists, likewise, could always draw a distinction between 'sinful'[4] foreign capitalism and their own contributions to national growth and stability. Class divisions could therefore be relatively easily overcome by the nationalist movement. For this reason, much Marxist analysis of political alignments in backward countries has been wide of the mark. Unity in the face of imperialism has, for the most part, over-ridden class hostilities; national independence taken priority over class struggle; for the nation as a whole, not merely its workers and peasants, has suffered – admittedly in different degrees and in different ways – from alien rule.

Similar antagonistic relationships between indigenous capital and foreign capital are visible in countries with much less-developed colonial economies. In Nigeria, for example, the United Africa Company dominated the economy.

By the late 1930s it controlled more than 40 per cent of Nigeria's import–export trade, and as late as 1949 it handled 34 per cent of commercial merchandise imports into Nigeria and purchased, on behalf of Nigerian marketing boards, 43 per cent of all Nigerian non-mineral exports.[5]

In association with five other firms, the U.A.C. formed the Association of West African Merchants which by 1949 handled about 66 per cent of Nigeria's imports and nearly 70 per cent of her exports.

4. G. McT. Kahin, *Nationalism and Revolution in Indonesia*, Oxford University Press, 1952, p. 73.

5. James S. Coleman, *Nigeria: Background to Nationalism*, University of California Press, 1958, p. 80, citing P. T. Bauer's *West African Trade*, Routledge, 1954.

Foreign domination on this scale was bound to produce conflicts in a society where indigenous trading was highly developed and had been for many centuries. During the inter-war period, it is estimated, no less than 100,000 people were engaged as middlemen in the marketing of major Nigerian exports.[6] The average net income of these traders was very high indeed for an 'underdeveloped' economy: £650 p.a.[7]

The economies of countries like these, then, were far from being pure subsistence economies. And increasingly, the national and international money economy made increasing inroads: by 1950, 79 per cent of the adult male population of Ghana was involved in the money economy; in Nigeria, 43 per cent; even in Kenya, 30 per cent were involved.[8]

The great bulk of these 'traders', however, were 'micro-traders': the 100,000 little men who clipped a few shillings off the handling of minute amounts of palm-oil; the tens of thousands of market women who made pennies or fractions of pennies out of selling relish, matches, fish, mirrors or kerosene in the markets. It is ridiculous to label them and wealthy giants like the United Africa Company as 'capitalist entrepreneurs'. Among the hundreds of thousands of African traders, there are indeed a few rich men; there are even more men of moderate wealth. Of the 8000 traders operating in Kumasi, Ghana, for example, 150 had a turnover of £500–£2000 a year, and a few of these as much as £100,000.[9] But the term 'bourgeois' – or even 'petty bourgeois' – can scarcely be used to describe the mass of petty traders and hucksters, such as those who form the bulk of the West African market trade. In Koforidua 3000 sellers – some 70 per cent of the female African population – participated in the market trade.[10]

6. ibid., p. 83.
7. Martin L. Kilson, Jr, 'The rise of nationalist organizations and parties in British West Africa', in John A. Davis (ed.), *Africa as Seen by American Negroes*, Paris, 1958, p. 55.
8. Guy Hunter, *The New Societies of Tropical Africa*, Oxford University Press, 1962, chs. 4–6.
9. ibid., p. 135, citing Peter Garlick's *African Traders in Kumasi*, Accra, 1959.
10. D. McCall, 'Trade and the role of wife in a modern West African town', in A. W. Southall (ed.), *Social Change in Modern Africa*, Oxford University Press, 1961.

Numerically, the great majority of these market traders will be small and poor, making a few shillings, sometimes a few pence in the day, pin money for women, a little cash from surplus vegetables or a handicraft. Their skill is in selling, in carrying in their head figures of pennies and halfpennies, in finding a bargain from each other and selling to a stranger. Few of them depend on trade alone. . . .[11]

This last characteristic is of great importance in understanding the readiness of these 'micro'-traders to support mass nationalist movements, for they are very commonly occupationally indeterminate, 'floating' between self-employment, employment of others and sale of their own labour-power. They do not constitute a distinctive and consolidated social class. The petty market-traders, and notably the women who, in accordance with traditional West African culture, predominate in this sector of the economy, were one of the principal groupings which assisted Nkrumah in his rise to power. The market-women of Lagos, too, were

. . . the main mass base of Nigeria's oldest political organization, the Nigerian National Democratic Party. . . . The market women were constituents whom any urban politician or nationalist leader would ignore at his peril.[12]

Nationalism in countries like Nigeria and the Gold Coast, therefore, though developed largely, originally, under the leadership of the small indigenous bourgeoisie proper, was also able to mobilize the numerically important micro-traders in common opposition to the big foreign interests. Its ideology, therefore, was much more populist than it was bourgeois. In a few territories, such as the Ivory Coast, relatively prosperous and differentiated, the prosperous farmer was dominant in the leadership. Its characteristic spokesman was Houphouët-Boigny. But though the son of a wealthy planter, and a chief and large planter himself, he led the great mass party of French West Africa, the Rassemblement Démocratique Africaine, into alliance with the French Communist Party – and into the 1949 violence at Dimboko, where thirteen people were killed and thirty-eight

11. Hunter, op. cit., p. 133.
12. Coleman, op. cit., p. 86.

wounded.[13] But the attraction of the Communist Party was its militancy, not its communism. The more bourgeoisified *élites*, once they have gained political control, quickly lose their radicalism, especially in the more prosperous territories. There is a great gulf between the socialist theory even of a Senghor and Dia and their social practice. After his flirtation with the P.C.F., Houphouët-Boigny settled down to a more congenial role as a pillar of the French Establishment. Before long, he was Minister in the Cabinet that planned Suez.

A fully developed *laissez-faire* ideology could scarcely flourish in the regulated world of the colonies. Something very close to it is reproduced in this passage from Awolowo, where Anglo-Saxon 'common sense', Puritan homilectic, Smiles-ian self-help and plain petty-bourgeoisdom find a congenial lodgment in the breast of a self-made Nigerian politician:

I read as widely as possible . . . Shakespeare, Dickens, R. L. Stevenson, Emerson, Lord Avebury, Sir Walter Scott, Hazlitt, Elbert Hubbard . . . But there were two books which helped me to evoke a philosophy of life to which, with some modifications which my experiences dictate, I still cling. The first book was *The Human Machine*, which was a free gift to anyone who took a correspondence course with Bennett College, Sheffield. The book was a collection of terse, powerful articles, loaded with the practical and well-tested doctrines of applied psychology . . . previously published . . . in . . . *John Bull*. The second book was written . . . by an American author, and its title was *It's Up to You*. The philosophy of the latter book is very simple, but also very true and fundamental. I will state it in a nutshell. . . . Take a jar, put in it small beans as well as big beans, making sure that each of the big beans is heavier in weight than each of the small beans; put the big beans at the bottom of the jar and the small beans at the top; shake the jar, and Behold! the small beans rattle to the bottom and the big beans shake to the top. . . . Now the world is like a mighty jar, and all of us are in it . . . like beans with varying sizes and weights. In normal circumstances, each of us is where he is because of his size and weight. By means of favouritism, or of some other deliberate and iniquitous tinkering with the contents of the jar, some beans which are small . . . may get to the top . . . but they are sure to rattle to the bottom sooner or later. Said the author in words which I vividly remember: 'Nobody

13. Virginia Thompson and Richard Adloff, *French West Africa*, Oxford University Press, 1958, pp. 123–31.

can fool the jar of life.' The *sine qua non* for anyone who wants to get to the top, therefore, is to increase his size and weight in his particular calling – that is mentally, professionally, morally, and spiritually. Getting to the top is one thing and remaining there is another. To maintain your place at the top you must make sure that you do not at any time shrink or lose in weight. . . . I am a firm believer in this philosophy.[14]

Here, Victorian drive is admixed with the American 'frontier' ethic of expansion and opportunity, plus lingering traces of the great Protestant Ethic, spiritually thinned down, as Weber has shown,[15] via the American sects, and finally secularized in the Rotary clubs and masonic lodges of the Mid-West,[16] and the whole infused with Nigerian business acumen.

But a bourgeoisie in close contact with thousands of micro-traders, face-to-face with the British Empire and the United Africa Company, could not be satisfied with a nineteenth-century ethic. Even in Europe, the 'small man' driven to the wall has turned to collective radicalism – even to the Nazis or Poujade. A purely bourgeois party could not hope to succeed, for whatever the numbers involved in the cash-economy, the mass of the people were only marginal producers of cash crops. The rest were subsistence producers. The really capitalized sector of the economy was controlled by foreigners. Even not-so-big business was commonly controlled by 'ethnic' trading 'castes': the Indians in East Africa, the 'Syrians' in West Africa, the Chinese in South-East Asia, Greeks and Armenians in the Middle East. These alien ethnic groupings were oriented, not to the internal and local markets, but to import–export trading. They established themselves in the seaports predominantly, and were usually in close 'compradore' dependence upon the overall colonial economic strategy.

They could be quite numerous and influential, but they could not easily form close ties with other, indigenous middle-class

14. Chief Obafemi Awolowo, *Awo: The Autobiography of Chief Obafemi Awolowo*, Cambridge University Press, 1960, pp. 69–70.

15. 'The protestant sects and the spirit of capitalism', in H. H. Gerth and C. W. Mills (eds.), *From Max Weber: Essays in Sociology*, Routledge, 1948, pp. 302–22.

16. See Robert S. Lynd and Helen Merrell Lynd, *Middletown: A Study in American Culture*, Constable, 1929, Sections 4–6, *passim*.

elements. In a society such as Egypt, for example, long involved in international trade, the 'middle classes' – described by Berger as composed of merchants, clerks, professionals, businessmen and agents, plus the 134,500 members of the 'agricultural' middle class (about 5 per cent of all landowners) – amounted to some 6–10 per cent of the gainfully occupied population in 1947 – around half a million people.[17] He goes on to point out, however, that these people did not constitute a very distinct *employing* class. Most of the smaller landowners, indeed, were self-employed or even employed. They might well be ranked on a wealth or status scale as 'middle class', but they are hardly a distinct class of small capitalists. Indeed, this 'middle-class' rag-bag includes a number of occupational groupings, like clerks and professionals, whose economic interests, whether in terms of ownership, job-situation, market-situation or work-situation,[18] or in terms of status, educational level, style of life, etc., were not at all similar. Sharply-marked-off bourgeois or petty-bourgeois classes, with their appropriate political organs, were unlikely to emerge among ambiguous, fragmented and ethnically divided middle strata of this kind. Not only do they lack definition and corporate identity as a class, but, for many of them, their alien ethnic status makes it dangerous to draw attention to themselves corporately and politically: they would invite attack as foreigners. Foreign-ness thus disqualifies these active and powerful elements from giving the leadership that an effective 'national bourgeoisie' might have provided.

The pattern of 'ethnic' monopolization of business opportunities where 'economic class becomes coterminous with ethnic group',[19] means that the educated indigenous population has to find alternative outlets for the exercise of its talents and for the satisfaction of its desires for wealth, power and status.

In the more backward countries, where business was poorly developed, the only other openings normally available to the ambitious and the capable were in the public service. In many

17. Morroe Berger, 'The middle class in the Arab world', in Walter Z. Laqueur (ed.), *The Middle East in Transition*, London, 1958, pp. 61–71.

18. See David Lockwood, *The Black-Coated Worker*, Allen and Unwin, 1958, Conclusion.

19. Fatma Mansur, *The Process of Independence*, Routledge, 1962, p. 13.

colonies, too, teaching, medicine, social work, were largely government jobs, not 'free professions'. But even in more advanced colonies, government service was the main avenue of upward mobility. In Indonesia, for example, the Chinese trading-class, early entrenched in the traditional trade between China and Indonesia, became under the Dutch régime of the 'Company System' and its successors, the hated operators of a government-controlled system of forced deliveries, forced labour and monopolies. The earliest Indonesian nationalist movement therefore developed out of the struggle of Javanese entrepreneurs to break the Dutch–Chinese stranglehold on business, with the formation in 1911 of the trading-association, *Sarekat Dagang Islam* (The Islamic Trading Society), an organization which then gave rise to a political movement, *Sarekat Islam*, in the following year.

By 1919 it had completely changed its character. It had turned into a mass movement with two and a half million members. In the following year, the Indonesian Communist Party was formed. Middle-class traders were clearly unsuitable leaders for dynamic mass movements of this kind. Instead, the leadership came increasingly from a new and more militant social stratum – the Western-educated government officials. *Sarekat Islam*, typically, had been founded by a merchant, Tjokroaminoto; the young man who stepped into his shoes, and who built the new movement into a mass organization, was a young engineer called Soekarno.[20] He was able to draw on vast reserves of talent, resentment and enthusiasm amongst young, Western-educated Indonesians barred from business by Dutch and Chinese monopolization.

They flooded into government service. By 1918 they occupied 98·9 per cent of the lowest positions – but only 6·4 per cent of the highest. Europeans, on the other hand, occupied 92·2 per cent of the highest, and only 0·6 per cent of the lowest.[21] Bitterness at this blatant discrimination, reinforced by a deliberate system of dual rates of pay for the same job (as in Kenya and many other colonies), was exacerbated by long periods of high 'graduate unemployment' when as many as 25 per cent of them might be

20. Kahin, op. cit., pp. 27–8, 65–75.

21. W. F. Wertheim, *Indonesian Society in Transition*, The Hague, 1959, p. 149.

unable to fill their stomachs with rice despite their Western education. Inevitably, then, they rapidly became consciously and militantly nationalistic.

It was a similar story elsewhere; and improvements were slow:

In 1946 in India the proportion of Indians to British in the senior ranks was 504 to 623, and in Ghana the same year, 36 to 171. In Nigeria in 1949 there were 245 Nigerians to 2541 British. In French West Africa, Frenchmen held the 5000 senior posts. The remaining 37,000 posts were filled by Africans, a comparatively high figure. In Indonesia, also in 1940, Indonesians held 7 per cent of the higher positions.[22]

In the least-developed colonies, the 'new men' in the public service became particularly important as leaders of nationalism.

Their relationship to other segments of the middle classes emerges from this description of Leopoldville on the eve of the explosion in the Congo:

Normally the contradictory interests of a bourgeoisie and the wage-earning mass of [sic] which it depends finds one of its manifestations in the articulation of a self-consciousness, a *morale*; what we find in the Congo, and more especially in Leopoldville, is that a bourgeois psychology and consciousness is viable not so much among the shop-keepers and taxi-drivers as among the relatively educated neo-bourgeoisie which acted as subaltern intellectuals and administrators of colonialism. Traders and artisans of course do not constitute a bourgeoisie in the strict sense but are dependent on the creation by a European middle-class of a large, consumer proletariat; naturally, there was opposition created by their speculation at the expense of the wage-earner's consuming power, just as they resented the development of a relatively skilled worker *élite* whose incomes were in many cases equal to their own and more stable. It was in the educationally-privileged, white-collar staffs ... that a self-consciousness ... first ... appeared ... Lumumba was first politically active in the African Staff Association at Stanleyville. Black Trade Union organization commenced not with proletarians and depressed craftsmen, but with these professional associations of fonctionnaires. ... The conclusion remains that it is highly misleading to talk of social classes; at best, we can discern tendencies towards the creation of such groups, whose consolidation would depend on the relative stage of capital development. There can

22. Mansur, op. cit., p. 12.

be no proletarian as long as family and ethnic ties hold him psychologically and to some extent economically ... from total dependence on the sale of his own labour-force; there can be no African middle-class as long as Europeans monopolize properly bourgeois economic functions, and as long as the two discrete elements of the 'economic' and 'intellectual' Congolese neo-bourgeoisie do not harmonize into a self-conscious class with special interests, and as long as they remain responsive to traditional allegiances.[23]

The uneasy shift from 'bourgeoisie' to 'neo-bourgeoisie' indicates the ambiguity of this category, here used with an imprecision usually reserved for the term 'petty bourgeoisie', one of the spongiest catchalls in the Marxist vocabulary. Clerks, shopkeepers, taxi-drivers, sanitary inspectors, all sorts of strange bedfellows are caught within the net. And yet these 'intermediate strata' ('middle' classes) *are* indeterminate congeries of occupations which defy precise schematization. What the passage does indicate well is the importance of the Western-educated civil servants in the emerging nationalist *élite* leadership, and the comparative weakness both of the specifically *entrepreneurial* 'petty bourgeoisie' and of the 'working-class'.

The role of the Western-educated Civil Servant was even more crucial in the nationalist movements of French West Africa. Half the Grand Councillors in 1952, and 160 of the 227 deputies elected to Territorial Assemblies in that year, were civil servants (generally minor ones). On the occasion of the historic Conference of the R.D.A. held at Bamako from the 25th to the 30th September, 1957, 60 per cent of the delegates were in public service: out of 254 delegates, eighty-three were administrators, forty-four teachers and thirty-five health workers.[24]

As a result of the Lamine Guèye law, these were relatively privileged people. They were to continue to maintain this privileged status when independence had been attained. The new *élite* was often drawn from the traditional upper strata or the new wealthy. Traditional prestige was important: even on the Left, a

23. Aristide R. Zolberg, *Congo: Prelude to Independence*, London, 1960, pp. 29–30.

24. André Blanchet, *L'Itinéraire des Partis Africains Depuis Bamako*, Paris, 1958, p. 23. Blanchet also notes that sixty-one of the seventy members of the Ivory Coast Territorial Assembly, and forty out of the sixty members in Niger, were civil servants (p. 22).

Sékou Touré, despite his mass base in the trade unions and his Marxist proclivities, claimed descent from Almamy Samory, hero of resistance to French conquest in the nineteenth century. Traditional wealth and high status themselves opened new opportunities for Western education: the new *élite* was thus doubly imbued with a consciousness of the gulf between it and the ordinary people. The biographies of African leaders in former French West Africa reveals the importance, indeed, of a single school, the William Ponty school at Dakar, as a breeding-ground of the new *élite*.[25] French official policy, indeed, had encouraged sons of rulers and other upper-class individuals to acquire Western education from as early as 1856, when the quaintly named Écoles des Otages were set up.[26]

As a result, political leadership normally came from people accustomed to high status in their communities. But even if they could claim no traditional prestige, their new status as educated men gave them prestige enough. Even on the Left, the leadership was drawn from the ranks of this new intelligentsia. In Asia, Burma's entire postwar history has been shaped by Western-educated men like Aung San and Ko Nu, respectively Secretary and President of the Rangoon University Students' Union in 1935, the former a 'moderately prosperous' landowner's son, the latter son of a merchant.[27] And the theoretical notions developed during the struggle for independence were to bear the marks of their formulation by this kind of *élite*. In the case of India, Clemens Dutt had had to write to P. C. Joshi in 1928: 'I hope that you are finding it possible to draw in actual proletarian workers in to the W.P.P.' [Workers' and Peasants' Party: an open, legal mass organization in place of the then-banned Communist Party]. The situation had hardly improved by 1934: Soviet politico-Indologists were only able to produce, as evidence of the increasingly 'successful' Communist challenge to Congress, a rise in Party membership from around twenty to 150 during a whole year.[28] Even by 1945, when the membership had reached some 25,000,

25. See Ronald Segal (ed.), *Political Africa*, Stevens, 1961, *passim*.

26. Mansur, op. cit., p. 32.

27. Saul Rose, *Socialism in Southern Asia*, London, 1959, p. 96.

28. Gene D. Overstreet and Marshall Windmiller, *Communism in India*, University of California, 1959, pp. 129, 155.

eighty-six of the 139 delegates to the First Party Congress were intellectuals, as against twenty-two workers and twenty-five peasants; the high proportion of intellectuals was even more accentuated among the full-time leadership. The Indian Socialist Party, too, was overwhelmingly middle class.[29] Even in would-be mass Left parties, then, the leadership was overwhelmingly a leadership of intellectuals.

But in the less-developed societies, the intellectuals, despite their (normally brief) Western education, remained in close contact with the ordinary people. Increasingly, too, the sons of ordinary peasants found their way into the schools. A French sociologist who knew Patrice Lumumba well has described his return to his home village in Kasai after an absence of ten years (before Lumumba had become a major political figure):

> As we got nearer our destination, we had to stop more and more often. Relatives and friends from every direction and of all ages ... came to greet him delightedly. They snapped their fingers, smacked their thighs, ran their hands along the hero's forearm. Exclamations, congratulations, and laughter. Babies were brought for admiration, children had grown into adolescents, adolescents had become adults. ...
>
> Finally we arrived. The local boy returned was greeted in triumph. The whole village was there, his family, the chief, village notables, and the small fry. The old historian-genealogist is present, too. ... The news spreads like wildfire. It is carried hurriedly to neighbouring villages. Emotion is at its height, joy everywhere. ...
>
> For more than a month, I saw my friend living in his childhood surroundings. He had a word for everybody, he asked about everybody and everything; he was invited everywhere. He was a 'monsieur' now. ...[30]

Political leaders of this kind enjoy a special intimacy which is not lost despite their new status as 'messieurs', in which, rather, the villagers find vicarious satisfaction. For despite the efforts of colonists to build an African *élite* which would be European in outlook, kinship still tied the *élite* to the ordinary people, and the colour-bar constantly threw him back into the arms of his less-educated and privileged fellows.

29. Rose, op. cit., p. 39.
30. Pierre Clement, 'Patrice Lumumba (Stanleyville, 1952–1953)', *Présence Africaine*, vol. 40 (1962), pp. 69–70.

The new politicians therefore share many of the attitudes of the ordinary villager – or at least, understand their needs and likely reactions intimately. Patrice Lumumba, at the time of the visit described above, had only just begun to engage in public life. Even in a book written several years later, in 1956–7, he was still the young intellectual in transition, struggling to develop a political theory which would connect with the needs of the people of his country, but as yet quite unable to step beyond the intellectual limits of Belgian paternalism.[31] His demands are the classic limited demands of the *évolué*. The first demands of this kind of *élite* invariably reflect their particular concerns with their own problems: demands for 'indigenization' of the higher ranks of the Civil Service; for equal pay where 'natives' and 'expatriates' do the same work; claims for citizens' rights for 'civilized' men; or for better and wider educational facilities. As Lord Hailey accurately remarked of Nigeria in 1937:

Local politics ... has not proceeded beyond the ideals of early Victorian radicalism; its ambition is a larger representation in the legislature, and a greater share in Government employ; it seems to make little appeal to the uneducated or rural elements.[32]

Examination of the social background of the new *élite* abundantly confirms the predominance of the new intelligentsia, even in those countries where 'bourgeois' and 'petty bourgeois' strata are well developed. In the Indian Parliament in 1952–7, for example, lawyers were the most numerous occupational group (21·6 per cent), then landowners (9·2 per cent), then businessmen (7·4 per cent).

In less-developed Nigeria, paradoxically, the picture at first appears to be different, for business is strongly represented. In the Western Region Legislature in 1956, 32 per cent of the Members belonging to the dominant party, the Action Group, were 'traders or businessmen', and in the Legislature of the Eastern Region, 31 per cent of the Members of the dominant party there, the National Council of Nigeria and the Cameroons, were so classified.[33]

31. Patrice Lumumba, *Congo, My Country*, London, 1962.
32. Cited in Coleman, op. cit., p. 201.
33. Coleman, op. cit., Table 24, pp. 382–3.

Yet the most recent authoritative study of the Nigerian *élite* is quite emphatic on the lack of cohesiveness and self-consciousness of the business *élite*. Indeed, they comment, 'As yet, there is only a nucleus of a business *élite* . . . the business *élite* of Nigeria in no sense . . . forms an economic " power *élite* ".' Nor do farming or organized labor constitute important organized interest-groups: they are 'under-represented' and 'weak'.[34]

'Business', then, despite its being strongly represented in the higher councils of the new nation, is not a self-conscious organized grouping displaying classic capitalist attitudes, as is more often the case in more developed economies. Mechanistic political science which relates ideology directly to one or two simple attributes of social groups, usually to self-interest as implied in class position, cannot adequately cope with the problem of analysing the complexity of historically conditioned attitudes such as those of the Nigerian business *élite* in politics.

In the colonial situation, foreign rule has cut across the sectional class interests of 'business'. Indigenous business, confronted with the entrenched power of large-scale foreign-owned commerce, becomes much more radical and nationalistic than the business class in developed economies. Because the business leadership is attached to a 'trading proletariat' of hundreds of thousands of 'micro-traders', it constitutes a mass force with radical tendencies. In those regions where entrenched 'feudal' rulers resist modernization, the radicalism of 'business' is even more marked. A classic instance is Northern Nigeria, where the programme of the Northern Elements Progressive Union is couched in a distinctly socialist idiom. This party finds its main support among the alien urban enclaves of traders and wage workers in the large Northern cities, and appeals also for the support of the *talakawa* peasantry. Other modernizing urban minority groups, such as the Action Group and the Bornu Youth Movement, have supported minor opposition parties on an ethnic basis.

In the Northern Region Legislature of 1956, however, 56 per cent of the Members of the N.E.P.U. and Bornu Youth Movement party-tickets, and 50 per cent of the Action Group Members, were

34. H. H. Smythe and M. M. Smythe, *The New Nigerian Élite*, Stanford University Press, 1960, pp. 83, 85.

'traders or businessmen'. 49 per cent of the reactionary Northern People's Congress, in contrast, were 'central officials', another 24 per cent 'district heads'. These were not the new bureaucrats we have been discussing, but pillars of the old-entrenched 'feudal' order, as the eduational data indicate more accurately: only 3 per cent of the N.P.C. Members were 'headmasters or principal teachers', as against 25 per cent of the United Middle Belt Congress Members, for instance. Here, the 'new men', the business interests and the urban masses come together: the result is a radical programme with a socialist tinge.

N.E.P.U. claims to speak in the name of 'the simple people of Nigeria: the teachers, the clerks, the petty traders, the farm peasants, the lorry drivers, the truck pushers, the women and the ex-servicemen, etc.' (The order of groups is instructive.) N.E.P.U. attacks N.P.C. feudalism as a corrupt and inefficient ruling class régime, founded on 'first and last defence of property and privilege and rear-guard action against equality', and entrenched over the years by the 'Family Compact', the 'undemocratic electoral college system, and the evil of 10 per cent nomination'. It deplores the low educational and health standards in the Region, and advocates agricultural development, reform of the judicial system and the allocation of more civil service posts and contracts to Northerners. The problem of the chiefs is to be handled by adopting the Indian method of dealing with Princes, Maharajahs and other potentates (a model also followed in Ghana) – what one might call the 'honorific tactic': plenty of honour, but little power. They are to be accorded, N.E.P.U. says, 'special and glorified status in the Local Government System', and guaranteed 'dignity and respect outside party politics'.[35]

N.E.P.U. thus advocates instalments of modernization which might seem elementary enough outside the North, but which is revolutionary in the Northern context, since it means the dismantling of feudal political control, the introduction of political democracy, modern social services and the modernization of the agricultural economy. The socialist flavour of their language reflects this militancy. For N.E.P.U., the political struggle is essentially a 'class struggle':

35. *N.E.P.U. 'Sawaba' Manifesto, and Manifesto of the Northern Elements Progressive Union for the 1959 Federal Elections, passim.*

... All political parties are but the expression of class interest, and as the interest of the 'Talakawa' [peasantry] is diametrically opposed to the interest of all sections of the master class, both white and black, the party seeking the emancipation of the 'Talakawa' must naturally be hostile to the party of the oppressors ... this emancipation must be the work of the 'Talakawa' themselves.

... The Machinery of Government, including the armed forces of the nation, exist only to conserve the privilege of this selfish minority group, the 'Talakawa' must organize consciously and politically for the conquest of the powers of the Government – both national and local, in order that this machinery of Government, including these forces, may be converted from an instrument of oppression into the agent of emancipation and the overthrow of Bureaucracy and autocratic privilege.[36]

To label N.E.P.U., then, as a 'petty-bourgeois' party, simply because of the predominance of traders and businessmen in its ranks is singularly unilluminating. The majority of political leaders in most societies, historically, have always been drawn from the upper strata of society: wealth and education equip those who possess them with the capacity to lead others, to inspire respect in their followers, to become familiar with affairs of state. The wealthy and the educated are therefore highly represented both on the Left and on the Right, whether in Europe or in Africa. But an analysis of the social background of M.P.s, which had only this observation to make, would not take us very far in understanding the complexity of historical forces producing the very *different* ideologies of British Labour and British Conservatism, French Gaullism and French Socialism, African Caesarism and African Populism.

Business in Nigeria is clearly markedly different from European 'Big Business', or even Indian 'Big Business'. Its programme is not markedly distinct from the programmes of other groupings, and the 'business *élite*' is able to subscribe to 'populist' values. It displays the classic 'progressive' attributes that Marx described for the bourgeoisies of Western Europe, which also had to fight their way into the sun against the entrenched power of the landed nobility. But where all-important external business and trade is run by aliens, the progressive capability of the indigenous

36. *Sawaba Declaration of Principles*, Kano, n.d.

bourgeoisie is frustrated: it is isolated from the mass nationalist movement, and usually concentrates on preserving its own skin.

Even in a relatively 'bourgeoisified' country like Nigeria, however, the business *élite* is overshadowed by the 'new men' in the political leaderships. In every Regional Legislature they are well outnumbered by civil servants, teachers and lawyers. This predominance of the Western-educated professionals and government officials is again borne out by Table 1:

Table 1

Occupations of Two Groups of *Élite* Nigerians [1]

Occupation	Study of 156 (1958)		Who's Who in Nigeria (1956 edition)	
	Number	%	Number	%
Professions	90	57·7	340	35·6
Government and Politics	28	18·0	374*	39·1
Business	19	12·2	113	11·8
Clerical and Technical	13	8·3	59	6·1
Farming	3	1·9	28	2·9
Skilled Labour	—	—	11	1·2
Miscellaneous	3	1·9	31	3·2
Total	156	100·0	956	100·0

* Includes 126 who listed occupations solely as 'legislator' and 18 as 'government minister', both of which categories were omitted from the other sample in favour of listings of permanent occupations. If these are omitted from the category of government and politics, the total for this group is 218 and the percentage 26·9.

1. Table and footnotes from Smythe and Smythe, op. cit., table 15, p. 81.

Hunter's recent study of selected African territories shows that this predominance of teachers, professionals and civil servants, with a smaller admixture of traders and businessmen, is not

Table 2

Previous Occupation of Members of Parliament in Selected African Countries [1]

	Teachers	Trader business-man	Lawyer	Civil servant (a)	Professions (b)	Farming Fishing	Village or local chief	Clerical and co-operative	Miscellaneous (c)
Nigeria									
Federal	98	44	23	87	20	8	1	15	5
East	34	17	5	9	13	4	1	1	2
West	43	34	14	7	6	4	—	6	7
North	26	16	—	76	3	2	7	—	2
Ghana	38	24	9	22	7	6	—	—	3
Kenya	19	4	2	5	3	4	—	—	4
Tanganyika	11	7	—	7	1	1	3	6	12
Uganda	21	6	5	8	2	—	—	6	4
Senegal	21	9	12	23	5	—	—	5	4
Mali	22	8	1	9	13	—	—	20	4
Republic of Congo	18	9	—	—	6	3	—	13	9
Total	351	178	71	253	79	32	12	72	56

Notes: (a) 'Civil Servant' includes staff of Native Authorities, but 'Scribe' is included under 'Clerical'.
(b) 'Professions' include medical, journalist, engineer, Church, veterinary.
(c) Miscellaneous includes craftsmen, foremen, a few Trade Unionists, a political organizer and some 'unknown'.

1. Table and footnotes from Hunter, op. cit, table 12, p. 285.

peculiar to Nigeria, but fairly typical of the new African *élites* (see Table 2).

This predominance of professionals, teachers and lawyers in the Legislatures of the new countries is, as we remarked earlier, not peculiar to these countries. It is markedly the case in Britain, for example, where 48·4 per cent of the Labour M.P.s in the 1945 House of Commons, and 61 per cent of the Conservatives, were in the liberal professions, managers or officers. The reasons for this high level of participation of such occupational groupings are obvious enough: such people are guaranteed

a great deal of in-group interaction in many activities and roles . . . which involve leadership skills and knowledge about large problems, are more politically aware, vote more, and have a greater commitment to such occupationally linked organizations as trade-unions.[37]

The lawyer, for example, possesses a network of social contacts, oratorical skills, technical knowledge, high social status and authority, plus ample leisure, opportunity and financial independence, which place him in a supremely favoured position as candidate for public office, a fact well known to university students from the emergent countries, who, for many years, have contributed far more than their due proportion to the Law Departments of British Universities and to the Inns of Court. In addition,

. . . occupations like . . . law and journalism . . . are dispensable in the sense that the practitioner is able to leave them for extended periods and enter politics without any loss of skill during his period of absence (perhaps the opposite is true in the case of the lawyer) and return to the practice of his profession without too great a financial loss or dislocation.[38]

The law, too, opens the gateway to business and administration.

In the more backward colonies and ex-colonies, such occupations have often been unavailable to the indigenous people; they have been monopolized by foreigners, especially where a

37. S. M. Lipset, *Agrarian Socialism*, Berkeley, 1950, p. 193.
38. ibid., p. 370.

direct colour-bar has operated. Thus the world well knows that on the eve of independence, the Congo had only a dozen graduates out of a population of $13\frac{1}{2}$ millions. Until his meteoric rise to fame, Lumumba had never been outside the Congo. In one typical backward country, Nyasaland, the expected yield of graduates from internal sources – from the Sixth Forms of that country's secondary schools – has been calculated thus:[39]

1966	4	1969	8
1967	5	1970	11
1968	6	1971	12

'The number of African Sixth Forms in the whole of Nyasaland, Northern and Southern Rhodesia, and the three East African territories put together did not reach ten in 1960.'[40]

As a result, Tanganyika, Uganda and Kenya will have to fill more than half the 4000 or more senior posts in those countries with expatriates for several years to come.[41]

The point at issue here, however, is not the number of trained leaders, but their social composition. The former occupations of some current leaders of nationalist movements are instructive: Tom Mboya was an assistant sanitary inspector; Patrice Lumumba a postal clerk; Kenneth Kaunda a teacher; Joshua Nkomo a social welfare worker.

Because of the under-developed nature of the economy, the African *élite*, therefore, was commonly in peculiarly close *rapport* with the ordinary people. This does not, of course, prevent their adopting styles of life which, in extreme cases, like that of Houphouët-Boigny, amount to the demagogic flaunting of Hollywood-style luxury in the faces of poor people who get vicarious satisfaction – for a time – from their leaders' opulence. The temptation is equally great for leaders from relatively humble backgrounds; for them, education and political power opened the world's oyster.

But the new *élite* can use this special closeness to the ordinary

39. Hunter, op. cit., p. 252.
40. ibid., p. 245.
41. ibid., p. 255.

people, the kind of affection we saw revealed on the occasion of Lumumba's home-coming, to build a peculiarly strong backing for themselves by deliberately maintaining a simple, rather than a glamorous style of life. Their relationship to the masses is thus a two-edged one, at once intimate and distant.

Conventional discussions of the quality of 'inspired' leadership known as 'charismatic' concentrate on the personal and 'superhuman' aspects of such leadership. To be sure, without magnetic appeal, the politician is unlikely to make a mass leader. But there are many competent spell-binders who never become mass leaders; they remain oddities at Hyde Park Corners, prophets without honour or leaders of microscopic sects. To become a mass 'charismatic' leader, the personal qualities of the leader must be yoked to a social policy which engages the hearts and minds of men because it answers all their needs. To *persist* as a mass leader more than ecstatic religious or emotional appeal is needed. The analysis of these aspirations, and of the way in which they are harnessed to a political or religious programme, is crucial: the social and 'this-worldly' aspects of leadership, as well as the personal and 'superhuman', are thus central to sociological analysis. Without such analysis, all we are doing, in speaking of 'charismatic' qualities, is drawing attention to personal magnetism.

'Charismatic' appeal, then, does not derive solely from some mysterious, inexplicable quality: it also depends upon the political rapport the leader has with his followers, and on his ability to enunciate policies which connect with popular needs. Bonds of attachment between leader and followers are not based upon 'superhuman' qualities alone; rather, they depend for their efficacy on close identification. In so far as he is a Westernized 'monsieur' and later the powerful figurehead of a mass movement, the leader is remote. To succeed, he must remain 'one of the people'. It is this peculiar combination of mass rapport and social distance that characterizes populist leadership: it cannot rely on tradition and the 'deference vote'.

Once in power, too, this kind of *élite* leader faces problems of a different kind from those which beset traditional rulers. He becomes further distanced from his people. His education, his history as a government official and then as a party organizer, predispose him to bureaucratic modes of thinking and acting. The perils of rule by such privileged bureaucratic castes, now in charge of whole societies, have already manifested themselves.[42]

42. Majhemout Diop, in his *Contribution à l'Etude des Problèmes Politiques en Afrique Noire*, Paris, 1958, uses a Soviet style of analysis in asserting the presence of *objective* class divisions in African societies, even if 'subjective' class consciousness has not yet developed. His picture of the composition of the 'petty bourgeoisie', however, is interesting, starting as it does with intellectuals, and students, and the liberal professions; going on to artisans, employees and small tradesmen; and concluding with semi- and 'lumpen'-proletarians! When he comes to the bourgeoisie proper, he points out that it is a peculiarly 'bureaucratized', and not a 'compradore' bourgeoisie, consisting as it does of 'some 200 ministers, directors and chefs de cabinets ... whose material and social situation, in relation to the rest of the population, is relatively the same as that of the "200 Families" in France'. What he is describing, in fact, is a 'new class', a privileged political *élite* – not a classic 'bourgeoisie' (p. 245).

Part Six
Inequality in Simpler Societies

First-hand studies of the so-called primitive communities have provided many new insights into the nature of human society. They have shown above all that the problem of social inequality has a universal scope. Social inequality, like many other features of social life, is often ordered in these societies by the kinship system. Sahlins provides a general survey of stratification in Polynesian society, which for him is based essentially on kinship. Leach gives a more detailed account of rank and class among the Kachins of highland Burma where also kinship plays an important part. Among other things, Leach brings out the many inconsistencies between ideas and practice, a point which reappears in some of the other sections and which is of fundamental importance for understanding the problem of social inequality.

11 M. D. Sahlins

Social Stratification in Kinship Societies

Excerpt from M. D. Sahlins, *Social Stratification in Polynesia*, University of Washington Press, 1958, pp. 1–9.

Various degrees of stratification can be distinguished among societies organized by kinship. There are some showing marked status distinctions, some in which equality characterizes most social relations and a large range of intermediate types. A graduated series of different degrees of stratification could be determined for primitive societies. If the series were to be correlated with quantitative measures of significant ecological conditions, some general propositions relating these cultural phenomena might be stated. In this study we explore the possibility by consideration of adaptive variations in Polynesian stratification. The initial plan is to order Polynesian societies on a stratification gradient, and then to correlate the gradient with techno-environmental differences, especially productivity differences. In this chapter we attempt to obtain criteria for placing Polynesian societies on a stratification gradient.

What is egalitarianism and what is stratification? Theoretically, an egalitarian society would be one in which every individual is of equal status, a society in which no one outranks anyone. But even the most primitive societies could not be described as egalitarian in this sense. There are differences in status carrying differential privilege in every human organization.

Although differences in status are regular features of human organization, the qualifications for status are not everywhere the same. In certain societies, e.g. Australian aboriginal communities, the only qualifications for higher status are those which every society uses to some extent, namely, age, sex and personal characteristics. Aside from these qualifications, there may be no others.[1]

1. Other examples of societies of this type include pygmy groups scattered from the Philippines to the African Congo, the Sakai of Malaya, the Indians

A society in which the only principles of rank allocation are these universals can be designated 'egalitarian', first, because this society is at the stratification minimum of organized human societies; second, because, given these qualifications, every individual has an equal chance to succeed to whatever statuses may [be] open. But a society unlike this, that is, one in which statuses are fixed by a mechanism beyond the universals, e.g. inheritance, can be called 'stratified'.

Societies vary in the degree to which they are stratified. One society may be considered more stratified than another if it has more status classes, restricted by principles other than the universals, or if high rank bestows greater prerogatives in economic, social, political and ceremonial activities. Criteria for estimating stratification in a kin society are thus divisible into 'structural', the degree of status differentiation, and 'functional', the degree to which rank confers privilege.

In many primitive societies every person has a different rank; the hierarchy is graduated by very small steps from lowest to highest. However, in discussing the structure of the ranking system, it is best to deal with broad groups or categories of status, as these provide simple descriptive generalizations. Frequently the natives themselves categorize levels of status, and this may be an aid in determining the structural criterion of degree of stratification. Such groups of statuses might be and have been called 'social classes'. However, in contrast to the social classes of market-dominated societies, status differences in kinship societies do not, as a rule, depend on differences in private wealth. Status inequalities in primitive societies are not accompanied by entrepreneurial enterprise, and the complete separation of producers from the factors of production. Social relations of mastery and subordination are here not correlates of economic relations of owner and laborer. Modern sociological defini-

---

of the Great Basin region of North America, the Ona, Yahgan and other South American marginal peoples, and the Bushmen of South Africa. With minor modifications, slightly more advanced groups, even lower horticulturalists and pastoralists, could be included, such as Indians of the American Northeast, the Hottentots and many New Guinea peoples. See also Gunnar Landtman, *The Origin of the Inequality of the Social Classes*, Chicago, 1938, ch. 1.

tions of class which stress occupational standing, class antagonisms, differences of interest and the like are not applicable to societies of the primitive order. To maintain a distinction, therefore, between what are really different phenomena, categories of rank in kin societies will be designated 'status levels'; the term 'social classes' will be reserved for the social strata of market-dominated societies.

Functional criteria of stratification can be divided into three broad categories: economic, sociopolitical and ceremonial. The extent to which high rank is associated with control and privilege in production, distribution and consumption is subsumed by the economic criterion. The sociopolitical criterion considers the powers bestowed by rank in the regulation of interpersonal affairs, such as the authority to apply sanctions to wrongdoers. Ceremonial inequality would be manifest in differential access to the supernatural and in distinctive ritual behavior.

The functional aspects of stratification are inter-related. To a certain extent, the relationship is mutual and reciprocal. However, in many primitive societies, power, privilege and prestige appear to be generated primarily in the processes of goods distribution. Thus Thurnwald sees the distributive functions of primitive chiefs as the genesis of centralized political authority.[2] Almost universally, the chief is the center of the tribal economy, concentrating goods made available by the various households and reallocating them for community activities. Malinowski writes: 'I think that throughout the world we would find that the relations between economics and politics are of the same type. The chief, everywhere, acts as a tribal banker, collecting food, storing it, and protecting it, and then using it for the benefit of the whole community.'[3] The attribution of prestige and power to chiefly generosity seems equally widespread. The essentials of the following statement, which refers particularly to the Trobriand Islanders, could be duplicated from all over the primitive world: 'A man who owns a thing is naturally expected to share it, to distribute it, to be its trustee and dispenser. And the higher the

2. Richard Thurnwald, *Economics in Primitive Communities*, Oxford, 1932, pp. 107, 180–81.
3. Bronislaw Malinowski, 'Anthropology as the basis of social science', in R. B. Cattell *et al.*, *Human Affairs*, London, 1937, pp. 232–3.

rank the greater the obligation. . . . Thus the main symptom of being powerful is to be wealthy, and of wealth is to be generous.'[4]

The chief's role as central distributive agent not only gives him the prestige by which he might extend his influence to other activities, it naturally demands that his powers be spread into other aspects of the economy and society. If there is separation on the basis of status between producers and regulators of general distribution, certain consequences would follow regarding the separation of such statuses in many other operations. First, there would be a tendency for the regulator of distribution to exert some authority over production itself – especially over productive activities which necessitate subsidization, such as communal labor or specialist labor. A degree of control of production implies a degree of control over the utilization of resources, or, in other words, some pre-eminent property rights. In turn, regulation of these economic processes necessitates the exercise of authority in interpersonal affairs; differences in social power emerge. Finally, all these differentials would probably be validated in ideology and ceremony. Sacredness and ritual superiority become attributes of high rank.

Ethnographic descriptions of Polynesian cultures clearly exemplify the posited relationship between the functional aspects of stratification.[5] There was specialization in the administration of distribution. Surplus production, i.e. food and other material goods not used by the producers, was periodically accumulated by certain members of the community and then periodically redistributed by them in support of communal and craft labor, religious ceremonies and the like. The distinction between producers and distributors corresponds precisely to that between nonchiefs and chiefs. The latter were focal points for the collection and redistribution of goods – a process Polanyi labels, 'the redistributive form of economic integration'.[6] As dispensers of food and other goods, and in reward of their logistic support of

4. Bronislaw Malinowski, *Argonauts of the Western Pacific*, London, 1922, p. 97.

5. Annotated documentation on particular Polynesian societies may be found in the following chapters [of Sahlins's book].

6. Karl Polanyi, *The Great Transformation*, New York, 1944; see also Karl Polanyi, 'Semantics of general economic history', mimeographed, rev. edn, 1953.

community enterprise, chiefs gained in prestige and extended their political and ceremonial prerogatives.

When it is recognized that the aspects of stratification are thus related, the hypothesis connecting stratification and productivity differences can be stated more explicitly than before. Degree of stratification is directly related to the surplus output of food producers. The greater the technological efficiency and surplus production, the greater will be the frequency and scope of distribution. Complexity of distribution will also be greater, for example, distribution to more kinds of specialists. Increase in scope, frequency and complexity of distribution implies increasing status differentiation between distributor and producer. This differentiation will be manifest in other economic processes besides distribution, and in sociopolitical and ceremonial life. Therefore the hypothesis: other factors being constant, the degree of social stratification varies directly with productivity. It should be noted that other factors are rarely constant in culture. Although this does not necessarily affect the validity of the general statement, it may affect its applicability to specific cases. Comparisons within a group of historically related cultures, such as those in Polynesia, are therefore apt to be statistically more significant than cross-cultural comparisons.

The ethnographic accounts of Polynesian cultures do not treat social ranking according to the criteria we have outlined in this chapter; hence, it is necessary to give a detailed explanation of the procedure to be used to assess the degree of stratification in particular cultures.

Two or three categories of social standing, status levels, can be distinguished in most Polynesian societies. One cannot necessarily rely on the native's distinctions of social grade, nor even the ethnographer's – although both of these may provide valuable clues. Rather, an attempt is made to place all those who exercise comparable prerogatives on a comparable social level. For example, while an ethnographer might place a paramount chief in a class by himself, it is unnecessary from our point of view to segregate him from other chiefs relative to whom he is merely *primus inter pares*. In many societies considered, a scheme of social standing based on seniority of descent from a common ancestor pervades the entire group, so that every person has a different rank. The gradation between adjacent status levels is so subtle that both native and ethnographer have difficulty in determining where one category of rank leaves off and another begins.[7] Here the concept of status levels will be used to refer to extremes or to averages of social standing. As stated above, a society with a greater number of status levels than another can be considered more stratified. By definition, it must contain a more complex system of differential roles and privileges. Of course, where a group defined by egalitarian principles of status allocation, such as the elders of a community, has greater influence than hereditary high rank, a strong element of egalitarianism may be said to prevail.

The powers of those of high rank to determine the utilization of strategic resources must be considered.[8] The common form of Polynesian tenure may be termed 'stewardship'.[9] Plots of land, irrigation canals and areas of ocean are usually corporate estates of groups of people, but title is particularly associated with the group head. All members of the group have customary rights of use; however, the head has the prerogatives of administering utilization, which he does in the best interests of the group as a whole. In a few Polynesian societies, each small kin group composed of a few households is an independent proprietary unit, the kindred head being subordinate to no higher authority in his prerogatives of management. In the majority of islands, however, the right of the head of the small kin group to control use of a plot is subordinated to overriding claims of managership by persons of chiefly status. Thus chiefs may be stewards over a number of separate tracts, each having its own manager. This system can be designated 'overlapping stewardship' and, because of the differentiation by status involved, is considered a more stratified pattern than simple stewardship. One of the rights of stewardship is that of placing a tabu on the use of a resource area. Such tabus have the purpose of conserving the food supply

7. See chapter 8 [of Sahlins's book].

8. Hereafter, 'strategic' is used with reference to things directly useful for materially sustaining life.

9. This is Drucker's terminology. Phillip Drucker, 'Rank, wealth and kinship in North-West coast society', *American Anthropologist*, vol. 41 (1939), pp. 55–65.

against times of famine or for events requiring accumulation of large amounts of food. There are variations in the powers of different statuses to impose economic tabus and in the manner of enforcing them. A supernatural sanction usually accompanies a tabu, but breach of the prohibition in some societies brings secular punishment by persons of chiefly rank. The presence and absence of powers of dispossession, especially of lower ranking stewards by higher ones, should be noted. The existence of lands held in an undifferentiated or communal manner with free access to all members of the society may be considered an egalitarian trait.

Differences in supervision of production are implied by the stewardship pattern of tenure, especially by the tabuing powers of stewards. Control of production, however, sometimes takes more pronounced and direct forms in Polynesia. The planting arrangements of individual households may be supervised by members of high status levels. Inspections may be made and secular punishments imposed on those who neglect their fields. As compared to supervision by household heads, such arrangements may be considered indicative of greater stratification. Furthermore, persons of high rank may also control communal and craft production. They may be the only ones able to supply the food necessary to support such enterprises. The extent to which higher status confers the right to regulate communal and craft production is an indication of degree of stratification.

Another type of status differential associated with production is the segregation of chiefs from subsistence activities and their dependence upon the produce of other members of the society. A society in which the higher status members are divorced from production is taken to be more stratified than one where such is not the case.

As indicated above, Polynesian chiefs function as central agents in large-scale redistributions of food and other goods. All stewards, in fact, have this prerogative, but the higher the rank of the chief, the greater his distributive activities in terms of the amount of goods and people encompassed. The redistributive process provides the economic basis for the celebration of great religious ceremonies, including the rites of crisis in chief families, and for other community activities, such as warfare and communal labor. In many areas it also provides the mechanism for distributing food in famine periods. To engage in redistribution, chiefs must have call upon the goods produced in the households of the community. However, the sanctions behind this chiefly due vary. The degree to which chiefs use forceful confiscation or visit secular punishments on those who refuse to yield up goods is an index of stratification.

Throughout Polynesia rank confers differential prerogatives in the consumption of goods. A general feature is the reservation of choice foods for persons of high standing. The privilege to consume certain nonstrategic goods varies more widely from place to place. Some clothes, ornaments, mats and the like may have only élite circulation and serve as insignia of high rank. The elaboration of insignia of rank is a measure of stratification.

Passing now to sociopolitical aspects of status, account is taken of observers' general statements regarding the degree of 'arbitrariness', 'despotism', 'equality' and 'democracy' that characterize the social relations in particular islands. The vagueness and impressionistic nature of the terminology dictate that no great weight should be placed on such evidence. But sometimes valuable insights may be gained, especially if the impressions of a number of different observers of the same society show agreement. The actual power structure must be considered. How and from whom do important social decisions emanate? Where the low-standing persons are consulted on important matters, or where nonstratified status groups such as elders regulate sociopolitical affairs, the society is less stratified than one in which policies are laid down by the highest in rank.

The extent to which higher status allows physical force to be exercised with impunity in defense of one's rights is significant. Generally, collective kinship retaliation was the method of revenging injuries in Polynesia. Within this pattern, chiefs could usually muster the greatest body of supporters, and hence inflict the greatest damage, as well as evade punishment for injuries they committed against others. But variations in these prerogatives of upper status members occurred. The degree to which chiefs relied on supernatural sanctions to enforce orders and avenge injuries is an index of egalitarianism.

Important differences in stratification are revealed by tendencies toward intermarriage within the highest status level. In all

Polynesian societies, there was a preference, among chiefs, for intrastatus marriages, those which consolidate the economic, social and ceremonial prerogatives of high rank. In some societies this is rigidly enforced; close relatives are picked as mates, and marriage is not contracted with those of low rank. In other societies, intrachiefly marriage is merely a loose preference, often ignored.

The high position of certain members of Polynesian island communities is ceremonially indicated by the famous mana-tabu complex which surrounds them. Chiefs are direct descendants of divinity; consequently, they are imbued with certain sacred powers (mana). In many of the islands an elaborate system of tabus exists concerning touching these sacred persons, touching their possessions or otherwise violating their sanctity. Such tabus are extensions of a general phenomenon of ceremonial prestige surrounding the head of every family. The elaborateness of the tabu concerning members of high status levels is a measure of the mana they possess and hence may be used as a measure of stratification. Whether violations of these tabus are punished secularly or merely supernaturally is also significant.

Other ceremonial indications of stratification are customs of paying respect to chiefs, such as bowing and various forms of obeisance postures, and addressing or referring to persons of different rank and their possessions by unique sets of nouns and verbs. Sometimes high status is symbolized by exclusive participation in certain rituals, such as ceremonious kava drinking. Finally, the extent to which the life-crisis rites in high ranking families differ in kind and elaboration from those generally found in the society is an index of degree of stratification.

12 E. R. Leach

Concepts of Rank and Class among the Kachins of Highland Burma

Excerpt from E. R. Leach, *Political Systems of Highland Burma: A Study of Kachin Social Structure*, Bell, 1964, pp. 159–72.

What makes the Kachins particularly interesting from an anthropological point of view is that they have a society which is simultaneously segmentary and class stratified. In most types of lineage system that have so far been described in any detail, the process of lineage segmentation leads to a 'balanced opposition' between the resulting segments rather than to a status ranking, superior and inferior. For this reason, among others, the interesting typology of political systems which Fortes and Evans-Pritchard have suggested for African societies[1] would not cover Kachin *gumsa*[2] society.

The Tikopia, as described by Firth,[3] have indeed what may be considered a 'pure' lineage system associated with notions of a class hierarchy, but here the whole scale of social activities is on such a minute scale that analogy is not very useful. I think that there are plenty of societies in the world of the Kachin *gumsa* type, but it so happens that social anthropologists have not yet got round to looking at them. That makes it all the more difficult for me to achieve lucidity.

In what I am going to say now, I repeat to some extent what I have said already, but I am arguing from a different point of view. In the previous sections we have been concerned mainly with the nature of lineage segments and the status relations between them. Now we are concerned with how these same status relations are

1. M. Fortes and E. E. Evans-Pritchard (eds.), *African Political Systems*, London, 1940, Introduction. Southern Bantu lineages are often ranked; cf., e.g. Hilda Kuper, *An African Aristocracy*, 1947.

2. *Gumsa* and *gumlao* are the two modes of political organization among the Kachins. *Gumsa* is hierarchical and *gumlao* is egalitarian. [Ed.]

3. R. Firth, *Primitive Polynesian Economy*, London, 1939, ch. 6.

fitted into the Kachin's own notion that his society is stratified into classes of almost caste-like rigidity.

To be frank, Kachin *gumsa* theory about class differences is almost totally inconsistent with Kachin practice. I want then to explain not only what the Kachin theory is but also how the inconsistencies in actual behaviour affect the total social structure.

In theory rank depends strictly upon birth status; all legal rules are framed as if the hierarchy of aristocrats, commoners and slaves had a caste-like rigidity and exclusiveness. In Kachin theory rank is an attribute of lineage and every individual acquires his rank once and for all through the lineage into which he happens to be born. It is easy to see that this theory is a fiction, but less easy to understand just what kind of fiction is involved.

It would appear that in pre-British days a very high proportion of the total population – in places nearly half[4] – were classed as *mayam*, a term which the dictionary translates as 'slaves'. The British disapproved of slavery and suppressed the institution of *mayam*. It is therefore difficult to discover the exact nature of the original institution or to discover whether 'slavery' was an adequate description of it.[5]

What evidence there is suggests that Kachin slavery had a good deal of resemblance to the *tefa* system of the Central Chins,[6] the *sei* system of the *Lakher*,[7] the *boi* (*bawi*) system of the Lushai[8] and the *mughemi* system of the Sema,[9] or for that matter the 'slavery' of pre-British Burma.[10]

4. J. T. O. Barnard, 'The frontier of Burma', *J. Roy. Cen. As. Soc.*, vol. 17 (1930), p. 182.

5. The most detailed account available seems to be that given by J. H. Green, 1934. *The Tribes of Upper Burma North of 24° Latitude and their Classification* (Typescript dissertation, Haddon Library, Cambridge), pp. 86–91.

6. H. N. C. Stevenson, *The Economics of the Central Chin Tribes*, Bombay, 1943, pp. 176 ff.

7. N. E. Parry, *The Lakhers*, London, 1932, pp. 223 ff.

8. J. H. Hutton, *The Sema Nagas*, London, 1921, App. 4; J. Shakespear, *The Lushei Kuki Clans*, London, 1912, pp. 46 ff.

9. J. H. Hutton, op. cit., pp. 145 ff.

10. V. Sangermano, *The Burmese Empire a Hundred Years Ago as Described by Father Sangermano*. Introduction and Notes by John Jardine, London, 1893, pp. 156, 261 ff; D. Richardson, *The Damathat or the Laws of Menoo* (trans. from the Burmese), Rangoon, 1912 (1st edn dates from 1847); B. Lasker, *Human bondage in South-East Asia*, Chapel Hill, 1950.

Nearly all slaves were owned by the chief or village headman. In most cases the status of slave amounted to that of permanent debtor. But, as we have seen, the role of debtor in Kachin society is not necessarily one of disadvantage. The slave might be in debt bondage to his master; but he also had claims on his master. His overall position resembled that of an adopted son or bastard (*n-gyi*) of the chief, or even more perhaps that of a poor son-in-law (*dama*) working to earn his bride. Thus by a kind of paradox the 'slave' though reckoned to be the lowest social stratum stood nearer to the chief than the members of any other named class.

The chief disposed of the marriages of his slaves just as he did those of his real children. Where slave married slave the children were slaves to the father's master (since he had paid the bride price). Similarly, even if a male slave married a free woman the children were slaves to the master who paid the bride-price. But if a free man married a slave woman, the bride-price was paid to the slave's master and served to redeem the children.

During the nineteenth century most Kachin slaves seem to have been of Assamese origin. Assamese were captured in large numbers in the period of Burmese ascendancy in Assam just prior to 1824 and these captives and their descendants were traded all over the Kachin Hills. Thus in 1868 Anderson found that most of the Kachin and Shan slaves in the Bhamo area were of Assamese origin;[11] in 1910 Grant Brown found on the Upper Chindwin whole villages of Kachin speakers directly descended from Assamese slaves.[12] Even when the Hukawng Valley Kachin slaves were released in 1926 it was still to be noted that of the total 3466 released, 2051 were of Assamese origin.[13] But slaves of this type do not seem to have been treated any differently from bond 'slaves' who were themselves Kachins. Neufville writing in 1828 is interesting on this point:

When in their own country and before the plunder of Assam furnished them with slaves they appear to have cultivated their lands and carried on all other purposes of domestic life by means of a species of voluntary servitude entered into by the poorer and more destitute

11. J. Anderson, *A Report on the Expedition to Western Yunnan via Bhamo*, Calcutta, 1871.
12. R. Grant Brown, *Burma as I saw it*, London, 1925, p. 16.
13. J. T. O. Barnard, op. cit., p. 182.

individuals of their own people who, when reduced to want, were in the habit of selling themselves into bondage either temporarily or for life to their chiefs or more prosperous neighbours. They sometimes resorted to this step in order to secure wives of the daughters and in either case were incorporated into the family performing domestic and agricultural service but under no obligation. Singphos in this state were called gumlao.[14]

Neglecting for the moment the description of these 'slaves' as *gumlao*,[15] it is evident that Neufville's informants regarded the status of 'slave' as close to that of adopted son or poor *dama*.

Formal rules about the payment of *hpaga*[16] . . . usually differentiate only three classes, namely the chiefs (*du*); the free-born commoners (*darat*); the slaves (*mayam*). But there are also intermediate classes which blur the distinction between these categories. *Ma gam amyu* (eldest son lineage) denotes an aristocracy. Aristocratic lineages in this sense are not the lineages of chiefs but lineages sufficiently close to those of chiefs for their members to be able to claim that they are descended from chiefs and to feel that their descendants might one day become chiefs again. Similarly there is a category *surawng*[17] which comprises (in theory) the children of slave women by free-born men – a category which blurs the distinction between free and not-free. The commoners (*darat daroi*, *mayu maya*) are simply a residual category, the 'ordinary' lineages which are not aristocrats and not slaves.

Kachin class is not directly correlated with economic status, either in a ritual or an objective sense. The Kachin 'rich man' (*sut lu ai wa*) is, as we have seen, the man who possesses many *hpaga*, but this does not necessarily mean that he is wealthy in terms of ordinary economic goods. There is no suggestion in Kachin ideology that a 'rich' man is necessarily an aristocrat or that an aristocrat is necessarily 'rich'. There are rich chiefs and poor chiefs; though it is true that a powerful chief is also a rich one. Within any one domain there is no substantial difference in

---

14. J. B. Neufville, 'On the geography and population of Assam', *As. Res.*, vol. 16 (1828), p. 240. This is the first reference to the term *gumlao*.

15. See Note 2 above. [Ed.]

16. *Hpaga*, 'trade'; 'ritual wealth object'. [Ed.]

17. cf. Barnard cited in W. J. S. Carrapiett, *The Kachin Tribes of Burma*, Rangoon, 1929, p. 99.

standard of living between the aristocrats and the commoners – members of both classes eat the same food, wear the same clothes, practise the same skills. Master and slave live in the same house under almost the same conditions.

In theory Kachin class difference has attributes of caste – that is to say it is a ritual distinction. Individuals are born great. Persons of higher class than oneself are deserving of honour (*hkungga*) – and this is true even if the individual in question is poverty-stricken and an imbecile. Honour is expressed through deference, notably by offering gifts and by the use of an appropriate florid or poetical style of speech.

In theory then people of superior class receive gifts from their inferiors. But no permanent economic advantage accrues from this. Anyone who receives a gift is thereby placed in debt (*hka*) to the giver. The receiver for a while enjoys the debt (he has it, he drinks it: *lu*) but it is the giver who owns the debt (rules it: *madu*). Paradoxically therefore although an individual of high-class status is defined as one who receives gifts (e.g. 'thigh-eating chief') he is all the time under a social compulsion to give away more than he receives. Otherwise he would be reckoned mean and a mean man runs the danger of losing status. For though Kachins hold that a man is born to high rank and do not acknowledge that social climbing is possible, they readily admit that it is possible 'to go downhill' (*gumyu yu*) – i.e. lose class status.

In practice, it would appear to be equally possible to gain status. Since, in theory, rank is acquired at birth, it is clear that class is an attribute of whole lineages not of individuals. Therefore an individual who wishes to be recognized as of high birth must strive not simply for personal recognition, but for the recognition of his whole lineage. Usually this is not very difficult. Most commoner lineages can claim some sort of aristocratic connexion, and in all such cases there is room for manoeuvre and social improvement. However, a few lineages are notoriously 'common' – i.e. they have no connexion whatever with the royal 'chiefly' clans; – for these the *gumsa* system has nothing much to offer; – the leaders of such lineages aim to be recognized as *bawmung* or as priests rather than as chiefs.[18]

18. The question whether a commoner lineage can assert a claim to aristocracy is largely a matter of names. In the same way our College of

Where a commoner lineage has remote claims to aristocracy an ambitious individual can work his way up the social scale by repeatedly validating these claims. Such a man in Kachin terminology possesses *hpaji*. *Hpaji* is the counterpart of *sut* (riches), it is manifested by lavishness in hospitality and feast-giving. It can be translated as 'wisdom' or 'cunning'. Only the rich can afford to give feasts; only the wise and cunning know how to get rich. Wisdom in itself does not necessarily imply aristocracy but when it comes to social climbing, the cunning ones are at an advantage.

We have then a situation in which the class hierarchy is supposed to be rigid, but in fact is not. In such a situation great store will be set by the symbols which attach to rank, and the rights to use such symbols will be jealously guarded. We have already seen this process at work in our discussion of land tenure. We have seen, for example, that the political status of any lineage within a village is specified by the links of clanship and affinity that relate that lineage to the 'principal lineage' – that is to say the lineage of the founder ancestor of the village. For this reason the exact status relationships that originally existed between the different founder ancestors of the various lineages which now compose the village or village cluster are matters of paramount importance.

Great ingenuity is devoted to garbling the evidence upon this crucial matter. The Hpalang feud stories . . . are an excellent example. It is clear that in each generation each rival faction within a group reinterprets the traditions of the past to its own liking. How far any one individual realizes that this process of 'rewriting history' is going on, it is impossible to say.

Social climbing then is the product of a dual process. Prestige is first acquired by an individual by lavishness in fulfilling ritual obligations. This prestige is then converted into recognized status by validating retrospectively the rank of the individual's lineage. This last is largely a matter of manipulating the genealogical tradition. The complicated nature of Kachin rules of succession makes such manipulation particularly easy.

Heralds can usually provide a family tree for anyone with a name like Howorth, or Howarth, or Howard, but may be hard put to it if the applicant's name is Smith. I fancy that a really influential commoner family would always come to be recognized as of chiefly (*du-baw*) origin if they maintained their position long enough.

We have seen that by natural right the youngest son succeeds the father in his rights to make sacrifices to the ancestral deities of the lineage, and that though other members of the father's lineage may on occasion succeed, they must first 'purchase' the rights of office from the youngest son by making the appropriate ritual gifts. In course of time therefore the total lineage of a chief includes a number of collateral branches tracing descent from the elder brothers of chiefs. In such a case only the 'youngest son line' is, strictly speaking, *du baw amyu* – 'of chiefly sort'; the collateral lines are inferior, they are *ma gam amyu* – 'eldest son sort'.

Let me emphasize, however, that the next senior line after that of the *youngest* son is that of the *eldest* son. In the fictitious instance in Figure 1, A_1, A_2 and A_3 are youngest sons and each succeeds in turn by right of birth. But if A_3 dies without issue, his *eldest* brother B_3 is the next in line and not C_3. Moreover, this cannot be obviated by adoption as in some other societies. A_3 may adopt a son, but that will not affect the succession of ritual office. Going back a generation, the descendants of B_2 and C_2 will in time come to consider themselves separate lineages. Then in order of ranking, the descendants of B_2 will be senior to those of C_2. But of B_2's descendants, the line from D_3 will be senior to that from E_3. The rank order of the individuals shown in the third generation is thus: A_3, B_3, C_3, D_3, E_3 and F_3.

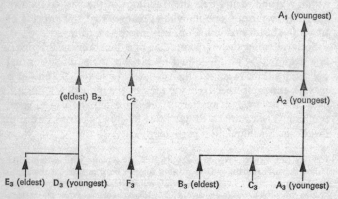

Figure 1 Diagram to illustrate principle of succession

To complicate things still further several additional criteria can be used to demonstrate that lineage A is decisively senior to lineage B or vice versa.

(a) In a situation of polygamy, the children of a chief wife (*latung num*) all rank superior to those of a second wife (*lashi num*) who in turn all rank superior to those of a third wife (*labai num*).

(b) A wife is not a wife until she has gone through the ceremony of *num shalai*. This can have important consequences. An important Kachin chief will not infrequently 'marry' a Shan princess but by Buddhist rites. It may then be contended that her offspring are illegitimate.

(c) Kachins practise levirate marriage. If a man dies, his widow is 'collected' by a lineage brother. It is sometimes contended that any offspring the woman has by this second marriage all rank lower than those by her first husband.

(d) Children born out of wedlock or as the result of adultery within wedlock are in the one case the legal offspring of the man paying the bastardy penalty (*sumrai hka*), and in the other of the legal husband of the mother. But such children, even when their status has been legitimized, rank lower than children of the same father born legitimate. For example, if a man A has illegitimate children by a woman B and then marries her (*num shalai*), the children born after marriage rank higher than the children born before marriage, though all are legitimate.

It follows therefore that the offspring of a man may fall into a considerable number of different categories; the heir (*uma*) of a chief is not simply his youngest son but 'the youngest son of the first wife with whom he went through the ceremony of *num shalai*', and that may easily be a matter of dispute.[19]

19. It is interesting to note that in the Tallensi lineage system studied by Fortes the usual form of lineage fission is for the descendants of a senior wife to hive off from the descendants of a junior wife, so that, in this very patrilineal society, the critical founder ancestor of a lineage is usually a woman. This is sometimes the case also with the Kachins, for it is frequently the marital status of the mother of the lineage founder which determines the rank of the lineage. Numerous examples of this can be seen in Kawlu Ma Nawng (1942), *History of the Kachins of the Hukawng Valley* (translation and notes by J. L. Leyden) (Bombay) (privately printed), pp. 2–10. Cf. M. Fortes, *The Dynamics of Clanship among the Tallensi*, London, 1945, pp. 198 ff.

These elaborate rules not only allow for much controversy, they also make it relatively easy for any influential aristocrat to reconstruct remote sections of his genealogy in his own favour. For example, to return to the hypothetical example given in Figure 1. As described above, F_3 and his descendants are in the junior line of the six lineages originating in A_1, B_2, C_2, E_3, B_3, C_3. They will thus soon be far removed from any chance of chiefly office. In a few generations they will come to form a lineage which no one will recognize as aristocratic, even if they themselves continue to boast of their chiefly connexions. The Kachins say of such a lineage that it has 'gone downhill' – *gumyu yu*.[20]

But if an individual in this F_3 line were by good fortune or strong personality to work himself and his family into a position of influence, he might well begin to assume the titles of a chief. It would then no doubt turn out that his ancestor A_1 had more than one wife and that of A_1's several children, only C_2 was the child of his chief wife, so that, after all, the real *uma* line passed through F_3! In Hpalang I found that there could be disagreements of this kind even with regard to persons as near as the great grandfather's generation. When it is realized that some chiefly genealogies purport to record history for the last forty generations or more, it will be appreciated that although a man's rank is in theory precisely defined by his birth, there is an almost infinite flexibility in the system as actually applied.

So far in this discussion I have been emphasizing that practice often deviates a long way from the structural ideal, and yet because of the flexibility of the native concepts Kachins can persuade themselves that they are keeping to the rules. I now want to make a different point – namely, that the structural ideal can itself be inconsistent, so that two or more quite different courses of action can both be equally 'right' (or 'wrong').

Inconsistency arises from the association of a rule of patri-local residence and a rule of succession by ultimogeniture.

The ideal of patri-local residence is consistent with the notion

20. cf. O. Hanson, *A Dictionary of the Kachin Language*, Rangoon, 1906, p. 103. *Dashi ni shawng e Lahtaw du rai ma ai dai hpang e gumyu yu mat ai*: 'formerly the Dashi were chiefs of the Lahtaw clan but afterwards they lost caste'.

that class is an attribute of whole lineage groups. The lineage is conceived of as a localized group identified with one particular place and having a special ranking status in respect to that place. Ultimogeniture cuts clean across this theory, being based on the assumption that the youngest son is the residual heir, the older brothers having gone off to seek their fortune elsewhere. If the older brothers stay at home an intolerable psychological situation is likely to arise. In our own society, the stereotype of a jealousy situation is with the mother-in-law or 'the lodger'. This stereotype is a reflection of the inconsistency between the ideal that each biological family should form a separate household, and the economic necessity of dependence on other people. The Kachin stereotype of a jealousy situation is between elder and younger brother. Slander and jealous speech (nsu nnawn) is thought of as a kind of sorcery which can bring misfortune to the person slandered, and where illness is diagnosed as being due to this cause, offerings are made to the nsu nat – 'the spirit of jealousy'. The mythical sanction supporting this offering is a tale about a quarrel between two brothers. In one version the elder brother at first uses his greater strength and knowledge of the world to deprive the younger brother of his rightful inheritance; then supernatural beings come to the aid of the younger brother who kills his elder brother by a trick and himself survives to become a rich chief.[21] The shades of the two brothers now constitute the nsu nat.

In other words, although Kachins maintain theoretically that an elder brother should live at home under the political suzerainty of his youngest brother, they recognize clearly enough that trouble is likely to ensue if he does.

The most obvious alternative to patrilocal residence is matrilocal (uxorilocal) residence. I have stressed already that in point of fact such residence is common. But if a married couple settle with the bride's parents (dama lung: 'the son-in-law climbs the hill') it is deemed a disgrace. The son-in-law thereby admits his social inferiority; he is working to earn his bride; he has virtually put himself in the position of bond-slave (mayam) to his

21. C. Gilhodes, *The Kachins; Religion and Customs*, Calcutta, 1922, p. 54. Alternative versions of this tale are considered later (in Leach's book).

mayu.[22] It is understandable therefore that, if questioned, Kachins will at first maintain that exceptions to the patri-local rule are rare.

In the real situation the corporate localized lineage segment seldom includes more than half a dozen or so separate individual families. This is clear evidence that, despite the ideal of lineage solidarity, the process of lineage fission must be going on all the time. This point I have made before, but what I am now stressing is that the mechanism of lineage fission is closely linked with ideas about class status, and that the process of lineage fission is, at the same time, a process of social mobility up and down the class hierarchy. The choice that an individual makes about his place of residence affects the class status prospects of his descendants.

This argument is important to my general analysis so I will recapitulate what has already been said on the subject of choice of residence so as to bring out the importance of this factor for class differentiation.

Choice of residence affects commoners and aristocrats rather differently. To take commoners first. Commoners really have a choice of four alternatives:

(a) A man and his wife can settle in the village of the man's parents. This is the orthodox procedure. The bride is then regarded as the woman of the whole local lineage group. If her husband dies she will be 'picked up' (*kahkyin*) as a levirate wife by one of her deceased husband's lineage kin. All members of the local lineage have probably helped in the provision of the bride-price (*hpu hpaga*) which is determined by the rank of the husband and they will all have shared in the return presents (*sharung shakau*) contributed by the bride's lineage and determined by the rank of the bride. The bridegroom's male relatives are thus interested in seeing that he makes as 'good' a marriage as possible. If the bride's lineage is of higher status than that of the bridegroom, then the status of the bridegroom's lineage is enhanced, and vice versa.

(b) Where a man was too poor to afford the bride-price for a wife it was formerly possible for him to become a voluntary slave

22. *Mayu*, relations through one's wife, being of superior status to oneself. [Ed.]

of some local notable; probably his own chief. He would then have the status of *ngawn mayam*.[23] His master would provide the capital to complete the bride-price transactions. In return the master would have a claim on the labour of the slave and his children and would be entitled to a share of the produce of his livestock and of the bride-price of his daughters. The advantage of this procedure from the slave's point of view was the security provided by the patronage of an influential chief. The slave's status *vis-à-vis* his master would appear to have been very similar to that of an illegitimate son or a poor son-in-law.[24]

(c) A man and his wife can settle in the village of the bride's parents (*dama lung*). By so doing the man repudiates the support of his own lineage and makes himself dependent upon the lineage of the bride. This situation usually originates in circumstances where the bridegroom is on bad terms with his relatives or else they are very poor. The bride's people (*mayu ni*) then agree to a reduced bride-price in return for an agreed number of years personal service from the bridegroom. After working for his bride in this way a man has 'lost face' in his own village and is likely to stay on as the dependant of his *mayu ni*. An unorthodox matri-local marriage of this kind initiates a new subordinate lineage in the village of the *mayu ni*. The *mayu–dama* relationship, it will be remembered, has continuity from one generation to another. Hence if two lineages of the same village are in *mayu–dama* relationship, the *dama* usually have an inferior status to the *mayu*. This inferiority rests on dual ground, firstly that the *mayu* 'were there first' and therefore have superior land title, and secondly that the founder of the *dama* lineage by adopting matri-local residence admitted his inferior status.

(d) A married couple can settle in an alien community. Empirically this seems to be rare. A man can only settle in an established community by permission of the village headman and since all approaches to persons of authority follow channels of kinship, it is really rather difficult to negotiate with people who are not kin

---

23. *Ngawn mayam:* Independent male householders in debtor status. Their wives. Their male and female children. It would appear that the master had few rights over the females in this group other than the right to take a share of the bride-price of the daughters.

24. cf. pp. 255–7.

at all. In Hpalang I only identified one household which had fairly certainly been complete strangers to everyone in the community when they first arrived. Although these people had only been living in Hpalang about five years, three of the children had already been married off or become betrothed to local families. The stranger family was thus already fully incorporated into the local kinship network of *mayu–dama* relationships. In saying that cases of this kind are rare, I am not suggesting that the total residential pattern of Kachin villages is stable. Individual families move frequently from one community to another, but the family head usually already has either agnatic or affinal kinsmen living in the community to which he moves.

In sum then the ordinary commoner has to choose between 'being orthodox' in which case he remains at home but comes under the ritual jurisdiction of his youngest brother, or 'being unorthodox' in which case he goes to live somewhere else but must then accept the position of an affinal relative (*dama*) in a subordinate position in the new community. A poor man can avoid this latter choice only by adopting the very similar course of making himself a voluntary bond slave.

The choices that face the elder sons of chiefs are rather different. There are again several alternatives but all of these are respectable and orthodox. We have already considered these alternatives . . .

(a) He may stay at home and submit to the overlordship of his youngest brother.

(b) He may collect a group of followers (*zaw*) and then go out to uninhabited country and carve out for himself a new territory. If he does this he may later purchase from his youngest brother the right to make offerings to the ancestral nats, etc., so that he may assume the status of a 'thigh-eating chief' in his new territory.

(c) He may, together with his followers, apply to the chief of an established domain for a village site. If this is granted he will have to purchase the 'ownership' rights in the manner already indicated and will thereafter be recognized as headman or petty chief of the new village as the case may be. In either case he is subordinate in certain respects to the chief from whom he purchases his rights. In consequence, the lineage segment of which he is the founder loses status slightly and becomes *ma gam amyu* as opposed to the *du baw amyu* of the parent stem. In describing this alternative under the head of Land Tenure I pointed out that the 'price' paid for the village land is similar to the bride-price of a chief's daughter. It would be normal for a *ma gam amyu* petty chief to become *dama* to his overlord at the first opportunity if he were not already a clan brother. Here again we see that within the context of the one community the *mayu–dama* relationship implies the subordination of the latter to the former.

Empirically it would seem that the second of these alternatives has great attractions for Kachin aristocrats. In the Kachin Hills Area west of the Irrawaddy and north of Myitkyina, and also in many other areas of notably low population density, there is a large preponderance of very small independent villages; the headman of each village claims to be an independent chief of full *du baw* status. This fact has been noted repeatedly and is the more remarkable in that the British administration was consistently opposed to such fragmented settlement. Such tiny settlements of three to a dozen households are clearly very weak both politically and economically; it would therefore seem that the prestige attaching to independent status is commonly valued more highly than economic prosperity.

In more densely settled areas there is no room for chiefs' sons to set up independent domains without infringing upon some other chief's existing rights. Therefore a chief's son, who is not content to stay at home, has no choice but to settle down in some subordinate capacity in the domain of a relative, asserting for himself as high a status as circumstances will permit.

In Hpalang, as we have seen, every village headman seemed excessively anxious to claim for himself the maximum possible degree of political independence to which some tortuous re-interpretations of tradition might seem to make him entitled. Such claims had very little real effect upon the political or economic power of the individuals concerned so that here again one must suppose that the issue at stake is purely one of prestige; recognition of one's class status by others being considered all important. So long as a petty chief or village headman can persuade other people to refer to him as a chief (*duwa*) and to credit his sons and daughters with the honorific Shan titles of Prince (*Zau*) and Princess (*Nang*), his lineage can still rank as chiefly (*du baw*), but once these titles are omitted the status of the lineage starts to go downhill and all will before long be rated simply as commoners.

Part Seven
Caste as a Form of Social Inequality

Caste is generally regarded as the prototype of rigid social inequality. It is both a form of social organization and a system of values. As a system of relations it is marked by a division of society into groups which are ranked in an elaborate hierarchy. As a system of values it is characterized by the legitimacy it accords to social inequality and the importance it assigns to the ideas of purity and pollution. The caste system is found in its most typical form in Indian society although 'caste-like' phenomena exist elsewhere. The essay by Srinivas gives a general account of the caste system while Béteille gives a more detailed picture of the way in which it operates within the context of an Indian village. Both accounts concentrate on the 'typical' features of caste as it existed in traditional India; many changes are now coming about in the system.

13 M. N. Srinivas

The Caste System in India

Excerpt from M. N. Srinivas, *Religion and Society among the Coorgs of South India*, Clarendon Press, 1952, pp. 24–31.

Caste is an institution of great complexity. It has its roots deep in history, and even today it governs the lives of 300 million Hindus in several important respects. It is popularly understood as the division of society into a fivefold hierarchy with the Brahmins at the head, followed in order by Kshatriyas, Vaishyas or traders, Shudras or servants and labourers, and, lastly, the Untouchables. The first three castes are called 'twice-born' (*dvija*) as they alone are entitled to undergo the ceremony of *upanayana* which constitutes spiritual rebirth. Only the twice-born castes are entitled to study the Vedas and to the performance of Vedic ritual on certain occasions. Caste in the above sense is referred to as *varṇa* and has an All-India application.

The idea of caste as the fivefold division of society represents a gross over-simplification of facts. The real unit of the caste system is not one of the five *varṇas* but *jāti*, which is a very small endogamous group practising a traditional occupation and enjoying a certain amount of cultural, ritual and juridical autonomy. Every *jāti*, or the members of a *jāti* in a particular village or a group of neighbouring villages, constitutes a caste court which punishes caste offences.

There are innumberable *jātis*. Professor Ghurye calculates that there are 2000 sub-castes (*jātis*) in each linguistic area.[1] This should give some idea of the total number of endogamous sub-castes in India as a whole. The importance of the *varṇa*-system consists in that it furnishes an All-India frame into which the myriad *jātis* in any single linguistic area can be fitted. It systematizes the chaos of *jātis* and enables the sub-castes of one region to be comprehended by people in another area by reference to a

1. *Caste and Race in India*, London, 1932, p. 27.

common scale. Further, the *varṇa*-system represents a scale of values, and *jātis* occupying the lower rungs have throughout tried to raise their status by taking over the customs and ritual of the top *jātis*. This has helped the spread of a uniform culture throughout Hindu society.

The attempt to fit the *jātis* of any region into the fivefold hierarchy is a very difficult affair. It is possible everywhere to say who are the Brahmins and Untouchables, but there is great confusion in the middle regions. Confining our remarks to South India for the moment, we find that the claims of local *jātis* to be Kshatriyas and Vaishyas are frequently questioned by others. For instance, it is well known that a ruling house claiming to be Kshatriyas were originally potters. Similarly, the claim of a local trading *jāti* to be Vaishya, one of the three twice-born *varṇas* of the Vedas, is hotly contested by the other castes in the area. It is not uncommon to find a *jāti* included under the Shudra *varṇa* claiming to be higher than the local *jātis* claiming to be Kshatriyas and Vaishyas. Disputes as to relative status are an essential feature of the caste system. This is especially so in the numerous *jātis* belonging to the fourth *varṇa* of Shudra. In south India the term 'Shudra' includes the vast majority of non-Brahmin *jātis* and even some reformist sects.

A man is *born* into a sub-caste (*jāti*) and this is the only way of acquiring membership. According to the traditional view, however, birth is not an accident. Certain Hindu theological notions like *karma* and *dharma* have contributed very greatly to the strengthening of the idea of hierarchy which is inherent in the caste system. The idea of *karma* teaches a Hindu that he is born in a particular sub-caste because he deserves to be born there. The actions he performed in a previous incarnation deserved such a reward or punishment, as the case might be. If he had performed better actions in his previous incarnation he would have been born in a higher caste. Thus the caste hierarchy comes to be an index of the state of an individual's soul. It also represents certain milestones on the soul's journey to God.

Thus the idea of deserts is associated with birth in a particular caste. A man is born in a high caste because of the good actions performed by him in his previous life, and another is born into a low caste because of bad actions performed in his previous life.

The other important concept is *dharma*, which has many meanings, one of which is 'that which is right or moral'. The existing moral code is identified with *dharma*. A man who accepts the caste system and the rules of his particular sub-caste is living according to *dharma*, while a man who questions them is violating *dharma*. Living according to *dharma* is rewarded, while violation of *dharma* is punished, both here and hereafter. If he observes the rules of *dharma*, he will be born in his next incarnation in a high caste, rich, whole and well endowed. If he does not observe them he will be born in a low caste, poor, deformed and ill endowed. Wordly position and success indicate the kind of life a man led in his previous incarnation.

One may also reap the reward of one's actions very soon after their performance. For purposes of such reward and punishment, a person is identified with his joint family. A man may become blind because his father, the head of the joint family, made money in the black market during the war.

The concept of pollution governs relations between different castes. This concept is absolutely fundamental to the caste system, and along with the concepts of *karma* and *dharma* it contributes to make caste the unique institution it is. Every type of inter-caste relation is governed by the concept of pollution. Contact of any kind, touching, dining, sex and other relations between castes which are structurally distant results in the higher of the two castes being polluted. Ordinarily, contact between members of the same caste, or between members of castes which are structurally very near each other, does not result in pollution. Where contact does result in pollution, however, the polluted member of the higher caste has to undergo a purificatory rite in order to be restored to normal ritual status. Such a purificatory rite is fairly simple where the structural distance between the castes is not very great and the type of contact is not serious. Sometimes, as when a Brahmin eats food cooked by an Untouchable, the resultant pollution is so great that he or she has to be excommunicated. Normally, in every caste, women observe the pollution rules much more strictly than men.

Contact is culturally defined. Touch is contact in all cases. Frequently the maintenance of a minimum distance between castes is insisted upon. This matter has received systematization in Kerala, where elaborate rules have been laid down requiring the minimum distance that should prevail between the various castes.

Aiyappan, in 1937, gives a scale of distance pollution for several castes: a Nayar must keep 7 feet from a Nambudri Brahman, an Iravan (Ilavan, Izhuvan, Tiyan) must keep 32, a Cheruman, 64 and a Nayadi 74 to 124. The respective distances between these lower castes are calculated by a simple process of subtraction: the Iravan must keep 25 feet from the Nayar and Cheruman 32 feet from the Iravan.[2]

The ban on contact between castes, and the solidarity of a sub-caste, express themselves in the spatial segregation of castes in a village. The Untouchables live everywhere at some distance from the others, while each of the other sub-castes occupies a street or a quarter of the village or town.

Normally, a man may accept cooked food and water from a member of the same or equal or superior caste. Food cooked by a member of a lower caste may not be eaten because such food defiles a man belonging to a higher caste. Mutual acceptability of cooked food denotes equality between the castes concerned, while the movement of food in one direction only indicates that the acceptor is inferior to the giver.

People living in rural areas, and the orthodox, exhibit a pre-occupation with the matter of acceptance or rejection of cooked food from different castes. The kind of food, the question whether it is cooked in butter or water, the caste of the person cooking it, and the place (whether temple or home) where the food is cooked, all go to determine its acceptability or otherwise. A tendency to define and systematize is obvious everywhere.

There is a general correlation between diet and status. Brahmins are usually vegetarians, abstaining even from eggs. The Shudra castes eat eggs and meat. Pork is inferior to mutton, and usually pork-eaters to mutton-eaters. Beef-eaters are the lowest of all. The consumption of toddy, too, begins at some point low down in the caste hierarchy.

Facts have been over-simplified in order to make some general statements. For instance, while Brahmins are usually vegetarians,

2. A Aiyappan, *The Anthropology of the Nayadis*, pp. 18 ff., quoted by J. H. Hutton, *Caste in India*, p. 70.

the Saraswat Brahmins of the west coast, and some Brahmins of Bengal, eat fish, while the Kashmiri Brahmins eat meat. Again, castes claiming to be Kshatriyas generally eat mutton. The Lingayats of south India, who are non-Brahmins, are vegetarians and teetotallers. It must be mentioned here that from the earliest times vegetarianism has been held up as an ethical ideal, it being considered wrong for an individual to kill other sentient creatures in order to keep himself alive. Vegetarianism goes hand in hand with teetotalism, the drinking of alcholic liquors being forbidden to the high castes.

The acceptance of cooked food by a high-caste man from an Untouchable constituted as serious an offence as having a liaison with an Untouchable, and in the old days both offences were punished, by the caste court concerned, with excommunication from caste. It is not only the high castes who are particular about the caste of the person from whom they accept food and water, but the Untouchables too are very particular. In Mysore, Untouchables do not accept food and water from smiths, and from Marka Brahmins. They believe such acceptance would defile them.

Each caste is traditionally associated with a separate occupation. Some of the earlier students of caste were so impressed with this feature of caste that they ascribed the origin of caste to the systematization of occupational differentiation. In rural India the bulk of the castes continue to practise their respective traditional occupations, though agriculture is common to all castes from the Brahmin to the Untouchable.

Some occupations are considered defiling because of the contact with some defiling object or other necessary to their practice. Swine-herding is defiling because swine defile. Leather defiles, and consequently the making and repairing of shoes is an occupation of the Untouchables. Certain other occupations, while not being defiling, are so strongly associated with low castes that no high caste man will take to them. The tapping of toddy would be a case in point. Finally, any occupation however remotely implying the destruction of sentient life in any form would be prohibited to the high castes. Thus not only butchery, the catching of fish and game, and the raising of sheep and fowls would be prohibited, but even the selling of dried fish and eggs would be regarded as an improper occupation for a high-caste man, especially a Brahmin. But, nowadays, under the influence of industrialization, the old association of caste with occupation is beginning to break down.

The members of a sub-caste tend to regard their traditional occupation as the natural one for them. Taking up any other occupation is regarded as improper. There is a pride in the skill required for the practice of the traditional occupation, and this skill is a secret which is not easily divulged to members of other castes. In fact, formerly castes tended to be guilds, and the members of castes regarded their traditional occupation as their monopoly. A violation of this monopoly would result in a fight. The matter could also be taken before the village court and before the king of the region.

Things associated with high caste, their houses, clothes, customs, manners and ritual, tend to become symbols of superior status. Consequently there is a ban on the lower castes taking them over and, formerly, such a ban was sanctioned by the political authority at the top. In Malabar, until 1865, only the Brahmins were allowed to clothe their bodies above the waist, even the women of the lower castes being prohibited from doing so. In many parts of India the lowest castes were not allowed to have tiled roofs for their houses. Nor were they allowed to build two-storied houses.

A consequence of the extreme stratification implied in the caste system is the tendency of each sub-caste, or each level of sub-castes, to live in a separate social world. The members of a sub-caste inhabit the same quarter of the village or town and frequently are all related to each other by agnatic or affinal links. They share a common culture and ritual idiom. They observe common restrictions regarding food and drink, and have certain caste festivals and rites not shared with others. They practise a common, traditional occupation, the secrets of which they do not share with others. They have caste courts and assemblies where elders of the sub-caste belonging to different villages assemble and decide matters of common concern. The members of a sub-caste share certain common values and are actively aware of this fact when they come into contact with other castes. The autonomy of a sub-caste does not, however, mean that it can live independently of other sub-castes. An Indian village usually consists of a few sub-castes which are mutually dependent and also possess certain interests in common.

The sub-caste or *jāti* is the unit of endogamy. Occasionally we find a *jāti* split up into several groups, each of which is endogamous. The rule about endogamy is still strictly observed, though a contemporary tendency among the educated members of the higher sub-castes is to marry into another sub-caste of the same level and sharing the same culture. Thus a member of the Mandyam division of the Sri Vaishnava Brahmins might nowadays marry a member of the Hebbar division of the same larger group, though formerly they would not have done so.

Hypergamous unions occasionally occur between castes. By this a man belonging to the higher caste takes a girl from the lower caste. It is never the other way about. Hypergamous marriages are common in Malabar and Bengal. They occur in other parts of India too.

The caste system is far from a rigid system in which the position of each component caste is fixed for all time. Movement has always been possible, and especially so in the middle regions of the hierarchy. A low caste was able, in a generation or two, to rise to a higher position in the hierarchy by adopting vegetarianism and teetotalism, and by Sanskritizing its ritual and pantheon. In short, it took over, as far as possible, the customs, rites and beliefs of the Brahmins, and the adoption of the Brahminic way of life by a low caste seems to have been frequent, though theoretically forbidden. This process has been called 'Sanskritization' in preference to 'Brahminization', as certain Vedic rites are confined to Brahmins and the two other 'twice-born' castes.

The tendency of the lower castes to imitate the higher has been a powerful factor in the spread of Sanskritic ritual and customs, and in the achievement of a certain amount of cultural uniformity not only throughout the caste scale, but over the entire length and breadth of India.

Another point which needs specially to be stressed is that the idea of hierarchy embodied in the caste system has been periodically questioned in India. Buddhism and Jainism questioned it quite early in the recorded history of caste. Lingayatism challenged it in the south in the twelfth century A.D. These attempts more or less met with failure, and occasionally the reformist sect either became a caste or reproduced within itself a caste system.

Many of the sanctions supporting the caste system tended to disappear under British rule. The British withdrew the explicit as well as implicit support which caste usually enjoyed under an Indian monarch. For instance, people who had been punished by caste courts could sue the caste elders responsible for defamation in courts established by the British.

Formerly, an offender against the code of the caste was punished with either a fine or, in very serious cases, excommunication from caste. Between themselves, caste councils and village councils completely controlled the conduct of an individual. Caste elders and village elders supported each other's authority.

Caste guarantees autonomy to a community, and at the same time it brings that community into relation with numerous other communities all going to form a hierarchy. The importance of such an institution is obvious in a vast country like India which has been the meeting-place of many different cultures in the past and which has always had considerable regional diversity. While the autonomy of a sub-caste was preserved it was also brought into relation with others, and the hierarchy was also a scale of generally agreed values. Every caste tended to imitate the customs and ritual of the topmost caste, and this was responsible for the spread of Sanskritization. When this process is viewed on a continental scale and over a period of at least 2500 years, it is easy to see how Sanskritic ideas and beliefs penetrated the remotest hill tribes in such a manner as not to do violence to their traditional beliefs. Caste enabled Hinduism to proselytize without the aid of a church.

Caste, which was so successful in absorbing autonomous groups everywhere, also provided the pattern for relations with non-Hindu groups. Christians and Muslims were regarded as castes, too, and they accepted such a status. Even revolutionary movements which had aimed at the overthrow of the caste system ended by either becoming castes themselves or reproduced the caste system within themselves. The main body of Hindus regarded these sects as castes and not as sects. Thus the caste system effectively neutralized all attempts to change it.

14 A. Béteille

Caste in a South Indian Village

Adapted from A. Béteille, *Caste, Class and Power: Changing Patterns of Stratification in a Tanjore Village*, University of California Press, 1965, pp. 45–65, 93–9.

I

In village Sripuram in the Tanjore district of South India the division of the community into a number of castes constitutes one of the most fundamental features of its social structure. In Hindu society, caste divisions play a part both in actual social interactions and in the ideal scheme of values. Members of different castes are, up to a point, expected to behave differently and to have different values and ideals. These differences are sanctioned by Hindu religion.

While some areas of social life in Sripuram have become relatively 'caste-free', there are many others which continue to be governed by caste. The individual's position in the caste structure is fixed by birth and is, to this extent, immutable. Formerly birth in a particular caste fixed not only one's ritual status, but, by and large, also one's economic and political positions. Today it is possible to achieve a variety of economic and political positions in spite of one's birth in a particular caste, although the latter is still very important in setting limits within which choice in the former is possible.

The term 'caste' itself requires some discussion. It has been used to mean different things by different people in a variety of situations. Indeed, it is doubtful whether much will be gained in clarity by giving to the word a single rigorous meaning at the outset. What people mean by caste in day-to-day life is different from the meaning it has in the traditional literature, or from what people consider to be its traditional and orthodox meaning. Sometimes by 'caste' people mean a small and more or less localized group; at other times the same word is used to refer to

273

a collection of such groups. Here we will see that this ambiguity in the use of the term reflects one of the basic features of the caste structure.

The English word 'caste' corresponds more or less closely to what is locally referred to as *jāti* or *kulam*. In addition to *jāti* and *kulam*, many of the villagers, particularly the Brahmins, are familiar with the concept of *varna*. Although the terms *jati* and *varṇa* refer normally to different things, the distinction is not consistently maintained. *Varṇa* refers to one of the four main categories into which Hindu society is traditionally divided; *jāti* refers generally to a much smaller group.[1] The English word 'caste' is used to denote both, not only by foreigners but also by villagers who are familiar with English. There is no real contradiction in this, for the word *jāti* has a series of meanings, and by extension it is applied to what, according to traditional usage, should be designated as *varṇa*. Thus, it is quite common for a person to say that such and such an individual is a Brahmin, or even a Kshatriya, by *jāti*. Within a given context such usage is intelligible, and does not generally lead to ambiguity.[2]

Some have tried to solve the problem by using the terms 'caste' and 'subcaste' to refer to primary divisions and their subdivisions. This is not altogether satisfactory, because the caste system is characterized by segmentation of several orders. Thus, if the Tamil Brahmins are referred to as a caste, then the Smarthas will be a subcaste, the Vadamas a sub-subcaste thereof, and the Vadadesha Vadamas a sub-sub-subcaste. To apply this usage consistently would be both difficult and tedious.

To begin with, caste may be defined as a small and named group of persons characterized by endogamy, hereditary membership and a specific style of life which sometimes includes the pursuit by tradition of a particular occupation and is usually associated with a more or less distinct ritual status in a hierarchical system, based on the concepts of purity and pollution. These terms require some discussion because a certain measure of ambiguity is attached to the definition of each.

1. M. N. Srinivas, *Caste in Modern India and Other Essays*, Bombay, 1962, pp. 63–9.

2. André Béteille, 'A note on the referents of caste', *European Journal of Sociology*, vol. 5 (1964), pp. 130–34.

The caste system gives to Hindu society a kind of segmentary character. The population of Sripuram is divided into a large number of castes or *jātis*, each having a certain measure of autonomy. A caste may be seen as a segment occupying a more or less specific position in a system of segments.[3] The structural distance of one caste from another may be great or small, depending upon their mutual positions, which are fixed within broad limits. Thus, the structural distance of Vadama from Brihacharanam is smaller than its structural distance from Shri Vaishnava, which is smaller than its structural distance from any Non-Brahmin caste. This way of looking at the mutual positions of castes is fruitful only up to a point; beyond this, such positions are both ambiguous and subject to change over time.

It will be seen that just as the total system can be broken down into a large number of castes, these in turn can be grouped together into a few broad divisions. These primary divisions are of great sociological significance, and a consideration of their nature provides a good starting point for our analysis.

II

Tamil society is characterized by a three-fold division into Brahmins, Non-Brahmins and Adi-Dravidas (or Untouchables). The importance of this division is reflected in the settlement pattern of the village in which each group of castes has its exclusive area of residence. The Brahmins live in brick and tile houses on a separate street known as the *agraharam*; the Adi-Dravidas live in thatched huts in their own hamlets which are called *cheris*; the Non-Brahmin houses, which are of mixed type, are located in between.

The territorial divisions of the village are clear and social values are attached to them. The *agraharam*, for instance, is not only a cluster of habitations, but also the centre of social life for the Brahmins. During marriages, and on the occasion of temple festivals arranged by the Brahmins the customary processions go only through the *agraharam*, although it is generally said that such processions go around the village. To the Brahmins the *agraharam*, in more ways than one, *is* the village.

3. See E. E. Evans-Pritchard, *The Nuer*, Oxford University Press, 1940.

The *cheri*, similarly, is not just another quarter of the village; it is a place which no Brahmin should enter. The concept of pollution attaches not only to groups and individuals, but also to places. The same is true of the concept of purity. The temple precincts are generally regarded as sacred. But not all of them have equal sanctity for every group in the village. Thus, for the Shri Vaishnava Brahmins, the venue of ceremonial gatherings during marriage or initiation is the Vishnu temple and not the Shiva temple, into which many of them will not even enter.

Brahmins, Non-Brahmins and Adi-Dravidas not only live in different parts of the village, but also in some measure regard themselves as having separate identities. Historically they have occupied different positions in the economic structure of the village, with Brahmins as landowners, Non-Brahmins mainly as tenants and Adi-Dravidas as agricultural labourers. These differences continue to exist, although a certain amount of levelling down has taken place in the last three decades. Politically there is some identification between these sections and the ideologies of certain parties. The three sections occupy different positions in the ritual hierarchy, the Brahmins at the top and the Adi-Dravidas at the bottom; the former are regarded as ritually the purest while the latter are considered as being in a permanent state of pollution.

In some ways the most striking difference between Brahmins on the one hand, and Non-Brahmins and Adi-Dravidas on the other, is in their physical appearance. This difference is summed up in various popular sayings, one of which runs as follows: *Parppan karuppum paraiyan sehappum ahadu* ('Dark Brahmins and light Paraiyas are not proper'). In the popular image the Brahmin is regarded not only as fair, but sharp-nosed, and as possessing, in general, more refined features. Although some Non-Brahmins also have features of this kind, they are rare among the cultivating and artisan castes who constitute the bulk of Non-Brahmins in Sripuram. Among Avi-Dravidas fair skin-colour is so conspicuous by its absence that normally a Brahmin would not be mistaken for a Palla or a Paraiya.

These differences are of significance because fair skin-colour and features of a certain type have a high social value not only in Sripuram, but in Tamil society in general, as indeed in the whole of India. The Brahmins are extremely conscious of their fair appearance and often contrast it with the 'black' skin-colour of the Kallas, or the Adi-Dravidas. A dark-skinned Brahmin girl is often a burden to the family because it is difficult to get a husband for her.

Traditionally, fair skin-colour has been associated with the 'Aryans' from whom the Brahmins claim descent and with whom they are now identified by leaders of certain separatist political parties. The *gotra* system, which is an essential feature of Brahmin social structure, links each one of them by putative ties of descent to one or another sage after whom the *gotra* is named. (The *gotra* is an exogamous division whose members are believed, particularly among the Brahmins, to be agnatically descended from a saint or a seer.) It is commonly believed that the Brahmins of an earlier generation, like the sages who were their forebears, were often endowed with *brahmatejas*, a quality which gave to their appearance a peculiar glow and serenity. This is frequently contrasted with the coarse and undistinguished features of the Non-Brahmins.

It seems probable that a particular upbringing and style of life leaves some impress on the appearance of people. A college-educated and urbanized Kalla, following a sedentary occupation such as the practice of law, has a different bearing and appears different from the generality of Kallas who are peasants and cultivators. He looks more 'refined' and 'cultivated'. And refinement of a particular kind, both in appearance and behaviour, has a high social value among Brahmins.

No doubt the popular belief that the Brahmins constitute a separate race is fallacious and will not bear examination from the anthropological point of view. But social movements and political ideologies are often based not on technically correct, but on popular conceptions, and to that extent the latter are real and require to be understood. The real physical differences of the Brahmins, and the popular belief that they constitute a separate race, have led to their being isolated socially and politically to a much greater extent in Tamiland and South India as a whole than in the north.

There are also typical differences in physical appearance between Non-Brahmins and Adi-Dravidas, as, indeed, there are between the different Non-Brahmin castes. On the whole the Pallas and Paraiyas appear to be darker, shorter and more broad-nosed than the Non-Brahmins, who, it must be remembered, constitute a very heterogeneous category both physically and culturally. These differences do not, however, have the same social significance as in the case of the Brahmins, for they have not generally been posed in racial terms or made the basis of any political ideology.

Dress also is in some ways distinctive of caste in the broader sense of the term. Among Brahmins, men are required by tradition to wear the eight-cubit piece of cloth or *veshti* after initiation. The traditional style of wearing the *veshti* by having the ends tucked at five places (*panchakachcham*) carries a ritual sanction among all Tamil Brahmins. Non-Brahmins or Adi-Dravidas, at least at Sripuram, do not wear the *veshti* in this way.

The Brahmins are rapidly giving up their traditional mode of dress. They now wear the four-cubit *veshti* by simply wrapping it around the waist, or they wear the eight-cubit *veshti* in this way without any *kachcham*. On ritual occasions such as marriage and *upanayanam* (initiation), however, they are required to wear the *veshti* in the traditional style. Temple priests also, at least while they are officiating, are required to wear the *panchakachcham*, as are priests who officiate at domestic ceremonies. In Sripuram there are about a dozen men, mostly past the age of fifty years, who normally dress in the traditional Brahminical style.

Differences between castes are carried further in the matter of women's dress. The principal garment used by all is a long piece of unsewn cloth known as the *podavai*, but there are important differences in the length of the cloth and in the manner in which it is worn. Among orthodox married Tamil Brahmin women the *podavai* is eighteen cubits in length and is worn with the *kachcham*, the ends being tucked in various ways. Non-Brahmin women do not usually have the *kachcham*, and among them the length varies between ten and twelve cubits, the garment generally reaching down to the ankles as with the Brahmins. Among the generality of Adi-Dravida women the *podavai* is considerably smaller in size and reaches just below the knee, leaving the legs uncovered.

Among Brahmin women especially, wearing the *podavai* in a

specific way symbolizes a particular culture or style of life. Minor distinctions of dress have been preserved with care and kept alive for generations, although, even in this, recent trends have been favouring a levelling down of differences. Tamil-, Telugu-, and Kannada-speaking Brahmin women have each their distinctive style of dress, and all these differences are in evidence even in a small village like Sripuram. Among Tamil Brahmins, again, a Shri Vaishnava (or Iyengar) woman will never wear her dress in the Smartha (or Iyer) style, nor will a Smartha woman adopt the Shri Vaishnava mode.

Today, however, there is a trend towards greater standardization of dress among women. Styles which were distinctive of particular castes are ceasing to be so, or are disappearing entirely. Married Brahmin women are slowly giving up their traditional mode of dress and beginning to take to the twelve-cubit *podavai* worn without a *kachcham*, as is common among Non-Brahmin women. It is true that in Sripuram such women constitute a small minority, but it is a minority which is increasing. The new style of dress blurs distinctions not only between Smarthas and Shri Vaishnavas, but also between Brahmins and Non-Brahmins. Yet even when married Brahmin women take to wearing the shorter, twelve-cubit garment, on ritual occasions they dress in the manner traditional to their caste. The more elaborate dress is called *madi saru* ('pure garment').

Among Adi-Dravida women, there seems to be a movement upwards, towards wearing longer garments like those worn by the Non-Brahmins. This is particularly true of the younger generation of Palla women in Sripuram. The older women continue to wear the shorter piece of cloth, especially while they work in the fields. The younger Adi-Dravida women have also started wearing blouses, whereas a generation ago the universal practice seems to have been to wear no separate upper garment. Thus in dress, and hence to some extent in outward appearance, differences between Non-Brahmin and Adi-Dravida women are tending to become smaller.

Whereas among Brahmin women the style of dress proclaims whether one is a Smartha or a Shri Vaishnava, the same purpose is served among men by the caste mark. Smartha men apply the *vibhuti*, which consists of three horizontal stripes made with consecrated ash, across the forehead and sometimes on other parts of the body as well. The *vibhuti* is an emblem of Shiva and its application has ritual significance. Similar ritual significance attaches among Shri Vaishnavas to the *namam*, which consists of a red (sometimes yellow) vertical stripe at the centre of the forehead, encased in a white U-shaped mark among the Vadagalai section and a Y-shaped mark among the Thengalai.

Although up to a point each subcaste, or caste, or group of castes maintains its distinctive identity, forces have been operating towards an ironing out of differences in dress and general appearance. In a large city like Madras it may be difficult to distinguish between a Brahmin and a Non-Brahmin, particularly if both are engaged in the same kind of occupation. But in a village such as Sripuram, in spite of the forces of secularization and the general influence of mass-produced consumers' goods, broad distinctions are still maintained.

III

It would perhaps be an exaggeration to say that Brahmins, on the one hand, and Non-Brahmins and Adi-Dravidas, on the other, represent two cultures. None the less one cannot but be impressed by the differences between them while examining their speech and language. In Tanjore District, particularly, Sanskrit has been a major influence on the Brahmins, both by way of enriching their thought and learning and by giving to their speech a particular character. It is well known that throughout Tamilnad Sanskritic scholarship has been a near monopoly of the Brahmins, while Non-Brahmins have specialized in Tamil studies.

The Brahmins of Sripuram are heirs to a long tradition of Sanskritic learning, whereas among the Non-Brahmins no such tradition has existed. Among the Adi-Dravidas literacy itself is a new phenomenon and is as yet confined to only a few persons. Some of the Vellalas, at least, have been familiar for generations with the devotional literature in Tamil, and perhaps it is no accident that the only professional Tamil *pundit* or teacher in Sripuram is a Vellala. It should, of course, be pointed out that virtually all adult Brahmins are literate in Tamil, which is, in fact, the language of their speech. The important point, however, is that even today they seem to attach greater value to Sanskrit, although only a few of them have more than a smattering of it.

The Brahmins are alive to the fact that the flow of events renders it increasingly difficult to transmit through the family their tradition of Sanskritic learning, and that ultimately it may become extinct. They require their sons and daughters to take up the study of Sanskrit in school, although it may be an optional subject. One of their principal grievances against the present educational system is that Sanskrit does not occupy within it the position of eminence which, according to them, it should.

A few years ago an informal school was started in the *agraharam* with a view to imparting some elementary knowledge of Sanskrit to the children and thereby keeping alive an ancient heritage. The school sits in the evening for about an hour on the verandah of one of the Brahmin residents who is a teacher in the Sanskrit College at Thiruvaiyar. He runs the school himself and charges only a nominal fee for the maintenance of petromax lanterns. The school is generally known as the *sahashranamam* class, but in addition to the *sahashranamam* (thousand names) of Vishnu, Lakshmi and so on, other *slokas* or verses in Sanskrit are taught. Both boys and girls between the ages of four and fourteen years attend the school, but it is open only to the Brahmin children of the *agraharam*.

Brahmins themselves regard their familiarity with Sanskrit as a sign of refinement, and a very high social value is attached to it. It sometimes enables them to engage in subtle arguments about abstract matters, since Sanskrit has a rich philosophical idiom. Moreover, the language of ritual among the Brahmins is almost entirely Sanskrit. This ritual is extremely elaborate in nature, even if one ignores entirely the complex temple rites and takes into account only those rites which the individual Brahmin is required to perform daily, monthly, annually and at various points of his life cycle.

There are minor distinctions of speech among Brahmins which the outsider, not familiar with the niceties of caste specialization, is likely to miss. Thus, the Iyers normally say *rasam* for pepper-water, whereas Iyengars have a special word, *sattumadu*. The Iyengars address the father's younger brother as *chittiya*, whereas among the Iyers he is called *chittappa*. The ceremony of washing the idol is known among Iyers as *abhishekham*, and among Iyengars as *thirumanjanam*. These distinctions, however slight they may appear, have been kept alive for generations, particularly in the vocabularies of kinship and ritual. Today there seems to be a tendency for words to be interchanged a little more freely and easily.

The Tamil which is spoken by the Non-Brahmin peasants of Sripuram is different both in vocabularly and accent from the speech of the Brahmins. This difference is much wider than the difference between Smarthas and Shri Vanishnavas. Adi-Dravidas in their turn have their own forms of intonation, and it is not difficult even for a Brahmin to distinguish an Adi-Dravida from a Non-Brahmin by his speech. As more and more Adi-Dravida children go to school and come into contact with both Non-Brahmin and Brahmin boys and girls, differences in speech tend to be levelled out, at least to some extent.

As against the comparatively simple and unsophisticated Tamil used by the Non-Brahmin peasantry, there is the trend towards a revival of Tamil in its pure or classical form. This trend has been associated with the Non-Brahmin movement, and today it is kept alive by the D.M.K., the Tamil Arasu Kazhagam, the Nam Tamizhar, and other parties and associations. Tamil of this variety is consciously de-Sanskritized, and it is often abstruse and difficult to comprehend. It has been given vitality through the speeches of the many eloquent D.M.K. leaders, and also in part through the films. The impact of this style on the Non-Brahmins of Sripuram has not been very significant, although the majority of them have been exposed to the influence of D.M.K. speeches as well as Tamil films.

The differential importance of the two languages, Sanskrit and Tamil, with regard to the styles of living of the Brahmins and Non-Brahmins, can be seen in the choice of personal names. Brahmins almost always have Sanskritic personal names. In a sense this is inevitable because names of men and women are chosen from among names of deities, and the major deities of the Brahmins, particularly the Shri Vaishnavas, are all Sanskritic. Non-Brahmins take their names from Tamil saints, local deities and local heroes, as well as from certain popular Sanskritic deities. Among

Brahmins, Shri Vaishnavas are more exclusive in their choice of personal names than Smarthas.

IV

Many of the important differences between Brahmins, on the one hand, and Non-Brahmins and Adi-Dravidas, on the other, are expressed in the sphere of rituals. Up to a point rituals can be regarded as standardized ways of expressing distinctive aspects of the style of life of a group or a category. Rituals serve to express in dramatic form not only the unity within a group, but also the cleavages between different sections of it. High points in the style of life of a particular community are often kept alive through ritual sanctions. Normally one group does not discard its particular rituals in favour of those of another unless it considers the style of life of the latter to be in some ways superior to its own.

The common meal has an extremely important social and ritual significance in Hinduism. When a large number of people gather together for a meal, ritual undertones are invariably associated with it. The common meal expresses symbolically both the unity of those who eat together and the cleavages between those who are required to eat separately. Ritual separation, having been elaborated to a high degree in Hindu society, serves to maintain the cleavages within the caste system. Generally two castes will not interdine unless the structural distance between them is small. Some castes are more exclusive in their commensal restrictions than others.

Broadly speaking, the higher the status of a caste, the more rigid it is in the matter of accepting food from the others. Thus, Brahmins do not accept cooked food from Non-Brahmins or Adi-Dravidas, although the latter accept it from them. This principle, however, is by no means a universal measure for the assessment of caste rank. Thus, orthodox Shri Vaishnavas do not accept food from Smarthas, or even sit for meals along with them, but the Smarthas are far less rigid in the matter of accepting food from the Shri Vaishnavas; yet it must not be inferred from this that Smartha Brahmins are lower in rank.

An examination of the manner in which the rules of commensality operate among the Brahmins of Sripuram will help us to gain some understanding of the nature of structural distance between different segments in the caste system. Since similar principles are operative in the case of Non-Brahmins and Adi-Dravidas, their part in the two latter cases will be indicated only briefly.

The Iyengars, who constitute the majority of Brahmins in Sripuram, are admitted to be the most exclusive in the matter of commensality. When a feast takes place in the *agraharam* on account of birth, marriage, death or some other occasion for ceremony, normally only Brahmins are invited to the meal. A few Non-Brahmins may be called, particularly if they are related to the family as servants or tenants, but they are given food separately in the backyard after the Brahmin guests have been served. Otherwise, particularly during marriage, a few influential Non-Brahmins may come to see the girl, and they are given betel leaves, areca nuts, bananas and coconuts, but not food in the proper sense of the term which includes cooked rice in one form or the other. Generally speaking, a Brahmin wedding at Sripuram, and the attendant feast, is a Brahmin affair; Non-Brahmins have very little to do with it, and still less Adi-Dravidas.

Brahmins do not dine at Non-Brahmin weddings. Generally they do not even attend, although the wedding may be taking place in the next street. If they go, they are given betel leaves, areca nuts and fruits – things which are not regarded as having any element of pollution attached to them. Orthodox Brahmins, particularly among Shri Vaishnavas, do not accept cooked food of any kind, including coffee, from Non-Brahmins. Some of the more 'progressive' and younger Brahmins, however, accept coffee and snacks when they visit their Non-Brahmin friends at Tanjore and elsewhere. For one thing, such Non-Brahmins, being town bred, are closer to them in their style of living than the peasants of Sripuram, and for another, social restrictions are more stringently observed in one's own village than outside.

When an important ceremony such as marriage takes place in the *agraharam*, it is obligatory on the part of the host to invite every family in the *agraharam* to the feast which forms a part of the occasion. Today, most of the Brahmins sit together and generally no distinction is made in the matter of serving. A generation or so ago, however, at wedding and other feasts Smarthas and

Shri Vaishnavas sat in separate rows, although they were served at the same time. The fact that Smarthas and Shri Vaishnavas of the younger generation freely interdine is another indication of the lessening of structural distance between the two communities to which reference was made earlier.

In examining the rules of commensality we find that the whole of society is broken up into segments, each segment forming a unit within which commensality is more or less freely allowed. In the broadest sense, the Brahmins together constitute such a segment, since commensality is by and large confined within it so far as the individual member is concerned. The broad Brahmin category is further segmented into Smarthas and Shri Vaishnavas, and for the orthodox, and for a considerable number of people in the older generation, the bonds of commensality often stop short at the boundary of each of these subdivisions. The Smarthas are further segmented into Vadama, Brihacharanam and so on, but segmentation at this level does not seem, at least in the recent past, to have been associated with commensal restrictions.

Commensal restrictions go hand in hand with a certain specialization of food habits which has been carried to a high degree by the Brahmins. Shri Vaishnavas, for instance, make use of silver utensils to a much greater extent than the others. In the Hindu scheme of values silver is considered to be, relatively speaking, 'pollutionproof'; in other words, the pollution attached to a utensil by another person eating or drinking out of it can be more easily removed if it is made of silver rather than bell metal, aluminium or stainless steel. Orthodox Shri Vaishnavas offer water to their Smartha guests in silver tumblers and food in silver plates. Smarthas are generally less particular about the rigidities of pollution.

In the kind of food eaten also there is a good deal of variation. All Tamil Brahmins are vegetarians, and the eating of meat, fish or eggs is considered polluting. The Adi-Dravidas eat meat of various kinds and also fish and eggs. Non-Brahmins show a wide range of variation. Most of them in Sripuram eat meat of certain kinds, although not regularly. A few of the Shaivite Vellalas do not eat meat at all, and some avoid eating it on particular days. The eating of meat or otherwise among the Vellalas of Sripuram cannot be exactly identified with caste since it is largely a matter of personal choice, although there are some Vellalas who refrain from eating meat as a group.

Differences in food habits, which are so clear between the broad Brahmin, Non-Brahmin and Adi-Dravida divisions, are also perceptible, although on a reduced scale, between the smaller subdivisions. Thus, among Adi-Dravidas, the Paraiyas eat beef, or did so until recently, whereas the Pallas refrain from beef, but eat pork. In Sripuram the Pallas not only do not inter-dine with the Paraiyas, but do not take water from the Paraiyas' wells or allow the Paraiyas to use theirs; this seems to be the general practice in the area as a whole.

The avoidance of meat by Brahmins, of pork by Vellalas, and of beef by Pallas has ritual sanctions. Sometimes, however, food habits are specialized along caste lines without any apparent ritual basis. Vegetarian food among Non-Brahmins has a different taste from that of the Brahmins, being generally more heavily spiced and hotter. Coffee is the most popular beverage among Brahmins, but Non-Brahmins, both in their homes and in restaurants, show a preference for tea. This is only partly explained by the fact that tea is less expensive.

V

We have seen that differentiation in styles of living has been developed to a very high degree within the caste system. Not only are there differences separating Brahmins from Non-Brahmins, but differences among Brahmins separate Shri Vaishnavas from Smarthas and, among Shri Vaishnavas, Vadagalai from Thengalai. The entire social world of Sripuram is thus divided and subdivided so as to constitute a segmentary structure in which each segment is differentiated from the other in terms of a number of criteria, major and minor. Further, in this structure the segments are not all equally separated from each other, but some are closer together and others further apart. For instance, the distance between Vadagalai and Thengalai Iyengar is smaller than the distance between either of them and any Non-Brahmin segment.

In the agrarian economy of Sripuram the three categories – Brahmin, Non-Brahmin and Adi-Dravida – have occupied rather different positions traditionally and are continuing to do so, by and large, even now. Very broadly speaking, one can characterize the Brahmins as landowners, the Non-Brahmins as cultivating tenants and the Adi-Dravidas as agricultural labourers. This characterization highlights only the typical positions. It holds true particularly with regard to Brahmins and Adi-Dravidas. Among the Non-Brahmins it admits of numerous exceptions since there are both landowners and agricultural labourers among them, and also there are Non-Brahmins of artisan and servicing castes who do not directly engage in agriculture.

Not all Brahmins are landowners, nor are all landowners Brahmins. The typical Brahmin in Sripuram is, none the less, a *mirasdar*, and it is he who sets the pattern for others to follow. In addition to landownership, Brahmins traditionally have engaged in various priestly functions, either as domestic priests or as temple priests. In Sripuram, however, the majority of Brahmins have been *mirasdars* devoted to the pursuit of learning and have not engaged in priesthood as a profession or a means of livelihood. There are today only three families in the *agraharam* which have priesthood as the principal source of livelihood.

Brahmins in general can be classified into three broad categories according to their calling and social position. The first category includes those who have been traditionally associated with the pursuit of learning and have lived on grants made by princes and patrons. These include the Smarthas proper and the Shri Vaishnavas. The term 'Vedic Brahmin' will be applied to this category, although the choice is not altogether a happy one.[4] The second category is made up of those who act as domestic priests for the Non-Brahmins; they are known as Panchangakkarans. The Panchangakkaran Brahmins in this area are Telugu-speaking. It should be emphasized that the Vedic Brahmins (the Shri Vaishnavas and the Smarthas proper) do not act as domestic priests for Non-Brahmins – at least, not in this area. The third category comprises temple priests or Archakars; it is made up of Kurukkals, or priests who officiate at Shiva temples, and Bhattachars, or those who officiate at Vishnu temples. These three

4. As an alternative I have thought of the term 'mirasdar Brahmin', which seems to be equally unsatisfactory. The general meaning of *mirasdar* is landowner or rentier.

categories of Brahmins constitute three endogamous divisions, each with further subdivisions.

The Brahmin has by tradition and scriptural injunction a number of roles: pursuit of learning; acceptance of alms; ministration to the spiritual needs of the populace. Although these roles may be combined in a single person, this is not always the case. The image of the Brahmin in the popular mind is of a person who lives by ministering to the religious needs of people. This image, as we have seen, is rather divorced from the real position of the Brahmins in Sripuram. In this village today there is only one Brahmin who acts as a *purohit*. But he ministers only to the religious needs of the *agraharam*, and only to the majority of Shri Vaishnavas, not to all the members of the *agràharam*. The Smarthas as well as certain other Shri Vaishnavas have *purohits* from among their own subcaste living at Thiruvaiyar and Tanjore.

The Vedic Brahmins of Sripuram do not today live by scholarship, although many of them can trace their descent from persons who did so in the past and were endowed with property for the purpose. Once a Brahmin scholar acquired property, it was handed down from generation to generation and the descendants became *mirasdars* by inheritance of ancestral property. It was not strictly obligatory on their part to keep up the family tradition, although many of them did so in practice. Thus, at the beginning of this century the Brahmins of Sripuram included a number of Sanskrit scholars pursuing their family traditions, and most of them owned at least a few acres of land. In course of the last sixty years the movement of population in and out of the *agraharam*, and the sale of land by many Brahmins, have reduced the number of *mirasdars* among them and, to some extent, disturbed the occupational homogeneity of the *agraharam*.

Today many Brahmins in the *agraharam* have taken up what may be considered new occupations. There are several clerks and schoolteachers among them. But one can easily see that in the choice of new occupations they have retained a certain continuity with the past and have not departed significantly from it. By and large, the most important element in their style of living has been preserved in their new occupations. No Brahmin has taken to any manual work in the real sense of the term. There is one person who has taken a job as a mechanic in a transport undertaking, but this is a recent occurrence and is regarded as exceptional.

Non-Brahmins, on the other hand, engage in various kinds of manual work. In Sripuram there are no big Non-Brahmin landowners, although there are absentee landlords among the Non-Brahmins living at Thiruvaiyar and Tanjore. The principal cultivating castes among the Non-Brahmins are the Vellalas, Padayachis and Kallas. Most of them are directly engaged in cultivation in one form or another. There is no ritual rule which prohibits the use of the plough by them as in the case of Brahmins; in fact, using the plough is their traditional occupation. There are some fairly prosperous Vellala and Kalla landowners who do not themselves till the soil, but supervise the work of agriculture. This practice, however, is exceptional rather than general; the Non-Brahmin cultivator in Sripuram adopts it only when he has acquired a good bit of land, and generally after he has passed a certain age.

In addition to these moderately well-to-do Vellala owner-cultivators, there are a few others who have taken to nonmanual occupations. These include the Tamil *pundit* referred to earlier, and a few shopkeepers and clerks. Up to now the adoption of these occupations has been exceptional among the Non-Brahmins of Sripuram, and it does not appear to have significantly affected their styles of living. There is only one Non-Brahmin family which is significantly different from the others in this regard. This is the Maratha family which owned at one time a good proportion of the land in Sripuram and whose members in their ways and habits are clearly *mirasdars* rather than peasants.

The Non-Brahmins of Sripuram also include artisan castes such as Potters and Carpenters, and servicing castes such as Barbers and Washermen. The artisan castes do not all perform their traditional occupation today. But manual work enters as an important component in their style of living in the large majority of cases. Finally, there are many Non-Brahmins who are engaged as cartmen, masons and labourers of one kind or another within and outside the village.

If manual labour plays an important part in the lives of Non-Brahmins, it does so to an even greater extent among the Adi-Dravidas. The Pallas not only engage in manual work, but their work in general is nonspecialized and unskilled, and less prestige is attached to it than to the work of the Non-Brahmin artisans. Occupations are graded by people in a more or less conscious manner, and the more degrading tasks such as hoeing, digging and carrying earth are reserved for Adi-Dravidas. Although there is a good deal of overlap between the work of Non-Brahmins and Adi-Dravidas, one can say, with some simplification, that the typical Non-Brahmin peasant in Sripuram is a sharecropper or a cultivator, whereas the typical Adi-Dravida is an agricultural labourer.

Occupation, however, is only one component, although an important one, in the style of life of a people. It has to be remembered that apart from the two families of temple priests there are no significant differences in traditional occupation among the Brahmins of Sripuram. Further, the new occupations adopted by them maintain a certain continuity with the past and seem to be more or less equally accessible to all varieties of Brahmins in the village. In spite of this, there are many differences among them, reflected particularly in their religious culture.

VI

Caste has often been viewed as the prototype of all hierarchical systems. Principles of caste rank rest essentially on conceptions of social esteem. Social esteem is attached to particular styles of life, and groups are ranked as high or low according to how or whether they pursue such styles. What is highly esteemed varies from one society to another and depends ultimately on the value-system of the society. In India ritual elements (and, in particular, the ideas of purity and pollution) have historically occupied an important place in styles of life which have enjoyed high social esteem.

Status in a caste hierarchy is based partly upon wealth, but not entirely. It is based upon wealth to the extent that the possession of a certain minimum of wealth is a necessary condition to the pursuit of a certain style of life. Beyond this minimum, however, it is not true that any caste which is in possession of more wealth is by this fact in a position of superior social rank.

Status, in addition to being associated with specific styles of life, has in every society a strong traditional bias. Hence it is not enough for a certain caste to adopt a particular style of life in order to achieve higher social rank. It has to legitimize its position by working this style of life into a tradition; it has to establish its association with the style over a number of generations.

Although it may be possible to list the different attributes which enter into styles of life that are highly esteemed, such listing would be of limited value. In the first place, people do not rank different castes in terms of a rational application of particular standards. Second, the standards themselves are ambiguous, variable, and subject to change over time.

Thus, although hierarchy is an important feature of the caste system, we must not assume that wherever there is segmentation we can rank the segments as higher or lower. There are conflicting claims to superior rank, and often it is impossible to speak of a consensus. It frequently happens that two castes put forward rival claims to superiority with regard to which members of other castes may be indifferent or may not regard themselves as competent to decide either way.

The important point to bear in mind about the hierarchy of the caste system is its ambiguities beyond a certain level. These ambiguities are essential in a system which seems always to have permitted a certain degree of mobility. They are further increased by the fact that the basis of social esteem, the entire value system on which the ranking of castes depends, has in recent times been undergoing important changes.

Ambiguities notwithstanding, one can say that the broad divisions, Brahmin, Non-Brahmin and Adi-Dravida, are associated with different degrees of social esteem. In the context of Sripuram, and perhaps of Tamilnad as a whole, there would be a wide measure of consensus that Brahmins rank higher socially than Non-Brahmins, who in turn rank higher than Adi-Dravidas. There are, no doubt, some Non-Brahmins who would challenge the relevance of such a system of grading; but most of them would accept it, and few would suggest a different order. Even though some Non-Brahmins may challenge the claim by Brahmins that they are superior in rank, this claim would certainly be acknowledged by the third party, the Adi-Dravidas. Thus, at the broadest level there is little ambiguity about social rank or the nature of the hierarchy.

Coming to subdivisions among the Brahmins, there would be fairly general agreement that the Smarthas and Shri Vaishnavas proper rank higher than the Panchangakkarans and the Kurukkals and Bhattachars. As between Panchangakkarans, on the one hand, and Kurukkals and Bhattachars, on the other, it is difficult to assign social precedence. The issue cannot in any case be decided with reference to Sripuram, since there are no Panchangakkaran Brahmins in the village.

The position of comparative inferiority of the Panchangakkarans and Archakars (i.e. Kurukkals and Bhattachars) may be partly explained by the fact that their occupation makes them dependent for their livelihood on services rendered to Non-Brahmins. Services to Non-Brahmins in a specific way do not enter into the style of life of the Smarthas and Shri Vaishnavas proper. Rather, their style of life revolves around the cultivation of scriptural knowledge and the performance of individual and family rites, both of which are associated with high social esteem.

Shri Vaishnavas and Smarthas make competing claims to the highest social rank. The claims cannot be judged in terms of any fixed or objective standards. Shri Vaishnavas tend to be more orthodox and exclusive, and they may even refuse to take water from the hands of Smarthas. But this is not necessarily accepted as a sign of superiority, since Smarthas as well as other Brahmins regard it as an extreme example of bigotry and sometimes hold it up to ridicule. Shri Vaishnavas claim superiority on the ground that they are more rigorous and orthodox in their ritual observances and that they do not worship non-Sanskritic deities as the Smarthas do. Smarthas maintain that Shri Vaishnavas are not Brahmins at all, but descendants of assorted people converted by Ramanuja.

It should be recognized that the actual position of a caste in the village is not based merely upon certain absolute standards of social estimation, but depends also upon local factors. In Sripuram the Shri Vaishnavas are in a dominant position by virtue of their strength of numbers and their control over various aspects of social life in the *agraharam*, including control of the Vishnu temple. The Smarthas are in a position of relative weakness. But there are other villages where Smarthas are in a position of strength and the presence of Shri Vaishnavas in the *agraharam* is accepted only on sufferance.

Determination of caste rank among the Non-Brahmins suffers similarly from ambiguity and the absence of universally accepted criteria. Conflicting claims to higher social rank are often expressed among the Non-Brahmins in the idiom of the *varna* scheme. Some of them claim to be Brahmins, some claim to be Kshatriyas and some claim to be Vaishyas. But the presentation of a claim does not necessarily, or even generally, lead to its acceptance. Thus, although the Padayachis claim to be Kshatriyas, and the Vellalas do not generally go above the Vaishya level in their claims, it is the Vellalas rather than the Padayachis who are, by and large, accepted as superior.

Such claims to Brahmin, Kshatriya and Vaishya status cannot be used as a basis for deciding questions of rank among the Non-Brahmins, because they are rarely, if ever, fully accepted. In the absence of a uniform set of principles for ranking castes it would perhaps be more meaningful to give some idea of the actual rank order as it exists among the Non-Brahmins in Sripuram.

There is a popular saying in Tamil: *Kallan, Maravan, Ahamudiyan, mella mella wandu Vellalar anar. Vellalar ahi, Mudaliyar shonnar.* ('Kallan, Maravan, and Ahamudiyan by slow degrees became Vellala. Having become Vellala, they called themselves Mudaliyar.') This saying illustrates two important features of the system: (1) that there is a hierarchical order which can be ascertained in broad terms for any given area, and (2) that it is possible for individual castes to move up this order with some success.

Mobility in the caste system may be sought either through the *varna* idiom, which has an all-India spread, or through the idiom of the local system of *jatis*. When the Padayachis claim to be Kshatriyas, they try to make use of the *varna* idiom. When, on the other hand, the Ahamudiyas claim to be Vellalas, they make use of an idiom which has a more local character. Both kinds of idiom have been extensively used over the last several decades.

In the context of Sripuram the hierarchy of castes among the Non-Brahmins is clear up to a point; beyond this point there is a good deal of ambiguity. One can roughly determine the upper and the lower rungs, but in the middle regions ranking is uncertain. Thus, it would be generally admitted that the Vellala (Peasant) group of castes occupies a high position, and that the Vannans (Washermen) and Ambattans (Barbers) rank rather low. The Tattans (Goldsmiths) and Tachchans (Carpenters) also occupy high positions, while the Nadars (Toddy-tappers) would be ranked near the bottom. The bulk of the cultivating castes rank somewhat lower than the Vellalas. Beyond this, very little can be said with any measure of certainty.

The position with regard to the Adi-Dravidas is somewhat similar in Sripuram. The Pallas, who constitute the bulk of them, are regarded by reason of their occupation and their food habits to be less degraded than the Paraiyas, Thottis and Chakkiliyas. Conversion to Christianity does not seem to make a real difference as far as the social rank of the Paraiyas is concerned. What is important is the style of life with which they have been traditionally associated and which still persists among them without very serious modifications.

Part Eight
Race and Social Stratification

Race in the broadest sense is closely associated with both the idea and the practice of social inequality. Although prejudice and discrimination based on race seem to be a common feature of many societies of both the past and the present, the importance of race in stratification has been heightened by two factors: slavery and colonialism. Today when other forms of social discrimination are on the decline, the importance of race seems to be on the increase. The essay by St Clair Drake examines the position of the Negro in the United States, discussing both the objective condition of the American Negro and the myths that have grown around him in a society which professes strongly equalitarian ideals. The contribution by van den Berghe analyses the pattern of racial discrimination in South Africa, in a historical perspective, and describes the social context out of which the policy of apartheid has emerged.

15 St Clair Drake

The Social and Economic Status of the Negro in the United States

St Clair Drake, 'The social and economic status of the Negro in the United States', *Daedalus*, vol. 94, no. 4 (1965), pp. 771–84, 805–10.

Caste, Class and 'Victimization'

During the 1930s, W. Lloyd Warner and Allison Davis developed and popularized a conceptual scheme for analysing race relations in the Southern region of the United States which viewed Negro–white relations as organized by a color-caste system that shaped economic and political relations as well as family and kinship structures, and which was reinforced by the legal system. Within each of the two castes (superordinate white and subordinate Negro), social classes existed, status being based upon possession of money, education and family background as reflected in distinctive styles of behavior. 'Exploitation' in the Marxist sense was present within this caste-class system, but also much more; for an entire socio-cultural system, not just the economic order, functioned to distribute power and prestige unevenly between whites and Negroes and to punish any individuals who questioned the system by word or behavior.[1]

Students of the situation in the North rarely conceptualized race relations in terms of caste, but tended rather to view specific communities as areas in which *ethnic* groups were involved in continuous competition and conflict, resulting in a hierarchy persisting through time, with now one, and again another, ethnic

1. The first systematic formulation of a caste-class hypothesis to explain American race relations appeared in an article by W. Lloyd Warner and Allison Davis, 'A comparative study of American caste', one of several contributions to a volume edited by Edgar Thompson, *Race Relations and The Race Problem*, Raleigh, N.C., 1939. The field research upon which much of the article was based was published later as Allison Davis, Burleigh Gardner and Mary Gardner, *Deep South*, Chicago, 1941. For a Marxist criticism of the caste-class interpretation of American race relations, see Oliver Cromwell Cox, *Caste, Class and Race*, New York, 1948.

group at the bottom as previous newcomers moved 'up'. Each ethnic group developed a social class structure within it, but as individuals acquired better jobs, more education and some sophistication, they and their families often detached themselves from immigrant colonies (usually located in slum areas) and sometimes from all ethnic institutions as well. They tended to become a part of the middle class. The Negroes who migrated North in large numbers during the First World War were the latest arrivals in this fluid and highly competitive situation, but their high visibility became a crucial factor limiting their upward mobility. Upwardly mobile Negroes could not 'disappear' into the middle class of the larger society as did European ethnics.[2]

Thus, on the eve of the Second World War, students of race relations in the United States generally described the status of Negroes as one in which they played subordinate roles in a caste system in the South and an ethnic-class system in the North. The actions of persons toward those of another race were explained not in terms of some vaguely defined emotions connected with 'prejudice', but rather in terms of the behavior they felt was expected of them by others in various positions within the social structure, and as attempts to protect and maximize whatever power and prestige accrued to them at their locus in the system. John Dollard, a psychologist, in his *Caste and Class in A Southern Town*, added an additional dimension. He analyses the situation in terms of the 'gains' and 'losses' – sexual, psychological, economic and political – which both Negroes and whites sustained at different levels in the Southern caste-class system.[3]

The caste-class analysis still provides a useful frame of refer-

2. Analysis of inter-ethnic mobility in terms of conflict, accommodation and assimilation characterized the work of 'The Chicago School' of Sociology during the 1920s and early 1930s. For more sophisticated analysis, note W. L. Warner and Leo Srole, *The Social Systems of American Ethnic Groups*, New Haven, Conn., 1946, in which studies of comparative mobility rates of various ethnic groups are made. Nathan Glazer and Patrick D. Moynihan, in *Beyond The Melting Pot*, Cambridge, Mass., 1963, have recently suggested that ethnic solidarities are much more enduring than earlier sociologists had expected them to be.

3. John Dollard, in association with Allison Davis, has added other dimensions to his analysis in *Children of Bondage*, Washington, D.C., 1940.

ence for studying the behavior of individuals and groups located at various positions in the social structure. It can also serve as a starting point for viewing the *processes* of race relations in terms of their consequences. Of the racial and ethnic groups in America only Negroes have been subjected to caste-deprivations; and the ethnic-class system has operated to their disadvantage as compared with European immigrants. In other words, Negroes in America have been subject to 'victimization' in the sense that a system of social relations operates in such a way as to deprive them of a chance to share in the more desirable material and non-material products of a society which is dependent, in part, upon their labor and loyalty. They are 'victimized', also, because they do not have the same degree of access which others have to the attributes needed for rising in the general class system – money, education, 'contacts', and 'know-how'.

The concept of 'victimization' implies, too, that some people are used as means to other people's ends – without their consent – and that the social system is so structured that it can be deliberately manipulated to the disadvantage of some groups by the clever, the vicious and the cynical, as well as by the powerful. The callous and indifferent unconsciously and unintentionally reinforce the system by their inaction or inertia. The 'victims', their autonomy curtailed and their self-esteem weakened by the operation of the caste-class system, are confronted with 'identity problems'. Their social condition is essentially one of 'powerlessness'.

Individual 'victims' may or may not accept the rationalizations given for the denial to them of power and prestige. They may or may not be aware of and concerned about their position in the system, but, when they do become concerned, victimization takes on important social psychological dimensions. Individuals then suffer feelings of 'relative deprivation' which give rise to reactions ranging from despair, apathy and withdrawal to covert and overt aggression. An effective analysis of the position of the Negro in these terms (although the word 'victimization' is never used) may be found in Thomas F. Pettigrew's *A Profile of the Negro American* (1964).

Concepts developed by Max Weber are useful for assessing the degree of victimization existing within the American caste-class system.[4] Individuals and groups can be compared by examining what he refers to as 'life chances', that is, the extent to which people have access to economic and political power. *Direct victimization* might be defined as the operation of sanctions which deny access to power, which limit the franchise, sustain job discrimination, permit unequal pay for similar work, or provide inferior training or no training at all. *Indirect victimization* is revealed in the consequences which flow from a social structure which decreases '*life chances*', such as high morbidity and mortality rates, low longevity rates, a high incidence of psychopathology or the persistence of personality traits and attitudes which impose disadvantages in competition or excite derogatory and invidious comparisons with other groups. Max Weber also compared individuals and groups in terms of differences in '*life styles*', those ways of behaving which vary in the amount of esteem, honor and prestige attached to them. Differences in 'life chances' may make it impossible to acquire the money or education (or may limit the contacts) necessary for adopting and maintaining prestigious life styles. The key to understanding many aspects of race relations may be found in the fact that, in American society, the protection of their familiar and cherished life styles is a dominating concern of the white middle classes, who, because many Negroes have life styles differing from their own, have tried to segregate them into all-Negro neighborhoods, voluntary associations and churches.[5] (Marxist sociologists tend to overemphasize protection of economic interests as a dynamic factor in American race relations, important though it is.)

4. For a discussion of these concepts, see Hans Gerth and C. Wright Mills, *From Max Weber: Essays in Sociology*, Routledge, 1946, chapter on 'Caste, class and party'.

5. The distinguished psychotherapist, Bruno Bettelheim, of the Orthogenic School of the University of Chicago, in a provocative and perceptive article in *The Nation*, 19 October 1963 ('Class, color and prejudice'), contends that protection of social class values is a more important variable than race prejudice in structuring relations between Negroes and whites in the North of the U.S.A.

The 'Ghettoization' of Negro Life

Pressure upon Negroes to live within all-Negro neighborhoods has resulted in those massive concentrations of Negro population in Northern metropolitan areas which bitter critics call 'concentration camps' or 'plantations' and which some social scientists refer to as 'Black Ghettos'.[6] Small town replicas exist everywhere throughout the nation, for the roots of residential segregation lie deep in American history. In older Southern towns slave quarters were transformed into Negro residential areas after Emancipation – a few blocks here, a whole neighborhood there, often adjacent to white homes. In newer Southern towns and cities a less secure upwardly mobile white population usually demanded a greater degree of segregation from ex-slaves and their descendants. Prior to the First World War, the residential patterns did not vary greatly between North and South, but the great northward migration of Negroes between 1914 and 1920 expanded the small Negro neighborhoods into massive Black Belts. Middle-class white neighbors used 'restrictive-covenants' as their main device for slowing down and 'containing' the expansion of Negro neighborhoods. Thus, with continued in-migration and restricted access to housing in 'white neighborhoods', the overcrowded Black Ghetto emerged with its substandard structures, poor public services, and high crime and juvenile delinquency rates.

Scholars know from careful research, and increasingly wider circles are becoming aware of the fact, that Negroes do not depress property values, but that middle-class white attitudes toward Negroes do.[7] As long as Negroes, as a group, are a

6. St Clair Drake and Horace R. Cayton, in *Black Metropolis*, Harper, 1962, use the term 'Black Ghetto' to refer to the involuntary and exploitative aspect of the all-Negro community and 'Bronzeville' to symbolize the more pleasant aspects of the segregated community. Robert C. Weaver, another Negro scholar, called his first book *The Negro Ghetto*, Russell, 1948. The term is widely used by contemporary Negro leaders with pejorative implications.

7. The most careful study of the effect of Negro entry into all-white neighborhoods is to be found in a book published by the University of California Press in 1961 which reports upon the results of research in Detroit, Chicago, Kansas City, Oakland, San Francisco, Philadelphia and Portland, Oregon – Luigi Laurenti's *Property Values and Race*, University of California Press, 1961.

symbol of lower social status, proximity to them will be considered undesirable and such social attitudes will be reflected in the market place. The problem is complicated by the fact that a very high proportion of Negro Americans actually does have lower-class attributes and behavior patterns. The upward mobility of white Americans, as well as their comfort and personal safety, is facilitated by spatial segregation. (Older cities in the South have been an exception.) The white middle class could protect its values by acting solely in terms of class, letting middle-class Negro families scatter into white neighborhoods irrespective of race. Instead, the white middle class in American cities protects its own neighborhoods from behavior patterns it disapproves of and from chronic social disorganization by 'ghettoizing' the Negro. Real-estate operators, black and white, have exploited the fears of the white middle class from the beginning of the northern migration by 'block busting', that is, by buying property for less than its normal market value and reselling it at a higher price to Negroes barred from the open market or by charging them higher rentals. Eventually the profit-potential in residential segregation was maximized by the institutions which controlled mortgage money and refused to finance property for Negro residence outside of the Black Belts except under conditions approved by them.

In 1948 the Supreme Court declared racial restrictive covenants unenforceable in the courts, but this action tended to accelerate rather than reverse the process of ghettoization, for many whites proceeded to sell to Negroes at inflated prices and then moved to the suburbs, or they retained their properties, moved away and raised the rents. The Court's decision was based partly upon a re-evaluation of the concept of civil rights and partly upon a recognition of the fact that serious economic injustice was a by-product of residential segregation, a situation summed up by Thomas Pettigrew:

While some housing gains occurred in the 1850s, the quality of Negro housing remains vastly inferior relative to that of whites. For example, in Chicago in 1960, Negroes paid as much for housing as whites, despite their lower incomes. . . . This situation exists because of essentially two separate housing markets; and the residential segregation that creates these dual markets has increased steadily over past decades until it has reached universally high levels in cities throughout the United States, despite significant advances in the socio-economic status of Negroes. . . .[8]

The trend has not yet been reversed despite F.H.A. administrative regulations and Supreme Court decisions.

The spatial isolation of Negroes from whites created Negro 'communities'. Within these Negro neighborhoods, church and school became the basic integrative institutions, and Negro entrepreneurs developed a variety of service enterprises – barbershops and beauty parlors, funeral homes and restaurants, pool parlors, taverns and hotels – all selling to what came to be called 'The Negro Market'. Successful banking and insurance businesses also grew up within some Negro communities. A Negro 'subculture' gradually emerged, national in scope, with distinctive variations upon the general American culture in the fields of literature, art, music and dance, as well as in religious ritual and church polity.

The spatial isolation of Negroes from whites in 'Black Belts' also increased consciousness of their separate subordinate position, for no whites were available to them as neighbors, schoolmates or friends, but were present only in such roles as schoolteachers, policemen and social workers, flat janitors and real-estate agents, merchants and bill collectors, skilled laborers involved in maintenance, and even a few white dentists and doctors with offices in the Black Belt. Such a situation inevitably generated anti-white sentiments (often with anti-Semitic overtones); and the pent-up feelings have occasionally erupted in anti-white riots. Normally, however, this intense racial consciousness finds expression in non-violent forms of social protest and is utilized by Negro leaders to sanction and reinforce Negro institutions and their own personal welfare. It has also lent powerful support to the segments of municipal political machines existing within Negro neighborhoods. As long as ghettos remain, race consciousness will be strong.

Residential segregation created the demographic and ecological

8. Thomas F. Pettigrew, *A Profile of the Negro American*, Van Nostrand, 1964, p. 190. His wife, Dr Ann Pettigrew, M.D., collaborated with him on the chapter dealing with health.

basis for 'balance of power' politics, since the possibility of a Negro bloc vote had to be recognized by both political parties. Northern Black Belt voters are not only occasionally the decisive factor in municipal elections, but have also sent a half-dozen Negroes to Congress. Indeed, it is ironic that one of the most effective weapons against segregation and discrimination in the South has been the political power generated in Negro precincts and wards of Northern Black Ghettos, thus reinforcing the direct action tactics of the civil rights movement. In the South, too, with the passage of the Civil Rights Act of 1964 and subsequent legislation, the political strength of newly enfranchised voters lies in their spatial concentration. There is some evidence that fear of this strength may operate as a factor in Northern cities to support 'open occupancy', desegregation being considered preferable to Negro dominance.[9]

While the development of machine politics has brought some gains to Negro communities, it has also resulted in various forms of indirect victimization. Local Negro leaders often co-operate with the city-wide machine in the protection of 'the rackets' – policy, dope and prostitution – and sacrifice group welfare to personal gain for self and party. They have not hesitated, in some places, even to drag their heels in the fight for residential desegregation rather than risk wiping out the base of their power. Being saddled with a 'bought leadership' is one of the greatest burdens Black Ghettos have had to bear. Economic victimization is widespread, too. In the 'affluent society' of the sixties, consumption-oriented and given to the 'hard sell', Negroes like other Americans are under social pressure to spend beyond their means. Given the lack of sophistication of many recent migrants and the very low median income of those with less than a high-school education, it is not surprising that loan sharks and dubious credit merchants (of all races) make the Black Ghetto a prime target. Negroes pay a high price for 'protection' of the white middle-class way of life, since those who aspire to leave the ghetto are trapped, and those who are content to stay develop a limited and restricted view of the world in which they live.

9. Though based upon only one community in Chicago, *The Politics of Urban Renewal*, by Peter Rossi and Robert A. Dentler, Free Press, 1961, analyses basic processes to be found in all Northern cities.

Folkways and Classways Within the Black Ghetto

Black Ghettos in America are, on the whole, 'run down' in appearance and overcrowded, and their inhabitants bear the physical and psychological scars of those whose 'life chances' are not equal to those of other Americans. Like the European immigrants before them, they inherited the worst housing in the city. Within the past decade, the white 'flight to the suburbs' has released relatively new and well-kept property on the margins of some of the old Black Belts. Here, 'gilded ghettos' have grown up, indistinguishable from any other middle-class neighborhoods except by the color of the residents' skin.[10] The power mower in the yard, the steak grill on the rear lawn, a well-stocked library and equally well-stocked bar in the rumpus room – these mark the homes of well-to-do Negroes living in the more desirable portions of the Black Belt. Many of them would flee to suburbia, too, if housing were available to Negroes there.

But the character of the Black Ghetto is not set by the newer 'gilded', not-yet run down portions of it, but by the older sections where unemployment rates are high and the masses of people work with their hands – where the median level of education is just above graduation from grade school and many of the people are likely to be recent migrants from rural areas.[11]

The 'ghettoization' of the Negro has resulted in the emergence of a ghetto subculture with a distinctive ethos, most pronounced, perhaps, in Harlem, but recognizable in all Negro neighborhoods. For the average Negro who walks the streets of any American Black Ghetto, the smell of barbecued ribs, fried shrimps and chicken emanating from numerous restaurants gives olfactory reinforcement to a feeling of 'at-homeness'. The beat of 'gut music' spilling into the street from ubiquitous tavern juke boxes and the sound of tambourines and rich harmony behind the crude folk art on the windows of store-front churches give auditory confirmation to the universal belief that 'We Negroes have

10. Professor Everett C. Hughes makes some original and highly pertinent remarks about new Negro middle-class communities in his introduction to the 1962 edition of Drake and Cayton's *Black Metropolis*.

11. Pettigrew, op. cit., pp. 180–81.

"soul"'. The bedlam of an occasional brawl, the shouted obscenities of street corner 'foul mouths', and the whine of police sirens break the monotony of waiting for the number that never 'falls', the horses that neither win, place nor show, and the 'good job' that never materializes. The insouciant swagger of teen-age drop-outs (the 'cats') masks the hurt of their aimless existence and contrasts sharply with the ragged clothing and dejected demeanor of 'skid-row' types who have long since stopped trying to keep up appearances and who escape it all by becoming 'winoes'. The spontaneous vigor of the children who crowd streets and playgrounds (with Cassius Clay, Ernie Banks, the Harlem Globe Trotters and black stars of stage, screen and television as their role models) and the cheerful rushing about of adults, free from the occupational pressures of the 'white world' in which they work, create an atmosphere of warmth and superficial intimacy which obscures the unpleasant facts of life in the overcrowded rooms behind the doors, the lack of adequate maintenance standards and the too prevalent vermin and rats.

This is a world whose urban 'folkways' the upwardly mobile Negro middle class deplores as a 'drag' on 'The Race', which the upper classes wince at as an embarrassment, and which race leaders point to as proof that Negroes have been victimized. But for the masses of the ghetto dwellers this is a warm and familiar milieu, preferable to the sanitary coldness of middle-class neighborhoods and a counterpart of the communities of the foreign-born, each of which has its own distinctive subcultural flavor. The arguments in the barbershop, the gossip in the beauty parlors, the 'jiving' of bar girls and waitresses, the click of poolroom balls, the stomping of feet in the dance halls, the shouting in the churches are all *theirs* – and the white men who run the pawnshops, supermarts, drug stores and grocery stores, the policemen on horseback, the teachers in blackboard jungles – all these are aliens, conceptualized collectively as 'The Man', intruders on the Black Man's 'turf'. When an occasional riot breaks out, 'The Man' and his property become targets of aggression upon which pent-up frustrations are vented. When someone during the Harlem riots of 1964 begged the street crowds to go home, the cry came back, 'Baby, we *are* home!'

But the inhabitants of the Black Ghetto are not a homogeneous mass. Although, in Marxian terms, nearly all of them are 'proletarians', with nothing to sell but their labor, variations in 'life style' differentiate them into social classes based more upon differences in education and basic values (crystallized, in part, around occupational differences) than in meaningful differences in income. The American caste-class system has served, over the years, to concentrate the Negro population in the low-income sector of the economy. In 1961 six out of every ten Negro families had an income of less than $4000.00 per year. This situation among whites was just the reverse: six out of every ten white families had *over* $4000.00 a year at their disposal. (In the South, eight out of ten Negro families were below the $4000.00 level.) This is the income gap. Discrimination in employment creates a job ceiling, most Negroes being in blue-collar jobs.

With 60 per cent of America's Negro families earning less than $4000.00 a year, social strata emerge between the upper and lower boundaries of 'no earned income' and $4000.00. Some families live a 'middle-class style of life', placing heavy emphasis upon decorous public behavior and general respectability, insisting that their children 'get an education' and 'make something out of themselves'. They prize family stability, and an unwed mother is something much more serious than 'just a girl who had an accident'; pre-marital and extra-marital sexual relations, if indulged in at all, must be discreet. Social life is organized around churches and a welter of voluntary associations of all types, and, for women, 'the cult of clothes' is so important that fashion shows are a popular fund raising activity even in churches. For both men and women, owning a home and going into business are highly desired goals, the former often being a realistic one, the latter a mere fantasy.

Within the same income range, and not always at the lower margin of it, other families live a 'lower-class life-style' being part of the 'organized' lower class, while at the lowest income levels an 'unorganized' lower class exists whose members tend always to become *dis*organized – functioning in an anomic situation where gambling, excessive drinking, the use of narcotics and sexual promiscuity are prevalent forms of behavior, and violent interpersonal relations reflect an ethos of suspicion and resentment which suffuses this deviant subculture. It is within this milieu that criminal and semi-criminal activities burgeon.

The 'organized' lower class is oriented primarily around churches whose preachers, often semi-literate, exhort them to 'be in the "world" but not of it'. Conventional middle-class morality and Pauline Puritanism are preached, although a general attitude of 'the spirit is willing but the flesh is weak' prevails except among a minority fully committed to the Pentecostal sects. They boast, 'We *live* the life' – a way of life that has been portrayed with great insight by James Baldwin in *Go Tell it on the Mountain* and *The Fire Next Time*.

Young people with talent find wide scope for expressing it in choirs, quartets and sextets, which travel from church to church (often bearing colorful names like The Four Heavenly Trumpets or the Six Singing Stars of Zion) and sometimes travelling from city to city. Such troups channel their aggressions in widely advertised 'Battles of Song' and develop their talent in church pageants such as 'Heaven Bound' or 'Queen Esther' and fund-raising events where winners are crowned King and Queen. These activities provide fun as well as a testing ground for talent. Some lucky young church people eventually find their fortune in the secular world as did singers Sam Cooke and Nat King Cole, while others remain in the church world as nationally known gospel singers or famous evangelists.

Adults as well as young people find satisfaction and prestige in serving as ushers and deacons, 'mothers', and deaconesses, Sunday-school teachers and choir leaders. National conventions of Negro denominations and national societies of ushers and gospel singers not only develop a continent-wide nexus of associations within the organized lower class, but also throw the more ambitious and capable individuals into meaningful contact with middle-class church members who operate as role models for the less talented persons who seek to move upward. That prestige and sometimes money come so easily in these circles may be a factor militating against a pattern of delaying gratifications and seeking mobility into professional and semi-professional pursuits through higher education.

Lower-class families and institutions are constantly on the move, for in recent years the Negro lower class has suffered from projects to redevelop the inner city. By historic accident, the decision to check the expansion of physical deterioration in metropolitan areas came at a time when Negroes were the main inhabitants of substandard housing. (If urban redevelopment had been necessary sixty years ago immigrants, not Negroes, would have suffered.) In protest against large-scale demolition of areas where they live, Negroes have coined a slogan, 'Slum clearance is Negro clearance'. They resent the price in terms of the inconvenience thrust upon them in order to redevelop American cities,[12] and the evidence shows that, in some cities, there is no net gain in improved housing after relocation.

At the opposite pole from the Negro lower class in both life styles and life chances is the small Negro upper class whose solid core is a group in the professions, along with well-to-do businessmen who have had some higher education, but including, also, a scattering of individuals who have had college training but do not have a job commensurate with their education. These men and their spouses and children form a cohesive upper-class stratum in most Negro communities. Within this group are individuals who maintain some type of contact – though seldom any social relations – with members of the local white power élite; but whether or not they participate in occupational associations with their white peers depends upon the region of the country in which they live. (It is from this group that Negro 'Exhibit A's' are recruited when white liberals are carrying on campaigns to 'increase interracial understanding'.) They must always think of themselves as symbols of racial advancement as well as individuals, they often provide the basic leadership at local levels for organizations such as the N.A.A.C.P. and the Urban League. They must lend sympathetic support to the more militant civil rights organizations, too, by financial contributions, if not action.[13]

The life styles of the Negro upper class are similar to those of the white upper *middle* class, but it is only in rare instances that

12. The issue of the extent to which Negroes have been victimized by urban redevelopment is discussed briefly by Robert C. Weaver in *The Urban Complex: Human Values in Urban Life*, Doubleday, 1964. See also Martin Anderson, *The Federal Bulldozer: A Critical Analysis of Urban Renewal: 1949–1962*, M.I.T. Press, 1964.

13. Drake and Cayton, op. cit., ch. 23, 'Advancing the race'.

Negroes have been incorporated into the clique and associational life of this group or have intermarried into it. (Their participation in activities of the white upper class occurs more often than with those whites who have similar life styles because of Negro upper-class participation as members of various civic boards and inter-racial associations to which wealthy white people contribute.) Living 'well' with highly developed skills, having enough money to travel, Negroes at this social level do not experience victimization in the same fashion as do the members of the lower class. Their victimization flows primarily from the fact that the social system keeps them 'half in and half out', preventing the free and easy contact with their occupational peers which they need; and it often keeps them from making the kind of significant intellectual and social contributions to the national welfare that they might make if they were white. (They are also forced to experience various types of nervous strain and dissipation of energy over petty annoyances and deprivations which only the sensitive and the cultivated feel. Most barbershops, for instance, are not yet desegregated, and taxi-drivers, even in the North, sometimes refuse Negro passengers.)

The Negro upper class has created a social world of its own in which a universe of discourse and uniformity of behavior and outlook are maintained by the interaction on national and local levels of members of Negro Greek-letter fraternities and sororities, college and alumni associations, professional associations and civic and social clubs. It is probable that if all caste barriers were dropped, a large proportion of the Negro upper class would welcome complete social integration, and that these all-Negro institutions would be left in the hands of the Negro middle class, as the most capable and sophisticated Negroes moved into the orbit of the general society. Their sense of pride and dignity does not even allow them to imagine such a fate, and they pursue their social activities and play their roles as 'race leaders' with little feeling of inferiority or deprivation, but always with a tragic sense of the irony of it all.

The Negro middle class covers a very wide income range, and whatever cohesion it has comes from the network of churches and social clubs to which many of its members devote a great deal of time and money. What sociologists call the Negro middle class is merely a collection of people who have similar life styles and aspirations, whose basic goals are 'living well', being 'respectable' and not being crude. Middle-class Negroes, by and large, are not concerned about mobility into the Negro upper class or integration with whites. They want their 'rights' and 'good jobs', as well as enough money to get those goods and services which make life comfortable. They want to expand continuously their level of consumption. But they also desire 'decent' schools for their children, and here the degree of victimization experienced by Negroes is most clear and the ambivalence toward policies of change most sharp. Ghetto schools are, on the whole, inferior. In fact, some of the most convincing evidence that residential segregation perpetuates inequality can be found by comparing data on school districts in Northern urban areas where *de facto* school segregation exists. (Table 1 presents such data for Chicago in 1962.)

Awareness of the poor quality of education grew as the protest movement against *de facto* school segregation in the North gathered momentum. But while the fight was going on, doubt about the desirability of forcing the issue was always present within some sections of the broad Negro middle class. Those in opposition asked, 'Are we not saying that our teachers can't teach our own children as well as whites can, or that our children can't learn unless they're around whites? Aren't we insulting ourselves?'

Table 1

Comparison of White, Integrated and Negro Schools in Chicago: 1962

Indices of comparison	Type of school		
	White	Integrated	Negro
Total appropriation per pupil	$342.00	$320.00	$269.00
Annual teachers' salary per pupil	$256.00	$231.00	$220.00
Per Cent uncertified teachers	12·00	23·00	49·00
No. of pupils per classroom	30·95	34·95	46·80
Library resource books per pupil	5·00	3·50	2·50
Expenditures per pupil other than teachers' salaries	$86.00	$90.00	$49.00

Adapted from a table in the U.S. Commission on Civil Rights report, *Public Schools, Negro and White*, Washington, D.C., 1962, pp. 241–8.

Those who want to stress Negro history and achievement and to use the schools to build race pride also express doubts about the value of mixed schools. In fact, the desirability of race consciousness and racial solidarity seems to be taken for granted in this stratum, and sometimes there is an expression of contempt for the behavior of whites of their own and lower income levels. In the present period one even occasionally hears a remark such as 'Who'd want to be integrated with *those* awful white people?'

Marxist critics would dismiss the whole configuration of Negro folkways and classways as a subculture which reinforces 'false consciousness', which prevents Negroes from facing the full extent of their victimization, which keeps them from ever focussing upon what they could be because they are so busy enjoying what they are – or rationalizing their subordination and exclusion. Gunnar Myrdal, in *An American Dilemma*, goes so far as to refer to the Negro community as a 'pathological' growth within American society.[14] Some novelists and poets, on the other hand, romanticize it, and some Black Nationalists glorify it. A sober analysis of the civil rights movement would suggest, however, that the striking fact about all levels of the Negro community is the absence of 'false consciousness', and the presence of a keen awareness of the extent of their victimization, as well as knowledge of the forces which maintain it. Not lack of knowledge but a sense of powerlessness is the key to the Negro reaction to the caste-class system.

Few Negroes believe that Black Ghettos will disappear within the next two decades despite much talk about 'open occupancy' and 'freedom of residence'. There is an increasing tendency among Negroes to discuss what the quality of life could be within Negro communities as they grow larger and larger. At one extreme this interest slides over into Black Nationalist reactions such as the statement by a Chicago Negro leader who said, 'Let all of the white people flee to the suburbs. We'll show them that the Black Man can run the second largest city in America better than the white man. Let them go. If any of them want to come back and integrate with *us* we'll accept them.'

14. See section on 'The Negro community as a pathological form of an American community', ch. 43 of Gunnar Myrdal, *An American Dilemma*, Harper, rev. edn 1962, p. 927.

It is probable that the Black Belts of America will increase in size rather than decrease during the next decade, for no city seems likely to commit itself to 'open occupancy' (although a committee in New York has been discussing a ten-year plan for dismantling Harlem).[15] And even if a race-free market were to appear Negroes would remain segregated unless drastic changes took place in the job ceiling and income gap. Controlled integration will probably continue, with a few upper- and upper-middle-class Negroes trickling into the suburbs and into carefully regulated mixed neighborhoods and mixed buildings within the city limits.[16] The basic problem of the next decade will be how to change Black Ghettos into relatively stable and attractive 'colored communities'. Here the social implications of low incomes become decisive.

The Myth of 'Separate but Equal'

Negroes have been 'victimized' throughout the three hundred and fifty years of their presence in the North American continent. The types of social systems which have organized their relations with whites have been varied – over two hundred years of slavery and indenture, ten years of post-Civil War Reconstruction in the South and eighty years of experimentation with a theory of 'separate but equal' ostensibly designed to replace caste relations with those of class. The 'separate but equal' doctrine has now been repudiated by the federal government and a broad section of public opinion as unjust and inimical to the national welfare. The period of desegregation has begun. Yet, the legacy of the past remains. As a transition to some new, and still undefined system of race relations takes place, it is relevant to examine the extent to which victimization persists, probing for its more subtle and covert manifestations. An estimate, too, should be made of whether or not what Merton has called 'the unintended consequences of purposive social action' carry a potential for new forms of victimization.

15. A report appeared on the front page of *The New York Times*, 5 April 1965, stating that a commission was at work trying to elaborate plans for 'integrating' Harlem by 1975. Columbia University was said to be co-operating in the research aspects of the project.

16. A successful experiment in 'controlled integration' has been described by Julia Abrahamson in *A Neighborhood Finds Itself*, New York, 1959.

By 1900 the doctrine had become firmly established that it was desirable for Negroes and whites to be members of two functionally related segments of a bi-racial society in which families, intimate friendship groups and voluntary associations (including churches) would be separate, although members of both races were participating in a common economic system and political order. Both Negro and white leaders emphasized the point that 'social equality' was not a Negro aspiration, and Booker T. Washington's famous Atlanta Compromise address delivered in 1895 made this point very explicit with his symbolism of the five fingers, separate and distinct, but joined together at the palm.

The theory of 'separate but equal' visualized a future in which Negroes would gradually acquire wealth and education on such a scale as to develop a social-class system within the Negro community paralleling that of the white community. Then, as the sociologist Robert Park once phrased it, Negroes and whites would 'look over and across' at each other, not 'up and down'. Defenders of 'bi-racialism' believed that although institutional life – including schools and neighborhoods – should remain separate, Negroes should be allowed to compete freely for jobs and should gradually acquire the full voting rights which they had lost in the South after 1875. It was considered unwise, however, to make a frontal assault upon segregation in public places since the key to the ultimate dissolution or transformation of the caste system lay in the acquisition of education and economic well-being – not in protest. The 'correct' behavior of an enlarged Negro middle class would eventually win acceptance by the white middle class. The doctrine of 'separate but equal' was given legal sanction in a number of Supreme Court decisions, the most famous being that of *Plessy v. Ferguson*, and it became the operating ideology among Southern white liberals between the two world wars.

During the first decade after the Second World War the doctrine of 'separate but equal' was abandoned as a guide to the formulation of public policy in so far as the armed forces, public transportation, public accommodations and public schools were concerned. Experience between the two world wars had demonstrated that, while it might be theoretically possible to achieve equality within the framework of a segregated school in the South, it seemed impossible in actual practice. In the field of public transportation, no matter how many shiny new coaches replaced the old rickety 'Jim Crow' coaches, Negroes did not consider them 'equal', and they never ceased to be resentful that there were two American armies instead of one. The cost of duplicating facilities to make public accommodations and schools truly equal would have been exorbitant even if Negroes welcomed the idea. Thus, a demand for change was in the air when the historic 1954 decision requiring school desegregation was taken, and the Court cut through to a fundamental question which had often been evaded: whether or not it was possible to maintain any kind of *forced* segregation in an open society without pejorative implications. Did not the very insistence upon separation imply inferiority? The caste-class system organizing race relations was recognized for what it really was – a system which, irrespective of the intent of individuals, resulted in the victimization of Negroes. Makers of national policy have now embarked upon a thorough-going program of desegregation coupled with an assault upon all institutionalized forms of racial discrimination. But the white public has not accepted the concept of 'total integration'.

Some paradoxes of progress

The abandonment of the doctrine of 'separate but equal' has forced consideration of many provocative questions, such as: 'Can the victimization resulting from unequal treatment of Negroes in the past be eliminated without preferential treatment for present-day victims?' There are those who contend that justice demands more than equality, that it requires a 'revolutionary breakthrough' in the form of preferential hiring, distinctive programs of education and special scholarship schemes. The existence of entrenched patterns of residential segregation also raises the question of the desirability and probability of the persistence of Negro neighborhoods and institutions. If *forced* separation eventually disappeared would separateness cease to be an index of victimization? Would it then lose its pejorative implications? Would the right to choose, if it ever came, mean that some Negroes will choose *not* to be 'integrated' except in the economic and political order?

New types of victimization are emerging which are not only

indirect but are also unintended consequences of actions designed to eliminate victimization. For instance, in several Northern cities an earnest effort is being made to facilitate and speed up the process of residential desegregation at the middle-class level. Negroes whose incomes and life styles approximate those of the white middle class are accepted into neighborhoods and apartment buildings in limited numbers in order not to excite fear and panic among white residents. The goal, as one Chicago neighborhood association states it, is 'an integrated neighborhood with high community standards', to reverse the process of ghettoization. However, without a commitment to 'open occupancy' at the city level, attainment of this goal demands a neighborhood-by-neighborhood approach, which calls for studying 'tipping points' and setting up 'benign quotas' in order to maintain a 'racial balance'. It may also involve a program which forces all lower-class residents to leave, irrespective of their color, while integrating a small number of middle-class Negroes into neighborhoods or specific apartment buildings. One effective technique has been clearance of slums followed by rebuilding at a high enough rent level to keep the proportion of Negroes automatically very low. This process is frequently called 'controlled integration'.[17] Actions such as these often result in the concentration of many lower-class Negroes into almost completely segregated public housing projects. What is gained for some in terms of better physical surroundings is lost in increased 'ghettoization'. Other displaced persons increase the degree of overcrowding in already overcrowded neighborhoods or filter into middle-class Negro neighborhoods and disorganize them.

Serious problems also arise within the middle class at the psychological level. In so far as Negro families have to co-operate actively in setting and maintaining quotas on the number of Negroes who enter, and in eliminating lower-class Negroes from the neighborhood, they become vulnerable to attack by other Negroes. Some sensitive individuals suffer from a feeling of guilt over manipulating the situation to maintain exclusiveness; others feel a loss of dignity in carrying on continuous discussion about race with white people. They dislike dealing with themselves as 'a problem'. A few people simply withdraw from such 'integrated'

17. Peter Rossi, op. cit.

situations into the comfort of the middle-class 'gilded ghetto'. This situation is only a special case of a more general problem confronting some Negroes in this Era of Integration – how to reconcile being a 'loyal Negro' or a 'Race Man' with new middle-class interracial relations or new occupational roles.

Rapid and fairly complete 'integration' of middle-class Negroes into neighborhoods, churches, educational and voluntary associations could have a profound effect upon Negro institutional life, 'skimming off the cream' of the Negro élites to the disadvantage of the larger Negro community. This would result in a kind of victimization of the Negro masses which would be permanent unless the conditions of life for the lower classes were drastically changed.

Unfortunately there are few signs of hope that the Negro masses will profit from current economic changes, for at the very moment when the civil rights movement has been most successful, and when access to training is being made more widely available to Negroes, forces are at work which could render these gains meaningless. Whitney Young, Jr, of the National Urban League, emphasizing economic problems facing Negroes, stated upon one occasion: 'Unless we identify these problems and take steps to meet them, we will find the masses of Negroes five years from today with a mouthful of rights, living in hovels with empty stomachs.'[18] About 12 per cent of the nonwhite labor force were unemployed in 1960, twice the rate for white workers.[19] In some urban areas it was between 15 and 20 per cent. It was higher for Negro men than women. Unemployment rates are particularly high for Negro youth. In 1961 nonwhite boys and girls between fourteen and nineteen had the highest unemployment rate of any age–color group in the nation, while the unemployment rate for Negro high-school graduates between the ages of sixteen and twenty-one was twice that for white youth and higher than the rate for whites who had *not* attended high school. One out of five

18. Quoted by James Reston in a column, 'The ironies of history and the American Negro', *The New York Times*, 15 May 1964.

19. See Norval D. Glenn, 'Some changes in the relative status of American non-whites: 1940–1960', *Phylon*, vol. 24, no. 2, Summer, 1963; and Marion Haynes, 'A century of change: Negroes in the U.S. economy, 1860–1960', *Monthly Labor Review*, U.S. Department of Labor Statistics, December 1962.

Negro high-school graduates were unable to find jobs.[20] If high-school graduates face such a situation, the plight of the untrained Negro is likely to be even worse. It was estimated in 1964 that automation was wiping out about 40,000 unskilled jobs a week, the sector of industry where Negro workers are concentrated. This trend is likely to continue for some time.[21]

If Negroes are not to become a permanent *lumpen-proletariat* within American society as a result of social forces already at work and increased automation, deliberate planning by governmental and private agencies will be necessary. Continued emphasis upon 'merit hiring' will benefit a few individuals, but, in the final analysis, structural transformations will have to take place.[22] There are those who feel that only a radical shift in American values and simultaneous adjustments of economy and society will wipe out, for ever, the victimization of the Negro. If such a situation does occur it is not likely to be the result of any cataclysmic proletarian upheaval, but rather through drift and piecemeal pragmatic decisions. One straw in the wind has been raised to test the temper of the time. Gunnar Myrdal and twenty-nine other scholars, writers and political scientists have released a statement on 'The Cybernation Revolution, the Weaponry Revolution, and Human Rights Revolution'. In discussing the need for adjustment to the effects of large-scale automation, they made a revolutionary suggestion:

We urge, therefore, that society, through its appropriate legal and governmental institutions, undertake an unqualified commitment to provide every individual and every family with an adequate income as a matter of right. . . .

Should this ever happen, Negroes would, of course, profit even more than whites, but demands for radical reforms of this type have not arisen from within the Civil Rights Movement whose leaders generally accept a middle-class work ethic which is incompatible with such a solution.[23]

20. Jacob Schiffman, 'Marital and family characteristics of workers, March 1962', *Monthly Labor Review*, U.S. Department of Labor, Bureau of Labor Statistics, Special Labor Force Report No. 26, January 1963.

21. Pettigrew, op. cit., p. 169.

22. ibid. 'Some needed societal reforms', pp. 168–76.

23. The author wishes to acknowledge with gratitude the assistance of Miss Odessa D. Thompson.

16 P. L. van den Berghe

Race and Racism in South Africa

Excerpt from P. L. van den Berghe, *Race and Racism: A Comparative Perspective*, Wiley, 1967, pp. 96-111.

If racism is an endemic disease in the United States, in South Africa it has become a way of life. Of all contemporary multi-racial societies, South Africa is the most complexly and rigidly stratified on the basis of race, the one in which race has greatest salience *vis-à-vis* other structural principles, and the one which is most ridden with conflict and internal contradictions.[1]

The 'white problem' of South Africa began in 1652 with the establishment by the Dutch East India Company of a refreshing station for its Asia-bound vessels at the Cape of Good Hope. The local population of what is now the western part of the Cape Province consisted of sparsely settled Hottentot pastoralists and Bushmen hunters and gatherers. At first race was not the basis for status differentiation between Europeans and indigenous people. Religion was the important criterion and baptism conferred legal and, to a considerable extent, social equality with the Dutch settlers. During the first years of Dutch settlement there were a few instances of Christian marriage between Dutchmen and Hottentot women.

Within a generation, however, color or race had supplanted religion as a criterion of membership in the dominant group, and by the end of the seventeenth century a rigid system of racial stratification existed at the Cape. In 1658 the first shipload of

1. [An] ... extensive bibliography and treatment of many of the ideas contained in this chapter can be found in my *South Africa, a Study in Conflict*, Wesleyan University Press, 1965. Also particularly germane are Leo Kuper's *An African Bourgeoisie*, Yale University Press, 1965; Leo Marquard's *The Peoples and Policies of South Africa*, Oxford University Press, 1952; C. W. De Kiewiet's *A History of South Africa, Social and Economic*, Oxford University Press, 1941; and Sheila Patterson's *Colour and Culture in South Africa*, London, 1953.

slaves entered Cape Town in response to the white settlers' clamor for servile help and to the scarcity and unreliability of the indigenous population for this purpose. The slave society of the Cape remained much more restricted in both area and number of people than that of the United States, Brazil or even Mexico.[2] Slavery was almost entirely confined to the towns and the settled agricultural districts of the Western Cape (i.e. to Cape Town and the surrounding towns of Stellenbosch, Paarl and Swellendam with their rural hinterland of vineyards, fruit orchards and wheat-fields). In 1700 the settlement consisted of only 1308 whites and 838 slaves; by 1805 it had grown to 25,757 whites, 29,545 slaves and an estimated 28,000 Hottentots. Slaves came mostly from eastern Africa, Madagascar and to a lesser extent from the Dutch East Indies. In 1795 Britain took over the Cape Colony (ceding it briefly again to Holland from 1803 to 1806) and in 1834 abolished slavery throughout her Empire.

The slave society of the Cape was not based on monoculture and on large plantations, but rather on medium-sized farms engaging in fairly diversified cash agriculture. It did, however, exhibit most characteristics of a paternalistic type of race relations, and showed many resemblances with the slave systems of the New World. The white farmer living on his autonomous estate constituted with his family and his retinue of slaves a large patriarchal unit in daily and intimate contact. The familiar pattern of the big house and the adjacent slave quarters was common, though in some cases slaves even lived in the basement of the big house. House slaves and skilled craftsmen who interbred extensively with their masters constituted a slave élite compared to the mass of field hands and to the 'public' slaves owned by the Dutch East India Company. Masters and house slaves lived together in the big house, played together as children and prayed and fornicated together as adults.

Spatial segregation was minimal, and what there was of it was

2. In addition to numerous travelogues, diaries and other eye-witness accounts that give a vivid picture of slavery at the Cape, the best secondary sources on South African slavery are C. G. Botha, *Social Life in the Cape Colony in the 18th Century*, Cape Town and Johannesburg, 1926; Isobel E. Edwards, *Towards Emancipation*, Cardiff, Wales, 1942; and J. S. Marais, *The Cape Coloured People*, London, New York, Toronto, 1939.

dictated by the dominant group's convenience and desire for privacy, rather than as a mechanism of social control. Unequal status was symbolized and maintained through an elaborate etiquette of race relations and through sumptuary regulations, in short, through mechanisms of *social* distance. A number of Dutch terms of reference and address (some of which have survived in modern Afrikaans) designate various sex and age statuses within both the dominant and the subordinate groups (e.g. *pay, jong, hotnot, booi, outa, aia, meid, skepsels, kleinjong, klonkie, baas, witman, nooi* and *seur*) and testify to a complex racial etiquette. When going to church, prosperous Dutch matrons were followed by a procession of slaves, one carrying their umbrella, another their prayer book, a third their foot-warmer or *stoofje*. Slaves were forbidden to walk in the streets with a lighted pipe or to wear shoes, for these objects were regarded as symbols of free status.

Miscegenation in the form of concubinage between Dutchmen and slave and Hottentot women was quite common and no stigma was attached to it. Dutch boys frequently had their first sexual experiences with slave girls. The East India Company condoned the use of its slave lodge in Cape Town as a notorious brothel for sailors and soldiers. (Curiously, it imposed a 9 p.m. curfew, perhaps more to keep their slaves fit for work than out of a sense of propriety.) The product of this extensive miscegenation between Dutchmen, slaves and free men of color, such as Hottentots and Malay political exiles from the East Indies, gave rise to the people now referred to as Cape Coloureds and who today are half as numerous as the whites, even though a great many light Coloureds have 'passed' into the white group.

The division of labor was clearly along racial lines, manual work being regarded as degrading by the whites and engaged in almost solely by slaves and Hottentots. Although there were some white craftsmen, they were in effect shop-owners supervising colored labor. Roles and statuses were unambiguously determined by race more than by any other criterion. Manumission was relatively infrequent (between 1715 and 1792, for example, there were only 893 cases in a slave population that grew from more than 2000 to nearly 15,000) and did not confer many privileges to the free person of color over the slave. Hottentots, although nominally free, lost both their pasture land and their cattle to the encroaching whites and thus were soon reduced to a condition of serfdom. Free people of color were subject to vagrancy laws and master-and-servant laws which greatly restricted their mobility and reduced them to a state of symbiotic dependence on the Dutch settlers that differed little from slavery.

Contrasted with the settled region around Cape Town in the Western Cape were the frontier districts into which the trek-boers ('travelling peasants') continuously expanded in search of new pastures and cattle to trade or steal from the Hottentot and Bantu. 'Trekking' began in the late seventeenth century and reached a climax in the Great Trek that started in 1836 and continued for a decade. The Boers (as the Dutch semi-nomads came to be known) were for the most part poorer farmers or younger sons who did not inherit land in the settled districts of the Cape; they expanded to the North, especially to the North-east along the coast, pushing further and further from the Cape as their sheep and cattle depleted the pastures. Until the 1770s they encountered mostly Hottentots and Bushmen on whose lands they encroached.

The Boers carried out a policy of genocide against the Bushmen, whom they hunted down in organized commandoes and whom they exterminated in the present area of South Africa. The Hottentots, who were pastoralists, had cattle and their skills as herdsmen to offer the Boers. In spite of a number of frontier skirmishes and cattle raids between them, the Hottentots were not wiped out. After they lost their pastures and cattle, they became herdsmen and servants to the Boers, with whom they eventually miscegenated themselves out of existence to give rise to a group of Coloureds known as 'Bastards'.[3] The relationship prevailing between the Boers and their Hottentot serfs was a rugged, frontier variety of paternalism. Contrary to the settled districts around Cape Town, where the whites relied mostly on slave labor, the frontier Boers were usually too poor to own slaves, and they depended almost solely on Hottentot labor. They regarded the Hottentots as slothful, unintelligent and irresponsible. Yet contact between masters and servants was very close, and the style of life of the Boers living in temporary thatched huts was not appreciably different from that of the indigenous nomads.

3. Marais, loc. cit.

Beginning in the 1770s Boer expansion was virtually stopped for over half a century at the Great Fish River when the whites encountered the Bantu-speaking nations who were in the process of migrating southward. The Bantu groups (whose descendants now comprise over two-thirds of South Africa's population and call themselves 'Africans') were organized in centralized states numbering hundreds of thousands of fairly densely settled people. The Bantu proved a much more formidable opponent than the Hottentots and Bushmen, and a whole series of frontier wars and cattle raids ensued between them and the whites.

With the establishment of British rule at the Cape, the settlement of about 5000 Britons in the Eastern Cape in 1820 and measures abolishing the vagrancy laws against the Hottentots in 1828 and emancipating the slaves in 1834, a new dimension of conflict was added to the South African scene. All subsequent history must be analysed in terms of a triangular conflict between the Boers (later known as 'Afrikaners') and the British, and between both of these white groups and the African majority. In 1836 the Boers started on their Great Trek and in a sweeping expansion invaded what is today the Province of Natal where they clashed with both the Zulu and the British. The British annexed Natal and most of the Afrikaners withdrew into what soon became the Boer Republics of the Transvaal and the Orange Free State. A series of conflicts between the whites and the African nations (Zulu, Ndebele, Sotho) ended in the elimination of the African nations as independent states and as military forces by 1880.

From that date the English and the Afrikaners ruled supreme over their respective parts of South Africa, and the conflict between the two white groups was intensified; the main economic stakes of the struggle were the control of the Kimberley diamond field (discovered in 1867) and the Witwatersrand gold deposits (opened in 1886). This contest between Boer expansionism and British imperialism culminated in the second Anglo-Boer War of 1899 to 1902 (a first Anglo-Boer War occurred on a much smaller scale in 1880) which ended in British victory and led in 1910 to the formation of the Union of South Africa as a politically autonomous state under the joint control of local English and Afrikaner settlers. The Africans, the Coloureds and the Indians

323

(who, beginning in 1860, were introduced by the English from India to work as indentured laborers on the sugar-cane plantations of Natal) were not consulted in the settlement between the two white groups and were given virtually no voice in the conduct of the new state's affairs (except for qualified franchise rights in the Cape Province). Only the European languages, English and Afrikaans (derived from Dutch), were given official standing. The Union (since 1961 Republic) of South Africa was launched on its career as a racist '*Herrenvolk* democracy', that is, as a state in which a white minority of 20 per cent ruled itself democratically but imposed its tyranny over a nonwhite majority of 80 per cent.

Although the political structure of South Africa has remained basically unchanged since 1910, profound economic transformations have made the country by far the most urbanized south of the Sahara and an industrial giant by African standards. The three largest cities in sub-Saharan Africa (Johannesburg, Cape Town and Durban) are located in South Africa; the economy became increasingly diversified, with manufacturing and services overshadowing both agriculture and mining; between 1912 and 1958 the national income increased over fifteen times.[4] These processes of urbanization and industrialization have been accelerated during the First and Second World Wars and have created conditions of intense racial competition as nonwhites became better skilled, educated and able to take over occupations held by whites, and as 'poor whites' were displaced from the land and forced to migrate to cities with few industrial skills.

South Africa is probably the most complex and the most conflict-ridden of the world's multiracial societies.[5] The most salient lines of cleavage are those of race. According to the dominant group's definition of the situation, the population is divided into four rigid color-castes: the Europeans or whites numbering slightly under 20 per cent; the Indians accounting for some 3 per cent; the Coloureds numbering somewhat less than 10 per cent; and the Africans who number 68 per cent of the total (see Table 1). The last three groups are collectively referred to as the 'non-Europeans' or 'nonwhites', and the caste-line between

4. van den Berghe, op. cit., pp. 89–90.

5. For more detailed accounts of contemporary South Africa, see van den Berghe, loc. cit.; Leo Marquard, loc. cit.; and Sheila Patterson, loc. cit.

whites and nonwhites is even more impermeable than that between the three nonwhite castes.

Contrary to government claims that these group boundaries are culturally defined, the castes are racially determined. Thus the Coloureds are completely Westernized (except for a small group of 'Cape Malays' who have remained Muslims); they are Christians, speak Afrikaans or English, and are culturally as indistinguishable from Europeans as Negro Americans are from white Americans. Yet they are regarded as non-Europeans by virtue of their physical characteristics. Similarly, Westernized Indians and Africans cannot lose their ascribed caste status. Membership in one of the four castes is by birth and for life. A person's race appears on his identity card and 'passing' is technically impossible. However, in the three centuries before the Population Registration Act was introduced in 1950 to prevent 'passing', tens if not hundreds of thousands of light Coloureds did enter the white group and a great many Africans passed for Coloured. Today the only caste where membership is not completely hereditary is the Coloured one; offspring of parents of different castes can be classified as Coloured.

Table 1

Racial Groups as Percentages of Total South African Population (1904–60)

Year	Whites	Africans	Asians	Coloureds	All non-whites	Total all races (in thousands)
1904	21·6	67·4	2·4	8·6	78·4	5,176
1911	21·4	67·3	2·5	8·8	78·6	5,973
1921	21·9	67·8	2·4	7·9	78·1	6,929
1936	20·9	68·8	2·3	8·0	79·1	9,590
1946	20·8	68·6	2·5	8·1	79·2	11,418
1951	20·9	67·5	2·9	8·7	79·1	12,648
1960	19·4	68·2	3·0	9·4	80·6	15,982

Miscegenation is severely condemned by the white group, both in law and in custom, although it continues to take place clandestinely on a small scale. Both intermarriage and 'indecent or immoral acts' between whites and nonwhites are forbidden by law and subject to severe penalties (up to seven years in prison.) Although intermarriage and sexual relations between the three nonwhite castes are not legally forbidden, they are uncommon, and all four racial groups may be regarded as virtually endogamous.[6]

The four castes are clearly in a hierarchy of power, wealth and prestige. Each race has a legally defined set of privileges or disabilities. Wide differences in standards of living, formal education, health, occupation and wages accompany the vastly unequal distribution of power. The whites retain a virtual monopoly of both power and wealth. With the exception of a residual and almost meaningless franchise exercised by the Coloureds in the Cape Province on a racially segregated voters' roll, the national electorate is entirely white; the bicameral parliament in Cape Town is all white, and so are the cabinet, the army, the navy, the judiciary and all the higher positions in the civil service (except for the machinery of puppet chiefs set up by the government in the Native Reserves now being restyled as Bantustans). The few political rights that the nonwhites enjoyed in 1910 were gradually eliminated, and South Africa is in effect a white government with an internal colonial empire in which the Africans (and increasingly the Coloureds and Indians) are dealt with administratively and arbitrarily without any representation on sovereign law-making bodies. The whites also monopolized the means of violence: military service and the right to carry firearms are limited to whites. (The police force uses nonwhites, but does not arm them with firearms.)

The political and military power of the Europeans has been translated into, and is further entrenched by, an impressive array of economic privileges. A rural white population of less than half a million owns 87 per cent of the land, whereas nearly four million Africans are squeezed into the remaining 13 per cent which make up the impoverished, eroded, overgrazed Native Reserves. The

6. In 1946, before the passage of the Prohibition of Mixed Marriages Act, only one white out of 714 married outside his 'race'. The respective figures for Coloureds, Indians and Africans were one in 20, one in 31 and one in 67. Cf. Pierre L. van den Berghe, 'Miscegenation in South Africa', *Cahiers d'Etudes Africaines*, 1960, p. 72.

whites keep for themselves almost all better-paying occupations, including skilled manual work. The nonwhites are left with domestic service, semiskilled and unskilled jobs in industry, mining and agriculture, some small-scale retail trade and petty white-collar occupations, mostly among Coloureds and Indians, and selected professions such as schoolteaching and nursing for 'their own people' in racially segregated institutions. When scarcity of white labor has forced industrialists to employ nonwhites in more skilled jobs, this is done surreptitiously and at greatly discriminatory rates of pay. The principle of unequal pay for equal work has even been applied by most religious denominations in paying widely different stipends for white and African clergymen. The mean family income of whites is approximately thirteen to fourteen times that of Africans and five times that of Coloureds and Indians. Numbering less than 20 per cent of the population, the whites earned 67 per cent of the national income in 1960.[7] Government educational expenditures per white pupil are ten times those per African pupil. In the towns the whites occupy all the better residential areas and throughout the country they enjoy a lion's share of all the public facilities. Indeed, the Reservation of Separate Amenities Act explicitly legalizes not only segregated facilities but also unequal ones; quite often no amenities at all are provided for nonwhites; thus in a park, for example, all benches are often labelled 'Europeans Only'.

Among the nonwhite groups the Coloureds suffer the smallest number of disabilities, although they are almost completely excluded from national policies. The Indians, on the average, are somewhat better off economically than the Coloureds, but they have been subjected to a more hostile government policy and to more restrictions than the Coloureds (though fewer than the Africans). Coloureds and Indians occupy an intermediate status between the whites and the Africans, but they are closer to the Africans than to the whites.

The Africans, who by themselves constitute more than two-thirds of the population, bear the brunt of political oppression and economic exploitation. Through their labor they create most of the country's wealth, but they receive only one-fourth of

7. van den Berghe, op. cit., p. 303.

the national income (26·5 per cent in 1960).[8] Although they are the poorest group, they pay a disproportionate share of taxes; they have no voting rights except in the puppet Bantustan of the Transkei where the white government can overrule any decision of the local African 'representatives' (most of whom are appointed rather than elected). Over a million Africans are arrested and convicted each year – the vast majority of them for purely technical offenses against discriminatory laws or regulations such as the 'pass laws' to which only nonwhites are subject. The geographical mobility of Africans, their family life and their freedom to seek work in the open market are severely limited by 'pass laws', 'influx control', 'job reservation', 'group area' laws and numerous other pieces of apartheid legislation. The entire lifetime of the African is spent under the burden of economic exploitation and the shadow of police surveillance, intimidation and brutality. In the urban ghettoes where Africans are forced to live, often separated by restrictive laws from their spouses and children, the inmates are free neither to come nor to go and are but one arbitrary step away from prison.

Next in importance to the racial lines of cleavage and their social, economic and political concomitants are the cultural or ethnic divisions in South Africa. Cultural or ethnic groups overlap only partly with racial groups. Race and culture are thus not only analytically distinct but also empirically so. To the extent that cultural criteria, foremost among which are language and religion, cut across the color castes, existing racial conflicts are further exacerbated. For example, Afrikaans- and English-speaking Coloureds have long aspired to become assimilated with their respective white language group, but they have been denied admission purely on the basis of race.

Politically the most important linguistic cleavage is between English- and Afrikaans-speaking whites who constitute respectively some 40 and 60 per cent of the dominant group. This old conflict has been most overt when the common threat of African opposition was felt to be most securely under control. With the post-Second World War emergence among Africans of mass militancy along modern political lines, the tension between the English and the Afrikaners has again receded into the background

8. ibid.

of South African politics. The slogan is for white unity against the 'black peril'. However, real conflicts of interest remain between these two white ethnic groups concerning the use of the two national languages in the government and the schools as well as the inequality of occupational and educational status between them. (The English-speaking whites tend to be of higher social class status than the Afrikaners.) In addition, the Afrikaners have since 1948 monopolized political power, whereas the English own the bulk of the country's extractive and manufacturing industries, and control much of banking, finance and commerce. Religiously, the whites are divided among the Protestants, Catholics and Jews; the Afrikaners are almost exclusively Protestants belonging to the Dutch Reformed Churches, while the English-speaking whites are religiously divided.

The main language and religious groups represented among whites are also present among nonwhites, since missionary activities and other forms of culture contact spread Christianity, the use of European languages and Western education. More nonwhites than whites speak English and/or Afrikaans, either as their mother tongue or as second language; similarly, for every white Christian there are approximately two nonwhite Christians. The Coloureds are overwhelmingly Afrikaans-speaking and Protestant; the Indians are mostly Hindus and Muslims and belong to five main Indian language groups, but almost all speak fluent English. The Africans are in majority Christians and speak several related Bantu languages (the major ones being Zulu, Xhosa and Sotho) as their mother tongues, but most urban men also know either English or Afrikaans, or both.

In spite of government attempts to revive the significance of ethnic distinctions among Africans through a policy of mother-tongue instruction in schools, linguistically based Bantustans, and government-sponsored revivalism and glorification of traditional African culture, language distinctions and ethnic chauvinism are rapidly subsiding in importance among urban Africans. What has been misleadingly and invidiously termed 'tribalism' is certainly more prevalent among whites than nonwhites. In fact, the very endeavor by the dominant whites to inculcate ethnic particularism among Africans has probably contributed to their drive toward Westernization and even deprecation of indigenous

African cultures. However, the existence of ethnic heterogeneity among nonwhites has been used by the government not only as a method of dividing and ruling but also as an alibi for racism. Faced with accusations of racial discrimination, the government fallaciously claims that apartheid is simply a policy of cultural pluralism.

In addition to the overlapping but discrete cleavages of race and ethnicity, the South African population is stratified into social classes. More precisely, each racial caste is subdivided according to status criteria which range from traditional ones (such as the Hindu caste system among South Africans of Indian origin) to modern socio-economic strata based on income, education, occupation and life-style. This leads to an extremely complex status system that space limitations prevent me from describing here.[9] Because of the all-encompassing and overwhelming importance of race, however, class distinctions tend to take a distinctly secondary place, or indeed a tertiary one, after both race and ethnicity. Similarity of class position across racial lines has never been a successful basis for political action in South Africa, and even the labor movement has been infected by racism. Not only is there an almost total lack of solidarity between white and nonwhite manual workers, but the prevailing feelings have been ones of bitterness and competition. The white worker is in such a pampered, protected and privileged position as to make his class status, in the Marxian sense of relationship to the means of production, nearly irrelevant.

The ubiquity of race, the confusion between race and culture by the dominant group, and the latter's insistence that racial consciousness and 'purity' are essential to its survival, make South Africa a society ridden with conflicts and contradictions. To mention but a few of the more obvious contradictions and sources of strain, a rigidly ascribed division of labor based on race is hardly the most efficient way of running a complex industrial economy; similarly, the government's insistence on the

9. More extensive accounts can be found in Leo Kuper's *An African Bourgeoisie*, Yale University Press, 1964, and in my own two books, *South Africa*, 1965, and *Caneville*, 1964, both Wesleyan University Press. Hilda Kuper's *Indian People in Natal*, Verry, 1960, gives a more detailed view of the Indian group.

maximum degree of spatial segregation compatible with the supply of African labor to 'white' industries entails an enormous waste of resources and productivity; the cost of the repressive apparatus needed to suppress African resentment against apartheid policies mounts yearly (e.g. between 1961 and 1964 the military budget increased from 112 million to 291 million dollars).

Yet, far from being resolved, these conflicts and contradictions have become increasingly acute as the dominant group has become more and more reactionary. The few rights of the nonwhites have been steadily eroded by legislation. Segregation measures became more and more inclusive, rigid and far-reaching as apartheid relentlessly extended from residential areas, primary and secondary schools, means of transport, waiting rooms, hospitals, cemeteries, toilets and sport facilities to universities, private associations and religious worship. Interracial contact, on a basis other than between master and servant, became increasingly penalized by methods ranging from ostracism to imprisonment. The desirability of apartheid and the inability of members of different races to live peacefully together became the official credo, and indeed the very process of enforcing racial segregation made intergroup conflict a self-fulfilling prophecy.

Mutual fear and hostility climbed; discourtesy, violence and brutality, both public and private, mounted; such tenuous nonutilitarian ties as existed between whites and nonwhites snapped under strain; the possibility of nondiscriminatory behavior, even for the few unprejudiced whites, disappeared; political opinions polarized; white racism called forth black racism; the use of terrorism by the police turned the nonwhite opposition away from Gandhian techniques of passive resistance and toward sabotage; the state steadily improved its machinery of oppression, invested in military hardware and passed more and more dictatorial legislation which destroyed the rule of law even for the white minority. Having engaged itself on the road to tyranny, the dominant minority soon reached the point of no return where any liberalization of policy might indeed open the floodgates of revolution and result in the extermination or expulsion of the ruling class. The white minority, to use a cliché, manoeuvered itself into the position of sitting on top of a self-created volcano of racial hatred with no other place to go. And it seeks its survival in what will probably bring about its demise – its monomaniacal racist compulsion.

This process of political repression can be analysed in terms of two principal components. The first consists of the apartheid program itself, that is, those pieces of legislation (such as the Group Areas Act, the Bantu Education Act, the Population Registration Act, the Prohibition of Mixed Marriages Act and many others) specifically aimed at bringing about maximum racial segregation while trying to minimize economic cost and disruption for the dominant white group. This apartheid program has ranged from 'macro-segregation' into monoracial regions (the 'Bantustans') to 'meso-segregation' into ghettoes within urban areas to 'micro-segregation' in the form of separate facilities in situations where close physical proximity is unavoidable, for example, on the job. This first aspect of government policy is part of a systematic, premeditated plan that has been meticulously perfected since the Afrikaner Nationalists came into office in 1948.

The second facet of Nationalist policies concerns the enforcement of this apartheid program. As the program generated increasing hostility among the nonwhites and mounting costs for the dominant Europeans, the government has passed a series of laws effectively abolishing the rule of law for *all* people, including the whites. Such laws as the Suppression of Communism Act, the Public Safety Act and the Criminal Law Amendment Act have been paradoxically nonracial in character, being also aimed at the few but annoying white radicals. Thus South Africa is in the process of resolving the basic duality of its traditional polity, namely as a democracy for the *Herrenvolk* and a colonial régime for the nonwhites. Tyranny is increasingly extending to the Europeans who are, by and large, willing to pay the price of freedom for their economic and social privileges.

South Africa has often been described as a Fascist state. This characterization shows little understanding of the situation. South Africa is racist but not Fascist. To be sure, some of the police methods and of the legislation used to suppress opposition give the country a superficial similarity with Fascist states. South Africa, however, clearly lacks most crucial elements of

Fascism, notably the presence of a charismatic leader, a high degree of militarism, the endeavor to create a monolithic nation and to include all institutions within a single political party, and intensive propaganda in a collectivist ideology. Apartheid, on the other hand, aims to compartmentalize the country and to perpetuate distinct racial and ethnic groups. A much closer parallel to South Africa than Nazi Germany or Fascist Italy is the southern part of the United States at the height of Jim Crow.

Apartheid, in my opinion, ought to be interpreted as an endeavor to re-establish the old paternalistic master–servant relations that prevailed in the pastoral Boer Republics of the nineteenth century.[10] At the ideological level apartheid is a romantic leap into a half-mythical past when the Africans 'knew their place', when the evils of urbanization had not yet corrupted them and made them 'cheeky', when missionaries, liberals and 'outside agitators' had not yet meddled in South Africa's affairs, when the 'Bantu' were simple but noble savages and when white supremacy was unquestioned.

This formulation is, of course, oversimplified, and apartheid consists of quite an elaborate set of rationalizations, but apartheid is a living political dinosaur. It is basically an old-fashioned colonial régime coerced through the dynamics of industrialization into modernizing its repressive apparatus. Apartheid aims at reversing the Westernization of Africans by using mother-tongue instruction in schools; preventing as many nonwhites as possible from settling in the 'white' cities; tolerating Africans in cities only in so far as they provide menial labor for the whites; achieving the minimum amount of equalitarian contact between racial groups and the maximum amount of segregation consistent with economic development; and recreating a series of pseudo-traditional Bantustans established along ethnic lines, and ruled paternalistically through a system of indirect rule. This reactionary Utopia

10. The polemical and scholarly literature is abundant. For factual information and for interpretations differing from my own, see Gwendolen Carter, *The Politics of Inequality, South Africa Since 1948*, Praeger, 1958; Sheila Patterson, *The Last Trek*, Routledge, 1957; Jordan Ngubane, *An African Explains Apartheid*, Praeger, 1963; Muriel Horrell, *A Survey of Race Relations in South Africa*, Johannesburg, S. A. Institute of Race Relations, Annual; Albert Luthuli, *Let My People Go*, McGraw-Hill, 1962; and N. J. Rhoodie and H. J. Venter, *Apartheid*, Amsterdam, 1960.

would not have much chance of success even in the more agrarian countries to the north of the Limpopo. In a highly industrialized and urbanized country like South Africa, the preservation of a rigidly ascribed system of racial castes, of a series of ethnic groups living in cultural isolation and of a minority white settler régime is doomed to failure.

In the process of trying to implement their blueprint the Afrikaner Nationalist government has faced growing opposition and has resorted to an increasingly naked use of coercion. Whatever condescending and supercilious benevolence toward the 'Bantu' may have motivated the early architects of apartheid, and may still delude its academic proponents, has degenerated into an increasingly ruthless and efficient police state. In the words of Hilda Kuper in a recent book review, 'South Africa has become a vast and terrifying prison.' Consensus is almost totally absent, and South Africa is held together in a condition of 'static disequilibrium' through a grim mixture of political coercion and economic interdependence. However exploited the Africans are, they depend for sheer physical survival on wage employment in the money economy. To withdraw one's labor is to face nearly immediate starvation. The price of survival at the minimum subsistence level is exploitation, oppression and degradation. But three million people cannot indefinitely repress the frustration and fury of thirteen million people who live in their midst. A South Africa divided against itself awaits its impending doom.

Part Nine
Equality and Inequality: Ideals and Practice

Human societies betray many contradictions between ideals and practice. Nowhere in the modern world are these contradictions more evident than in regard to social inequality. Today every society proclaims the ideals of equality and this is viewed as an index of progress and modernity; yet marked social inequalities continue to exist in practice. Dumont examines the problem of caste from the viewpoint of values and argues that there is a basic difference between Negro–White relations in America and the traditional caste system in India; the former exists within a framework of equalitarian values while the latter accepts the values of inequality. Béteille offers a general survey of inequality as a social value and raises the question as to how far one can speak of a true decline of social inequality in the modern world.

17 L. Dumont

Caste, Racism and 'Stratification': Reflections of a
Social Anthropologist[1]

Excerpt from L. Dumont, *Contributions to Indian Sociology*, no. 5,
October 1961, pp. 20–43.

In a recent article Professor Raymond Aron writes about
sociology: 'what there exists of a critical, comparative, pluralist
theory is slight'.[2] This is indeed the feeling one has when, after
studying the caste system in India, one turns to comparing it
with other social systems and to seeing, in particular, how it has
been accommodated within the theory of 'social stratification'
as developed in America. To begin with, the problem can be put
in very simple terms: is it permissible, or is it not, to speak of
'castes' outside India? More particularly, may the term be
applied to the division between Whites and Negroes in the southern states of the United States of America? To this question a
positive answer has been given by some American sociologists[3] –
in accordance with the common use of the word – while most

1. [This is an English version of a paper first published in French in
Cahiers Internationaux de Sociologie, Paris, vol. 29 (1960), pp. 91–112.] The
following reflections have sprung mainly from the preparation of an article
on 'caste' for the *Vocabulary of Social Sciences* (UNESCO). The question
of the proximate extensions of the term 'caste', for instance to societies of
South-East Asia, is left out. Only a remote extension is considered which
appears to require that sociological and anthropological approaches be
confronted, even if in a somewhat hasty and temporary manner.

2. Raymond Aron, 'Science et conscience de la société', *Archives Européennes de Sociologie*, vol. 1 (1960), p. 29.

3. The tendency, which its only systematic opponent, O. C. Cox, has
called 'the Caste School of Race Relations' seems to have won the day.
Another more moderate tendency consists in applying the word 'caste' to
the U.S.A. in a monographic manner, without comparative prejudice
(Myrdal, etc., see below). – The dictionaries give, besides the proper sense
of the word, the extended meaning, e.g. *Shorter Oxford Engl. Dict.*, *s.v.: 3.
fig.* A class who keep themselves socially distinct, or inherit exclusive
privileges 1807. [The French text has here a reference to Littré instead of
O.S.D.]

anthropologists with Indian experience would probably answer it in the negative.[4] Ideally, this question might appear as a matter of mere terminological choice: either we accept the former alternative and adopt a very broad definition, and as a result we may have to distinguish sub-types, as some authors who have opposed the 'racial caste' (U.S.A.) to the 'cultural caste' (India); or we refuse any extension of the term and apply it exclusively to the Indian type precisely defined, and in this case other terms will be necessary to designate the other types. But in actual fact, a certain usage has been established, and perhaps it is only by criticizing its already manifest implications that a way can be opened to a better comparative view. I shall, therefore, begin by criticizing the usage which predominates in America in the hope of showing how social anthropology can assist sociology in this matter. Two aspects will particularly require attention: what idea the authors in question have formed of the Indian system, and which place they give to the concept of 'caste' in relation to neighbouring concepts such as 'class' and to the broad heading of 'social stratification' under which they often group the facts of the kind. Thereafter I shall tentatively outline the framework of a true comparison.

4. Yet, among recent authors who are familiar with the Indian system, a sociologist working in Ceylon insists on the fundamental difference between India and U.S. (Bryce Ryan, *Caste in Modern Ceylon*, New Brunswick, N.J., 1953, p. 18, note), while F. G. Bailey asserts *a priori* that this comparison must take place under the word 'caste' (*Contributions*, no. 3, p. 90). Morris Carstairs is less categorical, but he accepts, with Kroeber's definition (below), the American usage, because of its advantages as compared with 'race' (*The Twice-Born*, London, 1957, p. 23). Much earlier an Indian author, Ketkar, insisted on a hierarchical division of American society based on race and occupation, he enumerated 10 groups (based in fact on the country of origin). He did not use the word 'caste' but he underlined with some relish the features which in his view recalled the Indian system. (Shridar V. Ketkar, *The History of Caste in India*, vol. 1, Ithaca, N.Y., 1909, p. 100 n., 102 n., 115 n. 5.) The general question has recently been discussed in: E. R. Leach (ed.), *Aspects of Caste in South India, Ceylon and N.-W. Pakistan*, Cambridge, 1960, *Cambridge Papers in Social Anthropology*, no. 2, notably p. 5.

A. Caste as an Extreme Case of Class: Kroeber

A definition of caste given by Kroeber is rightly regarded as classical, for the whole sociological trend with which I am concerned here links up with it.

In his article on 'Caste' in the *Encyclopaedia of Social Sciences* (vol. 3, 1930, 254b–7a), he enumerates the characteristics of caste (endogamy, heredity, relative rank) and goes on to say:

> *Castes, therefore, are a special form of social classes,* which in tendency at least are present in every society. Castes differ from social classes, however, in that they have emerged into social consciousness to the point that custom and law attempt their rigid and permanent separation from one another. *Social classes are the generic soil from which caste systems have at various times and places independently grown up* . . . [my italics].

By 'caste systems' he means in what follows, apart from India, medieval Europe and medieval Japan. He implicitly admits, however, that the last two cases are imperfect: either the caste organization extends only to a part of the society, or, as in the Japanese 'quasi-caste system', the division of labour and the integration with religion remain vague.

For us, the essential point here is that 'caste' is considered as an extreme case of 'class'. Why? Probably in the first place because of the 'universality of anthropology', as Lloyd Warner says while accepting Kroeber's definition.[5] In the second place, because 'caste' is at once rigid and relatively rare, whereas 'class' is more flexible, vaguer and relatively very widespread. But the problem is only deferred, for in such a perspective it should be necessary to define 'class', which is much more difficult than to define 'caste'. Never mind, 'class', after all, is familiar to us, while 'caste' is strange. . . . We are landed at the core of the sociocentrism within

5. W. Lloyd Warner (Dir.), *Deep South, A Social Anthropological Study of Caste and Class*, Chicago, c. 1941, ed. 1946, p. 9. – G. S. Ghurye's position is close to that of Kroeber: well-marked status groups are common in indo-european cultures; comparatively, the Indian caste system represents only an extreme case (untouchability, etc.), see *Caste and Race in India*, New York, 1932, pp. 140, 142.

which the whole school of authors under discussion develops. Actually, if one were prepared to make light of the relative frequency with which the supposed 'class' occurs, and if one were solely concerned with conceptual clarity, the terms could just as well be reversed, and one could start from the Indian caste system, which offers in a clear and crystalline form what is elsewhere diluted and blurred in many ways. The definition quoted reduces a society's consciousness of itself to an epiphenomenon – although some importance is attached to it: 'they have emerged into social consciousness.' The case shows that to do this is to condemn oneself to obscurity.

B. Distinction between Caste, Estate and Class

The oneness of the human species, however, does not demand the arbitrary reduction of diversity to unity, it only demands that it should be possible to pass from one particularity to another, and that no effort should be spared in order to elaborate a common language in which each particularity can be adequately described. The first step to that end consists in recognizing differences.

Before Kroeber gave his definition, Max Weber had made an absolute distinction between 'class' and *Stand*, 'status-group', or 'estate' in the sense of pre-revolutionary France – as between economy on the one hand and 'honour' and 'social intercourse' on the other.[6] His definition of class as an economic group has been criticized, but it has the merit of not being too vague. Allowing that social classes as commonly referred to in our societies have these two aspects, the analytical distinction is none the less indispensable from a comparative point of view, as we shall see. In Max Weber as in Kroeber, caste represents an extreme case; but this time it is the status-group which becomes a caste when its separation is secured not only through convention and laws, but also ritually (impurity through contact). Is this transition

6. Max Weber, *Wirtschaft und Gesellschaft*, vol. 2, pp. 635–7. Discussed by Cox, *Caste, Class and Race*, p. 287, and 'Max Weber on social stratification', *Amer. soc. Rev.*, vol. 2 (1950), pp. 223–7; cf. also Hans Gerth, 'Max Weber vs. Oliver C. Cox', *Amer. soc. Rev.*, ibid., pp. 557–8 (as regards Jews and Castes).

from status-group to caste conceived as genetic or only logical?
One notes in passing that, in the passage of *Wirtschaft und
Gesellschaft* which I have in view here, Weber thinks that individual castes develop some measure of distinct cults and gods – a
mistake of Western common sense which believes that what
wishes to be distinguished must be different. Into the genesis of
caste, Weber introduces a second component, namely a reputedly
ethnic difference. From this point of view, castes would be closed
communities (*Gemeinschaften*), endogamous and believing their
members to be of the same blood, which would put themselves in
society (*vergesellschaftet*) one with the other. On the whole, caste
would be the outcome of a conjunction between status-group and
ethnic community. At this juncture a difficulty appears. For it
seems that Weber maintains the difference between *Gesellschaft*
and *Gemeinschaft*: on the one hand the *Vergesellschaftung* of a
reputedly ethnic group, a 'Paria people', tolerated only for the
indispensable economic services it performs, like the Jews in
Medieval Europe, on the other the *Gemeinschaft* made up of
status-groups or, in the extreme case, of castes. If I am not mistaken, the difficulty emerges in the concluding sentence, which has
to reconcile the two by means of an artificial transition from the
one to the other: 'Eine ungreifende *Vergesellschaftung* die
ethnisch geschiedenen Gemeinschaften zu einem spezifischen,
politischen *Gemeinschaftshandeln* zusammenschliesst' [my italics],
or, freely translated, the *societalization* of ethnically distinct
communities embraces them to the point of uniting them, on the
level of political action, in a *community* of a new kind'. The particular group then acknowledges a hierarchy of honour and at the
same time its ethnic difference becomes a difference of function
(warriors, priests, etc.). However remarkable the conjunction here
achieved between hierarchy, ethnic difference and division of
labour may be, one may wonder whether Weber's failure is not due
to the fact that to a hierarchical view he added 'ethnic' considerations through which he wanted to link up widespread ideas on
the racial origin of the caste system with the exceptional situation
of certain minority communities like Jews or Gypsies in Western
societies.

What remains is the distinction, as analytical as one could wish,
between economic group and status-group. In the latter category,

one can then distinguish more clearly, as Sorokin did,[7] between 'order' or 'estate' and caste. As an instance, the clergy in pre-revolutionary France did not renew itself from within, it was an open 'estate'.

C. 'Caste' in the U.S.A.

At first sight there is a paradox in the works of the two most notable authors who have applied the term 'caste' to the separation between Whites and Negroes in the U.S.A. While their purpose is to oppose the 'color line' to class distinctions, they both accept the idea that caste is a particular and extreme form of class, not a distinct phenomenon. We have seen that Lloyd Warner accepts Kroeber's idea of continuity; however he immediately insists, as early as his article of 1936, that while Whites and Negroes make up two 'castes', the two groups are stratified into classes according to a common principle, so that the Negroes of the upper class are superior from the point of view of class to the small Whites, while at the same time being inferior to them from the point of view of 'caste'.[8] Gunnar Myrdal also states that 'caste may thus in a sense be viewed as the extreme form of absolutely rigid class', in this sense 'caste' constitutes 'a harsh deviation from the ordinary American social structure and the American Creed'.[9] The expression '*harsh* deviation' is neces-

7. Pitrim A. Sorokin, *Society, Culture and Personality, Their Structure and Dynamics*, Cooper, c. 1947, p. 259 (the 'order' or 'estate' as a 'diluted caste', cf. what has been said above about class and caste). Max Weber distinguishes between open and closed status groups (*Ges. Aufs. z. Religions-soziologie*, vol. 2, edn 1923, pp. 41–2). It is to be noted that a recent work recognizes two fundamental types of 'social stratification', the caste type which comprises 'orders' or 'estates', and the open class type, related respectively to the poles of Talcott Parsons' alternative of particularism–universalism (Bernard Barber, *Social Stratification, A comparative Analysis of Structure and Process*, Harcourt, 1957).

8. W. Lloyd Warner, 'American caste and class', *American Journal of Sociology*, vol. 42 (1936), pp. 234–7.

9. Gunnar Myrdal, *An American Dilemma, The Negro Problem and Modern Democracy* (with the assistance of Richard Sterner and Arnold Rose), Harper c. 1944 (rev. 1962), p. 675; also p. 668: 'The scientifically important difference between the terms "caste" and "class" as we are using them is, from this point of view, *a relatively large difference in freedom*

sary here to correct the idea of continuity posited in the preceding sentence. In other words, the supposed essential identity between class and caste appears to be rooted in the fact that, once equality is accepted as the norm, any form of inequality appears to be the same as any other because of their common deviation from the norm. We shall see presently that this is fully conscious, elaborately justified in Myrdal. But, if from the standpoint of comparative sociology, one purports to describe these forms of inequality in themselves and if, moreover, one finds that many societies have a norm of inequality, then the presumed unity between class on the one hand and the American form of discrimination on the other becomes meaningless, as our authors themselves sufficiently witness.

The use of the term 'caste' for the American situation is justified by our two authors in very different ways. For Myrdal, the choice of a term is a purely practical matter. One should take a word of common usage – and not try to escape from the value judgments implicit in such a choice. Of the three available terms, 'class' is not suitable, 'race' would give an objective appearance to subjective justifications and prejudices, so there remains only 'caste' which is already used in this sense, and which can be used in a monographic manner, without any obligation to consider how far it means the same thing in India and in the U.S.A.[10] In point of fact, the pejorative coloration of the word by no means

---

of movement between groups' (his italics). Same justification for the use of the term (practical reasons, not indicating identity with the Indian facts), in Westie and Westie, *American Journal of Sociology*, vol. 63 (1957–8), p. 192 and n. 5.

10. op. cit., pp. 667–8. In a footnote, Myrdal takes up an objection made in particular by Charles S. Johnson: the word 'caste' connotes an invariable and stable system in which the tensions and frictions which characterize the relations between Whites and Blacks in the United States are not found; he replies that he does not believe that a caste system having such characteristics exists anywhere (pp. 1374–35, n. 2) and says earlier (p. 668) that Hindu society today does not show that 'stable equilibrium' that American sociologists, observing from a distance, have been inclined to attribute to it. We see here some trace of the equalitarian Creed. The author has, since, had first-hand experience of India and one wonders whether he would maintain this today, whether, even, he would continue to use the word 'caste' for American phenomena.

displeases Myrdal. While the word 'race' embodies a false justification, the word 'caste' carries a condemnation. This is in accordance with American values as defined by the author in the following pages. The American ideology is equalitarian to the extreme. The 'American Creed' demands free competition, which from the point of view of social stratification represents a combination of two basic norms, equality and liberty, but accepts inequality as a result of competition.[11] From this one deduces the 'meaning' of differences of social status in this particular country, one conceives classes as the 'results of the restriction of free competition', while 'caste', with its draconian limitations of free competition, directly negates the American Creed, creates a contradiction in the conscience of every White, survives only because of a whole system of prejudices, and should disappear altogether.

All this is fine, and the militant attitude in which Gunnar Myrdal sees the sole possibility of true objectivity could hardly be more solidly based. In particular, he has the merit of showing that it is in relation to values (a relation not expressed by Kroeber and Warner) that the assumed continuity of class and caste can be best understood. But was it really necessary in all this to use the word 'caste' without scientific guarantee?[12] Would the argument have lost in efficiency if it had been expressed in terms of 'discrimination', 'segregation', etc., only? Even if it had, ought one to risk obscuring comparison in order to facilitate action? Gunnar Myrdal does not care for comparison. Further, does he not eschew comparative theory, in so far as he achieves his objectivity only when he can personally share the values of the society he is studying?

Unlike Myrdal, Lloyd Warner thinks that 'caste' can be used

11. ibid., pp. 670–1. There is here an interesting judgment on the Lloyd Warner school: according to Myrdal, one must take account of the extreme egalitarianism in the 'popular national theory' in order to understand at the same time the tendency among these authors to exaggerate the rigidity of distinctions of class and caste in America, and the interest aroused by their works, which has been greater than their strictly scientific novelty.

12. It is a little surprising to find, next to the ideas here summarized, a rather narrow idea of the place of concepts in science: 'Concepts are our created instruments and have no other form of reality than in our usage. Their purpose is to help make our thinking clear and our observations accurate' (p. 667).

of the Southern U.S.A. in the same sense as it is used of India. This is seen from a 'comparative study' by Warner and Allison Davis,[13] in which the results of their American study are summed up, 'caste' defined, and two or three pages devoted to the Indian side. This Indian summary, though based on good authors, is not very convincing. The variability of the system in time and space is insisted upon to the point of stating that: 'It is not correct to speak of an Indian caste system since there is a variety of systems there.'

In general, caste here is conceived as a variety of class, differing from it in that it forbids mobility either up or down. The central argument runs as follows: in the Southern States, in addition to the disabilities imposed upon the Negroes and the impossibility for them to 'pass', there is between Whites and Negroes neither marriage nor commensality; the same is true in India between different castes. It is the same kind of social phenomenon. 'Therefore, for the comparative sociologist and social anthropologist they are forms of behaviour which must have the same term applied to them' (p. 233).

The formula has the virtue of stating the problem clearly, so that if we do not agree with Warner we can easily say why. A first reason, which might receive ready acceptance, is that under the label of 'behaviour pattern' or 'social phenomena' Warner confuses two different things, namely a collection of particular features (endogamy, mobility and commensality prohibition, etc.) and a whole social system, 'caste' in the case of India obviously meaning 'the caste system'. It is not asked whether the sum of the features under consideration is enough (to the exclusion of all the features left out of consideration) to define the social system: in fact there is no question of a system but only of a certain number of features of the Indian caste system which, according to the author, would be sufficient to define the system. There is really here a *choice* which there is no necessity to follow.[14]

13. W. Lloyd Warner and Allison Davis, 'A comparative study of American caste', in Edgar T. Thomson (ed.), *Race Relations and the Race Problem*, Durham, North Car., 1939, pp. 219–45; for India, see pp. 229–32.

14. The operation of this choice is clear in principle: the caste system of India has been characterized by only those of its traits that it is thought may be found in America, where however they do not constitute a complete system but only part of a system which is called a class-and-caste system.

Let me try to indicate the reasons against the proposed choice. It is generally admitted, at any rate in social anthropology, that particular features must be seen in their relations with the other particular features. There follows, to my mind, a radical consequence – that a particular feature, if taken not in itself but in its concrete position within a system (what is sometimes called its 'function'), can have a totally different meaning according to the position it occupies. That is to say, from a sociological standpoint it is *actually different*. Thus as regards the endogamy of a group: it is not sufficient to say that the group is 'closed', for this very closure is perhaps not, sociologically speaking, the same thing in all cases; in itself it is the same thing, but in itself it is simply not a sociological fact, as it is not, in the first place, a conscious fact. One is led inevitably to the ideology, overlooked in the behaviouristic sociology of Warner and others, which implicitly posits that, among the particular features to be seen in relation to each other, ideological features do not have the same status as the others. Nevertheless a great part of the effort of Durkheim (and of Max Weber as well) bore on the necessity of recognizing in them the same objectivity as in other aspects of social life. Of course this is not to claim that ideology is necessarily the ultimate reality of social facts and delivers their 'explanation', but only that it is the condition of their existence.

The case of endogamy shows very clearly how social facts are distorted through a certain approach. Warner and Davis treat it as a fact of behaviour and not as a fact of values. As such it would be the same as the factual endogamy of a tribe having no prejudice against intermarriage with another tribe, but which given circumstances alone would prevent from practising it. If, on the contrary, endogamy is a fact of values, we are not justified in separating it in the analysis from other facts of values, and particularly – though not solely – from the justifications of it the people give. It is only by neglecting this that racial discrimination and the caste system can be confused. But, one might say, is it not possible that analysis may reveal a close kinship between social facts outwardly similar and ideologically different? The possibility can be readily admitted, but only to insist the more vigorously that we are as yet very far indeed from having reached that point, and that the task for the moment is to take social facts as they are given, without imposing upon them a discrimination scientifically as unwarrantable as is, in American society, the discrimination which these authors attack. The main point is that the refusal to allow their legitimate place to facts of consciousness makes true sociological comparison impossible, because it carries with it a sociocentric attitude. In order to see one's own society from without, one must become conscious of its values and their implications. Difficult as this is always, it becomes impossible if values are neglected. This is confirmed here from the fact that, in Warner's conceptual scheme, the continuity between class and caste proceeds, as we have seen, from an unsuspected relation to the equalitarian norm, while it is presented as a matter of behaviour.

The criticism of the 'Caste School of Race Relations' has been remarkably carried out by Oliver C. Cox.[15] From the same sources as Warner, Cox, with admirable insight, has evolved a picture of the caste system which is infinitely truer than that with which Warner was satisfied. It is true that one cannot everywhere agree with Cox, but we must remember that he was working at second and even at third hand (for instance from Bouglé). Even the limits of Cox's understanding show up precisely our most rooted Western prejudices. He is insufficient mainly in what regards the religious moorings of the system (purity and impurity); because for the Westerner society exists independently of religion and he hardly imagines that it could be otherwise. On the other hand, Cox sees that one should not speak of the individual caste but of the system (pp. 3–4), and that it is not a matter of racial ideology: '. . . although the individual is born heir to his caste, his identification with it is assumed to be based upon some sort of psychological and moral heritage which does not go back to any fundamental somatic determinant' (p. 5).

Elsewhere he writes (p. 14): 'Social inequality is the keynote of the system . . . there is a fundamental creed or presumption [of inequality] . . . antithesis of the Stoic doctrine of human equality . . .' We see here how Cox strikes on important and

15. Oliver C. Cox, 'Race and caste, a distinction', *American Journal of Sociology*, vol. 50 (1944–5), pp. 306–8, and above all, *Caste, Class and Race, A Study in Social Dynamics*, New York, 1948 (Monthly Review edn 1959), to which the references in the text relate.

uncontrovertible points whenever he wishes to emphasize the difference between India and America. I will not enlarge on his criticism of Warner and his school; we have already seen that he makes the essential point: the Indian system is a coherent social system based on the principle of inequality, while the American 'color bar' contradicts the equalitarian system within which it occurs and of which it is a kind of disease.[16]

The use of the word 'caste' to designate American racial segregation has led some authors, in an effort to recognize at the same time the ideological difference, to make a secondary distinction. Already in 1937 John Dollard was writing: 'American caste is pinned not to cultural but to biological factors.'[17] In 1941, in an article called 'Intermarriage in Caste Society' in which he was considering, besides India, the Natchez and the society of the Southern United States, Kingsley Davis asked: how is marriage between different units possible in these societies, while stratification into castes is closely dependent on caste endogamy? His answer was, in the main, that a distinction must be made between 'racial caste system' in which hybrids present an acute problem, and a 'non-racial caste system' where this is not so. In India, hypergamy as defined by Blunt for the North of India, that is, marriage between a man of an upper sub-caste and a woman of a lower sub-caste within the same caste can be understood in particular as a factor of 'vertical solidarity' and as allowing for the exchange of prestige in return for goods (p. 386). (The last point actually marks an essential aspect of true hypergamy, in which the status or prestige of the husband as well as the sons is not affected by the relatively inferior status of the wife or mother.) Another difference between the two kinds of 'caste systems' is that the 'racial' systems rather oppose two groups only, whereas the other systems distinguish a great number of 'strata'. Finally, K. Davis remarks that the hypothesis of the racial origin of the Indian caste system is not proven and that at any rate it is not

16. Cox's thesis appears to have had little effect. Sorokin, however, refers to his article and takes a similar position: the relation between Blacks and Whites has some of the elements of relations between castes but it differs fundamentally (op. cit., p. 258, n. 12).

17. John Dollard, *Caste and Class in a Southern Town*, New York, c. 1937, edn 1940, p. 64; Kingsley Davis, 'Intermarriage in Caste Society', *American Anthropologist*, vol. 43 (1941), pp. 376–95.

racial today (note 22). It is strange that all this did not lead Davis to reflect upon the inappropriateness of using the same word to denote so widely different facts. For him caste, whatever its content may be, is 'an extreme form of stratification', as for others it was an extreme case of class. This brings us to the question of the nature of this category of 'stratification'.

D. 'Social Stratification'

Though the expression deserves attention in view of the proliferation of studies published under this title in the United States and the theoretical discussions to which it has given rise, it does not in effect introduce anything new on the point with which we are here concerned. We meet again the same attitude of mind we have already encountered, but here it runs up against difficulties. As Pfautz acknowledges in his critical bibliography of works published between 1945 and 1952, it is essentially a matter of 'class'.[18] However, Weber's distinction has made its way in the world: one can distinguish types of social stratification according to whether the basis of inequality is power, or prestige, or a combination of both, and classes are usually conceived of as implying a hierarchy of power (political as well as economic), castes and 'estates' a hierarchy of prestige (pp. 392–3). One notes, however, that the community studies of Warner and others conclude that the status hierarchy is a matter of prestige and not of power. Let us stress here the use of the word 'hierarchy', which appears to be introduced in order to allow distinguishing different species within the genus 'stratification'. But here are two strikingly different concepts: should the quasi-geological impassibility suggested by the latter give way to the consideration of values?

18. Harold W. Pfautz, 'The Current Literature on Social Stratification, Critique and Bibliography', *American Journal of Sociology*, vol. 58 (1953), pp. 391–418. The theory of stratification is approached, not starting from class, but from an absolutely general point of view, by Talcott Parsons in 'A Revised Analytical Approach to the Theory of Social Stratification' (R. Bendix and S. M. Lipset (eds.), *Class, Status and Power, A Reader in Social Stratification*, Glencoe, Ill., 1953). While it adopts the same label, the work is outside the current here criticized; the general conception (*in fine*) removes the habitual implications of the word. The argument proceeds from values and the hierarchy which necessarily results from them. The conceptual framework is that of the general theory.

A theoretical controversy in the columns of the *American Sociological Review* is very interesting for the light it throws on the preoccupations and implicit postulates of some sociologists.[19] The starting point was an article published in 1945 by Kingsley Davis and Wilbert E. Moore. Davis had, three years earlier, given basic definitions for the study of stratification (*status*, *stratum*, etc.). Here the authors raised the question of the 'function' of stratification. How is it that palpable inequalities as those referred to under the name of social classes are met in a society whose acknowledged norm is equality? Davis and Moore formulate the hypothesis that it is the result of a mechanism comparable to that of the market: inequality of rewards is necessary in a differentiated society in order that the more difficult or important occupations, those demanding a long training of special skills or involving heavy responsibilities, can be effectively carried out. Buckley objected that Davis and Moore had confused true stratification and pure and simple differentiation: the problem of stratification is not, or is not only, one of knowing how individuals potentially equal at the start find themselves in unequal positions ('achieved inequality'), but of discovering how inequality is maintained, since terms like stratum or stratification are generally taken as implying permanent, hereditary, 'ascribed' inequality. In a rejoinder to Buckley, Davis admitted the difference of points of view; he added that the critic's animosity seemed to him to be directed against the attempt to explain inequality functionally. In my opinion, Davis was right in raising the question of inequality; he was wrong, as Buckley seems to imply, in raising it where inequality is weakest instead of tackling it where it is strongest and most articulate. But in so doing he remained within the tradition we have observed here, which always implicitly refers itself to equality as the norm, as this controversy and the very use of the term 'inequality' show.

19. Kingsley Davis, 'A conceptual analysis of stratification', *American Sociological Review*, vol. 7 (1942), pp. 309–21; K. Davis and Wilbert E. Moore, 'Some principles of stratification', *A.S.R.*, vol. 10 (1945), pp. 242–9; W. Buckley, 'Social stratification and social differentiation', *A.S.R.*, vol. 23 (1958), pp. 369–75; K. Davis, 'A reply to Buckley', *A.S.R.*, vol. 24 (1959), p. 82; Dennis H. Wrong, *A.S.R.*, vol. 24 (1959), pp. 772–82. Reference will be found in the articles of Buckley and Wrong to other articles not used here.

In a recent article Dennis H. Wrong sums up the debate. He points out the limitations of Davis's and Moore's theory and quotes from a work of the former a passage which again shows his pursuit of the functional necessity of stratification, as illustrated for instance by the fact that sweepers tend to have an inferior status in all societies (he is thinking of India).[20] In the end, Wrong asks for studies on certain relations between the egalitarian ideal and other aspects of society, such as the undesirable consequences of an extreme equality or mobility (p. 780). It appears that equality and inequality are considered here as opposite tendencies to be studied on the functional level. Referring to the Utopians, Wrong recalls the difficulty of 'making the leap from history to freedom' (p. 775).

Something has happened then in this branch of American sociology. With the multiplication of studies on social classes, one has been led to introduce values and that value-charged word, 'hierarchy'; one has been led to search for the functions (and disfunctions) of what our societies valorize as well as of what they do not valorize ('in-equality') and which had been called for that reason by a neutral and even pejorative term, 'stratification'. What is in fact set against the equalitarian norm is not, as the term suggests, a kind of residue, a precipitate, a geological legacy, but actual forces, factors or functions. These are negated by the norm, but they nevertheless exist; to express them, the term 'stratification' is altogether inadequate. Nelson N. Foote wrote in a preface to a series of studies: 'The dialectical theme of American history . . . has been a counterpoint of the principles of hierarchy and equality.'[21] The 'problem' of social classes, or of 'social stratification' as it appears to our sociologists springs from the contradiction between the equalitarian ideal, accepted by all these scholars as by the society to which they belong, and an array of facts showing that the difference, the differentiation, tends even among us to assume a hierarchical aspect, and to

20. I was unfortunately unable to consult during the preparation of this article Kingsley Davis's book, *Human Society*, Macmillan, 1949, quoted by Wrong, and which would have been of particular interest since the author was concerned with India at that time (cf. *The Population of India and Pakistan*, Princeton, 1951).

21. Nelson N. Foote, 'Destratification and restratification', Editorial Foreword, *American Journal of Sociology*, vol. 58 (1953), pp. 325–6.

become permanent or hereditary inequality, or discrimination. As Raymond Aron says: 'At the heart of the problem of classes I perceive the antinomy between the fact of differentiation and the ideal of equality.'[22] There are here realities which are made obscure to us by the fact that our values and the forms of our consciousness reject or ignore them. (This is probably still more so for Americans.) In order to understand them better, it is advantageous to turn to those societies which on the contrary approve and emphasize them. In so doing we shall move from 'stratification' to hierarchy.

E. Hierarchy in India

It is impossible to describe the caste system in detail here. Rather, after briefly recalling its main features, I shall isolate more or less arbitrarily the aspect which concerns us. Bouglé's definition can be the starting point: the society is divided into a large number of permanent groups which are at once specialized, hierarchized and separated (in matter of marriage, food, physical contact) in relation to each other.[23] It is sufficient to add that the common basis of these three features is the opposition of pure and impure, an opposition of its nature hierarchical which implies separation and, on the professional level, specialization of the occupations relevant to the opposition; that this basic opposition can segment itself without limit; finally, if one likes, that the conceptual reality of the system lies in this opposition, and not in the groups which it opposes – this accounts for the structural character of these groups, caste and sub-caste being the same thing seen from different points of view.

It has been acknowledged that the hierarchy is thus rendered perfectly univocal in principle.[24] Unfortunately, there has sometimes been a tendency to obscure the issue by speaking of not only religious (or 'ritual') status, but also 'secular (or "social")

22. *Archives Européennes de Sociologie*, I, vol. 1 (1960), p. 14.

23. Celestin Bouglé, *Essais sur le Régime des Castes*, Paris, 1908, p. 4. The English translation of Bouglé's theses, and a commentary on his book together with that of Hocart, which poses the problem of power, is in *Contributions*, no. 2 (1958).

24. Talcott Parsons, loc. cit.

status' based upon power, wealth, etc., which Indians would also take into consideration. Naturally Indians do not confuse a rich man with a poor man but, as the specialists seem to become increasingly aware, it is necessary to distinguish between two very different things: the scale of statuses (called 'religious') which I name hierarchy and which is absolutely distinct from the fact of power on the one hand, and on the other the distribution of power, economic and political, which is very important in practice but is distinct from, and subordinate to, the hierarchy. It will be asked then how power and hierarchy are related to each other. Precisely, Indian society answers this question in a very explicit manner.[25] Hierarchy culminates in the Brahman, or priest; it is the Brahman who consecrates the king's power, which otherwise depends entirely on force (this results from the dichotomy). From very early times, the relationships between Brahman and king or Kshatriya are fixed. While the Brahman is spiritually or absolutely supreme, he is materially dependent; while the king is materially the master, he is spiritually subordinate. A similar relation distinguishes one from the other the two superior 'human ends', *dharma* (action conforming to) universal order and *artha* (action conforming to) selfish interest, which are also hierarchized in such a way that the latter is legitimate only within the limits set by the former. Again, the theory of the gift made to Brahmans, a pre-eminently meritorious action, can be regarded as establishing a means of transformation of material goods into values (cf. hypergamy, mentioned above, p. 348: one gets prestige from the gift of a girl to superiors).

This disjunction of power and status illustrates perfectly Weber's analytical distinction; its interest for comparison is great, for it presents an unmixed form, it realizes an 'ideal type'. Two features stand out: first, in India, any totality is expressed in the form of a hierarchical enumeration of its components (thus of the state or kingdom for example), hierarchy marks the conceptual integration of a whole, it is so to say its intellectual cement. Secondly, if we are to generalize, it can be supposed that hierarchy, in the sense that we are using the word here, and in

25. What follows is summarized from my chapter on the conception of Kingship in ancient India, to appear in L. Renou and J. Filliozat, *L'Inde Classique*, vol. 3.

accord with its etymology, never attaches itself to power as such, but always to religious functions, because religion is the form that the universally true assumes in these societies. For example, when the king has the supreme rank, as is generally the case, it is very likely not by reason of his power but by reason of the religious nature of his function. From the point of view of rank at any rate, it is the opposite to what one most often supposes, namely that power is the essential which then attracts to itself religious dignities or finds in them support and justification.

One may see in the hierarchical principle, as it appears in India in its pure state, a fundamental feature of complex societies other than our own, and a principle of their unity; not their material, but their conceptual or symbolic unity. That is the essential 'function' of hierarchy: it expresses the unity of such a society while connecting it to what appears to it to be universal, namely a conception of the cosmic order, whether or not it includes a God, or a king as mediator. If one likes, hierarchy integrates the society by reference to its values. Apart from the general reluctance which searching for social functions at this level is likely to meet with, it will be objected that there are societies without hierarchy, or else societies in which hierarchy does not play the part described above. It is true for example that tribes, if they are not entirely devoid of inequalities, may have neither a king nor, say, a secret society with successive grades. But that applies to relatively simple societies, with few people, and where the division of labour is little developed.

F. The Modern Revolution

There remain the societies of the modern Western type, which go so far as to inscribe the principle of equality in their constitutions. It is indeed true that, if values and not behaviour alone are considered, a profound gap has to be acknowledged between the two kinds. What has happened? Is it possible to take a simple view of it? The societies of the past, most societies, have believed themselves to be based in the order of things, natural as well as social; they thought they were copying or designing their very conventions after the principles of life and the world. Modern society wants to be 'rational', to break away from nature in order to set up an autonomous human order. To that end, it is enough to take the true measure of man and from it to deduce the human order. No gap between the ideal and the real: like an engineer's blue print, the representation will create the actuality. At this point society, the old mediator between man in his particularity and nature, disappears. There are but human individuals, and the problem is how to make them all fit together. Man will now draw from himself an order which is sure to satisfy him. As the source of this rationality, Hobbes posits, not an ideal, always open to question, but the most general passion, the common generator of human actions, the most assured human reality. The individual becomes the measure of all things, the source of all 'rationality'; the equalitarian principle is the outcome of this attitude, for it conforms to reason, being the simplest view of the matter, while it most directly negates the old hierarchies.[26]

As against the societies which believed themselves to be natural, here is the society which wants itself to be rational. While the 'natural' society was hierarchized, finding its rationality in setting itself as a whole within a vaster whole, and was unaware of the 'individual', the 'rational' society on the other hand, recognizing only the individual, that is, seeing universality, or reason, only in the particular man, places itself under the standard of equality and is unaware of itself as a hierarchized whole. In a sense, the 'leap from history into freedom' has already been made, and we live in a realized Utopia.

Between these two types which it is convenient to contrast directly, there should apparently be located an intermediary type, where nature and convention are distinguished and where social conventions are susceptible of being judged by reference to an ideal model accessible to reason alone. But whatever may be the transitions which make for the evolution of the second type from the first, it is in the modern revolution which separates the two types, in fact the two leaves of the same diptych, that the

26. On Hobbes and the artificial society, 'rational' in the sense of being devised according to the reality of man (the individual) and not inspired by an ideal order, cf. Leo Strauss, *Natural Right and History*, University of Chicago Press, 1953, chapt. 5; Elie Halévy, *La Formation du Radicalisme philosophique*, 3 vols., Paris, 1901–4, vol. 1, pp. 3, 41, 53, 90; vol. 3, pp. 347–8; etc.

central problem of comparative sociology most probably lies: how can we describe in the same language two 'choices' so diametrically opposed to each other, how can we take into account at once the revolution in values which has transformed modern societies as well as the 'unity of anthropology'? Certainly this cannot be done by refusing to acknowledge the change and reducing everything to 'behaviour', nor by extending the obscurity from one side to the other, as we should by talking of 'social stratification' in general. But we remark that where one of the leaves of the diptych is obscure and blurred, the other is clear and distinct; use can be made of what is conscious in one of the two types of society in order to decipher what is not conscious in the other.

G. From Hierarchy to Discrimination

One can attempt, in broad terms, to apply this comparative perspective to the American racist phenomenon. It is obvious on the one hand that society did not completely cease to be society, as a hierarchized whole, on the day it willed itself to be simply a collection of individuals. In particular, the tendency to make hierarchical distinctions continued. On the other hand, racism is more often than not understood to be a modern phenomenon. (Economic causes of its emergence have sometimes been sought, while much closer and more probable ideological connexions were neglected.) The simplest hypothesis therefore is to assume that racism fulfils an old function under a new form. It is as if it were representing in an equalitarian society a resurgence of what was differently, and more directly and naturally expressed in a hierarchical society. Make distinction illegitimate, and you get discrimination; suppress the former modes of distinction and you have a racist ideology. Can this view be made more precise and confirmed? Societies of the past knew a hierarchy of status bringing with it privileges and disabilities, among others the total juridical disability of slavery. Now the history of the United States tells just this, that racial discrimination succeeded the slavery of the Negro people once the latter was abolished. (One is tempted to wonder why this all-important transition has not been more systematically studied, from a sociological point of view, than it seems to have been, but perhaps one's ignorance is the answer.[27]) The distinction between master and slave was succeeded by the discrimination of the White against the Black. To ask why does racism appear is already to have in part answered the question: the essence of the distinction was juridical; by suppressing it the transformation of its racial attribute into racist substance was encouraged. For things to have been otherwise the distinction itself should have been overcome.

In general, racism has certainly more complex roots. Besides the internal difference of status, traditional societies knew an external difference, itself coloured by hierarchy, between the 'we' and the others. It was normally social and cultural. For the Greeks as for others, foreigners were barbarians, strangers to the civilization and society of the 'we'; for that reason they could be enslaved. In the modern Western world not only are citizens free and equal before the law, but a transition develops, at least in popular mentality, from the moral principle of equality to the belief in the basic identity of all men, because they are no longer taken as samples of a culture, a society or a social group, but as *individuals* existing in and for themselves.[28] In other words, the recognition of a cultural difference can no longer ethnocentrically justify inequality. But it is observed that in certain circumstances, which it would be necessary to describe, a hierarchical difference

27. cf. Gunnar Myrdal, ibid., pp. 581 ff., the 'Jim Crow Laws', etc. The reaction to the abolition of slavery was not immediate but developed slowly. Discrimination appears as a simple separation under the slogan 'separate but equal'. For the period before the civil war also, Myrdal gives a succinct history, but the analysis, apparently, remains to be done. It promises to be fruitful, see, for example, the declarations of Jefferson and Lincoln (cf. *Times Literary Supplement*, 22 July 1960, pp. 457–8, according to J. W. Schulte-Nordholt, *The People That Walk in Darkness*, Starke, 1960). Recent articles by P. L. van den Berghe partly satisfy my wish. Cf. the last one: 'Apartheid, une interprétation sociologique de la ségrégation raciale', *Cahiers Internationaux de Sociologie*, vol. 28, nouv. ser., 7e année, 1960, pp. 47–56. According to this author, segregation has replaced etiquette as a mode of social distance. The change would correspond to the movement from slavery to racism.

28. The fact that the transition from 'equality' to 'identity' operates chiefly at the level of popular mentality makes it more difficult to seize on than if it were present in the great authors. I propose nevertheless to study elsewhere more closely this particular complementarity between equalitarianism and racism.

continues to be posited, which is this time attached to somatic characteristics, physiognomy, colour of the skin, 'blood'. No doubt, these were at all times marks of distinction, but they have now become the essence of it. How is this to be explained? It is perhaps apposite to recall that we are heirs to a dualistic religion and philosophy: the distinction between spirit and matter, body and soul, permeates our entire culture and especially the popular mentality. Everything looks as if the equalitarian–identitarian mentality was situated within this dualism, as if once equality and identity bear on the individual *souls*, distinction could only be effected with regard to the *bodies*. What is more, discrimination is collective, it is as if only physical characteristics were essentially collective where everything mental tends to be primarily individual. (Thus mental differences are attributed to physical types.) Is this far-fetched? It is only emphasizing the Christian ancestry of modern individualism and equalitarianism: the individual only has fellow-men (even his enemies are considered, not only as objects, but also as subjects), and he believes in the fundamental equality of all men taken severally; at the same time, for him, the collective inferiority of a category of men, when it is in his interest to state it, is expressed and justified in terms of what physically differentiates them from himself and people of his group. To sum up, the proclamation of equality has burst asunder a mode of distinction centred upon the social, but in which physical, cultural and social characteristics were indiscriminately mixed. To re-affirm inequality, the underlying dualism demanded that physical characteristics be brought to the fore. While in India heredity is an attribute of status, the racist attributes status to 'race'.

All this may be regarded as an arbitrary view of the abstract intellect. Yet, the hypothesis is confirmed at least in part in Myrdal's work. Dealing with the American facts, this author discovers a close connexion between equalitarianism and racism. To begin with, he notes in the philosophy of the enlightenment the tendency to minimize innate differences; then, generally everywhere and especially in America, the essentially moral doctrine of the 'natural rights' of man rests on a biological equalitarianism: all men are 'created equal'. The period 1830–60 sees the development of an ideology for the defence of slavery: slavery being condemned in the name of natural equality, its champions argue against this the doctrine of the inequality of races; later the argument is used to justify discrimination, which becomes established from the moment when, about 1877, the North gives up enforcing assimilation. The author's conclusions are worth pondering upon:

> The dogma of racial inequality may, in a sense, be regarded as a strange fruit of the Enlightenment. . . . The race dogma is nearly the only way out for a people so moralistically equalitarian, if it is not prepared to live up to its faith. A nation less fervently committed to democracy could probably live happily in a caste system . . . race prejudice is, in a sense, a function [a perversion] of equalitarianism.[29]

If this is so, it is permissible to doubt whether, in the fight against racism in general, the mere recall of the equalitarian idea, however solemn it may be, and even though accompanied by a scientific criticism of racist prejudices, will be really efficient. It would be better to prevent the passage from the moral principle of equality to the notion that all men are identical. One feels sure that equality can, in our day, be combined with the recognition of differences, so long as such differences are morally neutral. The means for conceptualizing differences must be provided to the people. The diffusion of the pluralistic notions of culture, society, etc., affording a counterweight and setting bounds to individualism, is an obvious indication.[30] Finally if the tendency to hierarchize still exists, if the affirmation of the modern ideal is not sufficient to make it disappear but, on the contrary, by a complicated mechanism, can on occasion make it ferocious and morbid, the antagonisms and interests which exploit it should not be lost sight of – but this is beyond our subject.

Cutting short here the attempt to define racism comparatively, I should like to recall, albeit too briefly, a structural relation which is essential to the possible developments of comparison. Equality and hierarchy are not, in fact, opposed to each other in

29. Gunnar Myrdal, ibid., pp. 83 ff., the quotations are from p. 89. Myrdal also takes account of the development of the biological view of man: *Homo sapiens* as a species in the animal world; cf. also p. 591: 'The persistent preoccupation with sex and marriage in the rationalization . . . is, to this extent, an irrational escape on the part of the whites from voicing an open demand for difference in social status . . . for its own sake.'

30. cf. Claude Lévi-Strauss, *Race et Histoire*, UNESCO, c. 1952.

the mechanical way which the exclusive consideration of values might lead one to suppose: the pole of the opposition which is not valorized is none the less present, each implies the other and is supported by it. Talcott Parsons draws attention, at the very beginning of his study, to the fact that the distinction of statuses carries with it and supposes equality within each status (op. cit., p. 1). Conversely, where equality is affirmed, it is within a group which is hierarchized in relation to others. So in the Greek cities or, in the modern world, the British democracy and imperialism, the latter being tinged with hierarchy (e.g. incipient racism in India in the second half of the nineteenth century).[31] It is this structural relation that the equalitarian ideal tends to destroy, the result of its action being what is most often studied under the name of 'social stratification'. In the first place the relation is inverted: equality contains inequalities instead of being contained in a hierarchy. In the second place a whole series of transformations happen which can perhaps be summarized by saying that hierarchy is repressed, made non-conscious: it is replaced by a manifold network of inequalities, matters of fact instead of right, of quantity and gradualness instead of quality and discontinuity. Hence, for a part, the well-known difficulty of defining social classes.

H. Conclusion

To conclude in general terms, comparative sociology requires concepts which take into account the values that different societies have, so to speak, chosen for themselves. A consequence of this choice of values is that certain aspects of social reality are clearly and consciously elaborated, while others are left in the dark. In order to express what a given society does not express, the sociologist cannot invent concepts, for when he attempts to do so he only manages, as in the case of 'social stratification', to translate in a way at once pretentious and obscure the prejudices of his own society. He must therefore have recourse to societies which have

31. Machiavelli observes that a 'republic', which wishes to extend its empire and not remain small and stagnant, should like Rome confide the defence of liberty to the people and not, like Sparta and Venice, to the great. (*Discourses on the first Decade of T. Livy*, vol. 1 ch. 5–6.)

expressed those same aspects. A general theory of 'inequality', if it is deemed necessary, must be centred upon those societies which give it a meaning and not upon those which, while presenting certain forms of it, have chosen to disavow it. It must be a theory of hierarchy in its valorized, or simple and direct forms, as well as in its non-valorized or devalorized, or complex, hybrid, covert forms. (Let us note, following Talcott Parsons,[32] that such a theory is only one particular way of considering the total social system.) In so doing one will of course in no way impose upon one society the values of another, but only endeavour to set reciprocally 'in perspective'[33] the various types of societies. One will try to see each society in the light not only of itself but of the others. From the point of view of social anthropology at any rate, this appears to be not only the formula for an objective comparison, but even the condition for understanding every particular society.

32. cf. Note 17.
33. E. E. Evans-Pritchard, *Social Anthropology*, Cohen, 1951, p. 129.

18 A. Béteille

The Decline of Social Inequality?

An original paper published here for the first time.

I

The existence of social inequality (in the broadest sense) is perhaps a common condition of all human societies. Social inequality is also one of the most sensitive areas of human existence. It is therefore not surprising that most people who have sought to examine its nature and basis have adopted what to others appear as partisan views. Either they have attacked certain institutions considered by them to be the source of inequality in their own or in other societies; or they have conceived future societies which can be organized on a basis of fundamental equality. Those who have written about social inequality have found it difficult to escape the vision of a classless Utopia.

The difficulty of obtaining an impartial view becomes evident when we examine the debate over social inequality between scholars representing the two major types of industrial society. East European sociologists argue that the abolition of private property has led to much greater social equality in their societies than is present in the West; inequalities of income have been reduced and the prestige rating of occupations depends increasingly on factors other than income. American students of the Soviet system point out that economic inequalities there are almost as great as in their own society; further, that under totalitarianism the political régime creates new forms of inequality which are far more oppressive than those in the West.

Western sociologists are themselves not unanimous in their views about the decline of inequality in their own society. The majority would certainly argue that this decline has been both real and substantial. They point to the rising wages of the working classes and to the equalization of educational and occupational opportunities. Some have begun to ask whether the concept of class has not become obsolete in mid twentieth-century Europe and America. One of the first issues of the influential *European Journal of Sociology* (vol. 1, no. 2) was in fact subtitled, 'À la recherche des classes perdues.'

There are others, however, who adopt a more sceptical if not critical point of view. Thus, Richard Titmuss[1] has presented an impressive body of data to show that during the last two or three decades equalization of income in Britain has been more apparent than real. Speaking in more general terms, John Westergaard[2] has challenged the view that there is any real basis for saying that social inequalities in Britain have been substantially reduced since the War. And there is the well-known view of Wright Mills[3] that in mid twentieth-century America class divisions are becoming more and not less rigid.

It thus appears that a certain ambiguity inheres in answers even to simple questions such as the distribution of income or the concentration of property. This ambiguity is increased by the ideological idiom in which the answers are evaluated. In Western countries those who argue that social inequalities are not being reduced tend to be characterized as radicals; adherents of left-wing ideologies in their turn feel obliged to show that their society is not as equalitarian as it should be or is made out to be. This debate is sometimes carried on with such vigour and sophistry that the layman and the outsider often find it impossible to decide what the real position is even on areas from which it should be possible to eliminate ambiguity.

Whatever the differences between the different types of industrial society – socialist or capitalist – these appear to be small when viewed against the problem of social inequality within the underdeveloped countries. This is a context in which many would

1. R. M. Titmuss, *Income Distribution and Social Change*, Allen & Unwin, 1962.

2. J. H. Westergaard, 'The withering away of class, a contemporary myth', in Perry Anderson *et al.*, *Towards Socialism*, London, 1965.

3. C. Wright Mills, *White Collar*, Oxford University Press, 1953; *The Power Elite*, Oxford University Press, 1959.

be tempted to agree with Aron[4] that the development of an industrial social order has a logic of its own, whether the path followed is that of socialism or of capitalism. And for many European scholars (both from the East and the West) the real problem of social inequality today lies not in their own society but in the Third World.

Among the factors believed to bring about the decline of social inequality, a special place is generally assigned to economic growth. Economic growth is at once concrete and measurable and it is undeniable that the most palpable forms of social inequality are to be found in the economically backward countries. As Myrdal has recently written:

> In South Asia there is a correlation between the severity, the rigidity of caste or semi-caste relations, and the economic level. That in the Western countries social equalization goes together with economic growth in circular causation, and with cumulative effects, is to me quite evident.[5]

The faith in the equalizing effect of economic growth is shared alike by adherents of socialism and capitalism. It is, if anything, even stronger among the leaders of the underdeveloped countries. Several of these countries have adopted programmes of planned economic change. The chief attraction of economic growth for many of their leaders is the belief that it will create the necessary conditions for an equalitarian society.

There can be no question that many of the more obtrusive forms of social inequality have become obsolete in the advanced industrial societies. Yet even here one encounters remarkable expressions of social discrimination as in the relations between Negroes and Whites in the United States or, increasingly, in the attitudes towards coloured immigrants in Britain. How far economic development will in itself solve what appears to be one of the most deep-rooted problems of social existence is a question which I shall leave aside for the time being. Even the most highly developed countries have not yet attained the conditions under

4. Raymond Aron, *Dix-huit Leçons sur la Société Industrielle*, Paris, 1962.

5. G. Myrdal, 'Chairman's introduction' in Anthony de Reuck and Julie Knight (eds.), *Caste and Race*, Churchill, 1967, p. 4.

which full social equality is possible. For the rest, there are countries in Asia, Africa, Latin America (and even in parts of Europe) where economic growth has barely touched the surface of traditional forms of social inequality.

II

There are two ways in which the problem of social inequality may be viewed. In the first case we examine the actually existing differences between individuals in terms of property, income or occupation. Several such criteria may be used, either singly or in combination. Most studies in social stratification are in fact concerned with attempts to divide up the population into hierarchically arranged layers in this way. In modern Western society, income and occupation are the criteria most frequently used so that in the popular mind social inequality is often identified with economic inequality. Actually, individuals may also be graded on the basis of a variety of 'non-economic' criteria such as education, accent or skin colour.

There is, however, another way in which the problem of social inequality may be studied. In most hitherto existing societies inequalities between strata have not only existed in fact but have also been accepted as normal and legitimate:

The rich man in his castle,
The poor man at his gate, .
God made them high or lowly
And ordered their estate.

Thus, social inequality belongs not only to the domain of facts which can be represented on statistical tables; it belongs also to the domain of values and norms.

In this essay I shall be concerned primarily with social inequality as a system of values and norms. This is a complex and difficult problem. Values and norms cannot be objectified in the same way as economic variables such as property and income. Largely on account of this it is extremely difficult to make comparisons between the value systems of different societies. One can say, for instance, that income is more equitably distributed in

Japan than in Indonesia. It would be far more difficult to demonstrate that the former has a more equalitarian value system than the latter.

A second difficulty arises from the fact that the values of a society are not always consistent with each other. Sometimes there are unstated values which are sharply at variance with the ones explicitly stated. One of the most persistently articulated values of American society is that of the equality of all human beings; yet in the minds of most Americans, Negroes are not considered as the equals of Whites, or Jews as the equals of Gentiles. When the basic values of a society are at variance with each other it becomes difficult to make a balanced assessment of their relative importance. Here again much depends on the sympathies of the investigator. East European sociologists are inclined to attach greater importance to the Negro problem in the United States than are their American counterparts.

Historically, different societies have varied greatly in the extent to which they have explicitly sanctioned social inequality. They have differed also in their relative emphases on the types of social inequality that have been sanctioned. Some have sanctioned inequality on the basis of colour, others in terms of refinement and 'culture' and yet others on the basis of ritual purity. Until recently some of the most powerful sanctions for social inequality derived from religious systems. Yet most of the world religions have also contained messages asserting the equality of men. Even Hinduism, which provided the ideological basis of caste, has had its equalitarian *bhakti* movements.

In spite of the great diversity of patterns, certain trends seem to emerge from a consideration of the events of the last hundred and fifty years. Everywhere there seems to have come about a steady erosion in the legitimacy accorded to social inequality. If social inequality continues to exist as a fact, it is no longer accepted by all as a part of the natural order but is challenged, or at least questioned, at every point. For students of social stratification, this decline in the legitimacy of social inequality is perhaps the most important feature of the nineteenth and twentieth centuries.

The decline in the legitimacy of social inequality did not start everywhere at the same time and has not proceeded equally far in every society. But today there are very few societies in the world where an ideology of inequality would be allowed to pass unchallenged. Even in India, where traditional conceptions of hierarchy are still very much alive, the constitution has declared itself squarely in favour of a 'casteless and classless society'. We have only to go back a few hundred years in European history or to consider the value systems of some of the non-European societies to see how novel the present situation is.

One of the first of the great modern thinkers who studied equality as a sociological problem was Alexis de Tocqueville. His work, which was based on his experience of American society in the early 1830s, is full of prognoses about the future.[6] What impressed de Tocqueville was not merely the greater equality in the material conditions of existence in America but also the absence there of a tradition of feudal estates and the tremendous force in social life of equalitarian values and norms. He was convinced that this was the general direction in which European societies would be moving in the future.

While it is true that economic factors have played a major part in the decline of certain forms of social inequality, it would be wrong to ignore the part played in this process by political ideology. Ossowski has pointed out that Marx's theory of social class (which has profoundly influenced contemporary theories of social inequality) was formulated under conditions in which market forces and 'the economic factor' appeared supreme. In the industrial societies of today, particularly in the socialist countries, political ideology is an active agent in altering not only the distribution of income but also the allocation of 'the privileges that are most essential for social status'.[7]

The influence of political factors is even more conspicuous in the underdeveloped countries. It is commonly said that whereas in the West, economic development preceded political change, in the ex-colonial countries of Africa and Asia modern political institutions and ideologies were taken over without the emergence of appropriate economic infrastructures. These countries are thus confronted by a number of paradoxes: sharp (and sometimes

6. Alexis de Tocqueville, *Democracy in America*, Vintage, 1956, 2 vols.

7. Stanislaw Ossowski, *Class Structure in the Social Consciousness*, Routledge, 1963, p. 184.

growing) differences of income and wealth coupled with increasing participation of the masses in politics; deeply ingrained values supporting social hierarchy co-existing with formal commitments to social equality.

It would be wrong to dismiss lightly the urge for social equality in the societies which are variously described today as 'underdeveloped', 'backward' or 'traditional'. In most of these countries, equalitarian ideologies developed in close association with nationalist movements aimed at overthrowing the colonial system. Clearly, these ideologies drew much of their inspiration from Western political thought. But in most cases there were attempts to give them an indigenous dressing and to claim for them an indigenous origin. The appeal to equalitarian values was perhaps a necessary condition for the success of nationalist movements. But these values and ideologies did not disappear with the end of colonial rule. If anything, they have taken firmer roots in post-colonial societies where they are coming into conflict at every point with traditional conceptions of hierarchy.

III

I have said earlier that social inequality can be studied both as fact and as value. It is possible to apply another dichotomy in the study of this problem. In analysing any system of social inequality, one can distinguish what is general or universal in it from what is unique and culturally specific. This distinction is in some ways related to the one between fact and value.

The question as to the generality or uniqueness of a given system of social inequality has been raised by a number of social anthropologists in relation to the study of caste. Leach asked in 1960 whether caste could best be understood as a structural phenomenon or as a unique expression of the Hindu cultural system. His answer was that the latter approach provided the more correct perspective.[8] Dumont has expressed the same point of view even more forcefully.[9] Both Leach and Dumont argue

8. E. R. Leach (ed.), *Aspects of Caste in South India, Ceylon and North-West Pakistan*, Cambridge University Press, 1962, Introduction.
9. L. Dumont, *Homo Hierarchicus*, Paris, 1966.

that a correct understanding of caste can be achieved only through an appreciation of its uniqueness; and that this uniqueness consists in the fact that the caste system is based on the recognition of inequality as a fundamental value.

It would appear reasonable to say that there are certain inequalities which are common to all societies. Most important among these are the inequalities which derive from the distribution of power. Inequalities of this kind are truly universal; even in the most primitive and undifferentiated societies power is unequally distributed between the old and the young and between the sexes. Inequalities which derive from the distribution of income are also a nearly universal feature of human societies; it is difficult to visualize a large and complex society in which everyone will have the same income.

Another very important source of inequality in a large number of societies arises from the distribution of property. The socialist societies of Eastern Europe have abolished the private ownership of the means of production. But here one may say, with a certain degree of oversimplification, that inequalities in the economic domain have been transferred to the political domain; instead of inequalities in the ownership of property we have inequalities in the control of the productive system.

Not all societies attach equal weight to the differences deriving from income, wealth and power. In fact, the values attached to property are diametrically opposite in socialist and capitalist societies. It seems further that income is less important as a basis of social inequality in socialist as contrasted with capitalist systems, whereas the opposite is probably true in the case of power. Generally speaking, the possession or control of material resources has a high social value in industrial societies. Conversely, poverty is a source of social opprobrium; to be poor in an affluent society is to show a lack of worth. Riches and poverty have not been evaluated in the same way in all societies; to take one example, in traditional India, the poor were by no means always disreputable.

Beyond income, wealth and power, there are sources of social inequality which are more specifically associated with particular cultural systems. It has sometimes been argued that these factors play a less important part in industrial as opposed to agrarian or 'traditional' societies. And further, as more and more societies become industrialized, they will all have the same bases of inequality which will be defined increasingly in terms of rational, organizational needs, that is, in terms of disparities, which derive from the unequal distribution of power and of skill. According to this argument other bases of inequality will be reduced to a marginal or residual position. But to talk in this way is to speculate; the industrial societies of today – however advanced – are far from attaining such a pattern of organization.

A very important scheme of classification, deriving from Max Weber, differentiates between inequalities deriving from class, status and power. In Weber's scheme, class and power appear to be generalized categories: the former arises from unequal life chances in a market situation and the latter from the nature of domination which is present in one form or another in all societies. Status, on the other hand, seems to be a kind of residual category. It is to a consideration of this that I now turn my attention.

Weber was struck by the fact that in all societies – including the capitalist societies of the West – social honour is based on something more than just wealth or power. He makes a distinction between status and class, arguing that status honour 'normally stands in sharp opposition to the pretentions of sheer property',[10] or, one may add, of any form of power whether economically determined or otherwise. However, he is compelled to concede that '. . . *today* the class situation is by far the predominant factor, for of course the possibility of a style of life expected for members of a status group is usually conditioned economically'.[11]

If status honour is not determined exclusively by economic or political power, what are its other determinants? Weber does not give a clear answer beyond saying that the question of social honour belongs to the realm of values as opposed to material interests. He also links it with the specific styles of life associated with particular sections of society. But the notion of style of life is extremely vague and it is hard to find a basis for saying why styles of life are evaluated differently in a given society or why

10. H. H. Gerth and C. W. Mills (eds.), *From Max Weber: Essays in Sociology*, London, 1948, p. 187.

11. ibid., p. 190 (italics added).

societies differ in according the highest social value to a particular style of life.

In pre-industrial societies styles of life were sharply differentiated and often there were legal or ritual sanctions against the adoption by members of the lower strata of the styles of life of the higher. These formal sanctions have been eliminated from modern industrial societies and elsewhere also they are on their way out. The elimination of formally defined privileges and disabilities is generally attended by an increase in the pace of individual mobility. In combination these two processes lead to a decrease in the visibility of social differences even where such differences continue to exist.

The style of life of a status group includes both material and non-material components. Non-material components such as modes of speech or literary and artistic tastes are in some ways more difficult to acquire than the material ones. In the case of the latter it has always been possible within limits to translate economic advantages into advantages of status. The industrial economic system with its mass-produced consumer goods and its media of mass communication greatly increases these possibilities. The expansion of education and an increase in the uniformity of its content is likely to have a similar effect on the non-material components of exclusive styles of life. In English society accent and speech play an important part in maintaining distances between social groups. If a uniform system of school and university education is established, these distinctions are likely to become less conspicuous.

There are various reasons why it may be difficult to translate economic advantages into status advantages. An exclusive style of life cannot be acquired by an individual in isolation; in order to acquire it he has to be a part of a social milieu. Social circles in which exclusive styles of life are cultivated usually resist the intrusion of outsiders. This resistance is itself an indication of the value attached to social inequality. In a society where equality is universally accepted as a basic value there would be no parvenus.

Tradition plays an important part in sanctioning the association between a group and its distinctive style of life. Thus it is not enough to have the material resources or even the cultural skills that are needed for the adoption of a particular style of life. The adoption has to be legitimized in terms of traditional association. Even in the United States the histories of local communities are full of the tensions between the old and the new rich. The role of tradition in providing legitimacy to the claims of status is of course much more important in pre-industrial societies.

IV

The question of tradition introduces another set of factors which are of great importance to any consideration of social honour. These centre around descent, lineage and race. All the three terms are ambiguous and I will not attempt to define them here. What they share in common is a belief that certain qualities – both physical and 'spiritual' – are fixed in the human individual by heredity and cannot be acquired except by birth. These beliefs – or rather sentiments – are not always rationally or even systematically formulated but they are deeply held even by people who have been taught the scientific argument that culture has nothing to do with heredity.

The hereditary principle is of course the basis of all caste and estate systems. If one gives a broad meaning to these terms, most pre-industrial societies were based on estates or castes of some kind. The hereditary principle continues to play an important part in contemporary agrarian societies. Attachment to the soil seems to have a universal association with respect for tradition and heredity: as Michael Young has written, 'The soil grows castes; the machine makes classes.'[12] Estate traditions may, however, outlive agrarian modes of production. Britain was the first country to change from agrarian to industrial production, yet an estate tradition has been kept alive there to a greater extent than in most West European countries.

The high social value placed on descent may be expressed in a variety of cultural idioms. There is first of all the polarity of honour and shame which seem to be two of the fundamental values of Mediterranean societies. Secondly, there is the polarity of purity and pollution which gives to the Hindu caste system its distinctive character. Finally, the values placed on skin colour

12. Michael Young, *The Rise of Meritocracy*, Thames and Hudson, 1961, p. 24. (Penguin edn, 1961.)

play an important part in ordering social hierarchies in a variety of contemporary societies, irrespective of their economic or ideological advancement.

Recently a group of social anthropologists have made intensive studies of Mediterranean peasant communities in Spain, Greece, Cyprus and Algeria.[13] These studies show the intense pre-occupation of the Mediterranean countryman with the notion of honour and its counterpart, shame. Honour and shame are complex ideas, whose meanings, although they vary greatly with context and situation, are in the end socially defined. They are among the fundamental qualities in terms of which individuals and their families (in the widest sense) are evaluated. From these studies we do not always get a clear picture as to how these concepts are related to the social hierarchy but such a relationship is implicit.

Julio Caro Baroja has made an interesting historical analysis of the changing conceptions of honour and shame in Spanish society from medieval times to the present. He argues that these conceptions derive from three principal sources, 'the classical world, the Germanic or barbarian cultures, and Christianity';[14] consequently, it is only to be expected that they bristle with contradictions. The Christian conception of honour is at many points opposed to the conception developed by the traditions of chivalry; honour among the peasantry never meant the same thing as it did among the nobility; there were great differences in the conception of honour as applying to men and women among all classes.

Honour could, of course, be achieved by the individual; but among all classes, honour also derived from one's family, lineage and ancestry. In medieval Spain the conception of honour was closely related to pride of birth and it provided a basis for the social ranking of families and lineages. A similar situation prevails among contemporary Mediterranean peasants.

Between the fifteenth and eighteenth centuries important distinctions were made in Spain between 'old Christians' and 'new

13. Julian Pitt-Rivers (ed.), *Mediterranean Countrymen*, Paris, 1963; J. G. Peristiany (ed.), *Honour and Shame, The Values of Mediterranean Society*, University of Chicago Press, 1966.

14. Julio Caro Baroja, 'Honour and shame: a historical account of several conflicts' in Peristiany, op. cit., p. 83.

Christians'; the latter were mainly converts from among Moors and Jews. The distinction between old and new Christians was not only socially important but was legally defined in the 'statutes of purity'. The Jews were in many cases economically powerful but for social and political reasons they sought absorption into the Christian community. The distinction between old and new Christians not only shows the importance of 'race' in social stratification but also brings out some of the tensions between honour and wealth.

To what extent do these concepts of honour and shame – so characteristic of medieval society – persist in modern Europe? It would seem that their presence is far less conspicuous today than in the past, outside of peasant communities. Peristiany has tried to explain in structural terms this decline in the social significance of honour and shame in modern industrial society.

Honour and shame are the constant preoccupation of individuals in small scale, exclusive societies where face to face personal, as opposed to anonymous, relations are of paramount importance and where the social personality of the actor is as significant as his office.[15]

In a world where social life is fragmented and impersonal and where there is multiplicity of standards, these values are likely to be basically transformed.

Caro Baroja brings out the association in medieval Spain between 'honour', 'purity' and 'cleanliness of blood'.[16] The cement that held the three together was of course the predominance of the lineage as a basis for the ordering of social hierarchies. The concept of purity was perhaps also nourished by Christianity as providing a basis and a justification for the distinction between Christians and Jews. In a different context Bastide[17] has also argued that medieval Christianity viewed the distinction between purity and impurity of blood partly in terms of the concept of sin.

The fullest elaboration of the concepts of purity and pollution is of course to be found in the Hindu system of ideas centring around caste. Purity as understood in the Hindu caste system

15. Peristiany, op. cit., p. 11.

16. Caro Baroja, op. cit., p. 101.

17. Roger Bastide, 'Colour, racism, and Christianity', *Daedalus*, vol. 96, no. 2, 1967.

means much more than purity and cleanliness of blood. Ritual purity can be lost in many ways and not merely through contamination of blood. But it is true none the less that the most severe rules against pollution applied to marriage or sexual contact between women of higher castes and men of lower. Even today, among all the strictures associated with caste the ones relating to endogamy have been the least affected by change.

The styles of life which were accorded the highest social value and the criteria by which status was evaluated in traditional India differed in many ways from their counterparts in Mediterranean society. Among the Hindus a much greater value was attached than elsewhere to the correct observance of restrictions relating to food, drink and contact of various kinds. It should be pointed out, however, that the preoccupation with purity and pollution was particularly conspicuous among the Brahmins whose influence was not equally great in every part of India. In fact, the Rajputs, who were the dominant group in large parts of Western and Northern India, had concepts of honour and shame which were not very different from those of medieval Spain.

The distinction between ritual status and secular dominance was made very clearly in Hinduism. Dumont has gone so far as to argue that the distinctiveness of Hinduism lay in its absolute separation *in principle* between the gradation of status and the distribution of power.[18] In practice, of course, the two were often closely associated. However, the wealthy and the powerful were by no means always the ones who enjoyed the highest status and the Brahmins, who had the highest status, were not always wealthy or powerful. In fact, Hinduism perhaps went further than any other social system in the extent to which it allowed status to be maintained independently of wealth or power.

The divisions and subdivisions within the caste system were both rigid and elaborate. At every point these divisions were reinforced by a variety of ritual sanctions. The traditional caste system can be viewed as a series of groups, each separated from the other by a greater or lesser ritual distance. Between some no intermarriage was possible but commensality prevailed; between others commensality was not allowed but other forms of social

18. Dumont, op. cit.

interchange were permitted; between the two extremes as represented by Brahmins and Untouchables, social relations were limited by a large number of ritual restrictions.

Central to the conception of caste is the notion of birth or descent; in fact, the word *jati* (caste) is derived from *jan* which means 'to give birth to'. A number of earlier anthropologists had argued that in its origin the caste system was based on racial distinctions. This view is no longer tenable. But the ideas of birth and descent play a crucial part in maintaining the structure of caste. They give to the individual caste a basis for unity and they also serve to maintain distances between different castes which, according to the principle, derive from different stocks.

Major changes have come about in the caste system in India in course of the last hundred and fifty years. It has been argued that this system could persist only under conditions of social and economic stagnation and that the economic and political transformations taking place in the country are bound to shake its very foundations. It is too early as yet to say that the caste system is on its way out but certain structural changes in Indian society are now too evident to be ignored. The association between caste and occupation is breaking down and individual social mobility is becoming increasingly possible. Individual castes are no longer as homogeneous in their styles of life as they had been in the past. Even though caste endogamy is still the general practice, the legal sanction behind this has been withdrawn. The ritual sanctions which supported the system are being steadily eroded. Finally, the principle of inherited inequality, which provided the ideological basis of caste, has not only been repudiated by the new constitution, but is being challenged at every point by the new political system.

Although formally rejected, the principle of inherited inequality continues to be one of the stubborn facts of real social interchange. Perhaps nowhere is this more evident today than in the sphere of race relations. Racial distinctions continue to be a basis of social inequality not only in the economically backward countries but also in the most advanced industrial societies.

The problem of race has today acquired tremendous political significance. Race riots in the United States and the policy of apartheid in South Africa are widely discussed as essentially political problems. Nor is racial conflict confined to the relations between Black and White. As the *Economist* wrote not very long ago:

The week of the Los Angeles riots was also the week when Malaysia broke apart because brown men could not control their dark suspicions of yellow men, and when black and brown men resumed their efforts to slug it out in southern Sudan. All the evidence is that there is potential trouble wherever people of different colours rub shoulders uneasily together.[19]

But race relations cannot be understood only in political terms; they have to be viewed in the context of the general problem of social inequality. The violence and conflict that are expressed in the political field follow from certain deprivations which have deeper social and cultural roots. Where there are sharp physical differences in the population these are often socially evaluated. The most common form of this kind of evaluation is the one which assigns a high social value to fair and a low one to dark skin colour. These values are reinforced by the real differences of income, occupation and education that often exist between Black and White. While a good deal of racial discrimination can be explained in economic terms, it is obvious that the values attached to skin colour in part exist independently of economic factors.

What makes skin colour such a persistent basis of social discrimination is its visibility. In estate societies people were sometimes required to carry distinctive badges in accordance with their station in society. Dress, ornaments or even hair style might serve to identify the social stratum to which the individual belonged. These external marks of status can now be given up, but it is hard to discard one's skin colour.

The social evaluation of skin colour or of physical features in general does not seem to have the same importance in all societies. As van den Berghe has observed:

Allowing then, for the independent discovery of racism in a number of societies, it remains true that the Western strain of the virus has eclipsed all others in importance. Through the colonial expansion of Europe racism spread widely over the world. Apart from its geographical spread, no other brand of racism has developed such a

19. Quoted in *Daedalus*, vol. 96, no. 2 (1967), p. 3.

flourishing mythology and ideology. In folklore as well as in literature and science, racism became a deeply ingrained component of the Western *Weltanschauung*.[20]

Perhaps it is no accident that the growing importance of race as a source of social inequality has been associated with the decline of other forms of invidious social distinctions.

Those who maintain that in Western society there has been a progressive decline in the value placed on social inequality will, clearly, meet their hardest test in the field of race relations. Western sociologists often seem to argue that the social value placed on race in their own culture is of limited or even marginal significance. Sociologists from Asian and African countries are likely to take a different view. At any rate it is well to remember the point made by Ossowski that the basic cleavage in American society as perceived by the people themselves is not between the propertied and the propertyless but between Negroes and Whites.[21]

There are two historical factors which have given a preponderant place to skin colour as a basis of social gradation. These are slavery and colonialism. In both cases economic and political differences were reinforced by palpable differences in skin colour. The institutions of slavery and colonialism confronted Western society with a paradox. While the French and the Industrial Revolutions were leading to a steady erosion of inequality as a social value, the same value it seems was being reintroduced through the back door by these two institutions.

The traditional societies of Asia were generally based on an acceptance of inequality as a fundamental social value. It has rightly been argued that the first really substantial basis for the recognition of the principle of social equality was provided in these societies by colonial rule. Yet colonial rule also introduced almost everywhere invidious social distinctions on the basis of skin colour or race. In India it was the British who introduced in the nineteenth century the principle of equality before the law; and it was also they who created laws which discriminated against people on the basis of skin colour.

20. Pierre L. van den Berghe, *Race and Racism: A Comparative Perspective*, Wiley, 1967, p. 13.
21. Ossowski, op. cit., p. 36.

A. Béteille

The Indian writer, Nirad C. Chaudhuri, has contrasted the values of the British in India with their values in their own society. He also notes that while the British were inclined to treat all Indians alike and to apply to them a uniform standard of justice, when it came to relations between the two races, their behaviour was coloured by prejudice and arrogance:

It is strange that while dealing out justice between Indian and Indian they were outstandingly successful, especially before the nationalist movement queered the pitch of impartiality, in regard to relations between themselves and us, the British in India lost all sense of right and wrong, truth and falsehood, charity and malice, and paraded a racial arrogance whose mildest form was a stony silence or in the case of unavoidable meetings an abrupt, businesslike termination without even any wishing back to an Indian's wish, and the worst was an obstreperous violence.[22]

Colonial rule is now virtually ended but the colonial experience has left a profound impact not only on the internal systems of a number of societies but also on certain crucial areas of international relations. In certain regions such as the West Indies and Latin America colonial rule injected foreign racial elements into the population in large numbers. In such societies today economic divisions correspond fairly well with the stratification on the basis of skin colour: by and large, those who are at the top are light-skinned and those who are at the bottom are dark. And because the lighter people also represent a 'higher' culture, their superior position is often viewed as a matter of breeding and race and not just of better economic opportunities.

Today the division of the human population into dark and fair is acquiring a new significance because of its correspondence with the division of the world into poor nations and rich. The fact that the dark races are also poor and backward gives them a certain moral and symbolic, if not real, unity: witness the growth of the cult of *négritude* in Francophone Africa; the increasing rift between the Black and White countries of the Commonwealth; and the emergence of the Afro-Asian idea in the United Nations. In White countries (including perhaps the U.S.S.R.) one encounters feelings of condescension and discrimination towards Asians

22. Nirad C. Chaudhuri, *The Continent of Circe*, Chatto, 1965, p. 122.

and Africans and a growing attitude of intolerance and suspicion between the two races which goes far beyond economic disparities. As Philip Mason writes:

Many white people associate with non-whites poverty, inefficiency and backwardness, while non-whites, looking at the whites, remember colonialism and slavery, think of riches and power and their selfish misuse. Each attributes to the other cruelty and sexual maladjustment.[23]

Thus, the value placed on social inequality acquires a new dimension in the context of international relations. The disparities between the rich nations and the poor are not likely to be substantially reduced in the near future. So long as these disparities continue, the impulse will remain to distinguish between superior and inferior people not only in terms of wealth but on the basis of culture and perhaps also of race as this is popularly conceived. The decline of social inequality will be measured not only by the values which govern the internal relations between people in the industrial societies of the West but also by the attitudes such people adopt towards other races and other cultures.

23. Philip Mason, 'The revolt against Western values', *Daedalus*, vol. 96, no. 2 (1967), p. 329.

Further Reading

Part One The Nature and Types of Social Inequality

Among the many recent books dealing with the nature and types of social inequality perhaps the most comprehensive is Reinhard Bendix and Seymour Martin Lipset (eds.), *Class, Status and Power: A Comparative Perspective*, 2nd edn, Free Press, 1966, Routledge & Kegan Paul, 1967. Another recent collection is J. A. Jackson (ed.), *Social Stratification*, Cambridge University Press, 1968. Gerhard E. Lenski, *Power and Privilege: A New Theory of Stratification*, McGraw-Hill, 1966, covers a broad range of problems within a single theoretical framework. A fascinating discussion on the nature of inequality in a non-Western society is provided by Louis Dumont, *Homo Hierarchicus: Essai sur le Système des Castes*, Gallimard, 1966.

Part Two Different Conceptions of Class

Among the many works dealing with the different conceptions of class, T. B. Bottomore, *Classes in Modern Society*, Allen & Unwin, 1965, Pantheon Books, 1966, and Kurt B. Mayer, *Class and Society*, revised edn, Random House, 1955, sum up very well the points of view prevalent in Britain and the U.S.A. A somewhat different viewpoint, representing the tradition of European Marxism, is presented in G. Gurvitch, *Le Concept des Classes Sociales* (mimeographed), Centre de Documentation Universitaire, Paris, 1965.

Part Three Classes and Strata in Industrial Society

Two of the most important books on classes and strata in industrial society are Ralf Dahrendorf, *Class and Class Conflict in an Industrial Society*, Routledge & Kegan Paul, 1959, Stanford University Press, 1959, and Raymond Aron, *La Lutte de Classes*, Gallimard, 1964. Useful accounts of classes and strata in particular industrial societies are available in *Transactions of the Third World Congress of Sociology*, vol. 3, International Social Science Association, London, 1956.

Part Four Stratification in Agrarian Systems

A concise account of the different types of agrarian class structure is available in Arthur L. Stinchcombe, 'Agricultural enterprise and rural class structure' in R. Bendix and S. Lipset (eds.), *Class, Status and Power: A Comparative Perspective*, 2nd edn, Free Press, 1966, Routledge & Kegan Paul, 1967. Gunnar Myrdal, *Asian Drama: An Inquiry into the Poverty of Nations*, Pantheon Books, 1968, Allen Lane The Penguin Press, 1968, Penguin Books, 1968, vol. I, chapters 10 and 12, gives a general account of the nature and conditions of inequality in South Asian agriculture from a broad economic point of view. The five case studies in Julian Steward *et al.*, *The People of Puerto Rico*, University of Illinois Press, 1966, Book Centre, 1966, in particular the ones by Eric R. Wolf and Sidney W. Mintz, contain graphic anthropological accounts of the internal and external relations of social classes in the plantation system. Barrington Moore Jr, *Social Origins of Dictatorship and Democracy: Lord and Peasant in the Making of the Modern World*, Beacon Press, 1966, Allen Lane The Penguin Press, 1967, contains a provocative historical account of agrarian social stratification in Europe, America and Asia.

Part Five Colonialism and the Emergent Countries

Guy Hunter, *The New Societies of Tropical Africa*, Oxford University Press for the Institute of Race Relations, 1962, Frederick A. Praeger, 1964, and W. F. Wertheim, *Indonesian Society in Transition*, Institute of Pacific Relations, 1956, W. van Hoeve, 1956, describe the impact of colonial rule and the problems of social transition in Africa and South-East Asia. J. H. Broomfield, *Elite Conflicts in a Plural Society: Twentieth Century Bengal*, University of California Press, 1968, provides a case study of a province that is now divided between India and Pakistan.

Part Six Inequality in Simpler Societies

Michael G. Smith, 'Pre-industrial stratification systems' in Neil J. Smelser and Seymour Martin Lipset (eds.), *Social Structure and Mobility in Economic Development*, Aldine Publishing Co., 1966,

Routledge & Kegan Paul, 1966, pp. 141–76, presents a general account of social inequalities in tribal and peasant societies. Another general account is given by R. Bastide, *Formes Élémentaires de la Stratification Sociale* (mimeographed), Centre de Documentation Universitaire, Paris, 1965. Two interesting monographs on specific tribal communities or groups of communities are Jacques J. Maquet, *The Premise of Inequality in Ruanda*, Oxford University Press for the International African Institute, 1961, and Marshall D. Sahlins, *Social Stratification in Polynesia*, University of Washington Press, 1958.

Part Seven Caste as a Form of Social Inequality

J. H. Hutton, *Caste in India*, 3rd edn, Oxford University Press, 1963, provides a useful introduction to the subject for the Western student. E. R. Leach (ed.), *Aspects of Caste in South India, Ceylon and North-West Pakistan*, Cambridge University Press Papers in Social Anthropology, 1960, discusses caste in the village context in three Asian countries. André Béteille, *Castes: Old and New, Essays in Social Structure and Social Stratification*, Asia Publishing House, 1969, deals with problems of status and power in contemporary India. A set of interesting discussions linking caste, race and slavery is available in Anthony de Reuck and Julie Knight (eds.), *Caste and Race: Comparative Approaches*, Churchill, 1967.

Part Eight Race and Social Stratification

Pierre L. van den Berghe, *Race and Racism: A Comparative Perspective*, Wiley, 1967, discusses the relationship between race and social inequality in general and comparative terms. A recent collection of essays dealing with the problem of race in many countries is John Hope Franklin (ed.), *Color and Race*, Houghton Mifflin, 1968. Sheila Patterson, *Dark Strangers*, Tavistock, 1963, University of Indiana Press, 1964, Penguin Books, 1965, discusses the problems of coloured immigrants in Britain.

Part Nine Equality and Inequality: Ideas and Practice

Stanislaw Ossowski, *Class Structure in the Social Consciousness*, Free Press, 1963, Routledge & Kegan Paul, 1963, is a classic study of the different ways in which social inequalities have been perceived, justified and condemned in European society from early times to the present. The same problem is discussed with particular reference to the contemporary situation by Raymond Aron in *Progress and Disillusion: The Dialectics of Modern Society*, Pall Mall Press, 1968, particularly in Part I, 'The dialectic of equality'. Gunnar Myrdal's well-known book, *An American Dilemma*, 2nd edn, Harper & Row, 1962, McGraw-Hill, 1964, discusses the tensions in American society between the ideals of equality and the facts of racial discrimination. Louis Dumont, *La Civilisation Indienne et Nous: Esquisse de Sociologie Comparée*, Colin, 1964, is about a society whose traditional values provided the most elaborate justification of inequality.

Acknowledgements

Permission to reprint the papers published in this volume is acknowledged from the following sources:

Reading 1   Stanford University Press
Reading 2   Routledge & Kegan Paul and University of California Press
Reading 3   Raymond Aron
Reading 4   International Sociological Association
Reading 5   Routledge & Kegan Paul and Stanford University Press
Reading 6   *Sociologie du Travail*
Reading 7   Oxford University Press
Reading 8   University of Illinois Press
Reading 9   N.V. Uitgeverij W. van Hoeve
Reading 10   Weidenfeld & Nicolson Ltd and the University of Chicago Press
Reading 11   University of Washington Press
Reading 12   The London School of Economics
Reading 13   Asia Publishing House and M. N. Srinivas
Reading 14   University of California Press
Reading 15   *Daedalus*
Reading 16   John Wiley & Sons Inc.
Reading 17   Presses Universitaires de France

Author Index

Subject Index

Some books on Sociology and Anthropology published in Penguin Books